Extraordinary Praise for
The Memory Keeper's Daughter

"[An] extraordinary debut."   —*Chicago Tribune*

"Kim Edwards has written a novel so mesmerizing that I devoured
it in a single gulp, reading far into the wee hours. Her characters
will hold you spellbound as you watch a marriage founded on the
sweetest of intimacies destroyed by unexamined concepts of con-
ventional wisdom, by lies and by secrecy. From the ashes grow new
lives strong enough to defy convention and to define family simply
as supportive love. Terror, pity, redemption—what reader can ask
for more? This beautifully written novel has it all."

—Sena Jeter Naslund

"In *The Memory Keeper's Daughter*, Kim Edwards has created a tale
of regret and redemption, of honest emotion, of characters haunted
by their past. Crafted with language so lovely you have to reread the
passages just to be captivated all over again . . . this is simply a beautiful book—I can't wait to see what she writes next."

—Jodi Picoult

"First-time novelist Edwards . . . has written a heart-wrenching
book, by turns light and dark, literary and suspenseful. A natural
for book discussions groups; recommended."

—*Library Journal*

"*The Memory Keeper's Daughter* unfolds from an absolutely mesmerizing premise, drawing you deeply and irrevocably into the en-
tangled lives of two families and the devastating secret that shapes
them both. I loved this riveting story with its intricate characters
and beautiful language."   —Sue Monk Kidd

"An auspicious debut novel. . . . *The Memory Keeper's Daughter* is a
page-turner, a wonderfully crafted tale. . . . Highly recommended."

—Bookreporter.com

W8-BSJ-836

"*The Memory Keeper's Daughter* is a gift, filled with radiant mystery. Kim Edwards writes with great wisdom and compassion about family, choices, secrets, and redemption. This is a wonderful, heartbreaking, heart-healing novel."　　　—Luanne Rice

"[A] tightly woven tale of love, loss and redemption."
　　　　　　　　　　　　　　　　　　—*Orlando Sentinel*

"A gripping novel, beautifully written. With amazing compassion, Kim Edwards explores the impact of a family secret that challenges the limits of love and redemption."　　　—Ursula Hegi

"This unusual novel is exciting, probing, dashing, and filled with surprises. The writing is memorable and smart. A keeper!"
　　　　　　　　　　　　　　　　　—Bobbie Ann Mason

"Anyone would be struck by the extraordinary power and sympathy of *The Memory Keeper's Daughter*."　　　—*The Washington Post*

PENGUIN BOOKS

THE MEMORY KEEPER'S DAUGHTER

Kim Edwards is the author of the short story collection *The Secrets of the Fire King*, which was an alternate for the 1998 PEN/ Hemingway Award, and she has won both the Whiting Award and the Nelson Algren Award. A graduate of the Iowa Writer's Workshop, she is an assistant professor of English at the University of Kentucky.

The
Memory Keeper's
Daughter

Kim Edwards

PENGUIN BOOKS

PENGUIN BOOKS

Published by the Penguin Group

Penguin Group (USA) Inc., 375 Hudson Street, New York, New York 10014, U.S.A.

Penguin Group (Canada), 90 Eglinton Avenue East, Suite 700, Toronto,
Ontario, Canada M4P 2Y3 (a division of Pearson Penguin Canada Inc.)

Penguin Books Ltd, 80 Strand, London WC2R 0RL, England

Penguin Ireland, 25 St Stephen's Green, Dublin 2, Ireland (a division of Penguin Books Ltd)

Penguin Group (Australia), 250 Camberwell Road, Camberwell,
Victoria 3124, Australia (a division of Pearson Australia Group Pty Ltd)

Penguin Books India Pvt Ltd, 11 Community Centre, Panchsheel Park, New Delhi – 110 017, India

Penguin Group (NZ), cnr Airborne and Rosedale Roads, Albany,
Auckland 1310, New Zealand (a division of Pearson New Zealand Ltd)

Penguin Books (South Africa) (Pty) Ltd, 24 Sturdee Avenue,
Rosebank, Johannesburg 2196, South Africa

Penguin Books Ltd, Registered Offices:
80 Strand, London WC2R 0RL, England

First published in the United States of America by Viking Penguin,
a member of Penguin Group (USA) Inc. 2005
Published in Penguin Books 2006

5   7   9   10   8   6

Copyright © Kim Edwards, 2005
All rights reserved

PUBLISHER'S NOTE

This is a work of fiction. Names, characters, places, and incidents either are the
product of the author's imagination or are used fictitiously, and any resemblance to actual
persons, living or dead, business establishments, events, or locales is entirely coincidental.

ISBN 0 14 30.3714 5
CIP data available

Printed in the United States of America
Designed by Carla Bolte • Set in Granjon

For Abigail and Naomi

Acknowledgments

I'd like to express my deep appreciation to the pastors of Hunter Presbyterian Church for years of wisdom on matters seen and unseen; thanks especially to Claire Vonk Brooks, who carried the seed of this story and entrusted it to me.

Jean and Richard Covert generously shared their insights and also read an early draft of this manuscript. I am grateful to them, as well as to Meg Steinman, Caroline Baesler, Kallie Baesler, Nancy Covert, Becky Lesch, and Malkanthi McCormick, for their candor and guidance. Bruce Burris invited me to teach a workshop at Minds Wide Open; my thanks to him, and to the participants that day, who wrote straight from their hearts.

I am very grateful to the Mrs. Giles Whiting Foundation for exceptional support and encouragement. The Kentucky Council on the Arts and the Kentucky Foundation for Women also provided sustaining grants in support of this book, and I thank them.

As always, enormous gratitude to my agent, Geri Thoma, for being so wise, warm, generous and steadfast. I'm very grateful also to all the people at Viking, especially my editor, Pamela Dorman, who brought such intelligence and engagement to editing this book, and whose insightful questions helped me walk more deeply into the narrative. Beena Kamlani's deft, perceptive editorial touch was invaluable as well, and Lucia Watson, with good cheer and precision, kept a thousand things in motion.

To writers Jane McCafferty, Mary Ann Taylor-Hall, and Leatha Kendrik, who read this manuscript with tough and loving eyes, heartfelt thanks. Special thanks also to my parents, John and Shirley

Edwards. To James Alan McPherson, whose teaching still informs my own, abiding gratitude. To Katherine Soulard Turner and her father, the late William G. Turner, for rich friendship, book talk, and Pittsburgh expertise, joyous thanks as well.

Love and thanks to all my family, near and far, especially to Tom.

The Memory Keeper's Daughter

1964

March 1964

I

THE SNOW STARTED TO FALL SEVERAL HOURS BEFORE HER labor began. A few flakes first, in the dull gray late-afternoon sky, and then wind-driven swirls and eddies around the edges of their wide front porch. He stood by her side at the window, watching sharp gusts of snow billow, then swirl and drift to the ground. All around the neighborhood, lights came on, and the naked branches of the trees turned white.

After dinner he built a fire, venturing out into the weather for wood he had piled against the garage the previous autumn. The air was bright and cold against his face, and the snow in the driveway was already halfway to his knees. He gathered logs, shaking off their soft white caps and carrying them inside. The kindling in the iron grate caught fire immediately, and he sat for a time on the hearth, cross-legged, adding logs and watching the flames leap, blue-edged and hypnotic. Outside, snow continued to fall quietly through the darkness, as bright and thick as static in the cones of light cast by the streetlights. By the time he rose and looked out the window, their car had become a soft white hill on the edge of the street. Already his footprints in the driveway had filled and disappeared.

He brushed ashes from his hands and sat on the sofa beside his wife, her feet propped on pillows, her swollen ankles crossed, a copy of Dr. Spock balanced on her belly. Absorbed, she licked her index finger absently each time she turned a page. Her hands were slender, her fingers short and sturdy, and she bit her bottom lip lightly, intently, as she read. Watching her, he felt a surge of love and wonder: that she was his wife, that their baby, due in just three weeks, would soon be born. Their first child, this would be. They had been married just a year.

She looked up, smiling, when he tucked the blanket around her legs.

"You know, I've been wondering what it's like," she said. "Before we're born, I mean. It's too bad we can't remember." She opened her robe and pulled up the sweater she wore underneath, revealing a belly as round and hard as a melon. She ran her hand across its smooth surface, firelight playing across her skin, casting reddish gold onto her hair. "Do you suppose it's like being inside a great lantern? The book says light permeates my skin, that the baby can already see."

"I don't know," he said.

She laughed. "Why not?" she asked. "You're the doctor."

"I'm just an orthopedic surgeon," he reminded her. "I could tell you the ossification pattern for fetal bones, but that's about it." He lifted her foot, both delicate and swollen inside the light blue sock, and began to massage it gently: the powerful tarsal bone of her heel, the metatarsals and the phalanges, hidden beneath skin and densely layered muscles like a fan about to open. Her breathing filled the quiet room, her foot warmed his hands, and he imagined the perfect, secret, symmetry of bones. In pregnancy she seemed to him beautiful but fragile, fine blue veins faintly visible through her pale white skin.

It had been an excellent pregnancy, without medical restrictions. Even so, he had not been able to make love to her for several months. He found himself wanting to protect her instead, to carry her up flights of stairs, to wrap her in blankets, to bring her cups of custard. "I'm not an invalid," she protested each time, laughing. "I'm not some fledgling you discovered on the lawn." Still, she was pleased by his attentions. Sometimes he woke and watched her as she slept: the flutter of her eyelids, the slow even movement of her chest, her outflung hand, small enough that he could enclose it completely with his own.

She was eleven years younger than he was. He had first seen her not much more than a year ago, as she rode up an escalator in a department store downtown, one gray November Saturday while he was buying ties. He was thirty-three years old and new to Lexington, Kentucky, and she had risen out of the crowd like some kind of vision, her blond hair swept back in an elegant chignon, pearls glimmering at her throat and on her ears. She was wearing a coat of dark green wool, and her skin was clear and pale. He stepped onto the escalator, pushing his way upward through the crowd, struggling to keep her in sight. She went to the fourth floor, lingerie and hosiery. When he tried to follow her through aisles dense with racks of slips and brassieres and panties, all glimmering softly, a sales clerk in a navy blue dress with a white collar stopped him, smiling, to ask if she could help. *A robe,* he said, scanning the aisles until he caught sight of her hair, a dark green shoulder, her bent head revealing the elegant pale curve of her neck. *A robe for my sister who lives in New Orleans.* He had no sister, of course, or any living family that he acknowledged.

The clerk disappeared and came back a moment later with three robes in sturdy terry cloth. He chose blindly, hardly glancing down, taking the one on top. *Three sizes,* the clerk was saying, and *a better selection of colors next month,* but he was already in the aisle, a coral-colored robe draped over his arm, his shoes squeaking on the tiles as he moved impatiently between the other shoppers to where she stood.

She was shuffling through the stacks of expensive stockings, sheer colors shining through slick cellophane windows: taupe, navy, a maroon as dark as pig's blood. The sleeve of her green coat brushed his and he smelled her perfume, something delicate and yet pervasive, something like the dense pale petals of lilacs outside the window of the student rooms he'd once occupied in Pittsburgh. The squat windows of his basement apartment were always grimy, opaque with steel-factory soot and ash, but in the spring there were lilacs blooming, sprays of white and lavender pressing against the glass, their scent drifting in like light.

He cleared his throat—he could hardly breathe—and held up the terry cloth robe, but the clerk behind the counter was laughing, telling a joke, and she did not notice him. When he cleared his throat again she glanced at him, annoyed, then nodded at her customer, now holding three thin packages of stockings like giant playing cards in her hand.

"I'm afraid Miss Asher was here first," the clerk said, cool and haughty.

Their eyes met then, and he was startled to see they were the same dark green as her coat. She was taking him in—the solid tweed overcoat, his face clean-shaven and flushed with cold, his trim fingernails. She smiled, amused and faintly dismissive, gesturing to the robe on his arm.

"For your wife?" she asked. She spoke with what he recognized as a genteel Kentucky accent, in this city of old money where such distinctions mattered. After just six months in town, he already knew this. "It's all right, Jean," she went on, turning back to the clerk. "Go on and take him first. This poor man must feel lost and awkward, in here with all the lace."

"It's for my sister," he told her, desperate to reverse the bad impression he was making. It had happened to him often here; he was too forward or direct and gave offense. The robe slipped to the floor and he bent to pick it up, his face flushing as he rose. Her gloves were lying on the glass, her bare hands folded lightly next to them. His discomfort seemed to soften her, for when he met her eyes again, they were kind.

He tried again. "I'm sorry. I don't seem to know what I'm doing. And I'm in a hurry. I'm a doctor. I'm late to the hospital."

Her smiled changed then, grew serious.

"I see," she said, turning back to the clerk. "Really, Jean, do take him first."

She agreed to see him again, writing her name and phone number in the perfect script she'd been taught in third grade, her teacher an ex-nun who had engraved the rules of penmanship in her small charges. Each letter has a shape, she told them, one shape in the world and no other, and it is your responsibility to make it perfect. Eight years old, pale and skinny, the woman in the green coat who would become his wife had clenched her small fingers around the pen and practiced cursive writing alone in her room, hour after hour, until she wrote with the exquisite fluidity of running water. Later, listening to that story, he would imagine her head bent beneath the lamplight, her fingers in a painful cluster around the pen, and he would wonder at her tenacity, her belief in beauty and in the authoritative voice of the ex-nun. But on that day he did not know any of this. On that day he carried the slip of paper in the pocket of his white coat through one sickroom after another, remembering her letters flowing one into another to form the perfect shape of her name. He phoned her that same evening and took her to dinner the next night, and three months later they were married.

Now, in these last months of her pregnancy, the soft coral robe fit her perfectly. She had found it packed away and had held it up to show him. *But your sister died so long ago,* she exclaimed, suddenly puzzled, and for an instant he had frozen, smiling, the lie from a year before darting like a dark bird through the room. Then he shrugged, sheepish. *I had to say something,* he told her. *I had to find a way to get your name.* She smiled then, and crossed the room and embraced him.

The snow fell. For the next few hours, they read and talked. Sometimes she caught his hand and put it on her belly to feel the baby move. From time to time he got up to feed the fire, glancing out the window to see three inches on the ground, then five or six. The streets were softened and quiet, and there were few cars.

At eleven she rose and went to bed. He stayed downstairs, reading the latest issue of *The Journal of Bone and Joint Surgery*. He was known to be a very good doctor, with a talent for diagnosis and a reputation for skillful work. He had graduated first in his class. Still, he was young enough and—though he hid it very carefully—unsure enough about his skills that he studied in every spare moment, collecting each success he accomplished as one more piece of evidence in his own favor. He felt himself to be an aberration, born with a love for learning in a family absorbed in simply scrambling to get by, day to day. They had seen education as an unnecessary luxury, a means to no certain end. Poor, when they went to the doctor at all it was to the clinic in Morgantown, fifty miles away. His memories of those rare trips were vivid, bouncing in the back of the borrowed pickup truck, dust flying in their wake. The dancing road, his sister had called it, from her place in the cab with their parents. In Morgantown the rooms were dim, the murky green or turquoise of pond water, and the doctors had been hurried, brisk with them, distracted.

All these years later, he still had moments when he sensed the gaze of those doctors and felt himself to be an imposter, about to be unmasked by a single mistake. He knew his choice of specialties reflected this. Not for him the random excitement of general medicine or the delicate risky plumbing of the heart. He dealt mostly with broken limbs, sculpting casts and viewing X-rays, watching breaks slowly yet miraculously knit themselves back together. He liked that bones were solid things, surviving even the white heat of cremation. Bones would last; it was easy for him to put his faith in something so solid and predictable.

He read well past midnight, until the words shimmered senselessly on the bright white pages, and then he tossed the journal on the coffee table and got up to tend to the fire. He tamped the charred fire-laced logs into embers, opened the damper fully, and closed the brass fireplace screen. When he turned off the lights, shards of fire glowed softly through layers of ash as delicate and white as the snow piled so high now on the porch railings and the rhododendron bushes.

The stairs creaked with his weight. He paused by the nursery door, studying the shadowy shapes of the crib and the changing table, the stuffed animals arranged on shelves. The walls were painted a pale sea green. His wife had made the Mother Goose quilt that hung on the far wall, sewing with tiny stitches, tearing out entire panels if she noted the slightest imperfection. A border of bears was stenciled just below the ceiling; she had done that too.

On an impulse he went into the room and stood before the window, pushing aside the sheer curtain to watch the snow, now nearly eight inches high on the lampposts and the fences and the roofs. It was the sort of storm that rarely happened in Lexington, and the steady white flakes, the silence, filled him with a sense of excitement and peace. It was a moment when all the disparate shards of his life seemed to knit themselves together, every past sadness and disappointment, every anxious secret and uncertainty hidden now beneath the soft white layers. Tomorrow would be quiet, the world subdued and fragile, until the neighborhood children came out to break the stillness with their tracks and shouts and joy. He remembered such days from his own childhood in the mountains, rare moments of escape when he went into the woods, his breathing amplified and his voice somehow muffled by the heavy snow that bent branches low, drifted over paths. The world, for a few short hours, transformed.

He stood there for a long time, until he heard her moving quietly. He found her sitting on the edge of their bed, her head bent, her hands gripping the mattress.

"I think this is labor," she said, looking up. Her hair was loose, a strand caught on her lip. He brushed it back behind her ear. She shook her head as he sat beside her. "I don't know. I feel strange. This crampy feeling, it comes and goes."

He helped her lie down on her side and then he lay down too, massaging her back. "It's probably just false labor," he assured her. "It's three weeks early, after all, and first babies are usually late."

This was true, he knew, he believed it as he spoke, and he was, in fact, so sure of it that after a time he drifted into sleep. He woke to find her standing over the bed, shaking his shoulder. Her robe, her hair, looked nearly white in the strange snowy light that filled their room.

"I've been timing them. Five minutes apart. They're strong, and I'm scared."

He felt an inner surge then; excitement and fear tumbled through him like foam pushed by a wave. But he had been trained to be calm in emergencies, to keep his emotions in check, so he was able to stand without any urgency, take the watch, and walk with her, slowly and calmly, up and down the hall. When the contractions came she squeezed his hand so hard he felt as if the bones in his fingers might fuse. The contractions were as she had said, five minutes apart, then four. He took the suitcase from the closet, feeling numb suddenly with the momentousness of these events, long expected but a surprise all the same. He moved, as she did, but the world slowed to stillness around them. He was acutely aware of every action, the way breath rushed against his tongue, the way her feet slid uncomfortably into the only shoes she could still wear, her swollen flesh making a ridge against the dark gray leather. When he took her arm he felt strangely as if he himself were suspended in the room, somewhere near the light fixture, watching them both from above, noting every nuance and detail: how she trembled with a contraction, how his fingers closed so firmly and protectively around her elbow. How outside, still, the snow was drifting down.

He helped her into her green wool coat, which hung unbuttoned, gaping around her belly. He found the leather gloves she'd been wearing when he first saw her, too. It seemed important that these details be right. They stood together on the porch for a moment, stunned by the soft white world.

"Wait here," he said, and went down the steps, breaking a path through the drifts. The doors of the old car were frozen, and it took him several minutes to get one open. A white cloud flew up, glittering, when the door at last swung back, and he scrambled on the floor of the backseat for the ice scraper and brush. When he emerged his wife was leaning against a porch pillar, her forehead on her arms. He understood in that moment both how much pain she was in and that the baby was really coming, coming that very night. He resisted a powerful urge to go to her and, instead, put all his energy into freeing the car, warming first one bare hand and then the other beneath his armpits when the pain of the cold became too great, warming them but never pausing, brushing snow from the windshield and the windows and the hood, watching it scatter and disappear into the soft sea of white around his calves.

"You didn't mention it would hurt this much," she said, when he reached the porch. He put his arm around her shoulders and helped her down the steps. "I can walk," she insisted. "It's just when the pain comes."

"I know," he said, but he did not let her go.

When they reached the car she touched his arm and gestured to the house, veiled with snow and glowing like a lantern in the darkness of the street.

"When we come back we'll have our baby with us," she said. "Our world will never be the same."

The windshield wipers were frozen, and snow spilled down the back window when he pulled into the street. He drove slowly, thinking how beautiful Lexington was, the trees and bushes so heavy with snow. When he turned onto the main street the wheels hit ice and the car slid, briefly, fluidly, across the intersection, coming to rest by a snowbank.

"We're fine," he announced, his head rushing. Fortunately, there wasn't another car in sight. The steering wheel was as hard and cold as stone beneath his bare hands. Now and then he wiped at the windshield with the back of his hand, leaning to peer through the hole he'd made. "I called Bentley before we left," he said, naming his colleague, an obstetrician. "I said to meet us at the office. We'll go there. It's closer."

She was silent for a moment, her hand gripping the dashboard as she breathed through a contraction. "As long as I don't have my baby in this old car," she managed at last, trying to joke. "You know how much I've always hated it."

He smiled, but he knew her fear was real, and he shared it. Methodical, purposeful: even in an emergency he could not change his nature. He came to a full stop at every light, signaled turns to the empty streets. Every few minutes she braced one hand against the dashboard again and focused her breathing, which made him swallow and glance sideways at her, more nervous on that night than he could ever remember being. More nervous than his in first anatomy class, the body of a young boy peeled open to reveal its secrets. More nervous than on his wedding day, her family filling one side of the church, and on the other just a handful of his colleagues. His parents were dead, his sister too.

There was a single car in the clinic parking lot, the nurse's powder-blue Fairlane, conservative and pragmatic and newer than his own. He'd called her, too. He pulled up in front of the entrance and helped his wife out. Now that they had reached the office safely they were both exhilarated, laughing as they pushed into the bright lights of the waiting room.

The nurse met them. The moment he saw her, he knew something was wrong. She had large blue eyes in a pale face that might have been forty or twenty-five, and whenever something was not to her liking a thin vertical line formed across her forehead, just between her eyes. It was there now as she gave them her news: Bentley's car had fishtailed on the unplowed country road where he lived, spun around twice on the ice beneath the snow, and floated into a ditch.

"You're saying Dr. Bentley won't be coming?" his wife asked.

The nurse nodded. She was tall, so thin and angular it seemed the bones might poke from beneath her skin at any moment. Her large blue eyes were solemn and intelligent. For months, there had been rumors, jokes, that she was a little bit in love with him. He had dismissed them as idle office gossip, annoying but natural when a man and single woman worked in such close proximity, day after day. And then one evening he had fallen asleep at his desk. He'd been dreaming, back in his childhood home, his mother putting up jars of fruit that gleamed jewellike on the oilcloth-covered table beneath the window. His sister, age five, sat holding a doll in one listless hand. A passing image, perhaps a memory, but one that filled him simultaneously with sadness and with yearning. The house was his but empty now, deserted when his sister died and his parents moved away, the rooms his mother had scrubbed to a dull gleam abandoned, filled only with the rustlings of squirrels and mice.

He'd had tears in his eyes when he opened them, raising his head from the desk. The nurse was standing in the doorway, her face gentled by emotion. She was beautiful in that moment, half smiling, not at all the efficient woman who worked beside him so quietly and competently each day. Their eyes met, and it seemed to the doctor that he knew her—that they knew each other—in some profound and certain way. For an instant nothing whatsoever stood between them; it was an intimacy of such magnitude that he was motionless, transfixed. Then she blushed severely and looked aside.

She cleared her throat and straightened, saying that she had worked two hours overtime and would be going. For many days, her eyes would not meet his.

After that, when people teased him about her, he made them stop. *She's a very fine nurse,* he would say, holding up one hand against the jokes, honoring that moment of communion they had shared. *She's the best I've ever worked with.* This was true, and now he was very glad to have her with him.

"How about the emergency room?" she asked. "Could you make it?"

The doctor shook his head. The contractions were just a minute or so apart.

"This baby won't wait," he said, looking at his wife. Snow had melted in her hair and glittered like a diamond tiara. "This baby's on its way."

"It's all right," his wife said, stoic. Her voice was harder now, determined. "This will be a better story to tell him, growing up: him or her."

The nurse smiled, the line still visible though fainter, between her eyes. "Let's get you inside then," she said. "Let's get you some help with the pain."

He went into his own office to find a coat, and when he entered Bentley's examination room his wife was lying on the bed, her feet in the stirrups. The room was pale blue, filled with chrome and white enamel and fine instruments of gleaming steel. The doctor went to the sink and washed his hands. He felt extremely alert, aware of the tiniest details, and as he performed this ordinary ritual he felt his panic at Bentley's absence begin to ease. He closed his eyes, forcing himself to focus on his task.

"Everything's progressing," the nurse said, when he turned. "Everything looks fine. I'd put her at ten centimeters; see what you think."

He sat on the low stool and reached up into the soft warm cave of his wife's body. The amniotic sac was still intact, and through it he could feel the baby's head, smooth and hard like a baseball. His child. He should be pacing a waiting room somewhere. Across the room, the blinds were closed on the only window, and as he pulled his hand from the warmth of his wife's body he found himself wondering about the snow, if it was falling still, silencing the city and the land beyond.

"Yes," he said, "ten centimeters."

"Phoebe," his wife said. He could not see her face, but her voice was clear. They had been discussing names for months and had reached no decisions. "For a girl, Phoebe. And for a boy, Paul, after my great-uncle. Did I tell you this?" she asked. "I meant to tell you I'd decided."

"Those are good names," the nurse said, soothing.

"Phoebe and Paul," the doctor repeated, but he was concentrating on the contraction now rising in his wife's flesh. He gestured to the nurse, who readied the gas. During his residency years, the practice had been to put the woman in labor out completely until the birth was over, but times had changed—it was 1964—and Bentley, he knew, used gas more selectively. Better that she should be awake to push; he would put her out for the worst of the contractions, for the crowning and the birth. His wife tensed and cried out, and the baby moved in the birth canal, bursting the amniotic sac.

"Now," the doctor said, and the nurse put the mask in place. His wife's hands relaxed, her fists unclenching as the gas took effect, and she lay still, tranquil and unknowing, as another contraction and another moved through her.

"It's coming fast for a first baby," the nurse observed.

"Yes," the doctor said. "So far so good."

Half an hour passed in this way. His wife roused and moaned and pushed, and when he felt she had had enough—or when she cried out that the pain was overwhelming—he nodded to the nurse, who gave her the gas. Except for the quiet exchange of instructions, they did not speak. Outside the snow kept falling, drifting along the sides of houses, filling the roads. The doctor sat on a stainless steel chair, narrowing his concentration to the essential facts. He had delivered five babies during medical school, all live births and all successful, and he focused now on those, seeking in his memory the details of care. As he did so, his wife, lying with her feet in the stirrups and her belly rising so high that he could not see her face, slowly became one with those other women. Her round knees, her smooth narrow calves, her ankles, all these were before him, familiar and beloved. Yet he did not think to stroke her skin or put a reassuring hand on her knee. It was the nurse who held her hand while she pushed. To the doctor, focused on what was immediately before him, she became not just herself but more than herself; a body like other bodies, a patient whose needs he must meet with every technical skill he had. It was necessary, more necessary than usual, to keep his emotions in check. As time passed, the strange moment he had experienced in their bedroom came to him again. He began to feel as if he were somehow removed from the scene of this birth, both there and also floating elsewhere, observing from some safe distance. He watched himself make the careful, precise incision for the episiotomy. A good one, he thought, as the blood welled in a clean line, not letting himself remember the times he'd touched that same flesh in passion.

The head crowned. In three more pushes it emerged, and then the body slid into his waiting hands and the baby cried out, its blue skin pinking up.

It was a boy, red-faced and dark-haired, his eyes alert, suspicious of the lights and the cold bright slap of air. The doctor tied the umbilical cord and cut it. *My son,* he allowed himself to think. *My son.*

"He's beautiful," the nurse said. She waited while he examined the child, noting his steady heart, rapid and sure, the long-fingered hands and shock of dark hair. Then she took the infant to the other room to bathe him and to drop the silver nitrate into his eyes. The small cries drifted back to them, and his wife stirred. The doctor stayed where he was with his hand on her knee, taking several deep breaths, awaiting the afterbirth. *My son,* he thought again.

"Where is the baby?" his wife asked, opening her eyes and pushing hair away from her flushed face. "Is everything all right?"

"It's a boy," the doctor said, smiling down at her. "We have a son. You'll see him as soon as he's clean. He's absolutely perfect."

His wife's face, soft with relief and exhaustion, suddenly tightened with another contraction, and the doctor, expecting the afterbirth, returned to the stool between her legs and pressed lightly against her abdomen. She cried out, and at the same moment he understood what was happening, as startled as if a window had appeared suddenly in a concrete wall.

"It's all right," he said. "Everything's fine. Nurse," he called, as the next contraction tightened.

She came at once, carrying the baby, now swaddled in white blankets.

"He's a nine on the Apgar," she announced. "That's very good."

His wife lifted her arms for the baby and began to speak, but then the pain caught her and she lay back down.

"Nurse?" the doctor said, "I need you here. Right now."

After a moment's confusion the nurse put two pillows on the floor, placed the baby on them, and joined the doctor by the table.

"More gas," he said. He saw her surprise and then her quick nod of comprehension as she complied. His hand was on his wife's knee; he felt the tension ease from her muscles as the gas worked.

"Twins?" the nurse asked.

The doctor, who had allowed himself to relax after the boy was born, felt shaky now, and he did not trust himself to do more than nod. *Steady,* he told himself, as the next head crowned. *You are anywhere,* he thought, watching from some fine point on the ceiling as his hands worked with method and precision. *This is any birth.*

This baby was smaller and came easily, sliding so quickly into his gloved hands that he leaned forward, using his chest to make sure it did not fall. "It's a girl," he said, and cradled her like a football, face down, tapping her back until she cried out. Then he turned her over to see her face.

Creamy white vernix whorled in her delicate skin, and she was slippery with amniotic fluid and traces of blood. The blue eyes were cloudy, the hair jet black, but he barely noticed all of this. What he was looking at were the unmistakable features, the eyes turned up as if with laughter, the epicanthal fold across their lids, the flattened nose. *A classic case,* he remembered his professor saying as they examined a similar child, years ago. *A mongoloid. Do you know what that means?* And the doctor, dutiful, had recited the symptoms he'd memorized from the text: flaccid muscle tone, delayed growth and mental development, possible heart complications, early death. The professor had nodded, placing his stethoscope on the baby's smooth bare chest. *Poor kid. There's nothing they can do except try to keep him clean. They ought to spare themselves and send him to a home.*

The doctor had felt transported back in time. His sister had been born with a heart defect and had grown very slowly, her breath catching and coming in little gasps whenever she tried to run. For many years, until the first trip to the clinic in Morgantown, they had not known what was the matter. Then they knew, and there was nothing they could do. All his mother's attention had gone to her, and yet she had died when she was twelve years old. The doctor had been sixteen, already living in town to attend high school, already on his way to Pittsburgh and medical school and the life he was living now. Still, he remembered the depth and endurance of his mother's grief, the way she walked up hill to the grave every morning, her arms folded against whatever weather she encountered.

The nurse stood beside him and studied the baby.

"I'm sorry, doctor," she said.

He held the infant, forgetting what he ought to do next. Her tiny hands were perfect. But the gap between her big toes and the others, that was there, like a missing tooth, and when he looked deeply at her eyes he saw the Brushfield spots, as tiny and distinct as flecks of snow in the irises. He imagined her heart, the size of a plum and very possibly defective, and he thought of the nursery, so carefully painted, with its soft animals and single crib. He thought of his wife standing on the sidewalk before their brightly veiled home, saying, *Our world will never be the same.*

The baby's hand brushed his, and he started. Without volition he began to move through the familiar patterns. He cut the cord and checked her heart, her lungs. All the time he was thinking of the snow, the silver car floating into a ditch, the deep quiet of this empty clinic. Later, when he considered this night—and he would think of it often, in the months and years to come: the turning point of his life, the moments around which everything else would always gather—what he remembered was the silence in the room and the snow falling steadily outside. The silence was so deep and encompassing that he felt himself floating to a new height, some point above this room and then beyond, where he was one with the snow and where this scene in the room was something unfolding in a different life, a life at which he was a random spectator, like a scene glimpsed through a warmly lit window while walking on a darkened street. That was what he would remember, that feeling of endless space. The doctor in the ditch, and the lights of his own house burning far away.

"All right. Clean her up, please," he said, releasing the slight weight of the infant into the nurse's arms. "But keep her in the other room. I don't want my wife to know. Not right away."

The nurse nodded. She disappeared and then came back to lift his son into the baby carrier they'd brought. The doctor was by then intent on delivering the placentas, which came out beautifully, dark and thick, each the size of a small plate. Fraternal twins, male and female, one visibly perfect and the other marked by an extra chromosome in every cell of her body. What were the odds of that? His son lay in the carrier, his hands waving now and then, fluid and random with the quick water motions of the womb. He injected his wife with a sedative, then leaned down to repair the episiotomy. It was nearly dawn, light gathering faintly in the windows. He watched his hands move, thinking how well the stitches were going in, as tiny as her own, as neat and even. She had torn out a whole panel of the quilt because of one mistake, invisible to him.

When the doctor finished, he found the nurse sitting in a rocker in the waiting room, cradling the baby girl in her arms. She met his gaze without speaking, and he remembered the night she had watched him as he slept.

"There's a place," he said, writing the name and address on the back of an envelope. "I'd like you to take her there. When it's light, I mean. I'll issue the birth certificate, and I'll call to say you're coming."

"But your wife," the nurse said, and he heard, from his distant place, the surprise and disapproval in her voice.

He thought of his sister, pale and thin, trying to catch her breath, and his mother turning to the window to hide her tears.

"Don't you see?" he asked, his voice soft. "This poor child will most likely have a serious heart defect. A fatal one. I'm trying to spare us all a terrible grief."

He spoke with conviction. He believed his own words. The nurse sat staring at him, her expression surprised but otherwise un-readable, as he waited for her to say yes. In the state of mind he was in it did not occur to him that she might say anything else. He did not imagine, as he would later that night, and in many nights to come, the ways in which he was jeopardizing everything. Instead, he felt impatient with her slowness and very tired all of a sudden, and the clinic, so familiar, seemed strange around him, as if he were walking in a dream. The nurse studied him with her blue unread-able eyes. He returned her gaze, unflinching, and at last she nod-ded, a movement so slight as to be almost imperceptible.

"The snow," she murmured, looking down.

. . .

But by midmorning the storm had begun to abate, and the distant sounds of plows grated through the still air. He watched from the upstairs window as the nurse knocked snow from her powder-blue car and drove off into the soft white world. The baby was hidden, asleep in a box lined with blankets, on the seat beside her. The doc-tor watched her turn left onto the street and disappear. Then he went back and sat with his family.

His wife slept, her gold hair splayed across the pillow. Now and then the doctor dozed. Awake, he gazed into the empty parking lot, watching smoke rise from the chimneys across the street, preparing the words he would say. That it was no one's fault, that their daugh-ter would be in good hands, with others like herself, with ceaseless care. That it would be best this way for them all.

In the late morning, when the snow had stopped for good, his son cried out in hunger, and his wife woke up.

"Where's the baby?" she said, rising up on her elbows, pushing her hair from her face. He was holding their son, warm and light, and he sat down beside her, settling the baby in her arms.

"Hello, my sweet," he said. "Look at our beautiful son. You were very brave."

She kissed the baby's forehead, then undid her robe and put him to her breast. His son latched on at once, and his wife looked up and smiled. He took her free hand, remembering how hard she had held onto him, imprinting the bones of her fingers on his flesh. He remembered how much he had wanted to protect her.

"Is everything all right?" she asked. "Darling? What is it?"

"We had twins," he told her slowly, thinking of the shocks of dark hair, the slippery bodies moving in his hands. Tears rose in his eyes. "One of each."

"Oh," she said. "A little girl too? Phoebe *and* Paul. But where is she?"

Her fingers were so slight, he thought, like the bones of a little bird.

"My darling," he began. His voice broke, and the words he had rehearsed so carefully were gone. He closed his eyes, and when he could speak again more words came, unplanned.

"Oh, my love," he said. "I am so sorry. Our little daughter died as she was born."

II

CAROLINE GILL WADED CAREFULLY, AWKWARDLY, ACROSS the parking lot. Snow reached her calves; in places, her knees. She carried the baby, swathed in blankets, in a cardboard box once used to deliver samples of infant formula to the office. It was stamped with red letters and cherubic infant faces, and the flaps lifted and fell with every step. There was an unnatural welling quiet in the nearly empty lot, a silence that seemed to originate from the cold itself, to expand in the air and flow outward like ripples from a stone thrown in water. Snow billowed, stinging her face, when she opened the car door. Instinctively, protectively, she curved herself around the box and wedged it into the backseat, where the pink blankets fell softly against the white vinyl upholstery. The baby slept, a fierce, intent, newborn sleep, its face clenched, its eyes only slits, the nose and chin mere bumps. You wouldn't know, Caroline thought. If you didn't know, you wouldn't. Caroline had given her an eight on the Apgar.

The city streets were badly plowed and difficult to navigate. Twice the car slid, and twice Caroline almost turned back. The interstate was clearer, however, and once Caroline got on it she made steady time, traveling through the industrial outskirts of

Lexington and into the rolling country of the horse farms. Here, miles of white fences made brisk shadows against the snow and horses stood darkly in the fields. The low sky was alive with fat gray clouds. Caroline turned on the radio, searched through the static for a station, turned it off. The world rushed by, ordinary and utterly changed.

Since the moment she had let her head dip in faint agreement to Dr. Henry's astonishing request, Caroline had felt as if she were falling through the air in slow motion, waiting to hit land and discover where she was. What he had asked of her—that she take his infant daughter away without telling his wife of her birth—seemed unspeakable. But Caroline had been moved by the pain and confusion on his face as he examined his daughter, by the slow numb way he seemed to move thereafter. Soon he'd come to his senses, she told herself. He was in shock, and who could blame him? He'd delivered his own twins in a blizzard, after all, and now this.

She drove faster, images of the early morning running through her like a current. Dr. Henry, working with such calm skill, his movements focused and precise. The flash of dark hair between Norah Henry's white thighs and her immense belly, rippling with contractions like a lake in the wind. The quiet hiss of the gas, and the moment when Dr. Henry called to her, his voice light but strained, his face so stricken that she was sure the second baby had been born dead. She had waited for him to move, to try to revive it. And when he didn't she thought suddenly that she should go to him, be a witness, so that she could say, later, *Yes, the baby was blue, Dr. Henry tried, we both tried, but there was nothing to be done.*

But then the baby cried, and the cry carried her to his side, where she looked and understood.

She drove on, pushing back her memories. The road cut through the limestone and the sky funneled down. She crested the slight hill and began the long descent to the river far below. Behind her, in the cardboard box, the baby slept on. Caroline glanced over her shoulder now and then, both reassured and distressed to see it had not moved. Such sleep, she reminded herself, was normal after the labor of entering the world. She wondered about her own birth, if she had slept so intently in the hours that followed, but both her parents were long dead; there was no one who remembered those moments. Her mother had been past forty when Caroline was born, her father already fifty-two. They had long since given up waiting for a child, had released any hope or expectation or even regret. Their lives were orderly, calm, content.

Until Caroline, startlingly, had arrived, a flower blooming up through snow.

They had loved her, certainly, but it had been a worried love, earnest and intent, layered with poultices and warm socks and castor oil. In the hot still summers, when polio was feared, Caroline had been made to stay inside, sweat beading on her temples as she stretched out on the daybed by the window in the upstairs hallway, reading. Flies buzzed against the glass and lay dead on the sills. Outside, the landscape shimmered in the light and heat, and children from the neighborhood, children whose parents were younger and thus less acquainted with the possibility of disaster, shouted to one another in the distance. Caroline pressed her face, her fingertips, against the screen, listening. Yearning. The air was still and sweat dampened the shoulders of her cotton blouse, the ironed waistband of her skirt. Far below in the garden, her mother, wearing gloves, a long apron, and a hat, pulled weeds. Later, in the dusky evenings, her father walked home from his insurance office, taking his hat off as he entered the still, shuttered house. Beneath the jacket, his shirt was stained and damp.

She was crossing the bridge now, her tires singing, the Kentucky River meandering far below and the high charged energy of the previous night melting away. She glanced again at the baby. Surely Norah Henry would want to hold this child, even if she couldn't keep her.

Surely this was none of Caroline's affair.

Yet she did not turn around. She turned on the radio again—this time she found a station of classical music—and drove on.

Twenty miles outside of Louisville, Caroline consulted Dr. Henry's directions, written in his sharp close hand, and left the highway. Here, so near the Ohio River, the upper branches of hawthorns and hackberry trees glittered with ice, though the roads were clear and dry. White fences enclosed the snow-dusted fields, and horses moved darkly behind them, their breath making clouds in the air. Caroline turned onto an even smaller road, where the land was rolling, unconfined. Soon, across a mile of pale hills, she glimpsed the building, built of red brick at the turn of the century, with two incongruous low-slung modern wings. It disappeared, now and again, as she followed the curves and dips of the country road, and then was suddenly before her.

She pulled into the circular driveway. Up close, the old house was in a state of mild disrepair. Paint was peeling on the wood trim and on the third floor a window had been boarded up, broken panes backed with plywood. Caroline got out of the car. She was wearing a pair of old flats, thin-soled and scuffed, kept in the closet and flung on hastily in the middle of last night when she couldn't find her boots. Gravel pushed up through the snow and her feet were immediately cold. She slung the bag she had prepared—containing diapers, a thermos bottle of warmed formula—over her shoulder, picked up the box with the baby, and entered the building. Lights of leaded glass, long unpolished, flanked the door on either side. There was an interior door with frosted glass and then a foyer, dark oak. Hot air, redolent with the scents of cooking—carrots and onions and potatoes—rushed and swirled around her. Caroline walked tentatively, floorboards creaking with every step, but no one appeared. A strip of threadbare carpet led across a wide-planked floor and into the back of the house to a waiting room with tall windows and heavy draperies. She sat on the edge of a worn velvet sofa, the box close by her side, and waited.

The room was overheated. She unbuttoned her coat. She was still wearing her white nurse's uniform, and when she touched her hair she realized she was still wearing her sharp white cap, too. She had risen at once when Dr. Henry called, dressing quickly and traveling out into the snowy night, and she had not stopped since. She unpinned the cap, folded it carefully, and closed her eyes. Distantly, silverware clattered and voices hummed. Above her, footsteps moved and echoed. She half dreamed of her mother, preparing a holiday meal while her father worked in the woodshop. Her childhood had been solitary, sometimes very lonely, but still she had these memories: a special quilt held close, a rug with roses beneath her feet, the weave of voices that belonged to her alone.

Distantly, a bell rang, twice. *I need you here right now,* Dr. Henry had called, strain and urgency in his voice. And Caroline had hurried, fashioning that awkward bed out of pillows, holding the mask on Mrs. Henry's face as the second twin, this little girl, slid into the world, setting something into motion.

Into motion. Yes, it could not be contained. Even sitting here on this sofa in the stillness of this place, even waiting, Caroline was troubled by the feeling that the world was shimmering, that things would not be still. *This?* was the refrain in her mind. *This now, after all these years?*

For Caroline Gill was thirty-one, and she had been waiting a long time for her real life to begin. Not that she had ever put it that way to herself. But she had felt since childhood that her life would not be ordinary. A moment would come—she would know it when she saw it—and everything would change. She'd dreamed of being a great pianist, but the lights of the high school stage were too different from the lights at home, and she froze in their glare. Then, in her twenties, as her friends from nursing school began to marry and have their families, Caroline too had found young men to admire, one especially, with dark hair and pale skin and a deep laugh. For a dreamy time she imagined that he—and, when he didn't call, that someone else—would transform her life. When years passed she gradually turned her attention to her work, again without despair. She had faith in herself and her own capabilities. She was not a person who ever got halfway to a destination and paused, wondering if she'd left an iron on and if the house was burning down. She kept on working. She waited.

She read, too, Pearl Buck's novels first and then everything she could find about life in China and Burma and Laos. Sometimes she let the books slip from her hands and gazed dreamily out the window of her plain little apartment on the edge of town. She saw herself moving through another life, an exotic, difficult, satisfying life. Her clinic would be simple, set in a lush jungle, perhaps near the sea. It would have white walls; it would gleam like a pearl. People would line up outside, squatting beneath coconut trees as they waited. She, Caroline, would tend to them all; she would heal them. She would transform their lives and hers.

Consumed by this vision, she had applied, in a great rush of fervor and excitement, to become a medical missionary. One brilliant late-summer weekend, she had taken the bus to St. Louis to be interviewed. Her name was put on a waiting list for Korea. But time passed; the mission was postponed, then canceled altogether. Caroline was put on another list, this time for Burma.

And then, while she was still checking the mail and dreaming of the tropics, Dr. Henry had arrived.

An ordinary day, nothing to indicate otherwise. It was late autumn by then, a season of colds, and the room was crowded, full of sneezes, muffled coughs. Caroline herself could feel a dull scratching deep in her throat as she called the next patient, an elderly gentleman whose cold would worsen in the next weeks, turning into the pneumonia that would finally kill him. Rupert Dean. He was sitting in the leather armchair, fighting a nosebleed, and he stood up slowly, stuffing his cloth handkerchief, with its vivid spots of blood, into his pocket. When he reached the desk he handed Caroline a photograph in a dark blue cardboard frame. It was a portrait, black and white, faintly tinted. The woman looking out wore a pale peach sweater. Her hair was gently waved, her eyes a deep shade of blue. Rupert Dean's wife, Emelda, dead now for twenty years. "She was the love of my life," he announced to Caroline, his voice so loud that people looked up.

The outer door of the office opened, rattling the glass-paneled inner door.

"She's lovely," Caroline said. Her hands were trembling. Because she was moved by his love and his sorrow, and because no one had ever loved her with this same passion. Because she was almost thirty years old, and yet if she died the next day there would be no one to mourn her like Rupert Dean still mourned his wife after more than twenty years. Surely she, Caroline Lorraine Gill, must be as unique and deserving of love as the woman in the old man's photo, and yet she had not found any way to reveal this, not through art or love or even through the fine high calling of her work.

She was still trying to compose herself when the door from the vestibule to the waiting room swung open. A man in a brown tweed overcoat hesitated in the doorway for a moment, his hat in his hand, taking in the yellow textured wallpaper, the fern in the corner, the metal rack of worn magazines. He had brown hair with a reddish tinge and his face was lean, his expression attentive, assessing. He was not distinguished, yet there was something in his stance, his manner—some quiet alertness, some quality of listening—that set him apart. Caroline's heart quickened and she felt a tingling on her skin, both pleasurable and irritating, like the unexpected brush of a moth's wing. His eyes caught hers—and she knew. Before he crossed the room to shake her hand, before he opened his mouth to speak his name, *David Henry,* in a neutral accent that placed him as an outsider. Before all this, Caroline was sure of a single simple fact: the person she'd been waiting for had come.

He had not been married then. Not married, not engaged, and with no attachments that she could ascertain. Caroline had listened carefully, both that day as he toured the clinic and later at the welcome parties and meetings. She heard what others, absorbed by the flow of polite conversation, distracted by his unfamiliar accent and sudden unexpected bursts of laughter, did not: that aside from mentioning his time in Pittsburgh now and then, a fact already known from his résumé and diploma, he never made reference to the past. For Caroline, this reticence gave him an air of mystery, and the mystery increased her sense that she knew him in ways the others did not. For her, their every encounter was charged, as if she were saying to him across the desk, the examination table, the beautiful, imperfect bodies of one patient or another, *I know you; I understand; I see what the others have missed.* When she overheard people joking about her crush on the new doctor, she flushed with surprise and embarrassment. But she was secretly pleased, too, for the rumors might reach him in a way that she, with her shyness, could not.

One late evening, after two months of quiet work, she had found him sleeping at his desk. His face was resting on his hands and he breathed with the light, even cadence of deep sleep. Caroline leaned against the doorway, her head tilted, and in that moment the dreams she'd nurtured for years had all coalesced. They would go together, she and Dr. Henry, to some remote place in the world, where they would work all day with sweat rising on their foreheads and instruments growing slippery in their palms, and where of an evening she would play to him on the piano that would be sent across the sea and up some difficult river and across the lush land to where they lived. Caroline was so immersed in this dream that when Dr. Henry opened his eyes she smiled at him, openly and freely, as she had never done before with anyone.

His clear surprise brought her to herself. She stood up straight and touched her hair, murmured some apology, blushed deep red. She disappeared, mortified but also faintly thrilled. For now he must know, now he would see her at last as she saw him. For a few days her anticipation of what might happen next was so great that she found it difficult to be in the same room with him. And yet when the days passed and nothing happened she was not disappointed. She relaxed and made excuses for the delay and went on waiting, unperturbed.

Three weeks later, Caroline had opened the newspaper to find the wedding photo on the society page: Norah Asher, now Mrs. David Henry, caught with her head turned, her neck elegant, her eyelids faintly curved, like shells. . . .

Caroline started, sweating in her coat. The room was overheated; she had almost drifted off. Beside her, the baby still slept. She stood and walked to the windows, the floorboards shifting and creaking beneath the worn carpet. Velvet drapes brushed the floor, remnants from the far-flung time when this place had been an elegant estate. She touched the edge of the sheer curtains beneath; yellow, brittle, they billowed dust. Outside, half a dozen cows stood in the snowy field, nosing for grass. A man wearing a red plaid jacket and dark gloves broke a path to the barn, buckets swinging from his hands.

This dust, this snow. It was not fair, not fair at all, that Norah Henry should have so much, should have her seamless happy life. Shocked at this thought, at the depth of her bitterness, Caroline let the curtains fall and walked out of the room, moving toward the sound of human voices.

She entered a hallway, fluorescent lights humming against the high ceiling. The air was thick with cleaning fluid, steamed vegetables, the faint yellow scent of urine. Carts rattled; voices called and murmured. She turned one corner, then another, descending a single step to enter a more modern wing with pale turquoise walls. Here the linoleum floor gave loosely against the plywood below. She passed several doors, glimpsing moments of people's lives, the images suspended like photographs: a man staring out a window, his face cast in shadows, his age indeterminate. Two nurses making a bed, their arms lifted high and the pale sheet floating for an instant near the ceiling. Two empty rooms, tarps spread, paint cans stacked in the corner. A closed door, and then the last one, open, where a young woman wearing a white cotton slip sat on the edge of a bed, her hands folded lightly in her lap, her head bent. Another woman, a nurse, stood behind her, silver scissors flashing. Hair cascaded darkly onto the white sheets, revealing the woman's bare neck: narrow, graceful, pale. Caroline paused in the doorway.

"She's cold," she heard herself saying, causing both women to look up. The woman on the bed had large eyes, darkly luminous in her face. Her hair, once quite long, now jutted raggedly at the level of her chin.

"Yes," the nurse said, and reached to brush some hair off the woman's shoulder; it drifted through the dull light and settled on the sheets, the speckled gray linoleum. "But it had to be done." Her eyes narrowed then as she studied Caroline's wrinkled uniform, her capless head. "Are you new here or something?" she asked.

Caroline nodded. "New," she said. "That's right."

Later, when she remembered this moment, one woman with a pair of scissors and the other sitting in a cotton slip amid the ruins of her hair, she would think of it in black and white and the image would fill her with a wild emptiness and yearning. For what, she was not certain. The hair was scattered, irretrievable, and the cold light fell through the window. She felt tears in her eyes. Voices echoed in another hall, and Caroline remembered the baby, left sleeping in a box on the overstuffed velvet sofa of the waiting room. She turned and hurried back.

Everything was just as she had left it. The box with its cheerful red cherubs was still on the sofa; the baby, her hands curled into small fists by her chin, was still sleeping. *Phoebe,* Norah Henry had said, just before she went under from the gas. *For a girl, Phoebe.*

Phoebe. Caroline unfolded the blankets gently and lifted her. She was so tiny, five and a half pounds, smaller than her brother though with the same rich dark hair. Caroline checked her diaper—tarry meconium stained the damp cloth—changed her, and wrapped her back up. She had not woken, and Caroline held her for a moment, feeling how light she was, how small, how warm. Her face was so small, so volatile. Even in her sleep, expressions moved like clouds across her features. Caroline glimpsed Norah Henry's frown in one, David Henry's concentrated listening in another.

She put Phoebe back into the box and tucked the blankets lightly around her, thinking of David Henry, edged with weariness, eating a cheese sandwich at his desk, finishing a cup of half-cold coffee, then rising to open the office doors again on Tuesday nights, a free clinic for patients who could not afford to pay him. The waiting room was always full on those nights, and he was often still there when Caroline finally went home at midnight, so weary herself that she could barely think. This was why she had come to love him, for his goodness. Yet he had sent her to this place with his infant daughter, this place where a woman had sat on the edge of a bed, her hair drifting into soft piles on the harsh cold light of the floor.

This would destroy her, he had said of Norah. *I will not have her destroyed.*

There were footsteps, drawing nearer, and then a woman with gray hair and a white uniform very much like Caroline's stood in the doorway. She was solidly built, agile for her size, no-nonsense. In another situation, Caroline would have been favorably impressed.

"Can I help you?" she asked. "Have you been waiting long?"

"Yes," Caroline said slowly. "I've been waiting for a long time, yes."

The woman, exasperated, shook her head. "Yes, look, I'm sorry. It's the snow. We're short-staffed today because of it. You get as much as an inch here in Kentucky, and the whole state shuts down. I grew up in Iowa, myself, and I don't see what all the fuss is about, but that's just me. Now, then. What can I do for you?"

"Are you Sylvia?" Caroline asked, struggling to remember the name on the paper below the directions. She'd left it in the car. "Sylvia Patterson?"

The woman's expression grew annoyed. "No. I am certainly not. I'm Janet Masters. Sylvia no longer works here."

"Oh," Caroline said, and then stopped. This woman didn't know who she was; clearly, she hadn't talked with Dr. Henry. Caroline, still holding the dirty diaper, dropped her hands to her sides to keep it out of sight.

Janet Masters planted her hands firmly on her hips, and her eyes narrowed. "Are you here from that formula company?" she asked, nodding across the room to the box on the sofa, the red cherubs smiling benignly. "Sylvia had something going with that rep, we all knew that, and if you're from the same company you can just pack up your things and go." She shook her head sharply.

"I don't know what you mean," Caroline said. "I'll just go," she added. "Really. I'm leaving. I won't bother you again."

But Janet Masters wasn't finished. "Insidious, that's what you people are. Dropping off free samples and then sending a bill for them a week later. This may be a home for the feebleminded, but it isn't run by them, you know."

"I know," Caroline whispered. "I'm truly sorry."

A bell rang, distantly, and the woman let her hands fall from her hips.

"See that you're out of here in five minutes," she said. "Out of here, and don't come back." Then she was gone.

Caroline stared at the empty doorway. A draft slid around her legs. After a moment she put the dirty diaper in the middle of the rickety piecrust table by the sofa. She felt in her pocket for her keys, then picked up the box with Phoebe in it. Quickly, before she could think about what she was doing, she went into the spartan hallway and through the double doors, the rush of cold air from the world outside as astonishing as being born.

She settled Phoebe in the car again and pulled away. No one tried to stop her; no one paid any attention at all. Still, Caroline drove fast once she reached the interstate, fatigue sluicing through her body like water down rock. For the first thirty miles she argued with herself, sometimes out loud. *What have you done?* she demanded severely. She argued with Dr. Henry, too, imagining the lines deepening in his forehead, the stray muscle in his cheek that leaped whenever he was upset. *What are you thinking?* he demanded to know, and Caroline had to confess that she had no idea whatsoever.

But the energy soon drained from these conversations, and by the time she reached the interstate she was driving mechanically, shaking her head now and then just to keep herself awake. It was late afternoon; Phoebe had been asleep for almost twelve hours. Soon she would need to be fed. Caroline hoped against hope they would be in Lexington before this happened.

She had just passed the last Frankfort exit, thirty-two miles from home, when the brake lights of the car ahead of her flared. She slowed, then slowed some more, then had to press down hard. Dusk was already beginning to gather, the sun a dull glow in the overcast sky. As she crested the hill, traffic came to a complete stop, a long ribbon of taillights that ended in a cluster flashing red and white. An accident: a pileup. Caroline thought she might weep. The gas gauge hovered below a quarter of a tank, enough to get back to Lexington but nothing extra, and this line of cars—well, they could be here for hours. She couldn't risk turning off the engine and losing the heat, not with a newborn in the car.

She sat still for several minutes, paralyzed. The last exit ramp was a quarter of a mile back, separated from her by a gleaming chain of cars. Heat rose from the Fairlane's powder-blue hood, shimmering faintly in the dusk, melting the few flakes of snow that had started to fall. Phoebe sighed, and her face tightened slightly and then relaxed. Caroline, following an impulse that would amaze her later, jerked the steering wheel and slid the Fairlane off the asphalt and onto the soft gravel shoulder. She put the car in reverse and then backed up, traveling slowly past the stalled line of cars. It was strange, as if she were passing a train. There was a woman with a fur coat; three children making faces, a man in a cloth jacket, smoking. She traveled slowly backward in the softening darkness, the stilled traffic like a frozen river.

She reached the exit without incident. It took her to route 60, where the trees were heavy with snow again. The fields were broken by houses, first a few and then many, their windows already glowing in the dusk. Soon Caroline was driving down the main street of Versailles, charmed by the brick shopfronts, searching for signs that would mark her way home.

A dark blue Kroger sign rose up a block away. That familiar sight, sale flyers decorating its bright windows, comforted Caroline and made her realize suddenly how hungry she was. And it was what, now—Saturday, not quite evening? The stores would be closed all day tomorrow, and she had very little food in her apartment. Despite her exhaustion, she pulled into the parking lot and turned off the car.

Phoebe, warm and light, twelve hours old, was wrapped in sleep. Caroline shouldered the diaper bag and tucked the baby beneath her coat, so small, curled close and warm. Wind moved over the asphalt, whisking the remnants of snow and a few new flakes, swirling them in corners. She picked her way through the slush, afraid of falling and hurting the baby, thinking at the same time, fleetingly, how easy it would be to simply leave her, in a garbage dumpster or on the steps of a church or anywhere. Her power over this tiny life was total. A deep sense of responsibility flooded through her, making her light-headed.

The glass door swung open, releasing a rush of light and warmth. The store was crowded. Shoppers spilled out, their carts piled high. A bag boy stood at the door.

"We're only still open on account of the weather," he warned, as she entered. "We're closing in half an hour."

"But the storm's over," Caroline said, and the boy laughed, excited and incredulous. His face was flushed with the heat pouring down over the automatic doors and spilling out into the evening.

"Didn't you hear? We're supposed to get hit again tonight, but good."

Caroline settled Phoebe in a metal cart and walked through the unfamiliar aisles. She pondered over formulas, a bottle warmer, over the rows of bottles with their selections of nipples, over bibs. She started to the checkout, then realized she had better get milk for herself, and some more diapers, and some kind of food. People passed her, and when they saw Phoebe they all smiled, and some even paused and moved the blanket aside to see her face. They said, "Oh, how sweet!" and "How old?" Caroline lied without compunction. Two weeks, she told them. "Oh, you shouldn't have her out in this," one woman with gray hair reprimanded her. "My! You should get that baby home."

In aisle 6, while Caroline was picking out cans of tomato soup, Phoebe stirred, her small hands jerking wildly, and began to cry. Caroline vacillated for a moment, then picked up the baby and the bulky bag and went to the restroom in the back of the store. She sat on an orange plastic chair in the corner, listening to water drip from the faucet, while she balanced the infant on her lap and poured formula from the thermos into a bottle. It took several minutes for the baby to settle down, because she was so agitated and because her sucking reflex was poor. Eventually, however, she caught on, and then Phoebe drank as she had slept: fiercely, intently, her hands in fists by her chin. By the time she relaxed, sated, they were announcing that the store was about to close. Caroline hurried to the checkout counter, where a single cashier waited, bored and impatient. She paid quickly, cradling the paper sack in one arm, Phoebe in the other. When she left, they locked the doors behind her.

The parking lot was nearly empty, the last few cars idling or pulling slowly out into the street. Caroline rested her paper sack of groceries on the hood and settled Phoebe in her box in the backseat. The faint voices of employees echoed across the lot. Scattered flakes swirled in the cones from the streetlights, no more or less than before. The forecasters so often got it wrong. The snow that had started before Phoebe was born—just last night, she reminded herself, though it seemed ages past—had not even been predicted. She reached into the paper sack and ripped open a loaf of bread, taking out a slice, for she had not eaten all day and was ravenous. She chewed as she shut the door, thinking with weary longing of her apartment, so spare and tidy, of her twin bed with its white chenille spread, everything in order and in place. She was halfway around the back of the car before she realized that her taillights were glowing weakly red.

She stopped where she was, staring. All that time, while she had dithered in the grocery aisles, while she had sat in the unfamiliar restroom quietly feeding Phoebe, this light had been spilling out across the snow.

When she tried the ignition it merely clicked, the battery so dead the engine wouldn't even groan.

She got out of the car and stood by the open door. The parking lot was empty now; the last car had driven away. She began to laugh. It wasn't a normal laugh; even Caroline could hear that: her voice too loud, halfway to a sob. "I have a baby," she said out loud, astonished. "I have a baby in this car." But the parking lot stretched quietly before her, the lights from the grocery store windows making large rectangles in the slush. "I have a baby here," Caroline repeated, her voice thinning quickly in the air. "A baby!" she shouted then, into the stillness.

III

NORAH OPENED HER EYES. OUTSIDE, THE SKY WAS FADING into dawn, but the moon was still caught in the trees, shedding pale light into the room. She had been dreaming, searching on frozen ground for something she had lost. Blades of grass, sharp and brittle, shattered at her touch, leaving tiny cuts on her flesh. Waking, she held her hands up, momentarily confused, but her hands were unmarked, her nails carefully filed and polished.

Beside her, in his cradle, her son was crying. In one smooth motion, more instinct than intention, Norah lifted him into the bed. The sheets beside her were cool, arctic white. David was gone then, called to the clinic while she slept. Norah pulled her son into the warm curve of her body, opened her nightgown. His small hands fluttered against her swollen breasts like moth wings; he latched on. A sharp pain, which subsided in a wave as the milk came. She stroked his thin hair, his fragile scalp. Yes, astonishing, the powers of the body. His hands stilled, resting like small stars against her aureolas.

She closed her eyes, drifting slowly between sleep and waking. A well deep within her was tapped, released. Her milk flowed and, mysteriously, Norah felt herself becoming a river or a wind, encompassing everything: the daffodils on the dresser and the grass grow-ing sweetly and silently outside, the new leaves pressing open against the buds of the trees. Tiny larvae, white as seed pearls and hidden in the ground, transforming themselves into caterpillars, inchworms, bees. Birds in winged flight, calling. All this was hers. Paul clenched his tiny fists below his chin. His cheeks moved rhyth-mically as he drank. Around them the universe hummed, exquisite and demanding.

Norah's heart surged with love, with vast unwieldy happiness and sorrow.

She had not cried about their daughter right away, though David had. *A blue baby,* he had told her, tears catching in the stubble of his one-day beard. A little girl who never took a breath. Paul was in her lap and Norah had studied him: the tiny face, so serene and wrinkled, the little striped knit cap, the infant fingers, so pink and delicate and curved. Tiny, tiny fingernails, still soft, translucent as the daylight moon. What David was saying—Norah could not take it in, not really. Her memories of the night before were distinct, then blurry: there was the snow, and the long ride to the clinic through the empty streets, and David stopping at every light while she fought against the rippling urge, seismic and intense, to push. After that she remembered only scattered things, strange things: the unfamiliar quietness of the clinic, the soft worn feel of a blue cloth across her knees. The coldness of the examination table slap-ping her bare back. Caroline Gill's gold watch glinting every time she reached to give Norah the gas. Then she was waking up and Paul was in her arms and David was beside her, weeping. She glanced up, watching him with concern and an interested detach-ment. It was the drugs, the aftermath of the birth, a hormonal high. Another baby, a blue one—how could that be? She remembered the second urge to push, and tension beneath David's voice like rocks in white water. But the infant in her arms was perfect, beauti-ful, more than enough. *It's all right,* she had told David, stroking his arm, *it's all right.*

It was not until they left the office, stepping tentatively into the chill, damp air of the next afternoon, that the loss had finally pene-trated. It was nearly dusk, the air full of melting snow and raw earth. The sky was overcast, white and grainy behind the stark bare branches of the sycamores. She carried Paul—he was as light as a cat—thinking how strange this was, to take an entirely new person to their home. She'd decorated the room so carefully, choosing the pretty maple crib and dresser, pressing the paper, scattered with bears, onto the wall, making the curtains, stitching the quilt by hand. Everything was in order, everything was prepared, her son was in her arms. Yet at the building entrance, she stopped between the two tapering concrete pillars, unable to take another step.

"David," she said. He turned, pale and dark-haired, like a tree against the sky.

"What?" he asked. "What is it?"

"I want to see her," she said, her voice a whisper, yet somehow forceful in the quiet of the parking lot. "Just once. Before we go. I have to see her."

David shoved his hands in his pockets and studied the pavement. All day, icicles had crashed from the zigzag roof; here they lay shattered near the steps.

"Oh, Norah," he said softly. "Please, just come home. We have a beautiful son."

"I know," she said, because it was 1964 and he was her husband and she had always deferred to him completely. Yet she could not seem to move, not feeling as she did, that she was leaving behind some essential part of herself. "Oh! Just for a moment, David. Why not?"

Their eyes met, and the anguish in his made her own fill with tears.

"She isn't here." David's voice was raw. "That's why. There's a cemetery on Bentley's family farm. In Woodford County. I asked him to take her. We can go there, later in the spring. Oh, Norah, please. You are breaking my heart."

Norah closed her eyes then, feeling something drain out of her at the thought of an infant, her daughter, being lowered into the cold March earth. Her arms, holding Paul, were stiff and steady, but the rest of her felt liquid, as if she too might flow away into the ditches and disappear with the snow. David was right, she thought, she didn't want to know this. When he climbed the steps and put his arm around her shoulders, she nodded, and they walked together across the empty parking lot, into the fading light. He secured the car seat; he drove them carefully, methodically, home; they carried Paul across the front porch and through the door; and they put him, sleeping, in his room. It had brought her a measure of comfort, the way David had taken care of everything, the way he'd taken care of her, and she had not argued with him again about her wish to see their daughter.

But now she dreamed every night of lost things.

Paul had fallen asleep. Beyond the window, dogwood branches, cluttered with new buds, moved against the paling indigo sky. Norah turned, shifted Paul to her other breast, and closed her eyes again, drifting. She woke suddenly to dampness, crying, sunlight full in the room. Her breasts were already filling again; it had been three hours. She sat, feeling heavy, weighted, the flesh of her stomach so loose it pooled whenever she lay down, her breasts stiff and swollen with milk, her joints still aching from the birth. In the hall, the floorboards creaked beneath her.

On the changing table Paul cried louder, turning an angry mottled red. She stripped off his damp clothes, his soaked cotton diaper. His skin was so delicate, his legs as scrawny and reddened as plucked chicken wings. At the edge of her mind her lost daughter hovered, watchful, silent. She swabbed Paul's umbilical cord with alcohol, threw the diaper in the pail to soak, then dressed him again.

"Sweet baby," she murmured, lifting him. "Little love," she said, and carried him downstairs.

In the living room the blinds were still closed, the curtains drawn. Norah made her way to the comfortable leather chair in the corner, opening her robe. Her milk rose up again with its own irresistible tidal rhythms, a force so powerful it seemed to wash away everything she had been before. *I wake to sleep,* she thought, settling back, troubled because she could not remember who had written this.

The house was quiet. The furnace clicked off; leaves rustled on the trees outside. Distantly, the bathroom door opened and shut, and water ran faintly. Bree, her sister, came lightly down the stairs, wearing an old shirt whose sleeves hung down to her fingertips. Her legs were white, her narrow feet bare against the wood floors.

"Don't turn on the light," Norah said.

"Okay." Bree came over and touched her fingers lightly to Paul's scalp.

"How's my little nephew?" she said. "How's sweet Paul?"

Norah looked at her son's tiny face, surprised, as always, by his name. He had not grown into it yet, he still wore it like a wrist band, something that might easily slip off and disappear. She had read about people—where? she could not remember this either— who refused to name their children for several weeks, feeling them to be not yet of the earth, suspended still between two worlds.

"Paul." She said it out loud, solid and definite, warm as a stone in sunlight. An anchor.

Silently, to herself, she added, *Phoebe*.

"He's hungry," Norah added. "He's always so hungry."

"Ah. He takes after his aunt, then. I'm going to get some toast and coffee. You want anything?"

"Maybe some water," she said, watching Bree, long-limbed and graceful, leave the room. How strange it was that her sister, who had always been her opposite, her nemesis, should be the one she wanted here, but it was so.

Bree was only twenty, but headstrong and so sure of herself that she seemed to Norah, often, the elder. Three years ago, as a junior in high school, Bree had run away with the pharmacist who lived across the street, a bachelor twice her age. People blamed the pharmacist, old enough to know better. They blamed Bree's wildness on losing her father so suddenly when she was in her early teens, a vulnerable age, everyone agreed. They predicted that the marriage would end soon and badly, and it had.

But if people imagined that Bree's failed marriage would subdue her, they were wrong. Something had begun to change in the world since Norah was a girl, and Bree had not come home as expected, chastened and embarrassed. Instead, she'd enrolled at the university, changing her name from Brigitte to Bree because she liked the way it sounded: breezy, she said, and free.

Their mother, mortified by the scandalous marriage and more

scandalous divorce, had married a pilot for TWA and moved to St. Louis, leaving her daughters to themselves. *Well, at least one of my daughters knows how to behave,* she had said, looking up from the box of china she was packing. It was autumn, the air crisp, full of golden raining leaves. Her white-blond hair was spun in an airy cloud, and her delicate features were softened with sudden emotion. *Oh, Norah, I'm so thankful to have one proper girl, you can't imagine. Even if you never marry, darling, you'll always be a lady.* Norah, sliding a framed portrait of her father into a carton, had flushed dark with annoyance and frustration. She too had been shocked by Bree's nerve, her daring, and she was angry that the rules seemed to have shifted, that Bree had more or less gotten away with it—the marriage, the divorce, the scandal.

She hated what Bree had done to them all.

She wished desperately that she'd done it first.

But it would never have occurred to her. She'd always been good; that was her job. She had been close to their father, an affable, disorganized man, an expert in sheep, who had spent his days in the closed-up room at the top of the stairs, reading journals, or out at the research station, standing amid the sheep with their strange and slanting yellow eyes. She'd loved him, and all her life she had felt a compulsion to make up, somehow: for his inattention to his family; and for her mother's disappointment in having married a man so alien, finally, to herself. When he died, this compulsion to make things right again, to fix the world, had only intensified. So she went on, studying quietly and doing what was expected of her. After graduation she had worked for six months at the telephone company, a job she'd not enjoyed and had given up quite happily when she married David. Their meeting in the lingerie department of Wolf Wile's department store, their whirlwind private wedding, had been the closest she'd come to wild, herself.

Norah's life, Bree was fond of saying, was just like a TV sitcom. *It's fine for you,* she'd say, tossing back her long hair, wide silver bracelets halfway to her elbow. *For me, I couldn't take it. I'd go nuts in about a week. A day!*

Norah smoldered, disdained and envied Bree, bit her tongue; Bree took classes on Virginia Woolf, moved in with the manager of a health-food restaurant in Louisville, and stopped coming by. Yet strangely, when Norah became pregnant, everything changed. Bree started showing up again, bringing lacy booties and tiny silver ankle bracelets imported from India; these, she'd found in a shop in San Francisco. She brought mimeographed sheets with advice on breast-feeding, too, once she heard that Norah planned to forgo bottles. Norah, by then, was glad to see her. Glad for the sweet, impractical gifts, glad for her support; in 1964 breast-feeding was radical, and she'd had a hard time finding information. Their mother refused to discuss the idea; the women in her sewing circle had told her they would put chairs in their bathrooms to ensure her privacy. At this, to her relief, Bree had scoffed out loud. *What a bunch of prudes!* she insisted. *Pay no attention.*

Still, while Norah was grateful for Bree's support, she was, at times, also secretly uneasy. In Bree's world, which seemed mostly to exist elsewhere, in California, or Paris, or New York City, young women walked around their houses topless, took pictures of themselves with babies at their enormous breasts, wrote columns advocating the nutritional benefits of human milk. *It's completely natural; it's in our nature as mammals,* Bree explained, but the very thought of herself as a mammal, driven by instincts, described by words like *suckling* (so close to *rutting,* she thought, reducing something beautiful to the level of a barn), had made Norah blush and want to leave the room.

Now Bree came back in carrying a tray with coffee, fresh bread, butter. Her long hair fell over her shoulder as she bent to put a tall glass of ice water on the table next to Norah. She slid the tray on the coffee table and settled onto the couch, tucking her long white legs beneath her.

"David's gone?"

Norah nodded. "I didn't even hear him getting up."

"You think it's good for him to be working so much?"

"Yes," Norah said firmly. "I do." Dr. Bentley had talked to the other doctors in the practice, and they had offered David time off, but David had refused. "I think it's good for him to be busy right now."

"Really? And what about you?" Bree asked, biting into her bread.

"Me? Honestly, I'm fine."

Bree waved her free hand. "Don't you think—" she began, but before she could criticize David again, Norah interrupted.

"It's so good you're here," she said. "No one else will talk to me."

"That's crazy. The house has been full of people wanting to talk to you."

"I had twins, Bree," Norah said quietly, conscious of her dream, the empty, frozen landscape, her frantic searching. "No one else will say a word about her. They act like since I have Paul, I ought to be satisfied. Like lives are interchangeable. But I had *twins*. I had a daughter too—"

She stopped, interrupted by the sudden tightness in her throat.

"Everyone is sad," Bree said softly. "So happy and so sad, all at once. They don't know what to say, that's all."

Norah lifted Paul, now asleep, to her shoulder. His breath was warm on her neck; she rubbed his back, not much bigger than her palm.

"I know," she said. "I know. But still."

"David shouldn't have gone back to work so soon," Bree said. "It's only been three days."

"He finds work a comfort," Norah said. "If I had a job, I'd go."

"No," Bree said, shaking her head. "No, you wouldn't, Norah. You know, I hate to say this, but David's just shutting himself away, locking up every feeling. And you're still trying to fill the emptiness. To fix things. And you can't."

Norah, studying her sister, wondered what feelings the pharmacist had kept at bay; for all her openness, Bree had never spoken of her own brief marriage. And even though Norah was inclined to agree with her now, she felt obligated to defend David, who through his own sadness had taken care of everything: the quiet unattended burial, the explanations to friends, the swift tidying up of the ragged ends of grief.

"He has to do it his own way," she said, reaching to open the blinds. The sky had turned bright blue, and it seemed the buds had swollen on the branches even in these few hours. "I just wish I'd seen her, Bree. People think that's macabre, but I do wish it. I wish I had touched her, just once."

"It's not macabre," Bree said softly. "It sounds completely reasonable to me."

A silence followed, and then Bree broke it awkwardly, tentatively, by offering Norah the last piece of buttered bread.

"I'm not hungry," Norah lied.

"You have to eat," Bree said. "The weight will disappear anyway. That's one of the great unsung benefits of breast-feeding."

"Not unsung," Norah said. "You're always singing."

Bree laughed. "I guess I am."

"Honestly," Norah said, reaching for the glass of water. "I'm glad you're here."

"Hey," Bree said, a little embarrassed. "Where else would I be?"

Paul's head was a warm weight, his fine thick hair soft against her neck. Did he miss his twin, Norah wondered, that vanished presence, his short life's close companion? Would he always feel a sense of loss? She stroked his head, looking out the window. Beyond the trees, faint against the sky, she glimpsed the faraway and fading sphere of the moon.

• • •

Later, while Paul slept, Norah took a shower. She tried on and discarded three different outfits, skirts that bound her waist, pants that strained across the hips. She had always been petite, slender and well-proportioned, and the ungainliness of her body amazed and depressed her. Finally, in despair, she ended up in her old denim maternity jumper, gratifyingly loose, which she had sworn she'd never wear again. Dressed but barefoot, she wandered through the house, room to room. Like her body, the rooms were spilling over, wild, chaotic, out of control. Soft dust had gathered everywhere, clothes were scattered on every surface, and covers spilled from the unmade beds. There was a clean trail in the dust on the dresser, where David had placed a vase of daffodils, brown already at the edges; the windows were cloudy too. In another day Bree would leave and their mother would arrive. At the thought of this, Norah sat helplessly on the edge of the bed, a tie of David's hanging limply in her hands. The disorder of the house pressed on her like a weight, as if the very sunlight had taken on substance, gravity. She didn't have the energy to fight it. What was more, and more distressing, she didn't seem to care.

The doorbell rang. Bree's sharp footsteps moved through the rooms, echoing.

Norah recognized the voices right away. For a moment longer she stayed where she was, feeling drained of energy, wondering how she could get Bree to send them away. But the voices came closer, near the stairwell, fading again as they entered the living room; it was the night circle from her church, bearing gifts, eager for a glimpse of the new baby. Two sets of friends had already come, one from her sewing circle and another from her china-painting club, filling the refrigerator with food, passing Paul from hand to hand like a trophy. Norah had done these same things for new mothers time and again, and now she was shocked to find she felt resentment rather than appreciation: the interruptions, the burden of thank-you notes, and she didn't care about the food; she didn't even want it.

Bree was calling. Norah went downstairs without bothering to put on lipstick or even brush her hair. Her feet were still bare.

"I look awful," she announced, defiant, entering the room.

"Oh, no," Ruth Starling said, patting the sofa by her side, though Norah noted, with a strange satisfaction, the glances being exchanged among the others. She sat down obediently, crossing her legs at the ankles, and folding her hands in her lap like she'd done in school as a little girl.

"Paul's just gone to sleep," she said. "I won't wake him up." There was anger in her voice, real aggression.

"It's all right, my dear," Ruth said. She was nearly seventy, with fine white hair, carefully styled. Her husband of fifty years had passed away the year before. What had it cost her, Norah wondered, what did it cost her now, to maintain her appearance, her cheerful demeanor? "You've been through such a lot," Ruth said.

Norah felt her daughter again, a presence just beyond sight, and quelled a sudden urge to run upstairs and check on Paul. I'm going crazy, she thought, and stared at the floor.

"How about some tea?" Bree asked, with cheery unease. Before anyone could answer, she disappeared into the kitchen.

Norah did her best to concentrate on the conversation: cotton or batiste for the hospital pillows, what people thought about the new pastor, whether or not they should donate blankets to the Salvation Army. Then Sally announced that Kay Marshall's baby, a girl, had been delivered the night before.

"Seven pounds exactly," Sally said. "Kay looks wonderful. The baby's beautiful. They named her Elizabeth, after her grandmother. They say it was an easy labor."

There was a silence, then, as everyone realized what had happened. Norah felt as if the quiet were expanding from some place in the center of her, rippling through the room. Sally looked up, flushed pink with regret.

"Oh," she said. "Oh, Norah. I'm so sorry."

Norah wanted to speak and set things in motion again. The right words hovered in her mind, but she could not seem to find her voice. She sat silently, and the silence became a lake, an ocean, where they all might drown.

"Well," Ruth said briskly, at last. "Bless your heart, Norah. You must be exhausted." She pulled out a bulky package, brightly wrapped, with a cluster of narrow ribbons in tight curls. "We took up a collection, thinking you probably had all the diaper pins a mother could want."

The women laughed, relieved. Norah smiled too and opened the box, tearing the paper: a jumper chair, with a metal frame and a cloth seat, similar to one she had once admired at a friend's house.

"Of course, he won't be able to use it for a few months," Sally was saying. "Still, we couldn't think of anything better, once he's on the move!"

"And here," said Flora Marshall, standing up, two soft packages in her hands.

Flora was older than the others in the group, older even than Ruth, but wiry and active. She knitted blankets for every new baby in the church. Suspecting from her size that Norah might have twins, she had knitted two receiving blankets, working on them during their evening sessions and the coffee hour at church, balls of soft bright yarn spilling from her bag. Pastel yellows and greens, soft blues and pinks intermingled—she wasn't about to lay any bets on whether they would be boys or girls, she joked. But twins, she'd been sure about that. No one had taken her seriously at the time.

Norah took the two packages, pressing back tears. The soft familiar wool cascaded onto her lap when she opened the first, and her lost daughter seemed very near. Norah felt a rush of gratitude to Flora who, with the wisdom of grandmothers, had known just what to do. She tore open the second package, eager for the other blanket, as colorful and soft as the first.

"It's a little big," Flora apologized, when the playsuit fell into her lap. "But then, they grow so fast at this age."

"Where's the other blanket?" Norah demanded. She heard her voice, harsh, like the cry of a bird, and she felt astonished; all her life she'd been known for her calm, had prided herself on her even temperament, her careful choices. "Where's the blanket you made for my little girl?"

Flora flushed and glanced around the room for help. Ruth took Norah's hand and pressed it hard. Norah felt the smooth skin, the surprising pressure of her fingers. David had told her the names of these bones once, but she could not remember them. Worse, she was crying.

"Now, now. You have a beautiful baby boy," Ruth said.

"He had a sister," Norah whispered, determined, looking around at all the faces. They had come here out of kindness. They were sad, yes, and she was making them sadder by the second. What was happening to her? All her life she had tried so hard to do the right thing. "Her name was Phoebe. I want somebody to say her name. Do you hear me?" She stood up. "I want someone to remember her name."

There was a cool cloth on her forehead then, and hands helping her lie down on the couch. They told her to close her eyes, and she did. Tears still slipped beneath her eyelids, a spring welling up, she couldn't seem to stop. People were speaking again, voices swirling

like snow in the wind, talking about what to do. It wasn't uncommon, someone said. Even in the best of circumstances, it wasn't
strange at all to have this sudden low a few days after birth. They
ought to call David, another voice suggested, but then Bree was
there, calm and gracious, ushering them all to the door. When they
had gone Norah opened her eyes to find Bree wearing one of her
aprons, the waistband with its rickrack trim tied loosely around her
slender waist.

Flora Marshall's blanket was on the floor amid the wrapping
paper, and she picked it up, weaving her fingers into the soft yarn.
Norah wiped her eyes and spoke.

"David said her hair was dark. Like his."

Bree looked at her intently. "You said you were going to have a
memorial service, Norah. Why wait? Why not do it now? Maybe it
would bring you some peace."

Norah shook her head. "What David says, what everyone says, it
makes sense. I should focus on the baby I have."

Bree shrugged. "Except you're not doing that. The more you try
not to think about her, the more you do. David's only a doctor," she
added. "He doesn't know everything. He's not God."

"Of course he's not," Norah said. "I know that."

"Sometimes I'm not sure you do."

Norah didn't answer. Patterns played on the polished wood
floors, the shadows of leaves digging holes in the light. The clock on
the mantel ticked softly. She felt she should be angry, but she was
not. The idea of a memorial service seemed to have stopped the
draining of energy and will that had begun on the steps of the clinic
and had not ceased until this moment.

"Maybe you're right," she said. "I don't know. Maybe. Something very small. Something quiet."

Bree handed her the telephone. "Here. Just start asking questions."

Norah took a deep breath and began. She called the new pastor
first and found herself explaining that she wanted to have a service,
yes, and outside, in the courtyard. Yes, rain or shine. *For Phoebe, my
daughter, who died at birth.* Over the next two hours, she repeated

the words again and again: to the florist, to the woman in classifieds at *The Leader,* to her sewing friends, who agreed to do the flowers. Each time, Norah felt the calm within her swell and grow, something akin to the release of having Paul latch on and drink, connecting her back to the world.

Bree left for class, and Norah walked through the silent house, taking in the chaos. In the bedroom, afternoon light slanted through the glass, showing every inattention. She had seen this disorder every day without caring, but now, for the first time since the birth, she felt energy rather than inertia. She pulled the sheets taut on the beds, opened the windows, dusted. Off came the denim maternity jumper. She searched her closet until she found a skirt that would fit and a blouse that didn't strain against her breasts. She frowned at her image in the mirror, still so plump, so bulky, but she felt better. She took time to do her hair too, a hundred strokes. Her brush was full when she finished, a thick nest of gold down, all the luxuriance of pregnancy falling away as her hormone levels readjusted. She had known it would happen. Still, the loss made her want to weep.

That's enough, she said sternly to herself, applying lipstick, blinking away the tears. *That's enough, Norah Asher Henry.*

She pulled on a sweater before she went downstairs and found her flat beige shoes. Her feet, at least, were slim again.

She checked on Paul—still sleeping, his breath soft but real against her fingertips—put one of the frozen casseroles into the oven, set the table, and opened a bottle of wine. She was discarding the wilted flowers, their stems cool and pulpy in her hands, when the front door opened. Her heart quickened at David's footsteps, and then he stood in the doorway, his dark suit loose on his thin frame, his face flushed from his walk. He was tired, and she saw him register with relief the clean house, her familiar clothes, the scent of cooking food. He held another bunch of daffodils, gathered from the garden. When she kissed him, his lips were cool against her own.

"Hi," he said. "Looks like you had a good day here."

"Yes. It was good." She nearly told him what she'd done, but instead she made him a drink: whiskey, neat, like he liked it. He leaned against the counter while she washed the lettuce. "How about you?" she asked, turning off the water.

"Not so bad," he said. "Busy. Sorry about last night. A patient with a heart attack. Not fatal, thankfully."

"Were bones involved?" she asked.

"Oh. Yes, he fell down the stairs. Broke his tibia. The baby's asleep?"

Norah glanced at the clock and sighed. "I should probably get him up," she said. "If I'm ever going to get him on a schedule."

"I'll do it," David said, carrying the flowers upstairs. She heard him moving above, and she imagined him leaning down to touch Paul's forehead lightly, to hold his small hand. But in a few minutes David came back downstairs alone, wearing jeans and a sweater. "He looked so peaceful," David said. "Let's let him sleep."

They went into the living room and sat together on the sofa. For a moment it was like before, just the two of them, and the world around them was an understandable place, full of promise. Norah had planned to tell David about her plans over dinner, but now, suddenly, she found herself explaining the simple service she had organized, the announcement she had placed. As she talked she was aware of David's gaze growing more intent, somehow deeply vulnerable. His expression made her hesitate; it was as if he'd been unmasked, and she was talking now to a stranger whose reactions she couldn't anticipate. His eyes were darker than she'd ever seen them, and she could not tell what was going on in his mind.

"You don't like the idea," she said.

"It's not that."

Again she saw the grief in his eyes; she heard it in his voice. Out of a desire to assuage it, she nearly took everything back, but she felt her earlier inertia, pushed aside with such great effort, lurking in the room.

"It helped me to do this," she said. "That isn't wrong."

"No," he said. "It isn't wrong."

He seemed about to say more, but then he stopped himself and stood up instead, walking to the window and staring out into the darkness at the little park across the street. "But damn it, Norah," he said, his voice low and harsh, a tone he had never used before. It frightened her, the anger underlying his words. "Why do you have to be so stubborn? Why, at least, didn't you tell me before you called the papers?"

"She died," Norah said, angry now herself. "There's no shame in it. No reason to keep it a secret."

David, stiff-shouldered, didn't turn. A stranger, holding a coral-colored robe over his arm in Wolf Wile's department store, he had seemed strangely familiar, like someone she had once known well and hadn't seen for years. Yet now, after a year of marriage, she hardly knew him at all.

"David," she said, "what is happening to us?"

He did not turn. Scents of meat and potatoes filled the room; she remembered the dinner, warming in the oven, and her stomach churned with a hunger she had denied all day. Upstairs, Paul began to cry, but she stayed where she was, waiting for his answer.

"Nothing's happening to us," he said at last. When he turned, the grief was still vivid in his eyes and something else—a kind of resolution—that she did not understand. "You're making a mountain out of a molehill, Norah," he said. "Which, I suppose, is understandable."

Cold. Dismissive. Patronizing. Paul was crying harder. The force of Norah's anger wheeled her around and she stormed upstairs, where she lifted the baby and changed him, gently, gently, all the time trembling with rage. Then the rocking chair, buttons, the blissful release. She closed her eyes. Downstairs, David moved through the rooms. He, at least, had touched their daughter, seen her face.

She would have the service, no matter what. She would do it for herself.

Slowly, slowly, as Paul nursed, as the light faded, she grew calm, became again that wide tranquil river, accepting the world and carrying it easily on its currents. Outside, the grass was growing slowly and silently; the egg sacs of spiders were bursting open; the wings of birds were pulsing in flight. *This is sacred,* she found herself thinking, connected through the child in her arms and the child in the earth to everything that lived and ever had. It was a long time before she opened her eyes, and then she was startled by both the darkness and the beauty all around: a small oblong of light, reflected off the glass doorknob, quivering on the wall. Paul's new blanket, lovingly knit, cascading like waves from the crib. And on the dresser David's daffodils, delicate as skin and almost luminous, collecting the light from the hall.

IV

ONCE HER VOICE DWINDLED TO NOTHING IN THE EMPTY parking lot, Caroline slammed the car door and started picking her way through the slush. After a few steps, she stopped and went back for the baby. Phoebe's thin wails rose in the darkness, propelling Caroline across the asphalt and past the wide blank squares of light, to the automatic doors of the grocery store. Locked. Caroline shouted and knocked, her voice weaving with Phoebe's cries. Inside, the brightly lit aisles were empty. A discarded mop bucket stood nearby; cans gleamed in the silence. For several minutes Caroline stood silently herself, listening to Phoebe's cries and the distant rush of the wind through the trees. Then she pulled·herself together and made her way to the back of the store. The rolling metal door off the loading platform was closed, but she walked up to it anyway, aware of the scent of rotting produce on the cold, greasy concrete where the snow had melted. She kicked hard at the door, so satisfied by its booming echo that she kicked it several more times, until she was breathless.

"If they're still in there, honey, which I kinda doubt, they aren't going to be opening up anytime soon."

A man's voice. Caroline turned and saw him standing below her, on the ramplike decline that allowed tractor trailers to back into the loading area. Even at this distance she could tell he was a large person. He wore a bulky coat and a wool knit hat. His hands were shoved into his pockets.

"My baby's crying," she said, unnecessarily. "My car battery is dead. There's a phone right inside the front door, but I can't get to it."

"How old's your baby?" the man asked.

"A newborn," Caroline told him, hardly thinking, the edge of tears and panic in her voice. Ridiculous, an idea she had always loathed, and yet here she was—a damsel in distress.

"It's Saturday night," the man observed, his voice traveling over the snowy space between them. Beyond the parking lot, the street was still. "Any garage in town is likely to be closed."

Caroline didn't answer.

"Look here, ma'am," he began slowly, the steadiness of his voice some kind of anchor. Caroline realized he was being deliberately calm, deliberately soothing; he might even think she was crazy. "I left my jumper cables with another trucker last week by mistake, so I can't help you that way. But it's cold out here, like you say. I'm thinking, Why don't you come sit with me in the rig? It's warm. I delivered a load of milk here a couple of hours ago, and I was waiting to see about the weather. I'm saying that you're welcome, ma'am. To sit in the truck with me. Might give you some time to think this through." When Caroline didn't immediately respond, he added, "I'm considering that baby."

She looked across the parking lot then, to its very edge, where a tractor trailer with a dark gleaming cab sat idling. She had seen it earlier, but she had not taken it in, the long dull silver box of it, its presence like a building at the edge of the world. In her arms Phoebe gasped, caught her breath, and resumed her crying.

"All right," Caroline decided. "For the moment, anyway." She stepped carefully around some broken onions. When she reached the edge of the ramp he was there, holding up a hand to help her down. She took it, annoyed but also grateful, for she felt the layer of ice beneath the rotting vegetables and snow. She looked up to see his face, thickly bearded, a cap pulled down to his eyebrows and, beneath it, dark eyes: kind eyes. Ridiculous, she told herself, as they walked together across the parking lot. Crazy. Stupid, too. He could be an ax murderer. But the truth was, she was almost too tired to care.

He helped her collect some things from the car and get settled in the cab, holding Phoebe while Caroline climbed into the high seat, then handing her up through the air. Caroline poured more formula from the thermos into the bottle. Phoebe was so worked up that it took her a few moments to realize that food had come, and even then she struggled to suck. Caroline stroked her cheek gently, and at last she clamped down on the nipple and started drinking.

"Kinda strange, isn't it," the man said, once she had quieted. He had climbed into the driver's seat. The engine hummed in the darkness, comforting, like some great cat, and the world stretched away to the dark horizon. "This kind of snow in Kentucky, I mean."

"Every few years it happens," she said. "You're not from here?"

"Akron, Ohio," he said. "Originally, that is. But I've been on the road five years now. I like to think of myself as being from the world, these days."

"Don't you get lonely?" Caroline asked, thinking of herself on a usual night, sitting alone in her apartment in the evening. She couldn't believe she was here, talking so intimately with a stranger. It was odd but thrilling too, like confiding in a person you met on a train or a bus.

"Oh, some," he admitted. "It's lonely work, sure. But just as often I get to meet someone unexpected. Like tonight."

It was warm in the cab, and Caroline felt herself giving in to it, settling back on the high comfortable seat. Snow still sputtered in the streetlights. Her car stood in the middle of the parking lot, a lone dark shape, brushed with snow.

"Where were you heading?" he asked her.

"Just to Lexington. There was a wreck on the interstate a few miles back. I thought I'd save myself some time and trouble."

His face was lit softly by the streetlight and he smiled. To her surprise, so did Caroline, and then they were both laughing.

"The best-laid plans," he said.

Caroline nodded.

"Look," he said, after a silence. "If it's only Lexington we're talking about, I could give you a lift. I might as well park the rig there as here. Tomorrow—well, tomorrow's Sunday, isn't it? But on Monday, first thing, you can call a towing service about your car. It'll be safe here, that's for sure."

Light from the streetlamp was falling across Phoebe's tiny face. He reached over and gently, gently, stroked her forehead with his large hand. Caroline liked his awkwardness, his calmness.

"All right," she decided. "If it doesn't put you out."

"Oh, no," he said. "Hell, no. Excuse my French. Lexington is on my way."

He collected the rest of the things from her car, the grocery sacks and blankets. His name was Al, Albert Simpson. He groped on the floor and found an extra cup beneath the seat. This he wiped out carefully with a handkerchief before he poured her coffee from his thermos. She drank, glad it was dark, glad for the warmth and the company of someone who didn't know a thing about her. She felt safe and strangely happy, though the air was stale and smelled of dirty socks, and a baby that did not belong to her lay sleeping on her lap. As he drove, Al talked, telling her stories of his life on the road, truck stops with showers and the miles sliding beneath the wheels as he pushed through one night after another.

Lulled by the hum of the tires, by the warmth and the snow rushing in the headlights, Caroline half drifted into sleep. When they pulled into the parking lot of her apartment complex, the trailer took five spaces. Al got out to help her down and left the truck idling while he carried her things up the exterior stairs. Caroline followed, Phoebe in her arms. A curtain flashed in a lower window—Lucy Martin, spying as usual—and Caroline paused, overcome for an instant by something like vertigo. For everything was just the same, but surely she was not the same woman who had left here in the middle of the previous night, wading through the snow to her car. Surely she had been transformed so completely that she should walk into different rooms, different light. Yet her familiar key slid into the lock, catching in the usual place. When the door swung open, she carried Phoebe into a room she knew by heart: the durable dark-brown carpet, the plaid sofa and chair she had gotten on sale, the glass-topped coffee table, the novel she'd been reading before bed—*Crime and Punishment*—neatly marked. She had left Raskolnikov confessing to Sonya, had dreamed of them in their cold garret, and had woken to the phone ringing and to snow filling the streets.

Al hovered awkwardly, filling up the doorway. He could be a serial killer, or a rapist, or a con man. He could be anything at all.

"I have a sofa bed," she said. "You're welcome to use it tonight."

After a moment's hesitation, he stepped inside.

"What about your husband?" he asked, looking around.

"I don't have a husband," she said, then realized her mistake. "Not anymore."

He studied her, standing with his wool hat in his hand, surprising dark curls sticking out of his head. She felt slow, yet hyperalert from the coffee and her fatigue, and she suddenly wondered how she must look to him—still in her nurse's uniform, her hair uncombed for hours, her coat gaping open, this baby in her arms, her tired arms.

"I don't want to be any trouble to you," he said.

"Trouble?" she said. "I'd still be stranded in a parking lot except for you."

He grinned then, went to his truck, and came back a few minutes later with a small duffel bag of dark green canvas.

"Someone was watching from a window downstairs. You sure I won't be causing you any grief, here?"

"That was Lucy Martin," Caroline said. Phoebe had been stirring, and she took the bottle from its warmer, tested the formula on her arm, and sat down. "She's a dreadful gossip. Trust me. You just made her day."

Phoebe wouldn't drink, however, but began to wail, and Caroline stood, pacing the room, murmuring. Al, meanwhile, got straight to work. In no time at all he had pulled out the sofa bed and made it up, sharp military folds at each corner. When Phoebe finally quieted, Caroline nodded at him and whispered good night. She closed the bedroom door quite firmly. It had occurred to her that Al would be the type to notice the absence of a crib.

During the drive Caroline had been making plans, and now she pulled a drawer from her dresser and dumped its neat contents in a pile on the floor. Then she folded two towels in the bottom and tucked a folded sheet around them, nestling Phoebe amid the blankets. When she climbed into her own bed, fatigue rolled over her like waves, and she slept at once, a hard and dreamless sleep. She did not hear Al snoring loudly in the living room, or the noise of snowplows moving through the parking lot, or the clatter of garbage trucks on the street. When Phoebe stirred, however, sometime in the middle of the night, Caroline was on her feet in an instant. She moved through the darkness as if through water, exhausted and yet with purpose, changing Phoebe's diaper, warming her bottle, concentrating on the infant in her arms and the tasks before her—so urgent, so consuming and imperative—tasks that now only she could do, tasks that could not wait.

. . .

Caroline woke to a flood of light and the smell of eggs and bacon. She stood, pulling her robe around her, and bent over to touch the baby's tranquil cheek. Then she went to the kitchen, where Al was buttering toast.

"Hey, there," he said, looking up. His hair was combed but still a little wild. He had a bald spot on the back of his scalp, and he wore a gold medallion on a chain around his neck. "Hope you don't mind my making myself at home. I missed dinner last night."

"It smells good," Caroline said. "I'm hungry too."

"Well, then," he said, handing her a cup of coffee. "Good thing I made plenty. It's a neat little place you've got here. Nice and tidy."

"Do you like it?" she asked. The coffee was richer and darker than she usually made it. "I'm thinking of moving."

Her own words surprised her, but once they were out, in the air, they seemed true. Ordinary light fell across the dark-brown carpet and the arm of her sofa. Water dripped from the eaves outside. She'd been saving money for years, imagining herself in a house or on an adventure, and now here she was: a baby in her bedroom and a stranger at her table and her car stranded in Versailles.

"I'm thinking of going to Pittsburgh," she said, surprising herself again.

Al stirred the eggs with a spatula, then lifted them onto plates. "Pittsburgh? Great town. What would take you there?"

"Oh, my mother had family there," Caroline said, as he put the plates on the table and sat down across from her. It seemed there was no end at all to the lies a person could tell, once she got started.

"You know, I've been meaning to say I'm sorry," Al said. His dark eyes were kind. "For whatever happened to your baby's father."

Caroline had half forgotten that she'd made up a husband, so she was surprised to hear in his voice that Al didn't believe she'd ever had one. He thought she was an unwed mother, she marveled. They ate without speaking much, passing remarks now and then about the weather and the traffic and Al's next destination, which was Nashville, Tennessee.

"I've never been to Nashville," Caroline said.

"No? Well, hop aboard, you and your daughter too," Al said. It was a joke, but within the joke was an offer. An offer not to her, not really, but rather to an unwed mother down on her luck. Still, for a moment Caroline imagined walking out the door with her boxes and her blankets and never looking back.

"Maybe next time," she said, reaching for the coffee. "I've got some things to settle here."

Al nodded. "Gotcha," he said. "I know how that goes."

"But thanks," she said. "I appreciate the thought."

"My infinite pleasure," he said seriously, and then he stood up to go.

Caroline watched from the window as he went to his truck, climbing up the steps into the cab and turning once to wave from the open doorway. She waved back, happy to see his smile, so ready and so easy, surprised by the tug in her heart. She had an impulse to run after him, remembering the narrow bed in the back of the cab where he sometimes slept and the way he'd touched Phoebe's forehead so gently. Surely a man who lived such a solitary life could keep her secrets, contain her dreams and fears. But his engine caught, and smoke billowed up from the silver pipe on his cab, and then he was pulling carefully out of the parking lot and onto the quiet street and away.

. . .

For the next twenty-four hours, Caroline slept and woke on Phoebe's schedule, staying up just long enough to eat. It was strange; she had always been particular about meals, fearing undisciplined snacking as a sign of eccentricity and self-absorbed solitude, but now she ate at odd hours: cold cereal straight from the box, ice cream spooned from the carton while standing at her kitchen counter. It was as if she had entered some twilight zone of her own, some state halfway between sleep and waking, where she would not have to consider too fully the consequences of her decisions, or the fate of the baby sleeping in her dresser drawer, or her own.

On Monday morning she got up in time to call in sick to work. Ruby Centers, the receptionist, answered the phone.

"Are you all right, honey?" she asked. "You sound awful."

"It's the flu, I think," Caroline said. "I'll probably be out a few days. Anything happening there?" she asked, trying to make her voice casual. "Dr. Henry's wife have the baby?"

"Well, I sure don't know," Ruby said. Caroline imagined her thoughtful frown, her desk swept clear and ready for the day, a little vase of plastic flowers on the corner. "No one else is in yet, except about a hundred patients. Looks to be everyone else has got your flu, Miss Caroline."

The minute Caroline hung up there was a knock on the front door. Lucy Martin, no doubt. Caroline was surprised it had taken her this long.

Lucy was wearing a dress with big bright pink flowers on it, an apron with ruffles edged in pink, and fuzzy slippers. When Caroline opened the door she stepped right in, carrying half a loaf of banana bread wrapped in plastic.

Lucy had a heart of gold, everyone said so, but her very presence set Caroline's teeth on edge. Lucy's cakes and pies and hot dishes were her tickets into the center of every drama: deaths and accidents, births and weddings and wakes. There was something not quite right about her eagerness, an eerie kind of voyeurism in her need for bad news, and Caroline usually tried to keep a distance.

"I saw your visitor," Lucy said now, patting Caroline's arm. "My goodness! Quite a good-looking fellow, wasn't he? I just couldn't wait to get the scoop."

Lucy sat down on the sofa bed, now folded up. Caroline took the armchair. The bedroom door, where Phoebe slept, stood open.

"You're not sick, dear?" Lucy was saying. "Because, come to think of it, usually you're long gone by this time in the morning."

Caroline studied Lucy's eager face, aware that whatever she said would travel swiftly through town—that in two days, or three, someone would come up to her in the grocery store or at church and inquire about the stranger who had spent the night at her apartment.

"That was my cousin you saw last night," Caroline said easily, amazed all over again at this sudden facility she'd developed, the fluidity and ease of her lies. They came to her whole; they didn't even make her blink.

"Oh, I *wondered,*" Lucy said, looking a little disappointed.

"I know," Caroline answered. And then, in a preemptive strike that amazed her when she thought about it later, she went on. "Poor Al. His wife is in the hospital." She leaned a little closer, lowered her voice. "It's so sad, Lucy. She's only twenty-five, but they think she might have brain cancer. She's been falling down a lot, so Al brought her in from Somerset to see the specialist. And they have this little baby. I told him, Look, go and be with her, stay in the hospital day and night if you have to. Leave the baby with me. And I think because I'm a nurse they felt comfortable with that. I hope you haven't been bothered with her crying."

For a few instants Lucy was stunned to silence, and Caroline understood the pleasure—the power—that comes from delivering a bolt from the blue.

"Poor, poor things, your cousin and his wife! How old is the baby?"

"Just three weeks," Caroline said, and then, inspired, she stood up. "Wait here."

She went into the bedroom and lifted Phoebe from the dresser drawer, keeping the blankets wrapped close around her.

"Isn't she beautiful?" she asked, sitting down next to Lucy.

"Oh, she is. She's lovely!" Lucy said, touching one of Phoebe's tiny hands.

Caroline smiled, feeling an unexpected surge of pride and pleasure. The features she had noted in the delivery room—the sloping eyes, the slightly flattened face—had become so familiar that she hardly noticed them. Lucy, with her untrained eye, didn't see them at all. Phoebe was like any baby, delicate, adorable, fierce in her demands.

"I love looking at her," Caroline confessed.

"Oh, that poor little mother," Lucy whispered. "Do they expect she'll live?"

"No one knows," Caroline said. "Time will tell."

"They must be devastated," Lucy said.

"Yes. Yes, they are. They've completely lost their appetites," Caroline confided, thereby heading off the arrival of one of Lucy's famous hot dishes.

•   •   •

For the next two days, Caroline did not go out. The world came to her in the form of newspapers, grocery deliveries, milkmen, the sounds of traffic. The weather changed and the snow was gone as suddenly as it had come, cascading down the sides of buildings and disappearing into drains. For Caroline, the broken days blurred together into a stream of random images and impressions: the sight of her Ford Fairlane, its battery recharged, being driven into the lot; the sunlight streaming through cloudy windows; the dark scent of wet earth; a robin at the feeder. She had her spells of worry, but often, sitting with Phoebe, she was surprised to find herself completely at peace. What she had told Lucy Martin was true: she loved looking at this baby. She loved sitting in the sunlight and holding her. She warned herself not to fall in love with Phoebe; she was just a temporary stop. Caroline had watched David Henry often enough at the clinic to believe in his compassion. When he had raised his head from the desk that night and met her eyes, she had seen in them an infinite capacity for kindness. She had no doubt that he would do the right thing, once he got over the shock.

Every time the phone rang she started. But three days passed with no word from him.

On Thursday morning there was a knock on the door. Caroline hurried to answer it, adjusting the belt of her dress, touching her hair. But it was only a deliveryman, holding a vase full of flowers: dark red and pale pink in a cloud of baby's breath. These were from Al. *My thanks for the hospitality,* he'd written on the card. *Maybe I'll see you on my next run.*

Caroline took them inside and arranged them on the coffee table. Agitated, she picked up *The Leader,* which she hadn't read in days, slipped off the rubber band, and skimmed through the articles, not really taking in any of them. Escalating tensions in Vietnam, social announcements about who had entertained whom the previous week, a page of local women modeling the new spring hats. Caroline was about to throw the paper down when a black-bordered square caught her eye.

> *Memorial Service*
> *For Our Beloved Daughter*
> *Phoebe Grace Henry*
> *Born and Died March 7, 1964*
> *Lexington Presbyterian Church*
> *Friday, March 13, 1964, at 9 a.m.*

Caroline sat down slowly. She read the words once and then again. She even touched them, as if this would make them clearer somehow, explicable. With the paper still in her hands, she stood up and went to the bedroom. Phoebe slept in her drawer, one pale arm outflung against the blankets. Born and died. Caroline went back into the living room and called her office. Ruby picked up on the first ring.

"I don't suppose you're coming in?" she said. "It's a madhouse here. Everyone in town seems to have the flu." She lowered her voice then. "Did you hear, Caroline? About Dr. Henry and his babies? They had twins after all. The little boy is fine; he's precious. But the girl, she died at birth. So sad."

"I saw it in the paper." Caroline's jaw, her tongue, felt stiff. "I wonder if you'd ask Dr. Henry to call me. Tell him it's important. I saw the paper," she repeated. "Tell him that, will you, Ruby?" Then she hung up and sat staring out at the sycamore tree and the parking lot beyond.

An hour later he knocked at her door.

"Well," she said, showing him in.

David Henry came in and sat on her sofa, his back hunched, turning his hat in his hand. She sat down in the chair across from him, watching him as if she'd never seen him before.

"Norah put the announcement in," he said. When he looked up she felt a rush of sympathy despite herself, for his forehead was lined, his eyes bloodshot, as if he hadn't slept in days. "She did it without telling me."

"But she thinks her daughter died," Caroline said. "That's what you told her?"

He nodded, slowly. "I meant to tell her the truth. But when I opened my mouth, I couldn't say it. At that moment, I thought I was saving her pain."

Caroline thought of her own lies, streaming out one after the other.

"I didn't leave her in Louisville," she said softly. She nodded at the bedroom door. "She's in there. Sleeping."

David Henry looked up. Caroline was unnerved, for his face was white; she had never before seen him shaken.

"Why not?" he asked, on the edge of anger. "Why in the world not?"

"Have you been there?" she asked, remembering the pale woman, her dark hair falling into the cold linoleum. "Have you seen that place?"

"No." He frowned. "It came highly recommended, that was all. I've sent other people there, in the past. I've heard nothing negative."

"It was awful," she said, relieved. So he hadn't known what he was doing. She wanted to hate him still, but she remembered how many nights he had stayed at the clinic, treating patients who couldn't afford the care they needed. Patients from the countryside, from the mountains, who made the arduous trip to Lexington, short on money, long on hope. The other clinic partners hadn't liked it, but Dr. Henry had not stopped. He wasn't an evil man, she knew that. He wasn't a monster. But this—a memorial service for a living child—that was monstrous.

"You have to tell her," she said.

His face was pale, still, but determined. "No," he said. "It's too late now. Do whatever you have to do, Caroline, but I can't tell her. I won't."

It was strange; she disliked him so much for these words, but she felt with him also at that moment the greatest intimacy she had ever felt with any person. They were joined together now in something enormous, and no matter what happened they always would be. He took her hand, and this felt natural to her, right. He raised it to his lips and kissed it. She felt the press of his lips on her knuckles and his breath, warm on her skin.

If there had been any calculation in his expression when he looked up, anything less than pained confusion when he released her hand, she would have done the right thing. She would have picked up the phone and called Dr. Bentley or the police, and she would have confessed it all. But he had tears in his eyes.

"It's in your hands," he said, releasing her. "I leave it to you. I believe the home in Louisville is the right place for this child. I don't make the decision lightly. She will need medical care she can't get elsewhere. But whatever you have to do, I will respect that. And if you choose to call the authorities, I will take the blame. There will be no consequences for you, I promise."

His expression was weighted. For the first time Caroline thought beyond the immediate, beyond the baby in the next room. It had not really occurred to her before that their careers were in jeopardy.

"I don't know," she said slowly. "I have to think. I don't know what to do."

He pulled out his wallet, emptying it. Three hundred dollars—she was shocked that he carried this much with him.

"I don't want your money," she said.

"It's not for you," he told her. "It's for the child."

"Phoebe. Her name is Phoebe," Caroline said, pushing away the bills. She thought of the birth certificate, left blank but for his signature in David Henry's haste that snowy morning. How easy it would be to type in Phoebe's name, and her own.

"Phoebe," he said. He stood up to go, leaving the money on the table. "Please, Caroline, don't do anything without telling me first. That's the only thing I ask. That you give me warning, whatever it is you decide."

He left, then, and everything was the same as it had been: the clock on the mantel, the square of light on the floor, the sharp shadows of bare branches. In a few weeks the new leaves would come, feathering out on the trees and changing the shapes on the floors. She had seen all this so many times, and yet the room seemed strangely impersonal now, as if she had never lived here at all. Over the years she had bought very few things for herself, being naturally frugal and imagining, always, that her real life would happen elsewhere. The plaid sofa, the matching chair—she liked this furniture well enough, she had chosen it herself, but she saw now that she could easily leave it. Leave all of it, she supposed, looking around at the framed prints of landscapes, the wicker magazine rack by the sofa, the low coffee table. Her own apartment seemed suddenly no more personal than a waiting room in any clinic in town. And what else, after all, had she been doing here all these years but waiting?

She tried to silence her thoughts. Surely there was another, less dramatic way. That's what her mother would have said, shaking her head, telling her not to play Sarah Bernhardt. Caroline hadn't known for years who Sarah Bernhardt was, but she knew well enough her mother's meaning: any excess of emotion was a bad thing, disruptive to the calm order of their days. So Caroline had checked all her emotions, as one would check a coat. She had put them aside and imagined that she'd retrieve them later, but of course she never had, not until she had taken the baby from Dr. Henry's arms. So something had begun, and now she could not stop it. Twin threads ran through her: fear and excitement. She could leave this place today. She could start a new life somewhere else. She would have to do that, anyway, no matter what she decided to do about the baby. This was a small town; she couldn't go to the grocery store without running into an acquaintance. She imagined Lucy Martin's eyes growing wide, the secret pleasure as she relayed

Caroline's lies, her affection for this discarded baby. *Poor old spinster,* people would say of her, *longing so desperately for a baby of her own.*

I'll leave it in your hands, Caroline. His face aged, clenched like a walnut.

. . .

The next morning, Caroline woke early. It was a beautiful day and she opened the windows, letting in the fresh air and the scent of spring. Phoebe had woken twice in the night, and while she slept Caroline had packed and carried her things to the car in the darkness. She had very little, as it turned out, just a few suitcases that would fit easily in the trunk and the backseat of the Fairlane. Really, she could have left for China or Burma or Korea at a moment's notice. This pleased her. She was pleased with her own efficiency, too. By noon yesterday she had made all the arrangements: Goodwill would take the furniture; a cleaning service would handle the apartment. She had stopped the utilities and the newspaper, and she had written letters to close her bank accounts.

Caroline waited, drinking coffee, until she heard the door slam downstairs and Lucy's car roar into life. Quickly, then, she picked Phoebe up and stood for a moment in the doorway of the apartment where she had spent so many hopeful years, years that seemed as ephemeral now as if they had never happened. Then she shut the door firmly and went down the stairs.

She put Phoebe in her box on the backseat and drove into town, passing the clinic with its turquoise walls and orange roof, passing the bank and dry cleaners and her favorite gas station. When she reached the church she parked on the street and left Phoebe asleep in the car. The group gathered in the courtyard was larger than she'd expected, and she paused at its outside edge, close enough to see the back of David Henry's neck, flushed pink from the cold, and Norah Henry's blond hair swept up in a formal twist. No one noticed Caroline. Her heels sank into the mud at the edge of the sidewalk. She eased her weight to her toes, remembering the stale smells of the institution Dr. Henry had sent her to last week. Remembering the woman in her slip, her dark hair falling to the floor.

Words drifted on the still morning air.

The night is as clear as day; the darkness and light are to thee both alike.

Caroline had woken at all hours. She'd stood eating crackers at the kitchen window in the middle of the night. Her days and nights had become indistinguishable, the comforting patterns of her life shattered once and for all.

Norah Henry wiped at her eyes with a lace handkerchief. Caroline remembered her grip as she pushed one baby out and then the other, and the tears in her eyes, then, too. This would destroy her, David Henry had declared. And what would it do if Caroline stepped forward now with the lost baby in her arms? If she interrupted this grief, only to introduce so many others?

Thou has set our misdeeds before thee, and our secret sins in the light of thy countenance.

David Henry shifted his weight as the minister spoke. For the first time Caroline understood in her body what she was about to do. Her throat closed and her breath grew short. The gravel seemed to press up through her shoes, and the group in the courtyard trembled in her sight, and she thought she might fall. Grave, Caroline thought, watching Norah's long legs bending, so graceful, kneeling suddenly in the mud. Wind caught at Norah's short veil, pulled at her pillbox hat.

For the things that are seen are transient, but the things that are unseen are eternal.

Caroline watched the minister's hand and, when he spoke again, the words, though faint, seemed addressed not to Phoebe but to herself, some kind of finality that could not be reversed.

We have committed her body to the elements, earth to earth, ashes to ashes, dust to dust. The Lord bless her and keep her, the Lord make his face to shine upon her and give her peace.

The voice paused, the wind moved in the trees, and Caroline pulled herself together, wiped her eyes with her handkerchief, and gave her head a swift shake. She turned and went to her car, where Phoebe was still sleeping, a wand of sunlight falling across her face.

In every end, then, a beginning. Soon enough she was turning the corner by the monument factory with its rows of tombstones, headed for the interstate. How strange. Wasn't it a bad omen to have a gravestone factory marking the entrance to a city? But then she was beyond it all, and when she reached the split in the highway she chose to go north, to Cincinnati and then to Pittsburgh, following the Ohio River to the place where Dr. Henry had lived a part of his mysterious past. The other road, to Louisville and the Home for the Feebleminded, disappeared in her rearview mirror.

Caroline drove fast, feeling reckless, her heart filling with an excitement as bright as the day. Because, really, what could ill omens matter now? After all, the child who rode beside her was, in the eyes of the world, already dead. And she, Caroline Gill, was vanishing from the face of the earth, a process that left her feeling light, then lighter, as if the car itself had begun to float high over the quiet fields of southern Ohio. All that sunny afternoon, traveling north and east, Caroline believed absolutely in the future. And why not? For if the worst had already happened to them in the eyes of the world, then surely, surely, it was the worst that they left behind them now.

1965

February 1965

Norah stood, barefoot and precariously balanced, on a stool in the dining room, fastening pink streamers to the brass chandelier. Chains of paper hearts, pink and magenta, floated down over the table, trailing across her wedding china, the dark red roses and gilded rims, the lace tablecloth, the linen napkins. As she worked the furnace hummed and strands of crepe paper wafted up, brushing against her skirt, then falling softly against the floor again, rustling.

Paul, eleven months old, sat in the corner beside an old grape basket full of wooden blocks. He had just learned to walk, and all afternoon he'd amused himself by stomping through this, their new house, in his first pair of shoes. Every room was an adventure. He had dropped nails down the registers, delighting in the echoes they made. He'd dragged a sack of joint compound through the kitchen, leaving a narrow white trail in his wake. Now, wide-eyed, he watched the streamers, as beautiful and elusive as butterflies, then pulled himself up on a chair and staggered in pursuit. He caught one pink strand and yanked, swaying the chandelier. Then he lost his balance and sat down hard. Astonished, he began to cry.

"Oh, sweetie, " Norah said, climbing down to pick him up.

"There, there," she murmured, running her hand over his soft dark hair.

Outside, headlights flashed and disappeared and a car door slammed. At the same time, the phone began to ring. Norah carried Paul into the kitchen and picked up the receiver just as someone knocked on the door.

"Hello?" She pressed her lips to Paul's forehead, damp and soft, straining to see whose car was in the driveway. Bree wasn't due for an hour. "Sweet baby," she whispered. And then into the phone she said again, "Hello?"

"Mrs. Henry?"

It was the nurse from David's new office—he'd joined the hospital staff a month ago—a woman Norah had never met. Her voice was warm and full: Norah pictured a middle-aged woman, hefty and substantial, her hair in a careful beehive. Caroline Gill, who had held her hand through the rippling contractions, whose blue eyes and steady gaze were inextricably connected for Norah to that wild and snowy night, had simply disappeared—a mystery, that, and a scandal.

"Mrs. Henry, it's Sharon Smith. Dr. Henry was called into emergency surgery just, I swear, as he was about to walk out the door and go home. There was a horrible accident out off Leestown Road. Teenagers, you know; they're pretty badly hurt. Dr. Henry asked me to call. He'll be home as soon as he can."

"Did he say how long?" Norah asked. The air was redolent with roast pork, sauerkraut, and oven potatoes: David's favorite meal.

"He didn't. But they say it was an awful wreck. Between you and me, honey, it may end up being hours."

Norah nodded. Distantly, the front door opened, shut. There were footsteps, light and familiar, in the foyer, the living room, the dining room: Bree, early, coming to pick up Paul, to give Norah and David this evening before Valentine's Day, their anniversary, to themselves.

Norah's plan, her surprise, her gift to him.

"Thank you," she told the nurse, before she hung up. "Thanks for calling."

Bree walked into the kitchen, bringing with her the scent of rain.

Below her long raincoat she wore black boots to her knees, and her thighs, long and white, disappeared in the shortest skirt Norah had ever seen. Her silver earrings, studded with turquoise, danced with light. She'd come straight from work—she managed the office for a local radio station—and her bag was full of books and papers from the classes she was taking.

"Wow," Bree said, sliding her bags on the counter and reaching for Paul. "Everything looks great, Norah. I can't believe what you've done with the house in such a short time."

"It's kept me busy," Norah agreed, thinking of the weeks she'd spent steaming off wallpaper and applying new coats of paint. They had decided to move, she and David, thinking that, like his new job, it would help them leave the past behind. Norah, wanting nothing else, had poured herself into this project. Yet it hadn't helped as much as she had hoped; often, still, her sense of loss stirred up, like flames out of embers. Twice in this last month alone she'd hired a babysitter for Paul and left the house, with its half-painted trim and rolls of wallpaper, behind. She had driven too fast down the narrow country roads to the private cemetery, marked with a wrought-iron gate, where her daughter was buried. The stones were low, some very old and worn nearly smooth. Phoebe's was simple, made from pink granite, with the dates of her short life chiseled deeply beneath her name. In the bleak winter landscape, the wind sharp in her hair, Norah had knelt in the brittle frozen grass of her dream. She'd been paralyzed with grief almost, too full of sorrow even to weep. But she had stayed for several hours before she finally stood up and brushed off her clothes and went home.

Now Paul was playing a game with Bree, trying to catch hold of her hair.

"Your mom's amazing," Bree told him. "She's just a regular Suzy Homemaker these days, isn't she? No, not the earrings, honey," she added, catching Paul's small hand in her own.

"Suzy Homemaker?" Norah repeated, anger lifting through her like a wave. "What do you mean by that?"

"I didn't mean anything," Bree said. She'd been making silly faces at Paul, and now she looked up, surprised. "Oh, honestly, Norah. Lighten up."

"Suzy Homemaker?" she said again. "I just wanted to have things look nice for my anniversary. What's wrong with that?"

"Nothing." Bree sighed. "Everything looks great. Didn't I just say so? And I'm here to babysit, remember? Why are you so angry?"

Norah waved her hand. "Never mind. Oh, darn it, never mind. David's in surgery."

Bree waited a heartbeat before she said, "That figures."

Norah started to defend him, then stopped. She pressed her hands against her cheeks. "Oh, Bree. Why tonight?"

"It's awful," Bree agreed. Norah's face tightened, she felt her lips purse, and Bree laughed. "Oh, come on. Be honest. Maybe it's not David's fault. But that's exactly how you feel, right?"

"It's *not* his fault," Norah said. "There was an accident. But okay. You're right. It does—it stinks. It absolutely stinks, okay?"

"I know," Bree said, her voice surprisingly soft. "It's really rotten. I'm sorry, Sis." Then she smiled. "Look, I brought you and David a present. Maybe it will cheer you up."

Bree shifted Paul to one arm and rummaged in her oversized quilted bag, pulling out books, a candy bar, a pile of leaflets about an upcoming demonstration, sunglasses in a worn leather case, and, finally, a bottle of wine, glimmering like garnets as she poured them each a glass.

"To love," she said, handing Norah one glass and raising the other. "To eternal happiness and bliss."

They laughed together and drank. The wine was dark with berries, faint oak. Rain dripped from the gutters. Years from now Norah would remember this evening, the gloomy disappointment and Bree bearing shimmering tokens from another world; her shiny boots, her earrings, her energy like a kind of light. How beautiful these things were to Norah, and how remote, how unreachable. Depression—years later she would understand the murky light she lived in—but no one talked about this in 1965. No one even considered it. Certainly not for Norah, who had her house, her baby, her doctor husband. She was supposed to be content.

"Hey—did your old house sell?" Bree asked, putting her glass on the counter. "Did you decide to take the offer?"

"I don't know," Norah said. "It's lower than we hoped. David wants to accept it, just to have it settled, but I don't know. It was our home. I still hate to let it go."

She thought of their first house, standing dark and empty with a FOR SALE sign planted in the yard, and felt as if the world had become very fragile. She held on to the counter to steady herself and took another sip of wine.

"So how's your love life these days?" Norah asked, changing the subject. "How are things with that guy you were seeing—what was his name—Jeff?"

"Oh, him." A dark expression crossed Bree's face, and she shook her head, as if to clear it. "I didn't tell you? I came home two weeks ago and found him in bed—in *my* bed—with this sweet young thing who worked with us on the mayoral campaign."

"Oh! I'm sorry."

Bree shook her head. "Don't be. It's not like I loved him or anything. We were just good, you know, together. At least I thought so."

"You didn't love him?" Norah repeated, hearing and hating her mother's disapproving voice coming from her own mouth. She did not want to be that person, drinking cups of tea in the orderly silent house of their childhood. But neither did she want to be the person she seemed to be becoming, set loose by grief into a world that made no sense.

"No," Bree was saying. "No, I didn't love him, though for a while I thought I might. But that's not even the point anymore. The point is he turned our whole thing into a cliché. I hate that more than anything—being part of a cliché."

Bree put her empty glass on the counter and shifted Paul into her other arm. Her face, unadorned, was delicate, finely boned; her cheeks, her lips, were flushed pale pink.

"I couldn't live like you do," Norah said. Since Paul was born, since Phoebe had died, she'd felt the need to keep a constant vigil, as if a second's inattention would open the door for disaster. "I just couldn't do it—break all the rules. Blow everything up."

"The world doesn't end," Bree said quietly. "Amazing, but it really doesn't."

Norah shook her head. "It could. At any given moment, anything at all could happen."

"I know," Bree told her. "Honey, I know." Norah's earlier irritation was washed away by a sudden rush of gratitude. Bree would always listen and respond, would not demand anything less than the truth of her experience. "You're right, Norah, anything can happen, any time. But what goes wrong is not your fault. You can't spend the rest of your life tiptoeing around to try and avert disaster. It won't work. You'll just end up missing the life you have."

Norah did not know how to answer this, so she reached for Paul, who was squirming in Bree's arms, hungry, his long hair—too long, but Norah couldn't bear to cut it—drifting slightly, as if underwater, whenever he moved.

Bree poured more wine for them both and took an apple from the fruit bowl on the counter. Norah cut up chunks of cheese and bread and banana, scattering them across the tray of Paul's high chair. She sipped from her wine as she worked. Gradually, the world around her became clearer somehow, more vivid. She noticed Paul's hands, like small starfish, spreading carrots in his hair. The kitchen light cast shadows through the back porch railing onto the grass, patterns of darkness and light.

"I bought David a camera for our anniversary," Norah said, wishing she could capture these fleeting instants, hold them forever. "He's been working so hard since he took this new job. He needs a distraction. I can't believe he has to work tonight."

"You know what?" Bree said. "Why don't I take Paul anyway? I mean, who knows, David might get home early enough for dinner. So what if it's midnight? Why not? You could just skip dinner then, sweep away the plates and make love on the dining room table."

"Bree!"

Bree laughed. "Please, Norah? I'd love to take him."

"He needs a bath," Norah said.

"That's okay," Bree said. "I promise not to let him drown in the tub."

"Not funny," Norah said. "Not funny at all."

But she agreed, finally, and packed Paul's things. His soft hair against her cheek, his large dark eyes watching her seriously as Bree walked out the door with him, and then he was gone. She watched from the window as Bree's taillights disappeared down the street, taking her son away. It was all she could do to keep herself from running after them. How was it possible to let a child grow up and go out into that dangerous and unpredictable world? She stood for several minutes, staring out into the darkness. Then she went into the kitchen, where she put foil over the roast and turned the oven off. It was seven o'clock. Bree's bottle of wine was nearly empty. In the kitchen, so silent she could hear the clock ticking, Norah opened another bottle, expensive and French, which she had bought for dinner.

The house was so quiet. Had she been alone, even once, since Paul was born? She did not think so. She had avoided such moments of solitude, moments of stillness when thoughts of her lost daughter might come rising up, unbidden. The memorial service, held in the church courtyard beneath the harsh light of the new March sun, had helped, but Norah sometimes still had the sense, inexplicably, of her daughter's presence, as if she might turn and see her on the stairs or standing outside on the lawn.

She pressed her hand flat against the wall and shook her head to clear it. Then, glass in hand, she walked through the house, her footsteps hollow on the newly polished floors, surveying the work she'd done. Outside, the rain fell steadily, blurring the lights across the street. Norah remembered another night, the swirling snow. David had taken her by the elbow, helping her into her old green coat, a raggy thing now but that she could not bring herself to discard it. The coat had fallen open around the fullness of her belly, and their eyes had met. He was so concerned, so serious, so charged with nervous excitement; in that moment Norah felt she knew him as she knew herself.

Yet everything had changed. David had changed. Evenings, when he sat beside her on the couch, browsing through his journals, he was no longer really there. In her former life, as a long-distance operator, Norah had touched the cool switches and metal buttons, listening for the distant ringing, the click of connection. *Hold, please,* she'd said, and words echoed, were delayed; people spoke at once and then stopped, revealing the wild static night that lay between them. Sometimes she had listened, the voices of people she would never meet spilling out their formal heartfelt news: of births or weddings, illnesses or deaths. She had felt the dark night of those distances and the power of her ability to make them disappear.

But it was a power she had lost—at least now, and where it mattered most. Sometimes, even after they had made love in the middle of the night and still lay together, heart beating against heart, she would look at David and feel her ears filling up with the dark distant roar of the universe.

It was after eight o'clock. The world had softened at the edges. She went back to the kitchen and stood at the stove, picking at the dried pork. She ate one of the potatoes straight from the pan, smashing it into the drippings with her fork. The broccoli-cheese dish had curdled and was beginning to dry; Norah tasted that too. It burned her mouth, and she reached for her glass. Empty. She drank a glass of water, standing at the sink, and then another, holding on to the edge of the counter because the world was so unsteady. *I'm drunk,* she thought, surprised and mildly pleased with herself. She had never been drunk before, though Bree had once come home from a dance and thrown up all over the linoleum. Her punch had been spiked, she told their mother, but to Norah she had confessed it all: the bottle in a brown-paper bag and her friends gathered in the bushes, their breath making sharp little clouds in the night.

The telephone seemed a long way away. Walking, she felt strange, as if she were somehow floating, just outside herself. She held on to the doorjamb with one hand and dialed with the other, the receiver pressed between her shoulder and her ear. Bree answered on the first ring.

"I know it's you," she said. "Paul's fine. We read a book and had a bath and now he's sound asleep."

"Oh, good. Yes, wonderful," Norah said. She had intended to tell Bree about this shimmering world, but now it seemed too private somehow, a secret.

"How about you?" Bree was saying. "Are you okay?"

"I'm fine," Norah said. "David's not here yet, but I'm fine."

She hung up fast, poured herself another glass of wine, and stepped onto the porch, where she lifted her face to the sky. A light mist hung in the air. Now the wine seemed to move through her like heat or light, spreading out through her limbs to her fingertips and toes. When she turned, her body once again seemed to float for an instant, as if she were sliding out of herself. She remembered their car, traveling over the icy roads as if airborne, swerving slightly before David got it under control. People were right; she couldn't remember the pain of labor, but she had never forgotten that feeling in the car of the world slipping, spinning, and her hands holding fast to the cold dashboard while David, methodical, stopped at every light.

Where was he, she wondered, sudden tears in her eyes, and why had she married him anyway? Why had he wanted her so much? Those whirlwind weeks after they met he'd been at her apartment every day, offering roses and dinners and drives in the country. Christmas Eve the doorbell rang and she went to answer it in her old robe, expecting Bree. Instead, she opened the door to find David, his face flushed with cold, brightly wrapped boxes in his arms. It was late, he said, he knew that, but would she come with him for a drive?

No, she said, and *You're crazy!* but all the time she was laughing at the wildness of it, laughing and stepping back and letting him in, this man on her steps holding his flowers and his gifts. She was amazed and pleased and a little astonished. There had been moments, watching others go off to sorority parties, or sitting on her stool in the windowless room of the telephone company while coworkers planned their weddings down to the last corsage and party mint, when Norah, so quiet and reserved, believed she would be single all her life. Yet here was David, handsome, a doctor, standing in the doorway of her apartment saying, *Come on, please, there's something special I want you to see.*

It had been a clear night, stars vivid in the sky. Norah sat on the wide vinyl front seat of David's old car. She was wearing a red wool dress and she felt beautiful, the air so crisp and David's hands on the wheel and the car traveling through the darkness, through the cold, traveling on smaller and smaller roads, into a landscape she did not recognize. He pulled to a stop beside an old flour mill. They stepped out of the car into the sound of rushing water. Black water caught the moonlight and poured over the rocks, turning the mill's great wheel. The building stood darkly against the darker sky, obscuring stars, and the air was filled with the rushing, spilling sounds of the water.

"Are you cold?" David asked, shouting over the stream, and Norah laughed, shivering, and said, No; no, she was not, she was fine.

"What about your hands?" he shouted, his voice ringing, cascading like the water. "You didn't bring any gloves."

"I'm fine," she shouted back, but he was already taking her hands in his, pressing them to his chest, warming them between his gloves and the dark flecked wool of his coat.

"It's beautiful here!" she called to him, and he laughed. Then he leaned down and kissed her, releasing her hands and letting his own slide inside her coat and up her back. Water rushed, echoing off the rocks.

"Norah," he shouted, his voice part of the night, rolling like the stream, the words clear and yet small amid the other sounds. "Norah! Will you marry me?"

She laughed, letting her head fall back, the night air pouring over her.

"Yes!" she shouted, pressing her palms against his coat again. "Yes, I will!"

He slid a ring on her finger, then: a thin white-gold band, exactly her size, its marquise diamond flanked by two tiny emeralds. To match her eyes, he said later, and the coat she'd worn when they met.

She was inside now, standing in the doorway of the dining room, turning this ring on her finger. Streamers drifted. One brushed her face; another had dipped into her wineglass. Norah watched, fascinated, as the stain spread slowly upward. It was, she noticed, almost exactly the same color as the napkins. Suzy Homemaker, indeed: she couldn't have found a closer match on purpose. Wine had splashed from her glass and spattered across the tablecloth too, staining the gold striped wrapping of her present to David. She picked this up and, on an impulse, tore the paper off. *I'm really very drunk,* she thought.

The camera was compact, a pleasing weight. Norah had debated for weeks about a suitable gift, until she'd seen this in the display case at Sears. Black and flashing chrome, with complex dials and levers and numbers etched around the rings, the camera had resembled David's medical equipment. The salesman, young and eager, had plied her with technical information about apertures and f-stops and wide-angle lenses. The terms washed over her like so much water, but she liked the weight of the camera in her hands, its cool textures, and the way the world was so precisely framed when she held it to her eye.

Tentatively, now, she pushed the silver lever. Click and then snap, loud in the room, as the shutter released. She turned the little dial, advancing the film—she remembered the salesman using that phrase, *advancing the film,* his voice rising up for a moment out of the stream of noise in the store. She looked through the viewfinder, framing the ruined table again, then turned two different dials to find the focus. This time, when she snapped the shutter, light exploded across the wall. Blinking, she turned the camera over and studied the bulb, now blackened and bubbled. She replaced it, burning her fingers, but somehow distant from that pain.

She stood and glanced at the clock: 9:45 P.M.

The rain was soft, steady. David had walked to work, and she imagined him trudging wearily home down the dark streets. On an impulse she got her coat and the car keys—she would go to the hospital and surprise him.

The car was cold. She backed out of the driveway, fumbling for the heat, and by old habit turned in the wrong direction. Even after she realized her mistake, she kept driving on the same narrow rainy streets, back to their old house, where she'd decorated the nursery with such innocent hope, where she'd sat nursing Paul in the dark. She and David had agreed about the wisdom of moving away, but the truth was she could not bear the idea of selling this place. She still went there almost every day. Whatever life her daughter had known, whatever Norah had experienced of her daughter, had happened in that house.

Except for being dark, the house looked much the same: the wide front porch with its four white columns, the rough-cut limestone and single light burning. There was Mrs. Michaels next door, just a few yards away, moving in her kitchen, washing dishes and staring out into the night; there was Mr. Bennett in his easy chair, the curtains open, the television on. Norah could almost believe, walking up the steps, that she lived here still. But the door opened into rooms that were bare, empty, shocking in their smallness.

Walking through the cold house, Norah struggled to clear her head. The effects of the wine seemed very much stronger now, and she was having trouble connecting one moment to another. She held David's new camera in one hand. A fact, not a decision. There were fifteen pictures left and spare flashbulbs in her pocket. She took a picture of the chandelier, satisfied, when the bulb flashed, because now she would always have that image with her; she would never wake up in the middle of the night in twenty years and not be able to remember this detail, these graceful sickles of gold.

She walked from room to room, still drunk but charged with purpose, framing windows, light fixtures, the swirling grain of the floor. It seemed vitally important that she record every detail. At one point, in the living room, a spent and blistered bulb slipped from her hand and shattered; when she stepped back, glass pierced her heel. She studied her stocking feet for a moment, amused and impressed by her degree of drunkenness—she must have left her wet shoes by the front door, out of old habit. She wandered through the house twice more, documenting light switches, windows, the pipe where gas had once come up to the second floor. It was only on her way downstairs that she realized her foot was bleeding, leaving a splotchy trail: grim hearts, bloody little valentines. Norah was shocked and also strangely thrilled at the damage she had managed to inflict.

She found her shoes, went outside. Her heel throbbed as she slid into the car, the camera still dangling from her wrist.

Later, she would not remember much about the drive, only the dark narrow streets, the wind in the leaves, light flashing on the puddles, and water spraying off her tires. She would not remember the crash of metal against metal, but only the sudden startling sight of a trash can, glittering, flying up in front of the car. Wet with rain, it seemed suspended for a long moment before it began to fall. She remembered that it hit the hood and rolled up to shatter the windshield; she remembered the car, bouncing over the curb and coming to a gentle stop in the median, beneath a pin oak. She did not remember hitting the windshield, but it looked like a spiderweb, the intricate lines fanning out, delicate, beautiful, and precise. When she pressed her hand to her forehead, it came away lightly smeared with blood.

She did not get out of the car. The trash can was rolling in the street. Dark shapes—cats—lurked at the edges of the trash, scattered in an arc. Lights flashed on in the house to her right, and a man came out in his robe and slippers, hurrying down the sidewalk to her car.

"Are you all right?" he asked, leaning down to look in the window as she rolled it slowly open. The cool night air lapped at her face. "What happened out here? Are you all right? Your forehead's bleeding," he added, pulling a handkerchief from his pocket.

"It's nothing," Norah said, waving away his handkerchief, suspiciously wrinkled. She pressed her palm gently to her forehead again, wiping away another smear of blood. The camera, still dangling from her wrist, tapped against the steering wheel. She slipped it off and put it carefully beside her on the seat. "It's my anniversary," she informed the stranger. "My heel's bleeding, too."

"Do you need a doctor?" the man asked.

"My husband's a doctor," Norah said, noting the man's uncertain expression, aware that she had perhaps not made much sense a moment earlier. Was, perhaps, not making much sense now. "He's a doctor," she repeated firmly. "I'll go find him."

"I'm not sure you should be driving," the man said. "Why don't you leave the car here and let me call an ambulance?"

At his kindness her eyes filled with tears, but then she imagined it, the lights and sirens and gentle hands, how David would come hurrying and find her in the ER, disheveled and bloody and somewhat drunk: a scandal and a disgrace.

"No," she said, becoming very careful of her words. "I'm fine, really. A cat ran out and startled me. But truly, I'm fine. I'll just go home now, and my husband will attend to this cut. It's really nothing."

The man hesitated for a long moment, the streetlight shining silver in his hair, before he shrugged and nodded once and stepped back onto the curb. Norah drove carefully, slowly, using her turn signals properly on the empty street. In the rearview mirror she saw him, arms folded, watching her until she turned the corner and disappeared.

The world was quiet as she drove back through the familiar streets, the effects of the wine beginning to ebb. Her new house was ablaze with lights in every window, upstairs and down, light pouring out like something liquid, something that had overflowed and could no longer be contained. She parked in the driveway and got out, standing for a moment on the damp grass, rain falling softly and beading on her hair, her coat. Inside, she glimpsed David sitting on the sofa. Paul was in his arms, sleeping with his head resting lightly on David's shoulder. She thought of how she'd left things, the spilled wine and trailing streamers, the ruined roast. She pulled her coat around her and hurried up the steps.

"Norah!" David met her at the door, still carrying Paul. "Norah, what happened to you? You're bleeding."

"It's okay. I'm okay," she said, refusing David's hand when tried to help her. Her foot hurt, but she was glad for the sharp pain; a counterpoint to the throbbing in her head, it seemed to run straight through her in a line and hold her steady. Paul was sound asleep, his breathing slow and even. She rested the palm of her hand lightly on his small back.

"Where's Bree?" she asked.

"She's looking for you," David said. He glanced into the dining room and she followed his gaze, saw the ruined dinner, the streamers all pooled on the floor. "When you weren't home, I panicked and called her. She brought Paul over, and then she went out looking for you."

"I was at the old house," Norah said. "I hit a trash can." She put her hand to her forehead and closed her eyes.

"You were drinking." He made the statement calmly.

"Wine with dinner. You were late."

"There are two empty bottles, Norah."

"Bree was here. It was a long wait."

He nodded. "Those kids tonight, the ones in the crash? There was beer all over the place. I was terrified, Norah."

"I wasn't drunk."

The phone rang and she picked it up, heavy in her hand. It was Bree, her voice swift as water, wanting to know what had happened. "I'm okay," Norah said, trying to speak calmly and clearly. "I'm fine." David was watching her, studying the dark lines on her palm where the blood had settled and dried. She pressed her fingers over them and turned away.

"Here," he said gently, once she hung up, touching her arm. "Come here."

They went upstairs. While David settled Paul into his crib, Norah eased off her ruined stockings and sat on the edge of the tub. The world was becoming clearer and steadier, and she blinked in the bright lights, trying to put the events of the evening in their proper order. When David came back, he brushed the hair from her forehead, his gestures gentle and precise, and started cleaning the cut.

"Hope you left the other guy in worse shape," he said, and she imagined that he might say this same thing to the patients who came through his office: small talk, banter, empty words as a distraction from the work he was doing.

"There was no one else," she said, thinking of the silver-haired man leaning into her window. "A cat startled me, and I swerved. But the windshield—oh!" she said, as he put antiseptic on her cut. "Oh, David, that hurts."

"It won't last long," he said, putting his hand on her shoulder for a moment. Then he knelt down by the tub and took her foot in his hand.

She watched him pick out the glass. He was careful and calm, absorbed in his thoughts. She knew he would attend to any patient with these same practiced motions.

"You are so good to me," she whispered, longing to bridge the distance between them, the distance she had made.

He shook his head and paused in his work and looked up.

"Good to you," he repeated slowly. "Why did you go to there, Norah, to our old house? Why don't you want to let it go?"

"Because it's the final thing," she said at once, surprised by the sureness and sorrow in her voice. "The final way we leave her behind."

In the brief instant before he looked away there was, on David's face, a flash of tension, of anger quickly repressed.

"What would you have me do that I'm not doing? I thought this new house would make us happy. It would make most people happy, Norah."

At his tone, fear rushed through her; she could lose him too. Her foot throbbed, and her head, and she closed her eyes briefly at the thought of the scene she had caused. She did not want to be stuck forever in this dark static night, David an unreachable distance away.

"All right," she said. "I'll call the realtor tomorrow. We should take that offer."

A film closed over the past as she spoke, a barrier as brittle and fragile as ice forming. It would grow and strengthen. It would become impenetrable, opaque. Norah felt this happening and she feared it, but now she feared more what would happen if it shattered. Yes, they would move on. This would be her gift, to David and to Paul.

Phoebe she would keep alive in her heart.

David wrapped her foot in a towel and sat back on his heels.

"Look, I don't see us moving back there," he said, gentler now that she'd conceded. "But we could. If you really wanted that, we could sell this place and move back."

"No," she said. "We live here now."

"But you're so sad," he said. "Please don't be sad. I didn't forget, Norah. Not our anniversary. Not our daughter. Not anything."

"Oh, David,' she said. "I left your present in the car." She thought of the camera, its precise dials and levers. *The Memory Keeper,* it said on the box, in white italic letters; this, she realized, was why she'd bought it—so he'd capture every moment, so he'd never forget.

"That's all right," he said, standing. "Wait. Wait right here."

He ran down the stairs. She sat on the edge of the tub for a moment longer, then stood and limped across the hall to Paul's room.

The carpet was dark blue and thick beneath her feet. She had painted clouds on the pale blue walls and hung a mobile of stars above the crib. Paul slept beneath the drifting stars, the blanket thrown off, his small hands outflung. She kissed him gently and tucked him in, running her hand over his soft hair, touching her index finger against his palm. He was so big now, walking and beginning to talk. Those nights almost year ago, when Paul had nursed so intently and David had filled the house with daffodils: where had they gone? She remembered the camera, and how she'd walked through their empty house determined to record every detail, a hedge against time.

"Norah?" David came into the room and stood behind her. "Close your eyes."

A cool line shimmered on her skin. She looked down to see emeralds, a long sequence of dark stones, caught in the gold stream of the chain against her skin. To match her ring, he was saying. To match her eyes.

"It's so beautiful," she whispered touching the warm gold. "Oh, David."

His hands were on her shoulders then, and for an instant she stood again amid the sound of rushing water from the mill, happiness as full around her as the night. *Don't breathe,* she thought. *Don't move.* But there was no stopping anything. Outside, rain fell softly, and seeds stirred in the dark wet earth. Paul sighed and shifted in his sleep. He would wake tomorrow, grow, and change. They'd live their lives day by day, each one taking them another step away from their lost daughter.

March 1965

THE SHOWER RUSHED AND STEAM SWIRLED, MISTING THE mirror and the window, clouding the pale moon. Caroline paced in the tiny purple bathroom, holding Phoebe close. Her breathing was light and rapid, her small heart beat so quickly. *Be well, my baby,* Caroline murmured, stroking her soft dark hair. *Be better, sweet girl, be well.* She paused, tired, to look out at the moon, a smear of light caught in the sycamore branches, and Phoebe's cough started again, deep in her chest. Her body grew rigid beneath Caroline's hands as she barked the air out of her constricted throat, the sounds sharp, wheezing. This was croup, a textbook case. Caroline stroked Phoebe's back, hardly bigger than her hand. When the coughing spell ended, she started walking again so she wouldn't sway herself to sleep on her feet. More than once this year she'd started awake to find herself standing and Phoebe, miraculously, still safe in her in her arms.

Stairs creaked, then floorboards, nearer, and then the purple door swung open in a rush of cool air. Doro, wearing a black silk robe over her nightgown, her gray hair falling loose around her shoulders, came in.

"Is it bad?" she asked. "It sounds just awful. Should I get the car?"

"I don't think so. But could you shut the door? The steam helps."
Doro pushed the door shut and sat on the edge of the tub.

"We woke you," Caroline said, Phoebe's soft breath against her neck. "Sorry."

Doro shrugged. "You know me and sleep. I was up anyway, reading."

"Anything interesting?" Caroline asked. She wiped at the window with the cuff of her robe; moonlight fell into the garden three floors below and shone like water on the grass.

"Science journals. Dull as dust, even for me. Sleep being the goal."

Caroline smiled. Doro had a PhD in physics; she worked in the university department her father had once chaired. Leo March, brilliant and well-known, was now in his eighties, physically strong but subject to lapses of memory and sense. Eleven months ago, Doro had hired Caroline as his companion.

A gift, this job: she knew that. She had emerged from the Fort Pitt tunnel onto the high bridge over the Monongahela River, emerald hills rising out of the river flats, the city of Pittsburgh gleaming suddenly before her, immediate, vivid, so startling in its vastness and its beauty that she had gasped and slowed, afraid of losing control of the car.

For one long month she had lived in a cheap motel on the edge of town, circling want ads and watching her savings dwindle. By the time she'd come to this interview, her euphoria had turned into dull panic. She rang the bell and stood on the porch, waiting. Bright yellow daffodils swayed against the overgrown spring grass; next door, a woman in a quilted housecoat swept soot from her steps. The people at this house had not bothered; Phoebe's car seat rested on the gritty accumulation of several days. Dust like blackened snow; Caroline's footprints were stark and pale behind her.

When Dorothy March, tall and slender in a trim gray suit, finally opened the door, Caroline ignored her wary glance at Phoebe, lifted the car seat, and stepped inside. She took a seat on the edge of an unsteady chair, its wine-velvet cushions faded to pink except for a few dark places near the upholstery studs. Dorothy March sat down across from her, on a couch of cracked leather supported on one end by a brick. She lit a cigarette. For several moments she studied Caroline, her blue eyes quick and alive. She did not say anything right away. Then she cleared her throat, exhaling smoke.

"Quite frankly, I wasn't counting on a baby," she said.

Caroline pulled out her résumé. "I've been a nurse for fifteen years. I'd bring a great deal of experience and compassion to this position."

Dorothy March took the papers in her free hand and studied them.

"Yes, you do seem to have a lot of experience. But it doesn't say here just *where* you've worked. You are not at all specific."

Caroline hesitated. She had tried a dozen different answers to this question at a dozen different interviews in these last weeks, and they had all come to nothing.

"That's because I ran away," she said, nearly giddy. "I ran away from Phoebe's father. And so I can't tell you where I'm from, and I can't give you any references. That's the only reason I don't already have a job. I'm an excellent nurse, and you'd be lucky to get me, frankly, given what you're offering to pay."

At this Dorothy March gave a sharp, startled laugh. "What a bold statement! My dear, it's a live-in position. Why in the world would I take such a chance on a perfect stranger?"

"I'll start now for room and board," Caroline persisted, thinking of the motel room with its peeling wallpaper and stained ceiling, the room she could not afford to keep another night. "For two weeks. I'll do that, and you can decide."

The cigarette had burned to nothing in Dorothy March's hand. She looked at it, then ground it out in the overflowing ashtray.

"But how would you manage?" she mused. "And with a baby too? My father is not a patient man. He will not be a patient patient, I assure you."

"A week," Caroline had replied. "If you don't like me in a week, I'll go."

Now nearly a year had passed. Doro stood up in the steam-softened bathroom. The sleeves of her black silk robe, printed with bright tropical birds, slipped down to her elbows. "Let me take her. You look exhausted, Caroline."

Phoebe's wheezing had abated and her color had improved; her cheeks were faintly pink, Caroline handed her over, feeling the sudden coolness of her absence.

"How was Leo today?" Doro asked. "Did he give you any grief?"

For a moment Caroline didn't answer. She was so tired, and she had traveled so far in this past year, one moment to the next, and her careful solitary life had been utterly transformed. Somehow she had come to be here in this tiny purple bathroom, a mother to Phoebe, a companion to a brilliant man with a failing mind, an unlikely but certain friend to this woman Doro March: the two of them strangers a year ago, women who might have passed each other on the street without a second glance or a glimmer of connection, their lives now woven together by the demands of their days and a cautious, sure respect.

"He wouldn't eat. He accused me of putting scouring powder in the mashed potatoes. So—a fairly typical day, I'd say."

"It's not personal, you know," Doro said softly. "He wasn't always like this."

Caroline turned off the shower and sat on the edge of the purple tub.

Doro nodded at the steamy window. Phoebe's hands were pale, like stars, against her robe. "That used to be our playground, over there on the hill. Before they put the freeway in. Herons used to nest in the trees, did you know that? My mother planted daffodils one spring, hundreds of bulbs. My father came home from work on the train every day at six o'clock, and he'd go straight over there and pick her a bunch of flowers. You wouldn't have known him," she said. "You don't."

"I know," Caroline said gently. "I realize that."

They were silent for a moment. The faucet dripped, and steam swirled.

"I think she's asleep," Doro said. "Will she be okay?"

"Yes. I think so."

"What's wrong with her, Caroline?" Doro's voice was intent now, her words a determined rush. "My dear, I know nothing about babies, but even I can sense that something's not right. Phoebe is so beautiful, so sweet, but there's something wrong, isn't there? She's nearly a year old and only now learning to sit up."

Caroline looked out the steam-streaked window at the moon and closed her eyes. As an infant, Phoebe's stillness had seemed, more than anything, a gift of quiet, of attentiveness, and Caroline could let herself believe nothing was wrong. But after six months, when Phoebe was growing but still small for her age, still slack in her arms, when Phoebe would follow a set of keys with her eyes and sometimes wave her arms but never reach to grab them, when she showed no signs of sitting on her own, Caroline had started taking Phoebe to the library on her day off. At the wide oak tables of the Carnegie, in the airy, spacious, high-ceilinged rooms, she stacked up the books and articles and began to read, grim journeys into gloomy institutions, shortened lives, no hope. It was a strange sensation, a pit opening in her stomach at every word. And yet there was Phoebe stirring in her car seat, smiling, waving her hands and cooing: a baby, not a case history.

"Phoebe has Down's syndrome," she forced herself to say. "That's the term."

"Oh, Caroline," Doro said. "I'm so sorry. This is why you left your husband, isn't it? You said he didn't want her. Oh, my dear, I'm so very, very sorry."

"Don't be," Caroline said, reaching to take Phoebe back. "She's beautiful."

"Oh, yes. Yes, she is. But Caroline. What will become of her?"

Phoebe was warm and heavy in her arms, her soft dark hair falling against pale skin. Caroline, fierce, protective, touched her cheek so gently.

"What will become of any of us? I mean, tell me honestly, Doro. Did you ever imagine that this would be your life?"

Doro looked away, an expression of pain her face. Years ago, her fiancé had been killed while jumping from a bridge into the river on a dare. Doro had mourned him and never married, never had the children she longed for.

"No," she said at last. "But this is different."

"Why? Why is it different?"

"Caroline," Doro said, touching her arm. "Let's not. You're tired. So am I."

Caroline settled Phoebe in her crib as Doro's footsteps sounded faintly down the stairs. Asleep in the dull glow of the streetlight, she looked like any child, her future as unmapped as the ocean floor, as rich with possibility. Cars rushed over the fields of Doro's childhood, their headlights playing on the wall, and Caroline imagined herons rising from the marshy field, their wings lifting in the pale gold light of dawn. *What will become of her?* In truth, Caroline sometimes lay awake at night, struggling with this same question.

In her own room the curtains, crocheted and hung in the windows decades ago by Doro's mother, cast delicate shadows; the moonlight was strong enough to read by. On the desk there was an envelope with three photographs of Phoebe, next to a paper folded twice. Caroline opened it and read what she had written.

Dear Dr. Henry,
I am writing to say that we are well, Phoebe and I. We are safe and happy. I have a good job. Phoebe is generally a healthy baby, despite frequent respiratory concerns. I am sending photos. So far, touch wood, she does not have any problems with her heart.

She should send this—she had written it weeks ago—but each time she went to mail it she thought of Phoebe, the soft touch of her hands or the cooing sounds she made when she was happy, and she could not do it. Now she put the letter away again and lay down, drifting quickly to the edge of sleep. Once she half dreamed of the clinic waiting room with its drooping plants, heat stirring the leaves, and started awake, uneasy, unsure of where she was.

Here, she told herself, touching the cool sheets. *I'm right here.*

· · ·

When Caroline woke in the morning, the room was full of sunlight and trumpet music. Phoebe, in her crib, was reaching, as if the notes were small winged things, butterflies or lightning bugs, that she might catch. Caroline got them both dressed and took her downstairs, pausing on the second floor, where Leo March was ensconced in his sunny yellow office, books tumbled all around the daybed, where he lay with his hands clasped behind his head, staring at the ceiling. Caroline watched him from the doorway—she was not allowed to enter this room except by invitation—but he did not acknowledge her. An old man, bald with a fringe of gray hair, still wearing his clothes from the day before, listening intently to the music that blared from his speakers, shaking the house.

"Do you want breakfast?" she shouted.

He waved his hand, indicating that he'd get it himself. Well, fine.

Caroline descended another flight to the kitchen and put the coffee on. Even here the trumpets sounded, faintly. She put Phoebe in her high chair, feeding her applesauce and egg and cottage cheese. Three times she handed her the spoon; three times it clattered on the metal tray.

"Never mind," Caroline said out loud, but her heart numbed. Doro's voice echoed: *What will become of her?* And what would? At eleven months, Phoebe should be able to grasp small objects.

She cleaned up the kitchen and went into the dining room to fold the laundry from the line; it smelled of wind. Phoebe lay on her back in the playpen, cooing, batting at the rings and toys Caroline had hung above her. Now and then Caroline paused in her work and went to adjust the bright objects, hoping that Phoebe, lured by their glitter, would roll over.

After about half an hour the music stopped abruptly, and Leo's feet appeared on the stairs in precisely tied and polished leather shoes, a swatch of pale undressed ankle flashing beneath his pant legs, which were several inches too short. Bit by bit he came entirely into view—a tall man, once thickly built and muscular, flesh now hanging loosely from his bony frame.

"Oh, good," he said, nodding at the laundry. "We've been needing a maid."

"Breakfast?" she asked.

"I'll get it myself."

"Go right ahead, then."

"I'll have you fired by lunchtime," he called from the kitchen.

"You go right ahead," she said again.

There was a cascade of falling pots, the old man swearing. Caroline imagined him stooped over to push the tangle of cookware back into the cupboard. She ought to go help him—but no, let him cope by himself. In her first weeks she'd been afraid to talk back, afraid not to jump whenever Leonard March called, until Doro had taken her aside. *Look, you're not a servant. You answer to me; you don't have to be at his beck and call. You're doing fine, and you live here too,* she had said, and Caroline had understood that her period of probation was over.

Leo came in, carrying a plateful of eggs and a glass of orange juice.

"Don't worry," he said, before she could speak. "I turned off the damned stove. And now I'm taking my breakfast upstairs to eat it in peace."

"Watch your language," Caroline said.

He grunted his answer and thumped up the stairs. She paused in her work, suddenly near tears, watching a cardinal land in the lilac bush outside the window, then fly away. What was she doing here? What yearning had driven her to this radical decision, this place of no return? And what, finally, would become of *her?*

After a few minutes, the trumpets started again upstairs and the doorbell rang twice. Caroline lifted Phoebe from the playpen.

"Here they are," she said, drying her eyes with her wrist. "Time to practice."

Sandra was standing on the porch, and when Caroline opened the door she burst in, holding Tim by one hand and hauling a big cloth bag in the other. She was tall, large-boned, blond, and forceful; she sat down without ceremony in the middle of the rug, dumping the stacking toys in a pile.

"Sorry I'm so late," she said. "The traffic's awful out there. Doesn't it drive you crazy, living this close to the crosstown? It would drive me nuts. Anyway, check out what I found. Look at these great stacking toys—plastic, different colors. Tim loves them."

Caroline sat down on the floor too. Like Doro, Sandra was an unlikely friend, someone Caroline would never have known in her old life. They'd met in the library one bleak January day when

Caroline, overwhelmed by experts and grim statistics, had slammed a book shut in despair. Sandra, two tables over amid her own stack of books, the spines and covers terribly familiar to Caroline, looked up. *Oh, I know just how you feel. I'm so angry I could break a window.*

They'd begun to talk, then: cautiously at first, then in a rush. Sandra's son, Tim, was nearly four. He had Down's too, but Sandra hadn't known it. That he was slower to develop than her three other children, this she had noticed, but to Sandra slow was only slow, and no excuse for anything. A busy mother, she'd simply expected Tim to do what her other children had done, and if it took him longer that was all right. He'd been walking by the time he was two, toilet trained by age three. The diagnosis had shocked her family; the doctor's suggestion—that Tim should be put into an institution—had angered her into action.

Caroline had listened intently, her heart lifting with every word.

They left the library and went for coffee. Caroline would never forget those hours, the excitement she'd felt, as if she were waking from a long, slow dream. What would happen, they conjectured, if they simply went on assuming their children would do *everything*. Perhaps not quickly. Perhaps not by the book. But what if they simply erased those growth and development charts, with their precise, constricting points and curves? What if they kept their expectations but erased the time line? What harm could it do? Why not try?

Yes, why not? They'd begun to meet, here or at Sandra's house with her older, rambunctious boys. They brought books and toys, research and stories, and their own experiences—Caroline's as a nurse, Sandra's as a schoolteacher and mother of four. A lot of it was simple common sense. If Phoebe needed to learn to roll over, put a bright ball just out of her reach; if Tim needed to work on coordination, give him blunt scissors and bright paper and let him cut. The progress was slow, sometimes invisible, but for Caroline, these hours had become a lifeline.

"You look tired today," Sandra said.

Caroline nodded. "Phoebe had croup last night. I don't know how long she'll hold out, actually. Any news about Tim's ears?"

"I liked the new doctor," Sandra said, sitting back. Her fingers were long and blunt; she smiled at Tim and handed him a yellow cup. "He seemed compassionate. Didn't just dismiss us. But the news isn't great. Tim has some hearing loss, so that's probably why his speech has been so slow. Here, sweetie," she added, tapping the cup he'd dropped. "Show Miss Caroline and Phoebe what you can do."

Tim was not interested; the nap of the carpet had his attention, and he ran his hands through it again and again, fascinated and delighted. But Sandra was firm, calm and determined. Finally, he took the yellow cup, pressed its edge to his cheek for a moment, then put it on the floor and started stacking others in a tower.

For the next two hours, they played with their children and talked. Sandra had strong opinions about everything and was not afraid to speak her mind. Caroline loved sitting in the living room and talking with this smart, bold woman, mother to mother. These days Caroline often longed for her own mother, dead almost ten years now, wishing she could call her up and ask advice or simply stop by to see her hold Phoebe in her arms. Had her mother felt all this—the love and the frustration—as Caroline grew up? She must have, and suddenly Caroline understood her childhood differently. The constant worry about polio—that, in its own strange way, was love. And her father's hard work, his careful concentration on their finances at night—that was love as well.

She did not have her mother but she had Sandra, and their mornings together were a highlight of her week. They told stories from their lives, shared ideas and suggestions about parenting, laughed together as Tim tried to stack the cups on their heads, as Phoebe reached and reached for a sparkly ball and finally, despite herself, rolled over. Several times that morning Caroline, still worried, dangled her car keys in front of Phoebe. They flashed, catching the morning light, and Phoebe's small hands flew open, her fingers waving, splayed like starfish. Music, motes of light: she reached for the keys as well. But no matter how she tried, she could not catch them.

"Next time," Sandra said. "Wait and see. It will happen."

At noon Caroline helped them carry things to the car, then stood on the porch with Phoebe in her arms, tired already but happy too, waving as Sandra pulled her station wagon out into the street.

When she went inside, Leo's record was skipping, playing the same three bars again and again.

Ornery old man, she thought, starting up the stairs. *Terrible old coot.*

"Couldn't you turn that down?" she began, exasperated, pushing open the door. But the record was skipping in an empty room. Leo was gone.

Phoebe began to cry, as if she had some sort of internal barometer for strife and tension. He must have slipped out the back when she was helping Sandra. Oh, he was clever, even though these days he sometimes left his shoes in the refrigerator. He took great pleasure in tricking her like this. Three times before Leo had slipped away, once stark naked.

Caroline hurried downstairs and shoved her feet into a pair of Doro's loafers, a size too small, cold. A coat for Phoebe, nestled in the stroller—for herself, she'd go without.

The day had turned overcast with low gray clouds. Phoebe whimpered, her small hands flailing, as they walked past the garage to the alley. *I know,* Caroline murmured, touching her head. *I know, sweetheart, I know.* She spotted one of Leo's footprints in a melting crust of snow, the large waffled sole of his boots, and felt a rush of relief. He had come this way, then, and he was dressed.

Well, at least he had his boots on.

At the end of the next block, she came to the 105 steps that led down to Koening Field. It was Leo who had told her how many there were, one night over supper when he was in a civil mood. Now he was at the bottom of the long cement cascade, his hands hanging at his sides, his white hair sticking out, looking so puzzled, so lost and so distressed, that her anger dissolved. Caroline did not like Leo March—he was not likable—but whatever animosity she held for him was complicated by compassion. For in moments like these she saw how the world looked at him and saw an old man, senile and forgetful, rather than the universe that had been, that was still, Leo March.

He turned and saw her, and after a moment confusion cleared from his face.

"Watch this!" he shouted. "Watch this, woman, and weep!"

Quickly, oblivious to the ice, a stilled stream down the middle of the steps, Leo ran up to her, legs pumping, fueled by some ancient adrenaline and need.

"I'll bet you never saw anything like that," he said, reaching the top, winded.

"You're right," Caroline said, "I never did. I hope I never do again."

Leo laughed, his lips a vivid pink against his bleached-pale skin.

"I got away from you," he said.

"You didn't get far."

"I could, though. If I had a mind. Next time."

"Next time take a coat," Caroline advised.

"Next time," he said, as they started walking, "I'll disappear in Timbuktu."

"You do that," Caroline said, a tide of weariness rushing in. Crocuses shouted purple and white against the bright grass; Phoebe was crying in earnest now. She was relieved to have Leo in tow, to have found him safe, grateful that disaster had been averted. Her fault, if he'd been lost or hurt, because she'd been so focused on Phoebe, who'd reached for weeks now and had still not learned to grasp.

They walked a few more feet in silence.

"You're a smart woman," Leo said.

She stopped on the bricks, astonished.

"What? What did you say?"

He looked at her, lucid, his eyes the same bright seeking blue as Doro's.

"I said you're smart. My daughter hired eight different nurses before you. None of them lasted more than a week. Bet you didn't know that."

"No," Caroline said. "No, I didn't."

. . .

Later, as Caroline cleaned up the kitchen and carried out the garbage, she thought of Leo's words. *I'm smart,* she said to herself, standing in the alley by the trash can. The air was damp and cool. Her breath came out in tiny clouds. *Smart won't get you a husband,* her mother said in sharp reply, but even this didn't dampen Caroline's pleasure in the first nice words Leo had ever said to her.

Caroline stood for a moment longer in the chilly air, grateful for the silence. Garages staggered, one after another, down the hill. Gradually, she became aware of a figure standing at the base of the alley. A tall man, in dark jeans and a brown jacket, colors so muted he nearly became another part of the late-winter landscape. Something about him—something about the way he stood and stared so intently in her direction—made Caroline uneasy. She put the metal lid back on the garbage can and folded her arms across her chest. He was walking toward her now, a big man, broad-shouldered and walking fast. His jacket was not brown at all, but a muted plaid with streaks of red. He pulled a bright red hat from the pocket and put it on. Caroline felt oddly comforted by this gesture, though she didn't know why.

"Hey, there," he called. "That Fairlane running okay for you these days?"

Her apprehension deepened, and she turned to look at the house, its dark brick rising into the white sky. Yes, there was her bathroom, where she had stood last night watching the moonlight on the lawn. There was her window, left partly open to the cold spring air, wind stirring the lacy curtains. When she turned back, the man had stopped just a few feet away. She knew him, and she understood this in her body, in her relief, before she could formulate it in thought. Then it was so bizarre she couldn't believe it.

"How in the world—" she began.

"It wasn't easy!" Al said, laughing. He had grown a soft beard, and his teeth flashed white. His dark eyes were warm, pleased and amused. She remembered him sliding bacon onto her plate, waving from the silver cab of his truck as he pulled away. "You are one tough lady to track down. But you said Pittsburgh. And I happen to have a layover here every couple of weeks. It kind of got to be a hobby, looking for you." He smiled. "Don't know what I'll do with myself now."

Caroline couldn't answer. There was pleasure at the sight of him but a great confusion too. For nearly a year she had not let herself think too long or too hard about the life she had left, but now it rose up with great force and intensity: the scent of cleaning fluid and sun in the waiting room and the way it felt to come home to her tranquil, orderly apartment after a long day, fix herself a modest meal, and sit down for the evening with a book. She had given up those pleasures willingly; she had embraced this change out of some deep unacknowledged yearning. Now her heart was pounding, and she stared wildly down the alley, as if she might suddenly see David Henry too. This, she understood suddenly, was why she had never sent that letter. What if he wanted Phoebe back—or Norah did? The possibility filled her with an excruciating rush of fear.

"How did you do it?" Caroline demanded. "How did you find me? Why?"

Al, taken aback, shrugged. "I stopped in Lexington to stay hello. Your place was empty. Being painted. That neighbor of yours told me you'd been gone three weeks. Guess I don't like mysteries, because I kept thinking of you." He paused, as if debating whether or not to go on. "Plus—hell, I liked you, Caroline, and I figured you were in some kind of trouble, to cut out like you did. You sure had trouble written all over you, standing in the parking lot that day. I figured maybe I could lend you a hand. I figured maybe you might need it."

"I'm doing just fine," she said. "So. What do you figure now?"

She hadn't meant the words to come out as they did, so tough and harsh. There was a long silence before Al spoke again.

"I guess I figure I was wrong about some things," Al said. He shook his head. "I thought we hit it off, you and me."

"We did," Caroline said. "I'm just shocked, that's all. I thought I'd cut my ties."

He looked at her then; his brown eyes met hers.

"It took me a full year," he said. "If you're worried about someone else tracking you down, remember that. And I knew where to start, and I had good luck. I started checking the motels I know, asking about a woman with a baby. Each time I went to a different place, and last week I hit pay dirt. The clerk at the place you stayed remembered you. She's retiring next week, by the way." He held his thumb and forefinger up, close together. "I came this close to missing you forever."

Caroline nodded, remembering the woman behind the desk with her white hair in a careful beehive, pearl earrings glimmering. The motel had been in her family for fifty years. The heat rattled all night, and the walls were constantly damp, peeling the paper. You never knew, anymore, the woman said, pushing a key across the counter, who was going to walk through the door.

Al nodded at the powder-blue hood of the Fairlane.

"I knew I'd found you the minute I saw that," he said. "How's your baby?"

She remembered the empty parking lot, all the light that had spilled into the snow and faded, the way his hand had rested, so gently, on Phoebe's tiny forehead.

"Do you want to come in?" she heard herself ask. "I was just about to wake her. I'll make you some tea."

Caroline took him down the narrow sidewalk and up the steps to the back porch. She left him in the living room and climbed the stairs, feeling giddy, unsteady, as if she'd suddenly become aware that the planet beneath her turned in space, shifting her world no matter how hard she tried to hold it still. She changed Phoebe and splashed water on her own face, trying to calm herself down.

Al was sitting at the dining room table, looking out the window. When she came down the stairs he turned, his face breaking into a wide grin. He reached for Phoebe at once, exclaiming over how big she'd grown, how beautiful she was. Caroline felt a rush of pleasure, and Phoebe, delighted, laughed, her dark curls falling down around her cheeks. Al reached into his shirt and pulled out a medallion, clear plastic over gilded turquoise letters that said GRAND OLE OPRY. He'd gotten it in Nashville. *Come with me,* he had said to her, all those long months ago, joking and yet not joking.

And here he was, having traveled all this way to find her.

Phoebe was making soft sounds, reaching. Her hands were brushing against Al's neck, his collarbone, his dark plaid shirt. At first, it didn't register with Caroline, what was happening; then, suddenly, it did. Whatever Al was saying receded, merging with Leo's footsteps upstairs and the rush of traffic outside, sounds that Caroline would forever afterward remember as being lucky.

Phoebe was reaching for the medallion. Not batting at air, as she had this morning, but using Al's chest for resistance, her small fingers scraping and scraping the medallion into her palm until she could close her fist around it. Rapt with success, she yanked the medallion hard on its string, making Al raise his hand to the chafing.

Caroline touched her own neck too, feeling the quick burn of joy. *Oh, yes,* she thought. *Grab it, my darling. Grab the world.*

May 1965

NORAH WAS AHEAD OF HIM, MOVING LIKE LIGHT, FLASHES of white and denim amid the trees: there, and then gone. David followed, leaning down now and then to pick up stones. Rough-skinned geodes, fossils etched in shale. Once, an arrowhead. He held each of these for a moment, pleased by their weight and shape, by the coolness of the stones against his palm, before he slipped them into his pockets. As a boy, the shelves of his room had always been littered with stones, and to this day he couldn't pass them up, their mysteries and possibilities, even though bending was awkward with Paul in a carrier against his chest and the camera scraping against his hip.

Far ahead, Norah paused to wave, then seemed to vanish straight into a wall of smooth gray stone. Several other people, wearing matching blue baseball caps, spilled suddenly, one by one, from this same gray wall. As David drew closer he realized that the stairway leading to the natural stone bridge rose up there, just out of sight. *Better watch your step,* a woman, descending, warned him. *It's steep like you wouldn't believe. Slippery too.* Breathless, she paused and held her hand on her heart.

David, noting her paleness, her shortness of breath, paused. "Ma'am? I'm a doctor. Are you all right?"

"Palpitations," she said, waving her free hand. "I've had them all my life."

He took her plump wrist and felt her pulse, swift but steady, slowing as he counted. Palpitations: people used the term freely, to talk about any quickening of the heart, but he could tell at once that the woman was in no real distress. Not like his sister, who had grown breathless and dizzy and was forced to sit anytime she so much as ran across the room. *Heart trouble,* the doctor in Morgantown had said, shaking his head. He had not been more specific, and it had not mattered; there was nothing he could do. Years later, in medical school, David had remembered her symptoms and read late into the night to make his own diagnosis: a narrowing of the aorta, or maybe an abnormality of the heart valve. Either way, June had moved slowly and fought to breathe, her condition worsening as the years passed, her skin pale and faintly blue in the months before she died. She had loved butterflies, and standing with her face turned to the sun, eyes closed, and eating homemade jelly on the thin saltines his mother bought in town. She was always singing, made-up tunes she hummed softly to herself, and her hair was pale, almost white, the color of buttermilk. For months after she died he had woken in the night, thinking he heard her small voice, singing like the wind in the pines.

"You say you've had this all your life?" he asked the woman gravely, releasing her hand.

"Oh, always," she said. "The doctors tell me it's not serious. Just annoying."

"Well, I think you'll be fine," he said. "But don't push yourself too hard."

She thanked him, touched Paul's head and said, *You watch out for that little one now.* David nodded and moved off, protecting Paul's head with his free hand as he climbed between the damp stone walls. He was pleased—it was good to be able to help people in need, to offer healing—something he could not seem to do for those he loved the most. Paul patted softly at his chest, grabbing at the envelope he'd stuffed in his pocket: a letter from Caroline Gill, de-livered that morning to his office. He had read it only once, swiftly, putting it away as Norah came in, trying to conceal his agitation. *We are well, Phoebe and I,* it had said. *So far, she does not have any problems with her heart.*

Now he caught Paul's small fingers in his own, gently. His son looked up, wide-eyed, curious, and he felt a deep swift rush of love.

"Hey," David said, smiling. "I love you, little guy. But don't eat that, okay?"

Paul studied him with wide dark eyes, then turned his head and rested his cheek against David's chest, radiating warmth. He wore a white hat with yellow ducks that Norah had embroidered in the quiet, watchful days after her accident. With the emergence of each duck, David had breathed a little easier. He had seen her grief, the space it had left in her heart, when he'd developed the spent roll of film in his new camera: room after empty room in their old house, close-ups of window frames, the stark shadows of the stair rail, the floor tiles, skewed and crooked. And Norah's footprints, those er-ratic, bloody trails. He'd thrown the photos out, negatives and all, but still they haunted him. He was afraid they always would. He had lied, after all; he had given away their daughter. That terrible consequences would follow seemed both inevitable and just. But days had passed, now nearly three months, and Norah seemed to be herself again. She worked in the garden, or laughed on the tele-phone with friends, or lifted Paul from his playpen with her lean, graceful arms.

David, watching, told himself she was happy.

Now the ducks bounced cheerfully with every step, catching the light as David emerged from the narrow stairs onto the natural stone bridge spanning the gorge. Norah, wearing denim shorts and a sleeveless white blouse, stood in the center of the bridge, the toes of her white sneakers flush with the rocky edge. Slowly, with a dancer's grace, Norah opened her arms and arched her back, eyes closed, as if offering herself to the sky.

"Norah!" he called out, appalled. "That's dangerous!"

Paul pushed his small hands against David's chest. *Doo,* he echoed, when he heard David say *dangerous,* a baby word applied to electrical outlets, stairs, fireplaces, chairs, and now to this sheer drop to the earth so far below his mother.

"It's spectacular!" Norah called back, letting her arms fall. She turned, causing pebbles to skid beneath her feet and slide over the edge. "Come see!"

Cautiously, he walked out onto the bridge and went to stand beside her at the edge. Tiny figures moved slowly on the path far below, where an ancient river had once rushed. Now hills rolled away into lush spring, a hundred different shades of green against the clear blue sky. He took a deep breath, fighting a wave of vertigo, afraid even to glance at Norah. He had wanted to spare her, to protect her from loss and pain; he had not understood that loss would follow her regardless, as persistent and life-shaping as a stream of water. Nor had he anticipated his own grief, woven with the dark threads of his past. When he imagined the daughter he'd given away, it was his sister's face he saw, her pale hair, her serious smile.

"Let me get a picture," he said, taking one slow step back, then another. "Come over to the middle of the bridge. The light's better."

"In a minute," she said, her hands on hips. "It's just so beautiful."

"Norah," he said. "You are really making me nervous."

"Oh, David," she said, tossing her head without looking at him. "Why are you so worried all the time? I'm fine."

He didn't answer, conscious of his lungs moving, the deep unsteadiness of his breathing. He'd had this same feeling when he opened Caroline's letter, addressed to his old office in her scraggy hand, half covered with a forwarding stamp. It was postmarked Toledo, Ohio. She had included three pictures of Phoebe, an infant in a pink dress. The return address was to a PO box, not in Toledo but in Cleveland. Cleveland, a place he had never been, a place where Caroline Gill was apparently living with his daughter.

"Let's move away from here," he said again, at last. "Let me take your picture."

She nodded, but when he reached the safe center of the bridge and turned, Norah was still near the edge, facing him, arms folded, smiling.

"Take it right here," she said. "Make it look like I'm walking on air."

David squatted, fiddling with the camera dials, heat radiating up from the bare golden rocks. Paul squirmed against him and started to fuss. David would remember all this—which went unseen and unrecorded—when the image rose up later in the developing fluid, taking slow shape. He framed Norah in the viewfinder, wind moving in her hair, her skin tan and healthy, wondering at all she kept from him.

The spring air was warm, softly fragrant. They hiked back down, passing cave entrances and sprays of purple rhododendron and mountain laurel. Norah led them off the main path and through the trees, following a creek, until they emerged in a sun-struck place she remembered for its wild strawberries. Wind moved lightly in the long grass, and the dark green leaves of the strawberry plants shimmered low against the earth. The air was full of sweetness, the hum of insects, heat.

They spread out their picnic: cheese and crackers and clusters of grapes. David sat down on the blanket, cradling Paul's head against his chest as he undid the baby carrier, thinking idly of his own father, stocky and strong, with skilled blunt fingers that covered David's hands as he taught him to heft an ax or milk the cow or pound a nail through the cedar shingles. His father, who smelled of sweat and resin and the dark hidden earth of the mines where he worked in the winter. Even when David was a teenager, boarding in town all week so he could go to high school, he had loved walking home on the weekend and finding his father there, smoking his pipe on the porch.

Doo, Paul said. Free, he immediately pulled off one shoe. He studied it intently, then dropped it almost at once and crawled off toward the grassy world beyond the blanket. David watched him yank a fistful of weeds and put them in his mouth, a look of surprise flashing across his small features at the texture. He wished, suddenly, fiercely, that his parents were alive to meet his son.

"Awful stuff, isn't it?" he said softly, wiping grassy drool from Paul's chin. Norah moved beside him, quietly, efficiently, taking out silverware and napkins. He kept his face turned; he didn't want her to see him so stirred by emotion. He took a geode from his pocket and Paul grasped it in both hands, turning it over.

"Should he have that in his mouth?" Norah asked, settling down beside him, so close he could feel her warmth, her scent of sweat and soap filling the air.

"Probably not," he said, retrieving the stone and giving Paul a cracker instead. The geode was warm and damp. He gave it a sharp crack on the rock, splitting it open to reveal its crystalline purple heart.

"So beautiful," Norah murmured, turning it in her hand.

"Ancient seas," David said. "The water got trapped inside and crystallized, over centuries."

They ate lazily, then picked ripe strawberries, sun-warmed and tender. Paul ate them by fistfuls, juice running down his wrists. Two hawks circled lazily in the deep blue sky. *Didi,* Paul said, lifting a chubby arm to point. Later, when he fell asleep, Norah settled him on a blanket in the grassy shade.

"This is nice," Norah observed, settling with her back against a boulder. "Just the three of us, sitting in the sun."

Her feet were bare and he took them in his hands, massaging them, delicate bones hidden beneath the flesh.

"Oh," she said, closing her eyes, "that's *really* nice. You'll put me to sleep."

"Stay awake," he said. "Tell me what you're thinking."

"I don't know. I was just remembering this little field by the sheep farm. When Bree and I were little we used to wait for our father there. We gathered huge bunches of black-eyed Susans and Queen Anne's lace. The sun felt just like this—like an embrace. Our mother put the flowers in vases all over the house."

"That's nice too," David said, releasing one of her feet and attending to the other. He ran his thumb, lightly, over the thin white scar the broken flashbulb had left. "I like thinking of you there." Norah's skin was soft. He remembered sunny days from his own childhood, before June got so sick, when the family had gone hunting for ginseng, a fragile plant hidden in the dusky light amid the trees. His parents had met on such a search. He had their wedding photo, and on the day of their own marriage Norah had presented it to him in a handsome oak frame. His mother, with clear skin and wavy hair, a narrow waist, a faint, knowing smile. His father, bearded, standing behind her, his cap in his hand. They had left the courthouse after the wedding and moved into the cabin his father had built on the mountainside overlooking their fields. "My parents loved being outside," he added. "My mother planted flowers everywhere. There was a cluster of jack-in-the-pulpit by the stream up from our house."

"I'm sorry I never met them. They must have been so proud of you."

"I don't know. Maybe. They were glad my life was easier."

"Glad," she agreed slowly, opening her eyes and glancing at Paul, who slept peacefully, dappled light falling on his face. "But maybe a little sorry too? I would be, if Paul grew up and moved away."

"Yes," he said, nodding. "That's true. They were proud and sorry both. They didn't like the city. They only visited me once in Pittsburgh." He remembered them sitting awkwardly in his single student room, his mother starting every time a train whistle sounded. June was dead by then, and as they sat sipping weak coffee at his rickety student table, he remembered thinking bitterly that they did not know what to do with themselves without June to care for. She had been the center of all their lives for so long. "They only stayed with me for one night. After my father died, my mother went to live with her sister in Michigan. She wouldn't fly, and she never learned to drive. I only saw her once, after that."

"That's too sad," Norah said, rubbing away a smear of dirt on her calf.

"Yes," David said. "Too sad indeed." He thought of June, the way her hair got so blond in the sun each summer, the scent of her skin— soap and warmth and something metallic, like a coin—filling the air when they squatted side by side, digging up the ground with sticks. He had loved her so much, her sweet laughter. And he had hated coming home to find her lying on a pallet on the porch on sunny days, his mother's face drawn with concern as she sat beside her daughter's limp form, singing softly, husking corn or shelling peas.

David looked at Paul, sleeping so deeply on the blanket with his head turned to the side, his long hair curling against his damp neck. His son, at least, he had sheltered from grief. Paul would not grow up, as David had, suffering the loss of his sister. He would not be forced to fend for himself because his sister couldn't.

This thought, and the force of its bitterness, shocked David. He wanted to believe he'd done the right thing when he handed his daughter to Caroline Gill. Or at least that he'd had the right reasons. But perhaps he had not. Perhaps it was not so much Paul he'd been protecting on that snowy night as some lost version of himself.

"You look so far away," Norah observed.

He shifted, moving closer to her, leaning against the boulder too.

"My parents had great dreams for me," he said. "But they didn't match my own dreams."

"Sounds like me and my mother," Norah said, hugging her knees. "She says she's coming to visit next month. Did I tell you? She's got a free flight."

"That's good, isn't it? Paul will keep her busy."

Norah laughed. "He will, won't he? That's her whole reason for coming."

"Norah, what do you dream about?" he asked. "What do you dream for Paul?"

Norah didn't answer right away. "I suppose I want him to be happy," she said at last. "Whatever in life makes him happy, I want him to have that. I don't care what it is, as long as he grows up to be good and true to himself. And generous and strong, like his father."

"No," David said, uncomfortable. "You don't want him to take after me."

She gave him an intent look, surprised. "Why not?"

He didn't answer. After a long, hesitant moment, Norah spoke again.

"What's wrong?" she asked, not aggressively but thoughtfully, as if she were trying to puzzle out the answer as she spoke. "Between us, I mean, David."

He didn't answer, struggling against a sudden surge of anger. Why did she have to stir things up again? Why couldn't she let the past rest and move on? But she spoke again.

"It hasn't been the same since Paul was born and Phoebe died. And yet you still won't talk about her. It's like you want to erase the fact that she existed."

"Norah, what do you want me to say? Of course life hasn't been the same."

"Don't get angry, David. That's just some kind of strategy, isn't it? So I won't talk about her anymore. But I won't back down. What I'm saying is true."

He sighed.

"Don't ruin the beautiful day, Norah," he said at last.

"I'm not," she said, moving away. She lay down on the blanket and closed her eyes. "I'm perfectly content with this day."

He watched her for a moment, sunlight catching in her blond hair, her chest rising and falling gently with each breath. He wanted to reach out and trace the delicate curved bones of her ribs; he wanted to kiss her at the point the bones met, stretching away like wings.

"Norah," he said. "I don't know what to do. I don't know what you want."

"No," she said. "You don't."

"You could tell me."

"I suppose I could. Maybe I will. Were they very much in love?" she asked suddenly, without opening her eyes. Her voice was still soft and calm, but he was aware of a new tension in the air. "Your father and your mother?"

"I don't know," he said, slowly, carefully, trying to determine the source of her question. "They loved each other. But he was away a lot. Like I said, they had hard lives."

"My father loved my mother more than she loved him," Norah said, and David felt an uneasiness stir in his heart. "He loved her, but he couldn't seem to show love in a way that was meaningful to her. She just thought he was offbeat, a little silly. There was a lot of silence in my house, growing up. . . . We're pretty silent in our house too," she added, and he thought of their calm evenings, her head bent over the little white hat with the ducks.

"A good silence," he said.

"Sometimes."

"And other times?"

"I still think about her, David," she said, turning on her side and meeting his gaze. "Our daughter. What she would be like."

He didn't answer, and as he watched she wept silently, covering her face with her hands. After a moment, he reached out and touched her arm; she wiped the tears from her eyes.

"And you?" she demanded, fierce now. "Don't you ever miss her too?"

"Yes," he said truthfully. "I think about her all the time."

Norah put her hand on his chest, and then her lips, berry-stained, were on his, a sweetness as piercing as desire against his tongue. He felt himself falling, the sun on his skin and her breasts lifting softly, like birds, against his hands. She sought the buttons on his shirt, and her hand brushed against the letter he had hidden in his pocket.

He shrugged off his shirt, but even so, when he slid his arms around her again, he was thinking, *I love you. I love you so much, and I lied to you.* And the distance between them, millimeters only, the space of a breath, opened up and deepened, became a cavern at whose edge he stood. He pulled away, back into the light and shadow, the clouds over him and then not, and the sun-warmed rock hot against his back.

"What is it?" she asked, stroking his chest. "Oh, David, what's wrong?"

"Nothing."

"David," she said. "Oh, David. Please."

He hesitated, on the edge of confessing everything, and then he could not.

"A problem from work. A patient. I can't get the case out of my mind."

"Let it go," she said. "I'm sick and tired of your work."

Hawks, lifting high on the updrafts, and the sun so warm. Everything circled, returning each time to the exact same point. He must tell her; the words filled his mouth. *I love you, I love you so much, and I lied to you.*

"I want to have another baby, David," Norah said, sitting up. "Paul's old enough now, and I'm ready."

David was so startled he didn't speak for a moment.

"Paul's only a year old," he said at last.

"So? People say it's easier to get all the diapers and things over with at once."

"What people?"

She sighed. "I knew you'd say no."

"I'm not saying no," David replied carefully.

She didn't answer.

"The timing seems wrong," he said. "That's all."

"You *are* saying no. You're saying no, but you don't want to admit it."

He was silent, remembering the way Norah had stood so close to the edge of the bridge. Remembering her photographs of nothing, and the letter in his pocket. He wanted nothing more than for the delicate structures of their lives to remain secure, for things to continue just as they were. For the world not to change, for this fragile equilibrium between them to endure.

"Things are fine right now," he said softly. "Why rock the boat?"

"How about for Paul?" She nodded to him, sleeping, still and peaceful, on his blanket. "He misses her."

"He can't possibly remember," David replied sharply.

"Nine months," Norah said. "Growing heart to heart. How could he not, at some level?"

"We're not ready," David said. "I'm not."

"It's not only about you," Norah said. "You're hardly home anyway. Maybe it's me who misses her, David. Sometimes, honestly, I feel like she's so close, just in the other room, and I've forgotten her. I know that must sound crazy, but it's true."

He didn't answer, though he knew exactly what she meant. The air was thick with the scent of strawberries. His mother had made preserves on the outdoor stove, stirring the foaming mixture as it cooked into syrup, boiling the jars and filling them to stand, jewel-like, on a shelf. He and June had eaten that jam in the dead of winter, stealing spoonfuls when their mother wasn't looking and hiding under the table's oilcloth cover to lick them clean. June's death had broken their mother's spirit, and David could no longer believe himself immune from misfortune. It was statistically unlikely that they'd have another child with Down's, but it was possible, anything was possible; and he couldn't take the risk.

"But it wouldn't fix things, Norah, to have another baby. That's not the right reason."

After a moment's silence she stood up, brushing her hands on her shorts, and waded off angrily through the field.

His shirt lay crumpled beside him, a corner of the white envelope visible. David did not reach for it; he did not need to. The note was brief, and though he had glanced at the photos only once, they were as clear to him as if he'd taken them himself. Phoebe's hair was dark and fine, like Paul's. Her eyes were brown, and she waved chubby fists in the air, as if reaching for something beyond the camera's view. Caroline, perhaps, wielding the camera. He had glimpsed her at the memorial service, tall and lonely in her red coat, and he'd gone straight to her apartment afterward, unsure of his intentions, knowing only that he had to see her. But by then Caroline was gone. Her apartment had looked exactly the same, with its squat furniture and plain walls; a faucet dripped in the bathroom. Yet the air was too still, the shelves bare. The bureau drawers and closets were empty. In the kitchen, a dull light pouring in across the black and white linoleum, David had stood listening to the beating of his own uneasy heart.

Now he lay back, the clouds moving over him, light and shadow. He had not tried to find Caroline, and since her letter had no useful return address, he could not imagine where to start. *It's in your hands now,* he had told her. But he found himself stricken at odd moments: alone in his new office; or developing photos, watching images emerge, mysteriously, on the sheets of blank white paper; or lying here on this warm rock while Norah, hurt and angry, walked away.

He was tired, and he felt himself drifting into sleep. Insects hummed in the sunlight, and he felt faintly anxious about bees. The stones in his pockets pressed against his leg. Nights in his childhood, he sometimes found his father in the porch rocker, the poplar trees glinting, alive with fireflies. On one such night his father handed him a smooth stone, an axhead he'd found while digging a trench. *Over two thousand years old,* he said. *Imagine that, David. It sat in other hands once, that eternally long ago, but beneath this very same moon.*

That was one time. There were other days when they went out to catch rattlesnakes. Dusk to dawn, they'd walked through the woods, carrying forked sticks, cloth bags over their shoulders and a metal box swinging from David's hand.

It always seemed to David that time paused on those days, the sun forever in the sky and the dry leaves moving under his feet. The world was reduced to just himself and his father and the snakes, but it was expanded, too, the sky opening vastly around him, higher and bluer with every step, and everything slowing down to the moment when he spotted a movement amid the colors of dirt and dry leaves, the diamondback pattern visible only when the snake began to move. His father had taught him how to go still, watching the yellow eyes, the flickering tongue. Each time a snake shed its skin the rattle grew longer, so you could tell by the loudness of the rattle in the forest silence how old the snake was, how big, and how much money it would bring. For the largest ones, coveted by zoos and scientists and sometimes by snake handlers, they might receive five dollars apiece.

Light fell through the trees and made patterns on the forest floor, and there was the sound of wind. Then there was the rattling, and the rearing head of the snake, and his father's arm, strong and solid, plunging a forked stick down to pin the snake by its neck. The fangs extended, striking hard into damp earth, the rattling wild and furious. With two strong fingers his father gripped the snake tightly behind its open jaw and picked it up: cool, dry, writhing like a whip. He slung the snake into a cloth bag and jerked it shut, and then the bag was a live thing, quivering on the ground. His father flipped it into a metal box and closed the lid. Without speaking they walked on, counting the snake money in their minds. There were weeks, in the summer and late fall, when they could make $25 this way. The money paid for food; when they went to the doctor in Morgantown, it paid for that too.

David!

Norah's voice came to him faintly, urgently, through the distant past and the forest and into the day. He rose up on his elbows and saw her standing on the far edge of the field of ripening strawberries, transfixed by something on the ground. He felt a rush of adrenaline and fear. Rattlesnakes liked sunny logs like the one by which she'd stopped; they laid their eggs in the fertile rotting wood. He glanced at Paul, still sleeping quietly in the shade, and then he was up and running, thistles scratching his ankles and strawberries bursting softly beneath his feet, already reaching into the pocket of his jeans and closing his fist around the largest stone. When he got close enough to glimpse the dark line of the snake, he threw it as hard as he could. The dull stone arched slowly through the air, turning. It fell six inches short of the snake and burst open, its purple heart alive and glittering.

"What in the world are you doing?" Norah asked.

He'd reached her by then. Panting, he looked down. It was not a snake at all but a dark stick resting against the dry skin of the log.

"I thought you called me," he said, confused.

"I did." She pointed to a cluster of pale flowers just beyond the line of shade. "Jack-in-the-pulpits. Like your mother used to have. David, you're scaring me."

"I thought it was a snake," he said, gesturing to the stick, shaking his head once more to try to clear away the past. "A rattlesnake. I was dreaming, I guess. I thought you needed help."

She looked puzzled, and he shook his head to clear away the dream. He felt terribly foolish, suddenly. The stick was a stick, nothing more. The day seemed absurdly normal. Birds called out, and the leaves began to move again in the trees.

"Why were you dreaming of snakes?" she asked.

"I used to catch them," he said. "For money."

"For money?" she repeated, puzzled. "Money for what?"

The distance was back between them, a chasm of the past that he could not cross. Money for food, and for those trips into town. She came from a different world; she would never understand this.

"They helped to pay my way through school, those snakes," he said.

She nodded and seemed about to ask more, but she did not.

"Let's go," she said, rubbing her shoulder. "Let's just get Paul and go home."

They walked back across the field and packed up their things. Norah carried Paul; he, the picnic basket.

. . .

As they walked, he remembered his father standing in the doctor's office, green bills falling like leaves on the countertop. With each one, David remembered the snakes, the whipping of their rattles and their mouths opening in a futile V, the coolness of their skin beneath his fingers, and their weight. Snake money. He was a boy, eight or nine, and it was one thing he could do.

That and protect June. *Watch your sister,* his mother would caution, looking up from the stove. *Feed the chickens and clean the coop and weed the garden. And watch June.*

David did, though not well. He kept June in sight but did not stop her from digging in the dirt and rubbing it through her hair. He didn't comfort her when she tripped over a rock and fell down, scraping her elbow. His love for her was so deeply woven with resentment that he could not untangle the two. She was sick all the time, from her weak heart and from the colds she got in every season, which made her wheeze and gasp for breath. Yet when he came up the path from school with his books slung over his back, it was June who was always waiting, June who looked into his face and understood what his day had been like, who wanted to know all about it. Her fingers were small and she liked to pat him, the breeze shifting her long lank hair.

And then one weekend he came home from school to find the cabin empty, still, a washrag hanging over the side of the tub and a chill in the air. He sat on the porch, hungry and cold, waiting. Very much later, near dusk, he glimpsed his mother walking down the hill with her arms folded. She did not speak until she reached the steps, and then she looked up at him and said, *David, your sister died. June died.* His mother's hair was pulled back tautly and a vein was pulsing in her temple and her eyes were red-rimmed from crying. She wore a thin gray sweater, pulled close, and she said, *David, she's gone.* And when he stood and hugged her she broke down, weeping, and he said, *When,* and she said, *Three days ago, on Tuesday, it was early in the morning and I went outside to get some water, and when I came back the house was quiet and I knew right away. She was gone. Stopped breathing.* He held his mother, and he could not think of anything more to say. The pain he felt was deep inside him, and above that was a numbness and he could not cry. He put a blanket around his mother's shoulders. He made her a cup of tea and went out to the hens and found the eggs she had not collected, and he gathered them. He fed the chickens and milked the cow. He did these ordinary things, but when he went inside the house was still dim, the air still silent, and June was still gone.

Davey, his mother said, a long time later, from the shadows where she sat, *You go off to school. Learn something that could help in the world.* He felt a resentment at that; he wanted his life to be his own, unencumbered by this shadow, this loss. He felt guilty because June was lying in the earth with a mound of dirt over her and he was still standing here; he was alive, and the breath moved in and out of his lungs; he could feel it, and his heart beat. *I'll be a doctor,* he said, and his mother didn't answer but after a while she nodded and rose, pulling her sweater close again. *Davy, I need you to take the Bible and go up there with me and say the words. I want the words said formally, and right.* And so they walked up the hillside together. It was dark by the time they got there, and he stood beneath the pines with the high wind whispering, and by the flickering light from the kerosene lamp he read, *The Lord is my shepherd. I shall not want. But I want,* he thought, as he spoke the words. *I want.* And his mother wept and they walked silently down the hill to the house, where he wrote a letter to his father, telling the news. He posted this on Monday when he went back to town, with its bustle and bright lights. He stood behind the counter, the oak worn smooth by a generation of commerce, and dropped the plain white letter in the mail.

. . .

When they finally reached the car, Norah paused to examine her shoulder, dark pink from the sun. She was wearing sunglasses, and when she looked up at him he could not read her expression.

"You don't have to be such a hero," she said. Her words were flat and practiced, and he could tell she had been thinking about them, rehearsing them, perhaps, during the walk back.

"I'm not trying to be a hero."

"No?" She looked away. "I think you are," she said. "It's my fault too. For a long time I wanted to be rescued, I realize that. But not anymore. You don't have to protect me all the time now. I hate it."

And then she took the car seat and turned away again. In the dappled sunlight, Paul's hand reached for her hair, and David felt a sense of panic, almost vertigo, at all he didn't know; at all he knew and couldn't mend. And anger: he felt that too, suddenly, in a great rush. At himself, but also at Caroline, who had not done what he'd asked, who had made an impossible situation even worse. Norah slid into the front seat and slammed the car door shut. He fished in his pocket for his keys and instead pulled out the last geode, gray and smooth, earth-shaped. He held it, warming in his palm, thinking of all mysteries the world contained: layers of stone, concealed beneath the flesh of earth and grass; these dull rocks, with their glimmering hidden hearts.

1970

May 1970

I

HE'S ALLERGIC TO BEES," NORAH TOLD THE TEACHER, watching Paul run across the new grass of the playground. He climbed to the top of the slide, sat for a moment with his short white sleeves flapping in the wind, and then sailed down, springing up with delight as he hit the ground. The azaleas were in dense bloom, and the air, warm as skin, hummed with insects, birds. "His father's allergic too. It's very serious."

"Don't worry," Miss Throckmorton replied. "We'll take good care of him."

Miss Throckmorton was young, just out of school, dark-haired and wiry and enthusiastic. She wore a full skirt and sturdy flat sandals, and her eyes never left the groups of children playing on the field. She seemed steady, competent, focused, and kind. Still, Norah did not completely trust her to know what she was doing.

"He picked up a bee," she persisted, "a *dead* bee; I mean, one that was just lying on the windowsill. Seconds later, he was swelling up like a balloon."

"Don't worry, Mrs. Henry," Miss Throckmorton repeated, a bit less patiently. She was already moving off, her clear voice calming, like a bell, to help a little girl with sand in her eyes.

Norah lingered in the new spring sun, watching Paul. He was playing tag, his cheeks flushed, running with his arms straight down by his sides—he'd slept that way, too, as an infant. His hair was dark, but otherwise he looked like Norah, people said, with the same bone structure and fair coloring. She saw herself in him, it was true, and David was there too, in the shape of Paul's jaw, the curve of his ears, the way he liked to stand with his arms folded, listening to the teacher. But mostly Paul was simply himself. He loved music and hummed made-up songs all day long. Though he was only six, he'd already sung solos at school, stepping forward with an innocence and confidence that astonished Norah, his sweet voice rising in the auditorium as clear and melodic as water in a stream.

Now he paused to squat beside another little boy who was skimming leaves from the dark water of a puddle with a stick. His right knee was skinned, the Band-Aid pulling off. Sunlight glinted in his short dark hair. Norah watched him, serious and utterly absorbed in his task, overcome by the simple fact of his existence. Paul, her son. Here in the world.

"Norah Henry! Just the person I wanted to see."

She turned to see Kay Marshall, dressed in slim pink pants and a cream and pink sweater, gold leather flats, and glimmering gold earrings. She was pushing her newborn in an antique wicker carriage while Elizabeth, her oldest, walked by her side. Elizabeth, born a week after Paul, in the sudden spring that had followed that strange and sudden snow. She was dressed this morning in pink dotted Swiss and white patent leather shoes. Impatiently, she pulled away from Kay and ran off across the playground to the swings.

"It's such a pretty day," Kay said, watching her go. "How are you, Norah?"

"I'm fine," Norah said, resisting the impulse to touch her hair, acutely aware of her plain white blouse and blue skirt, her lack of jewelry. No matter when or where Norah saw her, Kay Marshall was always like this: calm and cool, coordinated to the last detail, her children perfectly dressed and well-behaved. Kay was the sort of mother Norah had always imagined that she herself would be, handling every situation with a relaxed and instinctive calm. Norah admired her, and she envied her too. Sometimes she even caught herself thinking that if she could be more like Kay, more serene and secure, her marriage might improve; she and David might be happier.

"I'm fine," she repeated, looking at the baby, who gazed up at her with wide inquisitive eyes. "Look how big Angela is getting!"

Impulsively, Norah leaned down and picked up the baby, Kay's second daughter, dressed in frothy pink to match her sister. She was light and warm in Norah's arms, patting at Norah's cheeks with her small hands, laughing. Norah felt a rush of pleasure, remembering the way Paul had felt at this age, his scent of soap and milk, his soft skin. She glanced across the playground; he was running again, playing tag. Now that he was in school, he had his own life. He no longer liked to sit and cuddle with her unless he was sick or wanted her to read him a story before bed. It seemed impossible that he had ever been this small, impossible that he'd grown into a boy with a red tricycle who thrust sticks into puddles and sang so beautifully.

"She's ten months today," Kay said. "Can you believe it?"

"No," Norah said. "Time goes so fast."

"Have you been down by the campus?" Kay asked. "Have you heard what's happening?"

Norah nodded. "Bree called last night." She'd stood, the phone in one hand and the other on her heart, watching grainy news on TV: four students shot dead at Kent State. Even in Lexington, tension had been building for weeks, the newspapers full of war and protests and unrest, the world volatile and shifting.

"It's scary," Kay said, but her tone was calm, more disapproving than dismayed, the same voice she might have used to talk about someone's divorce. She took Angela, kissed her forehead, and put her gently back into the carriage.

"I know," Norah agreed. She used the same tone, but to her the unrest seemed deeply personal, a reflection of what had been going on within her heart for years. For a moment she felt another sharp, deep pang of envy. Kay lived in innocence, untouched by loss, believing that she would always be safe; Norah's world had changed when Phoebe died. All her joys were set into stark relief—by that loss and by the possibility of further loss she now glimpsed in every moment. David was always telling her to relax, to hire help, not to push herself so hard. He grew irritated with her projects, her committees, her plans. But Norah could not sit still; it made her too uneasy. So she arranged meetings and filled up her days, always with the desperate sense that if she let down her guard, even for a moment, disaster would follow. The feeling was worst in the late morning; she almost always had a quick drink then—gin, sometimes vodka—to ease her into the afternoon. She loved the calm, spreading through her like light. She kept the bottles carefully hidden from David.

"Anyway," Kay was saying. "I wanted to RSVP about your party. We'd love to come, but we'll be a little late. Is there anything I can bring?"

"Just yourselves," Norah said. "Everything's almost ready. Except I have to go home and take down a wasp's nest."

Kay's eyes widened slightly. She was from an old Lexington family and had "people," as she called them. Pool people and cleaning people and lawn people and kitchen people. David always said Lexington was like the limestone on which it was built: layers of stratification, nuances of being and belonging, your place in the hierarchy fixed in stone long ago. No doubt Kay had insect people too.

"A wasp's nest? Poor you!"

"Yes," Norah said. "Paper wasps. The nest is hanging off the garage."

It pleased her to shock Kay, even so mildly; she liked the concrete sound of the task before her. Wasps. Tools. The dismantling of a nest. Norah hoped it would take all morning. Otherwise, she might find herself driving, as she had so often in these last weeks, fast and hard, a silver flask in her purse. She could make it to the Ohio River in less than two hours. Louisville or Maysville or once, even, Cincinnati. She'd park on a river bluff and get out of the car, watching the distant ever-shifting water far below.

The school bell rang and the children began funneling inside. Norah searched for Paul's dark head, watched him disappear. "I just loved our two singing together," Kay said, blowing kisses to Elizabeth. "Paul has such a beautiful voice. A gift, really."

"He loves music," Norah replied. "He always has."

It was true. Once, at three months, while she talked with friends, he had suddenly begun to babble, a cascade of sounds pouring into the room like flowers spilling suddenly from a shaft of light, stopping the conversation entirely.

"Actually, that's the other thing I wanted to ask you, Norah. This fund-raiser I'm doing next month. It's a Cinderella theme, and I've been sent out to round up as many little footmen as I can. I thought of Paul."

Despite herself, Norah felt a surge of pleasure. She had given up hope of such an invitation years ago, after Bree's scandalous marriage and divorce.

"A footman?" she repeated, taking in the news.

"Well, that's the best part," Kay confided. "Not just a footman. Paul would sing. A duet. With Elizabeth."

"I see," Norah said, and she did. Elizabeth's voice was sweet but thin. She sang with forced cheer, like spring bulbs in January, her anxious eyes darting over the audience. Her voice wouldn't be strong enough without Paul's.

"It would mean such a lot to everyone if he would."

Norah nodded slowly, disappointed, annoyed with herself for caring. But Paul's voice was pure, winged; he would love to be a footman. And at least this party, like the wasps, would provide another anchor to her days.

"Wonderful!" Kay said. "Oh, marvelous. I hope you won't mind," she added, "I took the liberty of reserving a little tuxedo for him. I just knew you'd say yes!" She glanced at her watch, efficient now, ready to go. "Good to see you," she added, waving as she walked away, pushing the carriage.

The playground was empty. A candy wrapper flashed, pinwheeling, across the overgrown spring grass and caught in the flaming pink azaleas. Norah walked past the bright swings and slides to her car. The river, its calming swirl, called to her. Two hours, and she could be there. The lure of the fast drive, the rushing wind, the water, was nearly irresistible, so great that on the last school holiday she had been shocked to find herself in Louisville, Paul frightened and quiet in the backseat, her hair windswept and the gin already wearing thin. *There's the river,* she had said, standing with Paul's small hand in hers, looking at the muddy, swirling water. *Now we'll go to the zoo,* she'd announced, as if that had been her intention all along.

She left the school and drove into town through the tree-lined streets, past the bank and the jewelry store, her longing as vast as the sky. She slowed as she passed World Travel. Yesterday, she had interviewed for a job there. She'd seen the ad in the paper, and she'd been drawn into the low brick building by the glamorous signs in the windows: glittering beaches and buildings, vivid skies and colors. She had not really wanted the job until she got there, and then suddenly she did. Sitting in her printed linen sheath, holding her white purse on her lap, she had wanted this job more than anything. The agency was owned by a man named Pete Warren, fifty years old and bald across the top, who'd tapped a pencil on his clipboard and joked about the Wildcats. He had liked her, she could tell, even though her degree was in English and she had no experience. He was supposed to let her know today.

Behind her, someone honked a horn. Norah speeded up. This road went through town and intersected with the highway. But as she neared the university, traffic grew dense. The streets were so full of people she slowed to a crawl and then had to pull over entirely. She got out of the car and left it. Distantly, from deeper in the campus, came a dark swelling of voices, rhythmic and rising, a chant full of energy that was somehow akin to the buds bursting open on the trees. Her restlessness and longing seemed answered by this moment, and she fell into the current of moving people.

Scents of sweat and patchouli oil filled the air, and the sunlight was warm on her arms. She thought of the elementary school, just a mile away, the order there and the ordinariness, and she thought of Kay Marshall's disapproving tone, and yet she kept going. Shoulders and arms and hair brushed against her. The current began to slow and pool; there was a crowd gathering by the ROTC building, where two young men stood on the steps, one with a megaphone. Norah paused too, craning to see what was happening. One of the young men, wearing a suit jacket and tie, was holding an American flag aloft, the stripes fluttering. As she watched, the other young man, also nicely dressed, held his fist near the edge. The flames were invisible at first, an intensity of shimmering heat, and then they caught in the fabric, rising up against the leaves, the blue and greenness of the day.

Norah watched this happening as if in slow motion. Through the wavering air she saw Bree, moving along the perimeter of the crowd near the building, passing out leaflets. Her long hair was caught in a ponytail that swung against her white peasant top. She was so beautiful, Norah thought, glimpsing the determination and excitement on her sister's face in the instant before she disappeared. Envy rose in her again, flamelike: envy of Bree, for her sureness and her freedom. Norah pushed her way through the crowd.

She glimpsed her sister twice more—the flash of her blond hair, her face in profile—before she finally reached her. By then Bree was standing on the curb, talking to a young man with reddish hair, their conversation so intent that when Norah finally touched her arm Bree turned, puzzled and unseeing, her expression utterly blank for a long instant before she recognized her sister.

"Norah?" she said. She placed her hand on the red-haired man's chest, a gesture so sure and intimate that Norah's heart caught. "It's my sister," Bree explained. "Norah, this is Mark."

He nodded without smiling and shook Norah's hand, assessing her.

"They set the flag on fire," Norah said, conscious once again of her clothes, as out of place here as on the playground, for utterly different reasons.

Mark's brown eyes narrowed slightly and he shrugged.

"They fought in Vietnam," he said. "So I guess they had their reasons."

"Mark lost half his foot in Vietnam."

Norah found herself glancing down at Mark's boots, laced high up his ankles.

"The front half," he said, tapping his right foot. "The toes and then some."

"I see," Norah said, deeply embarrassed.

"Look, Mark, can you give us a minute?" Bree asked.

He glanced at the stirring crowd. "Not really. I'm the next speaker."

"It's okay. I'll be right back," she said, then took Norah's hand and pulled her a few yards away, ducking beneath a cluster of catalpa trees.

"What are you doing here?" she asked.

"I'm not sure," Norah said. "I had to stop, that's all, when I saw the crowd."

Bree nodded, her silver earrings flashing. "It's amazing, isn't it? There must be five thousand people here. We were hoping for a few hundred. It's because of Kent State. It's the end."

The end of what? Norah wondered, leaves fluttering around her. Somewhere, Miss Throckmorton was calling to the students and Pete Warren sat beneath the glossy travel posters, writing tickets. Wasps swam lazily in the sunny air by her garage. Could the world end on such a day?

"Is that your boyfriend?" she asked. "The one you were telling me about?"

Bree nodded, smiling a private smile.

"Oh, look at you! You're in love."

"I suppose so," Bree said softly, glancing at Mark. "I suppose I am."

"Well, I hope he's treating you well," Norah said, appalled to hear her mother's voice, right down to the intonation. But Bree was too happy to do anything but laugh.

"He treats me fine," she said. "Hey, can I bring him this weekend? To your party?"

"Sure," Norah said, though she wasn't sure at all.

"Great. Oh, Norah, did you get that job you wanted?"

The catalpa leaves moved like supple green hearts in the wind, and beyond them the crowd rippled and swayed.

"I don't know yet," Norah replied, thinking of the tasteful, colorful office. Suddenly her aspirations seemed so trivial.

"But how did the interview go?" Bree pressed.

"Well. It went well. I'm just not sure I want the job anymore, that's all."

Bree pushed a strand of hair behind her ear and frowned.

"Why not? Norah, just yesterday you were desperate for that job. You were so excited. It's David, isn't it? Saying that you can't."

Norah, annoyed, shook her head. "David doesn't even know. Bree, it was just a little box of an office. Boring. Bourgeois. You wouldn't be caught dead in it."

"I'm not you," Bree pointed out, impatient. "You're not me. You wanted this job, Norah. For the glamour. For heaven's sake, for the independence."

It was true, she had wanted the job, but it was also true that she felt anger flaring up again: fine for Bree, who was out here starting revolutions, to consign her to a nine-to-five life.

"I'd be typing, not traveling. It would be years and years before I earned any trips. It's not exactly what I imagined for my life, Bree."

"And pushing a vacuum cleaner is?"

Norah thought of the wild rush of wind, of the Ohio, swirling, only eighty miles away. She pressed her lips together and did not answer.

"You make me so crazy, Norah. Why are you afraid of change? Why can't you just *be* and let the world unfold?"

"I am," she said. I *am* being. You have no idea!"

"You're sticking your head in the sand. That's what I see."

"You don't see anything but the next available man."

"All right. We're done." Bree took a single step and was immediately swallowed by the crowd: a flash of color, then gone.

Norah stood for a moment beneath the catalpas, trembling with an anger she knew to be unaccountable. What was wrong with her? How could she envy Kay Marshall one moment and Bree the next, for such completely different reasons?

She made her way back through the crowd to her car. After the turbulence and drama of the protest, the city streets seemed flat, bleached of color, ominously ordinary. Too much time had passed; she had only two hours before she needed to fetch Paul. Not time enough for the river now. At home, in her sunny kitchen, Norah made herself a gin and tonic. The glass was solid and cool in her hand, and the ice tinkled with reassuring brightness. In the living room she paused before the photograph of herself standing on the natural stone bridge. When she remembered that day—their hike and their picnic—she never thought of this moment. Instead, she remembered the world spreading out below her, the sun and the air on her skin. *Let me take your picture,* David had called, insistent, and she'd turned to find him, kneeling, focusing, intent on preserving a moment that never really existed. She'd been right about that camera, to her own regret. David, fascinated to the point of obsession, had built a darkroom above the garage.

David. How was it that he grew more mysterious to her as the years passed, as well as more familiar? He had left a pair of amber cuff links on the console beneath the photos. Norah picked these up and held them in her palm, listening to the clock tick softly in the living room. The stones warmed in her hand; she was comforted by their smoothness. She found rocks everywhere, clustered in David's pockets, scattered on the dresser, tucked into envelopes in the desk. Sometimes she glimpsed David and Paul in the backyard, their heads bent together over some likely looking stone. Watching them, her heart always opened with a kind of wary gladness. Such moments were rare; David was so busy these days. Stop, Norah wanted to say. *Take a minute. Spend some time. Your son is growing so fast.*

Norah slipped the cuff links in her pocket and took her drink outside. She stood below the papery nest, watching the wasps circle it and disappear inside. Now and then one flew close to her, drawn to the sweet smell of gin. She sipped and watched. Her muscles, her very cells, were relaxing in a fluid chain reaction, as if she had swallowed the warmth of the day. She finished the drink, put the glass down on the driveway, and went to find her garden gloves and hat, stepping around Paul's tricycle. He was already too big for it; she should pack it away with the other things: his baby clothes, his outgrown toys. David did not want more children, and now that Paul was in school she had given up arguing with him about it. It was hard to imagine going back to diapers and 2 A.M. feedings, though she often longed to hold another baby in her arms: like Angela this morning, the sweet warmth and weight of her. How lucky Kay was and didn't even know it.

Norah pulled on her gloves and stepped back into the sun. She had no experience with wasps or bees, except for one sting on her toe when she was eight, which had hurt for an hour and healed. When Paul picked the dead bee off the floor and cried out in pain she'd felt no panic at all. Ice for the swelling, a long hug in the porch swing; all would be well. But the swelling and the redness had started in his hand and quickly spread. His face grew puffy, and she'd called for David with fear in her voice. He'd known right away what was happening, what shot to give. Within moments Paul began to breathe more easily. *No harm done,* David said. That was true, but it still made her sick with fear. What if David had not been home?

She watched the wasps for a few minutes, thinking of the protesters on the hill, the shimmering, unsteady world. She'd done what was expected of her, always. She had gone to college and taken a little job; she had married well. Yet since the birth of her children—Paul, careening down the slide with his arms outflung, and Phoebe, present somehow through her absence, arriving in dreams, standing on the unseen edge of every moment—Norah could no longer understand the world in the same way. Her loss had left her feeling helpless, and she fought that helplessness by filling up her days.

Now she studied the tools with purpose. She would deal with these insects herself.

The long-handled hoe was heavy in her hands. She lifted it slowly and took a bold swipe at the nest, the blade slicing easily through the papery skin. It thrilled her, the power of that initial strike. But as she pulled the hoe back, wasps, furious and determined, poured out of the torn nest and flew straight after her. One stung her wrist, another her cheek. She dropped the hoe and ran inside, slamming the door and standing with her back pressed against it, breathless.

Outside, the swarm circled, buzzing angrily around the ruined nest. Some wasps landed on the windowsill, their delicate wings moving lightly. Swarming, angry—they made her think of the students she had seen that morning; they made her think of herself. She went into the kitchen and made another drink, dabbing some gin on her cheek and her wrist, where the stings were beginning to swell. The gin was crisp, delightful, filling her with a warm, fluid sense of well-being and power. She had an hour, still, before she'd leave to pick Paul up.

"All right, you damned wasps," she said out loud. "You've had it now."

There was insect repellent in the closet, above the coats and shoes and the vacuum cleaner—a steel-blue Electrolux, brand new. Norah remembered Bree, brushing blond hair from her cheek. *Pushing a vacuum—is that what you want for your life?*

Norah was halfway out the door when she had the idea.

The wasps were busy, already reassembling the nest, and they seemed not to notice Norah when she came outside again, carrying the Electrolux. The machine sat in the driveway, as incongruous and odd as a steel-blue pig. Norah put her gloves back on, her hat, and a jacket. She wrapped a scarf around her face. She plugged the vacuum in and turned it on, letting it hum for a moment, sounding strangely small in the open air, before she picked up the nozzle. Boldly, she stuck it into what remained of the nest. The wasps buzzed and rushed with anger—her cheek and arm stung just at the sight of them—but they were quickly sucked in with a rattling sound, like acorns bouncing on the roof. She waved the nozzle in the air, a magic wand, collecting all the angry insects, shredding the delicate nest. Soon she had them all. She kept the vacuum running while she looked for some way to cover the nozzle; she didn't want these wasps, so industrious and single-minded, to escape. It was such a warm sunny day, and the drinks had left her so relaxed. She stuck the nozzle into the dirt, but the machine began to make a straining sound. Then she noticed the tailpipe of the car: yes, the nozzle fit on it perfectly. Deeply satisfied, overcome with accomplishment, Norah turned the machine off and went inside.

At the bathroom sink, sun pouring in through the frosted windows, she undid the scarf and took off her hat, studying her image in the mirror. Dark green eyes and blond hair and a face made thin by worry. Her hair was flattened, and her skin was filmed with sweat. An angry red welt rose on her cheek. She bit lightly at the inside of her lip, wondering what David saw when he looked at her. Wondering who was she, really, trying to fit in with Kay Marshall one minute and Bree's friends the next, driving wildly to the river, never in a place that felt like home? Which of those selves did David see? Or was it another woman entirely who slept beside him every night? Herself, yes, but not as she would ever see herself. And not as he had once seen her, either, anymore than she saw the man she had married each night when David came home, hung his suit jacket carefully over a chair, and snapped open the evening paper.

She dried her hands and went to put ice on her swollen cheek. The wasp nest hung tattered and empty from the eave of the garage. The Electrolux stood squatly in the driveway, connected to the tailpipe of the car by its long pleated hose, a silver umbilical cord that flashed in the sun. She imagined David coming home to find the wasps gone, the backyard decorated, the party planned down to the last perfect detail. He would be surprised, she hoped, and pleased.

She glanced at her watch. It was time to get Paul. On the back steps Norah paused, groping in her purse for the house keys. A strange noise from the driveway made her look up. It was a kind of buzzing, and at first she thought the wasps were starting to escape. But the blue air was clear, empty. The buzzing became a sizzling, and then there was the electrical scent of ozone, burning wires. These, Norah realized with a kind of slow wonder, were all coming from the Electrolux. She hurried down the steps. Her feet hit the blacktop, her hand was reaching through the bright spring air, when suddenly the Electrolux exploded and sprang out of reach, careening across the grassy lawn and hitting the fence so hard it broke a plank. The blue machine fell amid the rhododendrons, smoke billowing out in oily clouds, whining like a wounded animal.

Norah stood still with her hand outstretched, as frozen in time as any of David's photographs, trying to take in what had happened. A piece of the tailpipe had been pulled from the car. Seeing this, she understood: the gasoline fumes must have gathered in the vacuum cleaner's still-hot engine, causing it to explode. Norah thought of

Paul, allergic to bees, a boy with a voice like a flute, who might have been in its path if he'd been home.

As she watched, a wasp drifted out of the smoky tailpipe and flew off.

Somehow, this was too much for Norah. Her hard work, her ingenuity, and now, despite everything, the wasps were going to escape. She crossed the lawn. With one swift, unhesitating motion, she opened the Electrolux, reached in through the bloom of smoke to pull out the paper bag full of dust and insects, threw it on the ground, and began to stomp on it, a wild dance. The paper bag spilt along one edge and a wasp slipped out; her foot came down on it. It was Paul she was fighting for, but also for some understanding of herself. *You're afraid of change,* Bree had told her. *Why can't you just* be? But be what? Norah had wondered all day. Be *what?* She had known once: she had been a daughter and a student and a long distance-operator, roles she had handled with ease and assurance. Then she had been a fiancée, a young wife, and a mother, and she had discovered that these words were far too small ever to contain the experience.

Even after it was clear that all the wasps inside the bag must be dead, Norah kept dancing on the pulpy mess, wild and intent. Something was happening, something had changed, in the world and in her heart. That night, while the ROTC building on campus burned to the ground, bright flames flowering into the warm spring night, Norah would dream of wasps and bees, large dreamy bumblebees floating through tall grasses. The next day she would replace the vacuum cleaner without ever mentioning the incident to David. She would cancel the tuxedo for Kay's fund-raiser; she would accept that job. Glamour, yes, and adventure, and a life of her own.

All this would happen, but for the moment she did not consider anything but the movement of her feet and the bag slowly turning to a dirty pulp of wings and stingers. In the distance, the crowd of protesters roared, and the swelling sound traveled through the bright spring air to where she stood. Blood beat in her temples. What was happening there was happening here as well, in the quiet of her own backyard, in the secret spaces of her heart: an explosion, some way in which life could never be the same.

A single wasp buzzed near the fiery azaleas and moved angrily away. Norah stepped off the soggy paper sack. Dazed, cold sober, she walked across the lawn, fingering her keys. She got in the car, as if it were any other day, and drove off to get her son.

II

"DAD? DADDY?"

At the sound of Paul's voice, his quick light steps on the garage stairs, David looked up from the exposed sheet of paper he had just slipped into the developer.

"Hang on!" he called out. "Just a second, Paul." But even as he spoke the door burst open, spilling light into the room.

"Damn it!" David watched the paper darken rapidly, the image lost in the sudden burst of light. "Damn it, Paul, haven't I told you a million zillion *trillion* times not to come in when the red light is on?"

"Sorry. I'm sorry, Dad."

David took a deep breath, chastened. Paul was only six, and standing in the doorway he looked very small. "It's okay, Paul. Come on in. I'm sorry I yelled at you."

He squatted down and held out his arms, and Paul plunged into them, resting his head briefly on David's shoulder, the bristle of his new haircut both soft and stiff against David's neck. Paul was slight and wiry, strong, a boy who moved through the world like quicksilver, quiet and watchful and eager to please. David kissed his forehead, regretting that moment of anger, marveling at his son's shoulder blades, elegant and perfect, stretching out like wings beneath layers of skin and muscle.

"Okay. What was so important?" he asked, sitting back on his heels. "What was important enough to spoil my pictures?"

"Dad, look!" Paul said. "Look what I found!"

He unclenched his small fist. Several flat stones, thin disks with a hole in the center, rested on his palm, the size of buttons.

"These are great," David said, picking one up. "Where did you find them?"

"Yesterday. When I went with Jason to his grandfather's farm. There's a creek, and you have to be careful because Jason saw a copperhead last summer, but it's too cold for snakes now, so we were wading and I found these right by the edge of the water."

"Wow." David fingered the fossils; light and delicate, millennia old, time preserved more clearly than any photograph ever could. "These fossils were part of a sea lily, Paul. You know, a long time ago, a lot of Kentucky used to be under an ocean."

"Really? Neat. Is there a picture in the rock book?"

"Maybe. We'll check as soon as I clean up. How are we doing on time?" he added, stepping to the darkroom door and glancing outside. It was a beautiful spring day, the air soft and warm, dogwoods in bloom all around the perimeter of the garden. Norah had set up tables and covered them with bright cloths. She'd arranged plates and punch, chairs and napkins, vases of flowers. A maypole, fashioned around a lean poplar tree in the center of the backyard, streamed bright ribbons. She'd done this by herself too. David had offered to help, but she'd declined. *Stay out of the way,* she'd told him. *That's the best thing you can do right now.* So he had.

He stepped back into the darkroom, cool and hidden, with its pale red light and sharp scent of chemicals.

"Mom's getting dressed," Paul said. "I'm not supposed to get dirty."

"A tough order," David observed, sliding the bottles of fixer and developer onto a high shelf beyond Paul's reach. "Go on inside, okay? I'll be right there. We'll look up those sea lilies."

Paul ran down the stairs; David glimpsed him sprinting across the lawn, the screen door of the house slamming shut behind him.

He washed out the trays and set them to dry, then removed the film from the developer and put it away. It was peaceful in the darkroom, cool and quiet, and he stood there for a few seconds longer before he followed Paul. Outside, the tablecloths rippled in the breeze. May baskets, woven of paper and filled with spring flowers, adorned each plate. Yesterday, on the real May Day, Paul had taken baskets like these to the neighbors too, hanging them from each front door, knocking and running and hiding to watch them be discovered. Norah's idea: her artistry and energy and imagination.

She was in the kitchen, wearing an apron over a suit of coral-colored silk, arranging parsley and cherry tomatoes on a meat platter.

"Everything set?" he asked. "It looks great out there. Anything I can do?"

"Get dressed?" she suggested, glancing at the clock. She dried her hands on a towel. "But first put this platter in the fridge downstairs, okay? This one's already full. Thanks."

David took the platter, the glass cool against his hands. "Such a lot of work," he observed. "Why don't you have these parties catered?"

He had meant to be helpful, but Norah paused, frowning, on her way out the door.

"Because I enjoy this," she said. "The planning and the cooking—all of it. Because it gives me a lot of pleasure to pull something beautiful out of nothing. I have a lot of talents," she added, coolly, "whether you realize it or not."

"That's not what I meant." David sighed. These days they were like two planets in orbit around the same sun, not colliding but not drawing any closer either. "I just meant, Why not have some help? Hire a catering staff. We can certainly afford it."

"It's not about the money," she said, shaking her head, and stepped outside.

He put the platter away and went upstairs to shave. Paul followed him in and sat on the edge of the tub, talking a mile a minute and kicking his heels against the porcelain. He loved Jason's grandfather's farm, he had helped milk a cow there, and Jason's grandfather had let him drink some milk, still warm, tasting of grass.

David lathered on the soap with a soft brush, taking pleasure in listening. The razor blade slid in smooth clean strokes against his skin, sending quivering motes of light against the ceiling. For a moment the whole world seemed caught, suspended: the soft spring air and the scent of soap and the excited voice of his son.

"I used to milk cows," David said. He dried his face and reached for his shirt. "I used to be able to squirt a stream of milk straight into the cat's mouth."

"That's what Jason's pawpaw did! I like Jason. I wish he was my brother."

David, putting on his tie, watched Paul's reflection in the mirror. In the silence that was not quite silence—the sink faucet dripping, the clock ticking softly, the whisper of cloth against cloth—his thoughts traveled to his daughter. Every few months, shuffling through the office mail, he came across Caroline's loopy handwriting. Though the first few letters had come from Cleveland, now each envelope bore a different postmark. Sometimes Caroline enclosed a new post office box number—always in different places, vast impersonal cities—and whenever she did this David sent money. They had never known each other well, yet her letters to him had grown increasingly intimate over the years. The most recent ones might have been torn from her diary, beginning *Dear David* or simply *David,* her thoughts pouring forth in a rush. Sometimes he tried to throw the letters away unopened, but he always ended up fishing them from the trash and reading them quickly. He kept them locked in the filing cabinet in the darkroom so he would always know where they were. So Norah would never find them.

Once, years ago, when the letters first began to arrive, David had made the eight-hour drive to Cleveland. He'd walked through the city for three days, studying phone books, inquiring at every hospital. In the main post office he'd touched the little brass door numbered 621 with his fingertips, but the postmaster would not give him the owner's name or address. *I'll stand here and wait then,* David said, and the man shrugged. *Go ahead,* he said. *Better bring some food, though. Weeks can pass before some of these mailboxes get opened.*

In the end, he'd given up and come home, allowing the days to pass, one by one, as Phoebe grew up without him. Each time he sent money, he enclosed a note asking Caroline to tell him where she lived, but he did not press her, or hire a private investigator, as he sometimes imagined doing. It would have to come from her, he felt, the desire to be found. He believed he wanted to find her. He believed that once he did—once he could fix things—he would be able to tell Norah the truth.

He believed all this, and he got up every morning and walked to the hospital. He performed surgeries and examined X-rays and came home and mowed the lawn and played with Paul; his life was full. Yet even so, every few months, for no predictable reason, he woke from dreams of Caroline Gill staring at him from the clinic doorway or across the courtyard at the church. Woke, trembling, and got dressed and went down to the office or out to the darkroom, where he worked on his articles or slid his photographs into their chemical baths, watching images emerge where nothing had been.

"Dad, you forgot to look up the fossils," Paul said. "You promised."

"That's right," David said, pulling himself back to the present, adjusting the knot in his tie. "That's right, son. I did."

They went downstairs together to the den and spread the familiar books on the desk. The fossil was a crinoid, from a small sea animal with a flowerlike body. The buttonlike stones had once been plates forming the stem column. He rested his hand lightly on Paul's back, feeling his flesh, so warm and alive, and the delicate vertebrae just beneath his skin.

"I'm going to show Mom," Paul said. He grabbed the fossils and ran off through the house and out the back door. David got a drink and stood by the window. A few guests had arrived and were scattered across the lawn, the men in dark blue coats, the women like bright spring flowers in pink and vibrant yellow and pastel blue. Norah moved among them, hugging the women, shaking hands, managing the introductions. She had been so quiet when David first met her, calm and self-contained and watchful. He could never have imagined her in this moment, so gregarious and at ease, launching a party she had orchestrated down to the very last detail. Watching her, David was filled with a kind of longing. For what? For the life they might have had, perhaps. Norah seemed very happy, laughing on the lawn. Yet David knew this success would not be enough, not even for a day. By evening she would have moved on to the next thing, and if he woke in the night and ran his hand along the curve of her back, hoping to stir her, she would murmur and catch his hand in hers and turn away, all without waking.

Paul was on the swing set now, flying high into the blue sky. He wore the crinoids on a long piece of string around his neck; they lifted and fell, bouncing against his small chest, sometimes snapping against the chains of the swing.

"Paul," Norah called, her voice drifting in clearly through open screen. "Paul, take that thing off your neck. It's dangerous."

David took his drink and went outside. He met Norah on the lawn.

"Don't," he said softly, putting his hand on her arm. "He made it himself."

"I know. I gave him the string. But he can wear it later. If he slips while he's playing and it gets caught, it could choke him."

She was so tense; he let his hand fall.

"That's not likely," he said, wishing he could erase their loss and what it had done to them both. "Nothing bad is going to happen to him, Norah."

"You don't know that."

"Even so, David's right, Norah."

The voice came from behind. He turned to see Bree, whose wildness and passions and beauty moved like a wind through their house. She was wearing a spring dress of filmy material, which seemed to float around her as she moved, and holding hands with a young man, shorter than she: clean-cut, with short reddish hair, wearing sandals and an open collar.

"Bree, honestly, it could catch and he could choke," Norah insisted, turning too.

"He's swinging," Bree told her lightly, as Paul flew high against the sky, his head tipped back, sun on his face. "Look at him, he's so happy. Don't make him get down and get all worried. David's right. Nothing's going to happen."

Norah forced a smile. "No? The world could end. You said so yourself just yesterday."

"But that was yesterday," Bree said. She touched Norah's arm and they exchanged a long look, connected for a moment in a way that excluded everyone else. David watched with a rush of longing and with a sudden memory of his own sister, the two of them hiding under the kitchen table, peeking through the folds of oilcloth, stifling their laughter. He remembered her eyes and the warmth of her arm and the joy of her company.

"What happened yesterday?" David asked, pushing away the memory, but Bree ignored him, talking to Norah.

"I'm sorry, Sis," she said. "Things were a little crazy yesterday. I was out of line."

"I'm sorry too," Norah said. "I'm glad you came to the party."

"What happened yesterday? Were you at the fire, Bree?" David asked again. He and Norah had woken in the night to sirens, to the acrid smell of smoke and a strange glow in the sky. They had come outside to stand with their neighbors on the dark quiet lawns, their ankles growing wet with dew while on campus the ROTC building burned. For days the protests had been growing, layers of tension in the air, invisible but real, while in towns along the Mekong River bombs fell and people ran, cradling their dying children in their arms. Across the river in Ohio now, four students lay dead. But no one had imagined this in Lexington, Kentucky: a Molotov cocktail and a building in flames, police pouring into the streets.

Bree turned to him, her long hair swinging over her shoulders, and shook her head. "No. I wasn't there, but Mark was." She smiled at the young man beside her and slipped her slender arm through his. "This is Mark Bell."

"Mark fought in Vietnam," Norah added. "He's here protesting the war."

"Ah," David said. "An agitator."

"A protester, I believe," Norah corrected, waving across the lawn. "There's Kay Marshall," she said. "Will you excuse me?"

"A protester, then," David repeated, watching Norah walk away, the breeze moving lightly against the sleeves of her silk suit.

"That's right," Mark said. He spoke with self-mocking intentness and a faint familiar accent that reminded David of his father's voice, low and melodic. "The relentless pursuit of equity and justice."

"You were on the news," David said, remembering him all at once. "Last night. You were giving some kind of speech. So. You must be glad about the fire."

Mark shrugged. "Not glad. Not sorry. It happened, that's all. We go on."

"Why are you being so hostile, David?" Bree asked, fixing her green eyes on him.

"I'm not being hostile," David said, realizing even as he spoke that he was. Realizing, too, that he was beginning to flatten and extend his own vowels, called by the deep pull of language, patterns of speech as familiar and compelling as water. "I'm gathering information, that's all. Where are you from?" he asked Mark.

"West Virginia. Over near Elkins. Why?"

"Just curious. I had family there once."

"I didn't know that about you, David," Bree said. "I thought you were from Pittsburgh."

"I had family near Elkins," David repeated. "A long time ago."

"Is that so?" Mark was watching him less warily now. "They work coal?"

"Sometimes, in the winter. They had a farm. A hard life, but not as hard as coal."

"They keep their land?"

"Yes." David thought of the house he had not seen for nearly fifteen years.

"Smart. My daddy, now, he sold the home place. When he died in the mines five years later, we had nowhere to go. Nowhere at all." Mark smiled bitterly and thought for a moment. "You ever go back there?"

"Not in a long time. You?"

"No. After Vietnam I went to college. Morgantown, the GI bill. It got to be strange, going back. I belonged and I didn't belong, if you know what I mean. When I left I didn't think I was making a choice. But it turned out I was."

David nodded. "I know," he said. "I know what you mean."

"Well," Bree said, after a long moment of silence. "You're both here now. I'm getting thirstier by the second," she added. "Mark? David? Want a drink?"

"I'll come with you." Mark said, extending his hand to David. "Small world, isn't it? It's good to meet you."

"David is a mystery to us all," Bree said, pulling him away. "Just ask Norah."

David watched them merge into the bright milling crowd. A simple encounter, yet he felt strangely agitated, exposed and vulnerable, his past rising up like the sea. Each morning he stood for a moment in his office doorway, surveying his clean simple world: the orderly array of instruments, the crisp white length of cloth on the examination table. By every external measure he was a success, yet he was never filled, as he hoped to be, with a sense of pride and reassurance. *I suppose this is it,* his father had said, slamming the truck door and standing on the curb by the bus stop on the day David left for Pittsburgh. *I suppose this is the last we can expect to hear from you, moving up in the world and all. You won't have time for the likes of us anymore.* And David, standing on the curb with early leaves falling down around him, had felt a deep sense of desperation, because even then he sensed the truth of his father's words: whatever his own intentions were, however much he loved them, his life would carry him away.

"Are you all right, David?" Kay Marshall asked. She was walking by, carrying a vase of pale pink tulips, each petal as delicate as the edge of a lung. "You look a million miles away."

"Ah, Kay," he said. She reminded him a little of Norah, some kind of loneliness moving always beneath her carefully polished surface. Once, after drinking too much at another party, Kay had followed him into a dark hallway, slipped her arms around his neck, and kissed him. Startled, he had kissed her back. The moment had passed, and although he often thought about the cool, surprising touch of her lips on his, every time he saw her David also wondered that it had ever really happened. "You look ravishing as always, Kay." He raised his glass to her. She smiled and laughed and moved on.

He went into the coolness of the garage and up the stairs, where he took his camera from the cupboard and loaded a new roll of film. Norah's voice lifted above the crowd, and he remembered the feel of her skin when he'd reached for her that morning, the smooth curve of her back. He remembered the moment she'd shared with Bree, how connected they were, beyond any bond he'd ever share with her again. *I want,* he thought, slipping the camera around his neck. *I want.*

He moved around the edges of the party, smiling and saying hello, shaking hands, drifting away from conversations to catch moments of the party on film. He paused before Kay's tulips, focusing in close, thinking how much they really did resemble the delicate tissue of lungs and how interesting it would be to frame shots of both and stand them next to each other, exploring this idea he had that the body was, in some mysterious way, a perfect mirror of the world. He grew absorbed in this, the sounds of the party falling away as he concentrated on the flowers, and he was startled to feel Norah's hand on his arm.

"Put the camera away," she said. "Please. It's a party, David."

"These tulips are so beautiful," he began, but he was unable to explain himself, unable to put into words why these images compelled him so.

"It's a party," she repeated. "You can either miss it and take pictures of it, or you can get a drink and join it."

"I have a drink," he pointed out. "No one cares that I'm taking a few pictures, Norah."

"I care. It's rude."

They were speaking softly, and during the whole exchange Norah had not stopped smiling. Her expression was calm; she nodded and waved across the lawn. And yet David could feel the tension radiating from her, and the pressed-back anger.

"I've worked so hard," she said. "I organized everything. I made all the food. I even got rid of the wasps. Why can't you just enjoy it?"

"When did you take the nest down?" he asked, searching for a safe topic, looking up at the smooth, clean eaves of the garage.

"Yesterday." She showed him her wrist, the faint red welt. "I didn't want to take any chances with your allergies and Paul's."

"It's a beautiful party," he said. On an impulse he brought her wrist to his lips and gently kissed the place where she'd been stung. She watched him, her eyes widening in surprise and a flicker of pleasure, then pulled her hand away.

"David," she said softly, "for heaven's sake, not here. Not now."

"Hey, Dad," Paul called, and David looked around, trying to locate his son. "Mom and Dad, look at me. Look at me!"

"He's in the hackberry tree," Norah said, shading her eyes and pointing across the lawn. "Look, up there, about halfway up. How did he do that?"

"I bet he climbed up from the swing set. Hey!" David called, waving back.

"Get down right now!" Norah called. And then, to David, "He's making me nervous."

"He's a kid," David said. "Kids climb trees. He'll be fine."

"Hey, Mom! Dad! Help!" Paul called, but when they looked up at him, he was laughing.

"Remember when he used to do that in the grocery store?" Norah asked. "Remember, when he was learning to talk, how he used to shout out *help* in the middle of the store? People thought I was a kidnapper."

"He did it at the clinic once," David said. "Remember that?"

They laughed together. David felt a wave of gladness.

"Put the camera away," she said, her hand on his arm.

"Yes," he said. "I will."

Bree had wandered over to the maypole and picked up a royal purple ribbon. A few others, intrigued, had joined her. David started back to the garage, watching the fluttering ends of the ribbons. He heard a sudden rush and stirring of the leaves, a branch cracking loudly. He saw Bree lift her hands, the ribbon slipping from her fingers as she reached up into the open air. A silence grew for a long instant, and then Norah cried out. David turned around in time to see Paul hit the ground with a thud, then bounce once, slightly, on his back, the sea lily necklace broken, the treasured crinoids scattered on the ground. David ran, pushing through the guests, and knelt beside him. Paul's dark eyes, were full of fear. He grabbed David's hand, trying hard to breathe.

"It's okay," David said, smoothing Paul's forehead. "You fell out of the tree and lost your wind, that's all. Just relax. Take another breath. You're going to be okay."

"Is he all right?" Norah asked, kneeling down beside him in her coral suit. "Paul, sweetie, are you okay?"

Paul gasped and coughed, tears standing in his eyes. "My arm hurts," he said, when he could speak again. He was pale, a thin blue vein visible in his forehead, and David could tell he was trying hard not to cry. "My arm really hurts."

"Which arm?" David asked, using his calmest voice. "Can you show me where?"

It was his left arm, and when David lifted it carefully, supporting the elbow and the wrist, Paul cried out in pain.

"David!" Norah said. "Is it broken?"

"Well, I'm not sure," he said calmly, though he was nearly certain that it was. He rested Paul's arm gently on his chest, then put one hand on Norah's back to comfort her. "Paul, I'm going to pick you up. I'm going to carry you to the car. And then we're going to go to my office, okay? I'm going to show you all about X-rays."

Slowly, gently, he lifted Paul. His son was so light in his arms. Their guests parted to let him pass. He put Paul in the backseat, got a blanket from the trunk, and tucked it around him.

"I'm coming too," Norah said, sliding in the front seat beside him.

"What about the party?"

"There's lots of food and wine," she said. " They'll just have to figure it out."

They drove through the bright spring air toward the hospital. From time to time, Norah still teased him about the night of the birth, how slowly and methodically he had driven through the empty streets, but he could not bring himself to speed today either.

They passed the ROTC building, still smoldering. Wisps of smoke rose like dark lace. Dogwoods were in bloom nearby, the petals pale and fragile against the blackened wall.

"The world's falling to pieces, that's how it feels," Norah said softly.

"Not now, Norah." David glanced at Paul in the rearview mirror. He was quiet, uncomplaining, but tears streaked his pale cheeks.

In the ER, David used his influence to hurry the process of admission and X-ray. He helped Paul get settled in a bed, left Norah reading him stories from a book she'd grabbed in the waiting room, and went to pick up the X-rays. When he took them from the technician, he saw his hands were trembling, so he walked down the halls, strangely silent on this beautiful Saturday afternoon, to his office. The door swung shut behind him, and for a moment David stood alone in the darkness, trying to compose himself. He knew the walls to be a pale sea green, the desk scattered with papers. He knew that instruments, steel and chrome, were lined up in trays below the glass-fronted cupboards. But he could see nothing. He raised his hand and touched his palm to his nose, but even so close he could not see his own flesh, only feel it.

He groped for the light switch; it gave at his touch. A panel, mounted on the wall, pulsed and then filled with a steady white light that bleached things of their color. Against the light were negatives he'd developed the week before: a series of photos of a human vein, taken in sequence, in gradations of precisely controlled light, the level of contrast changing subtly with each one. What excited David was the precision he'd achieved, and the way the images did not resemble a part of the human body as much as other things: lightning branching down to earth, rivers moving darkly, a wavering expanse of sea.

His hands were shaking. He forced himself to take several deep breaths, then took the negatives down and slipped Paul's X-rays beneath the clips. His son's small bones, solid yet delicate, stood out with ghostly clarity. David traced the light-filled image with his fingertips. So beautiful, the bones of his small son, opaque yet appearing here as if they were filled with light, translucent images floating in the darkness of his office, as strong and as delicate as the intertwined branches of a tree.

The damage was simple enough: clear, straightforward fractures of the ulna and the radius. These bones ran parallel; the greatest danger was that, in healing, the two might fuse together.

He flipped on the overhead light and started back down the hall, thinking of the beautiful hidden world inside the body. Years ago, in a shoe store in Morgantown, while his father tried on work boots and frowned over the price tag, David had stood on a machine that X-rayed his feet, turning his ordinary toes into something ghostly, mysterious. Rapt, he'd studied the wands and bulbs of shadowy light that were his toes, his heels.

It was, though he would not realize it for years, a defining moment. That there were other worlds, invisible, unknown, beyond imagination even, was a revelation to him. In the weeks that followed, watching deer run and birds lift off, leaves fluttering and rabbits bursting suddenly from the undergrowth, David stared hard, seeking to glimpse their hidden structures. And June—sitting on the porch steps, calmly shelling peas or shucking corn, her lips parted with concentration—he had stared at her too. For she was like him yet not like him, and what separated them was a great mystery.

His sister, this girl who loved wind, who laughed at the sun on her face and was not afraid of snakes. She had died at age twelve, and by now she was nothing but the memory of love—nothing, now, but bones.

And his daughter, six years old, walked in the world, but he did not know her.

When he got back, Norah was holding Paul in her lap, though he was almost too big for such comfort, his head resting awkwardly on her shoulder. His arm was trembling with minor convulsions from the trauma.

"Is it broken?" she asked right away.

"Yes, I'm afraid so," David said. "Come and take a look."

He slipped the X-rays onto the light table and pointed out the darkened lines of fracture.

Skeletons in the closet, people said, and *bone dry,* and *I have a bone to pick with you.* But bones were alive; they grew and mended themselves; they could knit back together what had been torn apart.

"I was so careful about the bees," Norah said, helping him move Paul back to the examination table. "The wasps, I mean. I got rid of the wasps, and now this."

"It was an accident," David said.

"I know," she said, near tears. "That's the whole problem."

David didn't answer. He had taken out the materials for the cast, and now he concentrated on applying the plaster. It had been a long time since he'd done this—usually he set the bone and left the rest to the nurse—and he found it comforting. Paul's arm was small and the cast grew steadily, white as a bleached shell, as bright and seductive as a sheet of paper. In a few days it would be turning a dull gray, covered with bright childhood graffiti.

"Three months," David said. "Three months, and you'll have the cast off."

"That's almost the whole summer," Norah said.

"What about Little League?" Paul asked. "What about swimming?"

"No baseball," David said. "And no swimming. I'm sorry."

"But Jason and I are supposed to play Little League."

"I'm sorry," David said, as Paul dissolved into tears

"You said nothing would happen," Norah said, "and now he has a broken arm. Just like that. It could have been his neck. His back."

David felt tired all of a sudden, torn up about Paul, exasperated with Norah too.

"It could have been, yes, but it wasn't. So stop. Okay? Just stop it, Norah."

Paul had gone still and was listening intently, alert to the altered tones and cadences of their voices. What, David wondered, would Paul remember of this day? Imagining his son into the uncertain future, into a world where you could go to a protest and end up dead with a bullet in your neck, David shared Norah's fear. She was right. Anything could happen. He put his hand on Paul's head, the bristle of his crew cut sharp against his palm.

"I'm sorry, Dad," Paul said, his voice small. "I didn't mean to ruin the pictures."

David, after a second's confusion, remembered his roar hours earlier when the darkroom lights went on, Paul standing stricken with his hand on the switch, too scared to move.

"Oh, no. No, son, I'm not mad about that, don't worry." He touched Paul's cheek. "The pictures don't matter. I was just tired this morning. Okay?"

Paul traced his finger along the edge of the cast.

"I didn't mean to frighten you," David said. "I'm not upset."

"Can I listen to the stethoscope?"

"Of course." David slid the black wands of the stethoscope into Paul's ears and squatted down. The cool metal disk he placed on his own heart.

From the corner of his eye he saw Norah watching them. Away from the bright motion of the party, she carried her sadness like a dark stone clenched in her palm. He longed to comfort her, but he could think of nothing to say. He wished he had some kind of X-ray vision for the human heart: for Norah's and his own.

"I wish you were happier," he said softly. "I wish there were something I could do."

"You don't have to worry," she said. "Not about me."

"Don't I?" David breathed in deeply so that Paul could hear the rush of air.

"No. I got a job yesterday."

"A job?"

"Yes. A good job." She told him all about it then: a travel agency, mornings. She'd be home in time to pick Paul up from school. As she spoke, David felt as if she were flying away from him. "I've been going crazy," Norah added with a fierceness that surprised him. "Totally crazy with so much time on my hands. This will be a good thing."

"Okay," he said. "That's fine. If you want a job so much, take it." He tickled Paul and reached for his otoscope. "Here," he said. "Look in my ears. See if I left any birds in there."

Paul laughed, and the cool metal slid against David's lobe.

"I knew you wouldn't like this," Norah said.

"What do you mean? I'm telling you to take it."

"I mean your tone. You should hear yourself."

"Well, what do you expect?" he said, trying to keep his voice even, for Paul's sake. "It's hard not to see this as criticism."

"It would only be criticism if it were about you," she said. "That's what you don't understand. But it's not about you. It's about freedom. It's about me having a life of my own. I wish you could understand that."

"Freedom?" he said. She'd been talking to her sister again, he'd bet his life on it. "You think anyone is free, Norah? You think I am?"

There was a long silence, and he was grateful when Paul broke it.

"No birds, Dad. Just giraffes."

"Really? How many?"

"Six."

"Six! Good grief! Better check the other ear."

"Maybe I'll hate the job," Norah said. "But at least I'll know."

"No birds," Paul said. "No giraffes. Just elephants."

"Elephants in the ear canal," David said, taking the otoscope. "We'd better get home right away." He forced himself to smile, squatting down to pick Paul up, new cast and all. As he felt his son's weight, the warmth of his good bare arm around his neck, David let himself wonder what their lives would have been like if he'd made a different decision six years ago. The snow had fallen and he'd stood in that silence, all alone, and in one crucial moment he'd altered everything. *David,* Caroline Gill had written in her most recent letter, *I've got a boyfriend now. He's very nice, and Phoebe is fine; she loves to catch butterflies and sing.*

"I'm happy about the job," he told Norah as they waited in the hall for the elevator. "I don't mean to be difficult. But I don't believe this doesn't have to do with me."

She sighed. "No," she said. "You wouldn't believe it, would you?"

"What's that supposed to mean?"

"You see yourself as the center of the universe," Norah said. "The still point around which everything else revolves."

They gathered up their things and walked to the elevator. Outside it was still a beautiful day, late afternoon, clear and sunny. By the time they got home, the guests had dispersed. Only Bree and

Mark were left, carrying plates of food into the house. The ribbons of the maypole fluttered in the breeze. David's camera was on the table, and Paul's fossils were piled neatly beside it. David paused, surveying the lawn, scattered with chairs. Once, this whole world had been hidden beneath a shallow sea. He carried Paul inside and up the stairs. He gave him a drink of water and the orange chewable aspirin he liked and sat with him on the bed, holding his hand. So small, this hand, so warm and alive. Remembering the light-filled images of Paul's bones, David was filled with a sense of wonder. This was what he yearned to capture on film: these rare moments where the world seemed unified, coherent, everything contained in a single fleeting image. A spareness that held beauty and hope and motion—a kind of silvery poetry, just as the body was poetry in blood and flesh and bone.

"Read me a story, Dad," Paul said, so David settled himself on the bed, holding Paul in his arms, turning the pages of *Curious George*, who was in the hospital with a broken leg. Downstairs, Norah moved through the rooms, cleaning up. The screen door swung open and shut, open and shut again. He imagined her walking through it, dressed in a suit, heading for her new job and a life that excluded him. It was late afternoon, and a golden light filled the room. He turned the page and held Paul, feeling his warmth, his measured breathing. A breeze lifted the curtains. Outside, the dogwood was a bright cloud against the dark planks of the fence. David paused in his reading, watching the white petals fall and drift. He felt both comforted and troubled by their beauty, trying not to notice that they looked, from this distance, like snow.

June 1970

W ELL, PHOEBE CERTAINLY HAS YOUR HAIR," DORO OB-
served.

Caroline touched the nape of her neck, considering. They were
on the east side of Pittsburgh, in an old factory building that had
been converted into a progressive preschool. Light fell through the
long windows and splashed in motes and patterns on the plank
floor; it caught the auburn highlights in Phoebe's thin braids as she
stood before a big wooden bin, scooping lentils, letting them cascade into jars. At six, she was chubby, with dimpled knees and a
winning smile. Her eyes were a delicate almond shape, upslanted,
dark brown. Her hands were small. This morning she wore a
pink-and-white striped dress, which she had chosen and put on
by herself—backwards. She wore a pink sweater, too, which had
caused a spectacular tantrum at home. *She's certainly got your temper.*
Leo, dead now for almost a year, had been fond of muttering this,
and Caroline had always been astonished: not so much that he'd
seen a genetic connection where none could exist but that anyone
would define her as a woman with a temper.

"Do you think so?" she asked Doro, running her fingers through
the hair behind her ear. "Do you think her hair's like mine?"

"Oh, yes. Sure it is."

Phoebe was shoving her hands deep into the velvety lentils now, laughing with the little boy beside her. She lifted fistfuls and let them run through her fingers, and the boy held out a yellow plastic cup to catch them.

To the other children in this preschool Phoebe was simply herself, a friend who liked the color blue and Popsicles and twirling in circles; here, her differences went unnoticed. In the first weeks, Caroline had watched warily, braced against the sorts of comments she'd heard too often, on playgrounds, at the grocery store, in the doctor's office. *What a terrible shame! Oh, you're living my worst nightmare.* And once, *At least she won't live very long—that's a blessing.* Thoughtless or ignorant or cruel, it didn't matter; over the years these comments had rubbed a raw spot in Caroline's heart. But here the teachers were young and enthusiastic, and the parents had quietly followed their example: Phoebe might struggle more, go slower, but like any child she'd learn.

Lentils scattered on the floor as the boy dropped his shovel and ran into the hall. Phoebe followed, braids flying, headed for the green room with its easels and its pots of paint.

"This place has been so good for her," Doro said.

Caroline nodded. "I wish the Board of Education could see her here."

"You have a strong argument, and a good lawyer. You'll be fine."

Caroline glanced at her watch. Her friendship with Sandra had grown into a political force, and today the Upside Down Society, over 500 members strong, would ask the school board to include their children in public schools. Their chances were good, but Caroline was still very nervous. So much rested on this decision.

A speeding child careened past Doro, who caught him gently by the shoulders. Doro's hair was pure white now, in striking contrast to her dark eyes, her smooth olive skin. She swam every morning and she'd taken up golf, and lately Caroline often caught her smiling to herself, as if she had a secret.

"It's so good of you to come today to cover for me," Caroline said, pulling on her coat.

Doro waved her hand. "Don't mention it. I'd much rather be

here, actually, than fighting with the department over my father's papers." Her voice was weary, but a smile flickered across her face.

"Doro, if I didn't know better, I'd guess you were in love."

Doro only laughed. "What a bold conjecture," she said. "And speaking of love, can I expect Al this afternoon? It's Friday, after all."

The patterns of light and shadow in the sycamores were so soothing, like moving water. It was Friday, yes, but Caroline hadn't heard from Al all week. Usually he called from the road, from Columbus or Atlanta or even Chicago. He'd asked her to marry him twice this year; each time her heart had flared with possibility, and each time she'd said no. They had argued on his last visit—*You hold me at arm's length,* he'd complained—and he'd left angry, without saying goodbye.

"We're just close friends, Al and I. It's not that easy."

"Don't be ridiculous," Doro said. "Nothing's simpler."

So it *was* love, Caroline thought. She kissed Phoebe's soft cheek and went away in Leo's old Buick: black, vast, with a ride like a boat. In the last year of his life Leo had grown frail, spending most of his days in an armchair near the window with a book in his lap, gazing out at the street. One day Caroline had found him slumped, his gray hair sticking up at an awkward angle, his skin—even his lips—so pale. Dead. She knew this before she touched him. She took off his glasses, placed her fingertips on his eyelids, and drew them closed. Once they had taken his body away she sat in his chair, trying to imagine what his life had been like, the tree branches moving silently outside the window, her own footsteps, and Phoebe's, making patterns on his ceiling. "Oh, Leo," she'd said out loud, to the empty air. "I'm sorry you were so alone."

After his funeral, a quiet affair crowded with physics professors and gardenias, Caroline offered to leave, but Doro wouldn't hear of it. *I'm used to you. I'm used to the company. No, you stay. We'll take it day by day.*

Caroline drove across the city she had come to love, this tough, gritty, strikingly beautiful city with its soaring buildings and ornate bridges and vast parks, its neighborhoods tucked into every emerald hill. She found a parking spot on the narrow street and entered the building, its stone darkened by decades of coal smoke. She walked through the foyer with its high ceilings and intricate mosaic floor and climbed two flights of stairs. The wooden door was darkly stained, with a panel of cloudy glass and tarnished brass numbers: 304B. She took a deep breath—she had not been this nervous since her oral exams—and pushed the door open. The room's shabbiness surprised her. The big oak table was scratched and the windows were cloudy, making the day outside seem muted and gray. Sandra was already sitting with half a dozen other parents from the Upside Down board. Caroline felt a surge of affection. They had drifted into meetings one by one at first, people she and Sandra met in grocery stores and on buses; then the word had spread and people started calling. Their lawyer, Ron Stone, sat next to Sandra, whose blond hair was pulled severely back, her face serious and pale. Caroline took the remaining seat beside her.

"You look tired," she whispered.

Sandra nodded. "Tim has the flu. Of all days. My mother had to come from McKeesport to watch him."

Before Caroline could answer the door swung open again, and men from the Board of Education began to file in, relaxed, joking with one another, shaking hands. When everyone was settled and the meeting had been called to order, Ron Stone stood and cleared his throat.

"All children deserve an education," he began, his words familiar. The evidence he presented was clear, specific: steady growth, tasks accomplished. Still, Caroline watched the faces in front of her turn impassive, masked. She thought of Phoebe sitting at the table last night, a pencil gripped in one hand, writing the letters of her name: backwards, all over the page, wavering, but written. The men on the board shuffled papers and cleared their throats. When Ron Stone paused, a young man with dark wavy hair spoke up.

"Your passion is admirable, Mr. Stone. We on the board appreciate everything you say, and we appreciate the commitment and devotion of these parents. But these children are mentally retarded; that's the bottom line. Their accomplishments, significant though they may be, have taken place within a protected environment, with teachers capable of giving extra, perhaps undivided, attention. That seems a very significant point."

Caroline met Sandra's eye. These words were familiar too.

"Mentally retarded is a pejorative term," Ron Stone replied evenly. "These children are delayed, yes, no one's questioning that. But they are *not* stupid. No one in this room knows what they can achieve. The best hope for their growth and development, as for all children, is an educational environment without predetermined limits. We only ask for equity today."

"Ah. Equity, yes. But we haven't got the resources," said another man, thin, with sparse graying hair. "To be equitable, we would have to accept them all, a flood of retarded individuals that would overwhelm the system. Take a look."

He passed around copies of a report and began doing a cost-benefit analysis. Caroline took a deep breath. It would do no good for her to lose her temper. A fly buzzed, caught between the panes of glass in the old windows. Caroline thought again of Phoebe, such a loving quicksilver child. A finder of lost things, a girl who could count to fifty and dress herself and recite the alphabet, a girl who might struggle to speak but who could read Caroline's mood in an instant.

Limited, the voices said. *Flooding the schools. A drag on resources and on the brighter children.*

Caroline felt a rush of despair. They'd never really see Phoebe, these men, they would never see her as more than different, slow to speak and to master new things. How could she show them her beautiful daughter: Phoebe, sitting on the rug in the living room and making a tower of blocks, her soft hair falling around her ears and an expression of absolute concentration on her face? Phoebe, putting a 45 on the little record player Caroline had bought her, enthralled by the music, dancing across the smooth oak floors. Or Phoebe's soft small hand suddenly on her knee, at a moment when Caroline was pensive or distracted, absorbed by the world and its concerns. *You okay, Mom?* she would say, or simply, *I love you.* Phoebe, riding on Al's shoulders in the evening light, Phoebe hugging everyone she met. Phoebe having tantrums and stubbornly defiant, Phoebe dressing herself that morning, so proud.

The talk around the table had turned to numbers and logistics, the impossibility of change. Caroline stood up, trembling. Her dead mother's hand flew to her mouth in shock. Caroline herself could not quite believe it, how her life had changed her, what she had become. But there was no going back. A flood of the mentally retarded, indeed! She pressed her hands to the table and waited. One by one the men stopped speaking, and the room grew quiet.

"It's not about numbers," Caroline said. "It's about children. I have a daughter who is six years old. It takes her more time, it's true, to master new things. But she has learned to do everything that any other child learns to do: to crawl and walk and talk and use the bathroom, to dress herself, which she did this morning. What I see is a little girl who wants to learn, and who loves everyone she sees. And I see a roomful of men who appear to have forgotten that in this country we promise an education to every child—regardless of ability."

For a moment no one spoke. The tall window rattled slightly in the breeze. Paint was beginning to bubble and peel on the beige walls.

The voice of the dark-haired man was gentle.

"I have—we all have—great sympathy for your situation. But how likely is it that your daughter, or any of these children, will master any academic skills? And what would that do to her self-image? If it were me, I'd rather have her settled in a productive and useful trade."

"She's six years old," Caroline said. "She's not ready to learn a trade."

Ron Stone had been watching the exchange intently, and now he spoke.

"Actually," he said. "This entire discussion is beside the point." He opened his briefcase and took out a thick cluster of papers. "This is not just a moral or logistical issue. It's the law. This is a petition, signed by these parents and by five hundred others. It's appended to a class-action lawsuit filed on behalf of these families to allow the acceptance of their children into Pittsburgh's public schools."

"This is the civil rights law," the gray-haired man said, looking up from the document. "You can't use that. That's not the letter or the spirit of this law."

"You look those documents over," Ron Stone said, shutting his briefcase. "We'll be in touch."

Outside, on the old stone steps, they burst into talk; Ron was pleased, cautiously optimistic, but the others were ebullient, hugging Caroline to thank her for her speech. She smiled, hugging them back, feeling both drained and moved by a deep affection for these people: Sandra, of course, who still came over every week for coffee; Colleen, who with her daughter had gathered the names on the petition; Carl, a tall sprightly man whose only son had died young from heart complications related to Down's and who had given them office space in his carpet warehouse for their work. She'd known none of them four years ago except Sandra, yet they were bound to her now by many late nights, many struggles and small triumphs, and so much hope.

Agitated, still, from her speech, she drove back to the preschool. Phoebe jumped up from the circle group and ran to Caroline, hugging her knees. She smelled of milk and chocolate and there was a streak of dirt across her dress. Her hair was a soft cloud beneath Caroline's hand. Caroline told Doro briefly what had happened, the ugly words—*flood, drag*—still running through her mind. Doro, late for work, touched her arm. *We'll talk more tonight.*

The drive home was beautiful, leaves on the trees and lilacs blooming like drifts of foam and fire against the hills. It had rained the night before; the sky was a clear bright blue. Caroline parked in the alley, disappointed to see that Al hadn't yet arrived. Together, she and Phoebe walked beneath the flickering shade of the sycamores, through the piercing hum of bees. Caroline sat on the porch steps and turned on the radio. Phoebe started spinning on the soft grass, her arms held out and her head flung back, face to the sun.

Caroline watched her, still trying to shed the tension and acrimony of the morning. There was reason to hope, but after all these years of struggling to change the world's perceptions, Caroline made herself stay cautious.

Phoebe ran over and cupped her hands around Caroline's ear, whispering a secret. Caroline couldn't catch the words, just the breathless excited rush of air, and then Phoebe ran off into the sunshine again, twirling in her pale pink dress. The sunlight touched amber glints in her dark hair, and Caroline remembered Norah Henry beneath the bright clinic lights. For an instant she was stung with weariness and doubt.

Phoebe stopped in her twirling, arms held out to keep her balance. Then she gave a shout and ran headlong across the lawn and up the steps to where Al stood, looking down, a brightly wrapped package in one hand for Phoebe and bunch of lilacs that Caroline knew were for her.

Her heart lifted. He had courted her with a slow, persistent patience, showing up, solid and steady, week after week, offering a fistful of flowers or some other cheerful gift, the pleasure on his face so real that she could not bear to turn him away. Yet she'd held herself back from him, not trusting this love that had come so unexpectedly, from such an unexpected source. Now she stood, feeling a rush of pleasure. How afraid she'd been that this time he would stay away!

"Pretty day," he said, squatting to hug Phoebe, who flung her arms around his neck in welcome. The package contained a filmy butterfly net with a carved wooden handle, which she took at once, running off toward a bank of dark blue hydrangeas. "How did the meeting go?"

She told him the story and he listened, shaking his head.

"Well, school's not for everyone," he said. "I sure didn't like it much. But Phoebe's a sweet kid, and they shouldn't keep her out."

"I want her to have a place in the world," Caroline said, realizing suddenly that it wasn't Al's love for her she doubted, it was his love for Phoebe.

"Honey, she has a place. It's right here. But yeah, I think you're right. I think you're doing the right thing to fight for her so hard."

"I hope you had a better week," she said, noting the shadows beneath his eyes.

"Oh, same old, same old," he said, sitting on the steps beside her and picking up a stick, which he started to peel. Distantly, mowers hummed; Phoebe's little radio played "Love, Love Me, Do." "I logged 2,398 miles this week. A record, even for me."

He'll ask again, Caroline thought. This was the moment; he was road weary and ready to settle down, and he'd ask. She watched his hands move deftly, swiftly, stripping the bark, and her heart surged. This time she'd say yes. But Al didn't speak. The silence extended for so long that finally she felt pressured to break it.

"That was a nice gift," she said, nodding across the grassy space where Phoebe was running, the net making bright arcs in the air.

"Fellow in Georgia made it," Al said. "Nicest guy. Had a whole bunch of them he'd carved for his grandkids. We got to talking in the grocery store. He collects shortwave radios and invited me to stop by and see them. Spent the whole night talking, me and him. Now, that's the plus of the wandering life. Oh, yeah," he went on, reaching into his pants pocket and pulling out a white envelope. "Here's your mail from Atlanta."

Caroline took the envelope without comment. Inside there would be several twenty-dollar bills folded neatly into a plain white paper. Al brought them back from Cleveland, Memphis, Atlanta, Akron: cities he frequented on his runs. She told him simply that the money was for Phoebe, from her father. Al accepted this without comment, but Caroline's feelings were more complex. Sometimes she dreamed she was walking through Norah Henry's house, taking things from the shelves and the cupboards, filling a cloth bag, happy until she came upon Norah Henry standing by a window, her expression distant and infinitely sad. She'd wake, trembling, and get up and make herself some tea, sitting in the darkness. When the money came she put it in the bank and didn't think about it until the next envelope arrived. She had done this for five years now, and she had saved almost $7,000.

Phoebe was still running, chasing after butterflies, birds, motes of light, the fluttering notes spilling from the radio. Al was fiddling with the dial.

"The nice thing about this city is that you can really find some music. Some of those podunk little towns I stay in, all you get is the

Top Forty. Gets old, after a while." He began to hum along with "Begin the Beguine."

"My parents used to dance to this song," Caroline said, and for an instant she was sitting on the stairs of her childhood home, invisible, watching her mother, in a full-skirted dress, welcoming guests at the door. "I haven't thought of it in years. But every now and then they used to roll the rug up in the living room on a Saturday night and have some other couples in, and they'd dance."

"We ought to go dancing sometime," Al said. "You like to dance, Caroline?"

Caroline felt something shift in her then, some excitement. She couldn't place its source: something to do with her anger from the morning passing, and the vibrant day, and the warmth of Al's arm next to hers. The breeze fluttered the poplars, revealing the silvery undersides of their leaves.

"Why wait?" she asked, and stood, extending her hand.

He was puzzled, bemused, but then he was standing with his hand resting on her shoulder and they were moving on the lawn to the thin strains of the music, the background of rushing cars. Sunlight mingled in her hair, the grass was soft beneath her stocking feet, and they moved together so easily, dipping and turning, the tension she'd carried with her from the meeting dissipating with each step. Al smiled, pressing her close; sunlight struck her neck.

Oh, she thought, as he spun her again, *I'll say yes.*

There was the pleasure of the sunlight and Phoebe's floating laughter and Al's hands warm through the fabric on her back. They moved in the grass, turning with the music, connected by it. The traffic rushing by was as present and soothing as the ocean. Other sounds, thin, lifted through the strands of music, through the bright day. Caroline didn't register them at first. Then Al turned her, and she stopped dancing. Phoebe was kneeling in the soft warm grass by the hydrangeas, crying too hard to speak, holding up her hand. Caroline ran and knelt in the grass, studying the angry swollen circle on Phoebe's palm.

"It's a beesting," she said. "Oh, honey, it hurts, doesn't it?"

She pressed her face into Phoebe's warm hair. Soft, soft skin, and her chest, rising and falling; beneath that, the steady pattern of her heart. Here was the thing that couldn't be measured, couldn't be quantified or even explained: Phoebe was herself alone. You could not, finally, categorize a human being. You could not presume to know what life was or what it might hold.

"Oh, sweetie, it's all right," she said, smoothing Phoebe's hair.

But Phoebe's sobs were giving way to a wheezing like the croup she'd suffered as a child. Her palm was swelling; the back of her hand and her fingers too. Caroline felt herself grow still inside, even as she rose swiftly and called to Al.

"Hurry!" she cried, her voice so loud and strange. "Oh Al, she's allergic."

She was lifting Phoebe, heavy in her arms, and then she paused, bewildered, because her keys were in her purse on the kitchen counter and she couldn't figure out how to open the door while holding Phoebe, who was wheezing harder now. Then Al was there, taking Phoebe and running to the car, and Caroline had the keys somehow, the keys and her purse. She drove as fast as she dared through the city streets. By the time they reached the hospital, Phoebe's breath was coming in short, desperate gasps.

They left the car at the entrance and Caroline grabbed the first nurse she saw.

"It's an allergic reaction. We need to see a doctor *now.*"

The nurse was older, a bit heavyset, her gray hair turned under in a pageboy. She led them through a set of steel doors where Al put Phoebe gently, gently, on the gurney. Phoebe was struggling to breathe now, her lips faintly blue. Caroline, too, was having trouble breathing, fear pulled so tightly in her chest. The nurse swept Phoebe's hair back, touching her fingers to the pulse in her neck. And then Caroline watched her see Phoebe as Dr. Henry had seen her on that snowy night so long ago. She saw the nurse taking in the beautifully sloped eyes, the small hands that had gripped the net so hard as she ran after butterflies, saw her eyes narrow slightly. Still, she was not prepared.

"Are you sure?" the nurse asked, looking up and meeting her eyes. "Are you really sure you want me to call a doctor?"

Caroline stood fixed in place. She remembered the scents of boiled vegetables, and the day she had driven away with Phoebe, and the impassive expressions worn by the men on the board of education. In a rush of wild alchemy her fear transformed itself into anger, fierce and piercing. She raised her hand to slap the bland, impassive face of the nurse, but Al caught her wrist.

"Call the doctor," he said to the nurse. "Do it now."

He put his arm around Caroline and didn't let go, not when the nurse turned away or when the doctor appeared, not until Phoebe's breathing began to ease and some of the color returned to her cheeks. Then they went together to the waiting room and sat in the orange plastic chairs, hand in hand, nurses buzzing and voices coming over the intercom and babies crying.

"She could have died," Caroline said. Her calm broke; she began to tremble.

"But she didn't," Al said firmly.

Al's hand was warm, large and comforting. He had been so patient all these years, he had come back again and again, saying he knew a good thing when he saw it. Saying he'd wait. But he'd been away two weeks this time, not one. He hadn't called from the road, and though he'd brought her flowers as always, he hadn't proposed for six months. He could drive away in his truck and never come back, never give her another chance to say yes.

She raised his hand and kissed his palm, strong, so rough with calluses, so marked with lines. He turned, startled from his thoughts, as puzzled as if he'd just been stung himself.

"Caroline." His tone was formal. "There's something I want to say."

"I know." She placed his hand on her heart, held it there. "Oh, Al, I've been such a fool. Of course I'll marry you," she said.

1977

July 1977

L IKE THIS?" NORAH ASKED.

She was lying on the beach, and beneath her hip the gritty sand slid and shifted. Every time she took a deep breath and re- leased it, sand slithered out from under her. The sun was so hot, like a shimmering metal plate against her skin. She had been here for over an hour, posing and re-posing, the word *repose* like a taunt, for it was what she longed to do and could not. It was her vacation, after all—she had won two weeks in Aruba for selling the highest number of cruise packages in the state of Kentucky last year—and yet here she was: sand sticking to the sweat on her arms and neck as she lay still, pressed between sun and beach.

To distract herself, she kept her gaze on Paul, who was running along the shore, a speck on the horizon. He was thirteen, and he'd shot up like a sapling in this last year. Tall and awkward, he ran every morning as if he might escape from his own life.

Waves crashed slowly against the beach. The tide was turning, coming in, and the harsh noon light would soon change, making the picture David wanted impossible until tomorrow. A strand of hair was stuck against Norah's lip, tickling, but she willed herself to stillness.

"Good," David said, bent over his camera and clicking off a rapid series of shots. "Oh, yes, great, that's really very good."

"I'm hot," she said.

"Just a few more minutes. We're almost done." He was on his knees now, his thighs winter pale against the sand. He worked so hard, and spent long hours in his darkroom too, clipping images to dry on the clotheslines he'd strung from wall to wall. "Think about the sea. Waves in the water, waves in the sand. You're part of that, Norah. You'll see in the photo. I'll show you."

She lay still beneath the sun, watching him work, remembering days early in their marriage when they'd gone out for long walks in the spring evenings, holding hands, the air infused with scents of honeysuckle and hyacinths. What had she imagined, that younger version of herself, walking in the soft still light of dusk, dreaming her dreams? Not this life, certainly. Norah had learned the travel business inside out over the past five years. She'd organized the office, and gradually she'd started overseeing trips. She'd built a stable client list and learned to sell, pushing glossy brochures across her desk, describing in breathless detail places she herself had only dreamed of going. She'd become an expert at solving last-minute crises: lost luggage, misplaced passports, sudden bouts of giardiasis. Last year, when Pete Warren decided to retire, she'd taken a deep breath and bought the business. Now it was all hers, from the low brick building to the boxes of blank airline tickets in the closet. Her days were hectic, busy, satisfying—and every night she came home to a house full of silence.

"I still don't see it," she said, when David finally finished, when she was standing up and brushing sand from her legs and her arms, shaking sand from her hair. "Why take the photo of me at all, if you're hoping I'll just disappear into the landscape?"

"It's about perspective," David said, looking up from his equipment. His hair was wild, his cheeks and forearms flushed with noon sun. In the far distance Paul had turned and was on his way back, drawing nearer. "It's about expectations. People will look at this picture and see a beach, rolling dunes. And then they'll glimpse something a little odd, something familiar in your particular set of curves, or they'll read the title and look again, searching for the woman they didn't see the first time, and they'll find you."

There was intensity in his voice; the wind coming off the ocean moved through his dark hair. It made her sad, because he spoke of photography as he had spoken once of medicine, of their marriage, a language and tone that evoked the lost past and filled her with longing. *Do you and David talk about big things or small things?* Bree asked her once, and Norah was shocked to realize how many of their conversations were about things as perfunctory and necessary as household chores and Paul's schedule.

The sun was bright on her hair and the gritty sand had caught in the tender skin between her legs. David was absorbed in putting away his camera. Norah had hoped this dream vacation would be a path back to the closeness they'd once shared. This was what had compelled her to spend so many hours lying in the hot sun, holding herself still while David took roll after roll of photos, but they had been here three days now, and nothing but the setting was significantly different from home. Each day they drank their morning coffee in silence. David found ways to work; he was either taking pictures or fishing. He did read in the evenings, swinging in the hammock. Norah took walks and naps, puttered, and went shopping at the bright, overpriced tourist shops in town. Paul played his guitar, and he ran.

Norah shaded her eyes and looked down the golden curve of the beach. Closer now, the runner's shape had emerged, and she saw it was not Paul after all. The man running was tall, lean, maybe thirty-five or forty. He wore blue nylon shorts edged with white piping and no shirt. His shoulders, already tanned dark, were edged with a burn that looked painful. As he drew close to them, he slowed and then stopped, hands on his hips, breathing heavily.

"Nice camera," he said. Then, looking straight at Norah, he added, "Interesting shot." He was beginning to go bald; his eyes were dark brown, intense. She turned away, feeling their heat, as David began to talk: waves and dunes, sand and flesh, two conflicting images at once.

She gazed down the beach. Yes. There, barely visible, was

another running figure, her son. The sun was so bright. For a few seconds she felt dizzy, little silverfish of light flashing behind her eyelids just as it glanced across the edges of the waves. Howard: she wondered where he was from, where he'd gotten a name like that. He and David were talking intently now about apertures and filters.

"So you're the inspiration for this study," he said, turning to include Norah.

"I suppose," she said, brushing sand off her wrist. "It's a bit hard on the skin," she added, aware suddenly that the new bathing suit left her nearly naked. The wind moved over her, moved through her hair.

"No, you have beautiful skin," Howard said. David's eyes widened—he looked at her as if he'd never seen her before—and Norah felt a surge of triumph. *See?* she wanted to say. *I have beautiful skin.* But the intentness of Howard's gaze stopped her.

"You should see David's other work," Norah said. She gestured to the cottage, tucked low beneath the palms, bougainvillea cascading off the porch trellises. "He brought his portfolio." A wall, her words; also an invitation.

"I would like that," Howard said, turning back to David. "I'm interested in your study."

"Why not?" David said. "Join us for lunch."

But Howard had a meeting in town at one o'clock.

"Here comes Paul," Norah said. He was running very fast along the edge of the water, pushing through the last hundred yards, his arms and legs flashing in the light, the wavering heat. My son, Norah thought, the world opening for an instant as it sometimes did around the very fact of his presence. "Our son," she said to Howard. "He's a runner too."

"He has good form," Howard observed. Paul drew close and began to slow down. Once he reached them he bent down with his hands on his knees, dragging deep breaths into his lungs.

"And good time," David said, glancing at his watch. *Don't do it,* Norah thought; David couldn't seem to see how much Paul recoiled at David's suggestions for his future. *Don't.* But David pushed on. "I hate to see him miss his vocation. Look at that height.

Think what he could do on a court. But he doesn't give a damn about basketball."

Paul looked up, grimacing, and Norah felt a flare of familiar irritation. Why couldn't David understand that the more he pushed basketball, the more Paul would resist? If he wanted Paul to play, he ought to forbid it instead.

"I like running," Paul said, standing up.

"Who can blame you," Howard said, reaching to shake hands, "when you run like that?"

Paul shook his hand, flushing with pleasure. *You have beautiful skin,* he'd said to her, moments ago. Norah wondered if her own face had been so transparent.

"Come to dinner," she suggested impulsively, inspired by Howard's kindness to Paul. She was hungry, thirsty too, and the sun had made her light-headed. "Since you can't come for lunch, come for dinner. Bring your wife, of course," she added. "Bring your family. We'll build a fire and cook out on the beach."

Howard frowned, looking out over the shining water. He clasped his hands and put them behind his head, stretching. "Unfortunately," he said, "I am here alone. A retreat of sorts. I am about to be divorced."

"I'm sorry," Norah said, though she was not.

"Come anyway," David said. "Norah throws wonderful dinner parties. I'll show you the rest of the series I'm working on—it's all about perception. Transformation."

"Ah, transformation," Howard said. "I'm all for that. I'd love to come to dinner."

David and Howard talked for a few minutes while Paul paced along the waves, cooling down, and then Howard left. A few minutes later, standing in the kitchen, slicing cucumbers for lunch, Norah watched him walk far down the beach, there and gone and there again as the curtain caught the breeze. She remembered the dark burn on his shoulders, his penetrating eyes and voice. Water rushed in the pipes as Paul showered, and there was the soft rustling of paper as David arranged his photos in the living room. He'd seemed obsessed over the years, always seeing the world— seeing her—as if from behind the lens of a camera. Their lost

daughter still hovered between them; their lives had shaped themselves around her absence. Norah even wondered, at times, if that
loss was the main thing holding them together. She slid the cucum-
ber slices into a salad bowl and started peeling a carrot. Howard
was a pinprick in the distance, then gone. His hands were large, she
remembered, the palms and cuticles pale against his tan. *Beautiful
skin,* he'd said, and his eyes hadn't left hers.

After lunch, David dozed in the hammock and Norah lay down
on the bed beneath the window. An ocean breeze flowed in; she felt
abundantly alive, somehow connected to the sand and the sea by
this wind. Howard was just an ordinary person, almost scrawny
and beginning to go bald, yet he was mysteriously compelling too,
conjured perhaps from her own deep loneliness and wishing. She
imagined Bree, delighted with her, laughing.

Well, why not? she would say. *Really, Norah, why not?*

I'm a married woman, Norah replied, shifting to look out the window at the dazzling, shifting sand, eager for her sister to refute her.

*Norah, for heaven's sweet sake, you only live once. Why not have
some fun?*

Norah stood, walking softly on the old worn boards, and fixed
herself a gin and tonic with lime. She sat on the porch swing, lazy in
the breeze, watching David dozing, so unknown to her these days.
Notes from Paul's guitar floated through the soft air. She imagined
him, sitting cross-legged on the narrow bed, head bent in concentration over the new Almansa guitar that he loved, a gift from
David on his last birthday. It was a beautiful instrument, with an
ebony fretboard and rosewood back and sides, brass turners. David
tried, with Paul. He pushed too hard on sports, it was true, but he
also made time to take Paul fishing or hiking in the woods, on their
endless search for rocks. He'd spent hours researching this guitar,
ordering it from a company in New York, his face full of quiet pleasure as Paul lifted it reverently from the box. She looked at David
now, sleeping on the other side of the porch, a muscle working in
his cheek. *David,* she whispered, but he did not hear her. *David,* she
said a bit louder, but he did not stir.

At four o'clock she roused herself, dreamily. She chose a sun-
dress splashed with flowers, gathered at the waist, thin straps over

her shoulders. She put on an apron and began to cook, simple, but luxurious foods: oyster stew with crisp crackers on the side, corn yellowing on the cob, a fresh green salad, small lobsters she'd bought that morning at the market, still in buckets of seawater. As she moved in the tiny kitchen, improvising roasting pans from cake pans and substituting oregano for marjoram in the salad dressing, the crisp cotton skirt moved lightly against her thighs, her hips. The air, warm as breath, glanced across her arms. She plunged her hands into a sink of cold water, rinsing the lettuce leaf by delicate leaf. Outside, Paul and David worked to light a fire in the half-rusted grill, its holes patched with aluminum foil. There were paper plates on the weathered table, and wine poured into red plastic glasses. They would eat the lobster with their fingers, butter running down their palms.

She heard his voice before she saw him, another tone, slightly lower than David's and slightly more nasal, with a neutral northern accent; crisp air, edged with snow, floated into the room with every syllable. Norah dried her hands on the kitchen towel and went to the doorway.

The three men—it shocked her that she thought of Paul this way, but he stood shoulder to shoulder with David now, nearly grown and independent, as if his body had never had anything to do with hers at all—were clustered on the sand just beyond the porch. The grill gave off its aromas of smoke and resin, and the coals sent a wavering heat into the sky. Paul, shirtless, stood with his hands thrust into the pockets of his cutoffs, answering with awkward brevity the questions that came his way. They did not see her, her husband and her son; their eyes were on the fire and on the ocean, smooth as opaque glass at this hour. It was Howard, facing them, who lifted his chin to her and smiled.

For an instant, before the others turned, before Howard raised the bottle of wine and slid it into her hands, their eyes met. It was a moment real to only the two of them, something that could not be proven later, an instant of communion subject to whatever the future would impose. But it was real: the darkness of his eyes, his face and hers opening in pleasure and promise, the world crashing around them like the surf.

David turned, smiling, and the moment slammed shut like a door.

"It's white," Howard said, handing her the bottle. Norah was struck by how ordinary Howard seemed then, by the silly way his sideburns grew halfway down his cheeks. The hidden meaning of the earlier moment—had she imagined it then?—was gone. "I hope that's all right."

"Perfect," she said. "We're having lobster." Yes, so ordinary, this talk. The stunning moment was behind them now, and she was the gracious hostess, moving as easily in her role as she moved within her whisper of a dress. Howard was her guest; she offered him a wicker chair and a drink. When she came back, carrying bottles of gin and tonic and a bucket of ice on a tray, the sun had reached the edge of the water. Clouds billowed high in airy shades of pink and peach.

They ate on the porch. Darkness fell swiftly, and David lit the candles set at intervals along the railing. Beyond, the tide came in, waves rushing invisibly against the sand. In the flickering light, Howard's voice rose and fell and rose again. He talked about a camera obscura he had built. The camera obscura was a mahogany box that sealed out all light, except for a single pinpoint. This pinprick cast a tiny image of the world onto a mirror. The instrument was the precursor to the camera; some painters—Vermeer was one—had used it as a tool to achieve an extraordinary level of detail in their work. Howard was exploring this, too.

Norah listened, awash in the night, struck by his imagery: the world projected on a darkened interior wall, tiny figures caught in light but moving. It was so different from her sessions with David, when the camera seemed to pin her in place and time, hold her still. That, she realized, sipping her wine in the darkness, was the problem at the heart of everything. Somewhere along the way, she and David had gotten stuck. They circled each other now, fixed in their separate orbits. The conversation shifted, and Howard told stories about the time he'd spent in Vietnam, working as a photographer for the army, documenting battles. "A lot of it was boring, actually," he said, when Paul expressed his admiration. "A lot of it was just riding up and down the Mekong on a boat. It's an extraordinary river, though, an extraordinary place."

After dinner Paul went to his room. A few minutes later, notes from his guitar cascaded amid the sounds of the waves. He had not wanted to come on this vacation; he had given up a week at music camp, and he had an important concert to play just a few days after they got home. David had insisted that he come; he did not take Paul's musical ambitions seriously. As an avocation it was fine, but not as a career. But Paul was passionate about the guitar, determined to go to Juilliard. David, who had worked so hard to give them every comfort, got tense every time the subject came up. Now Paul's notes fell through the air, winged and graceful but each one a little cut, too, the point of a knife piercing flesh.

The conversation moved from optics to the rarefied light of the Hudson River Valley, where Howard lived, and southern France, where he liked to visit. He described the narrow road, a thin dust rising, and the fields of pulsing sunflowers. He was all voice, hardly more than a shadow next to her, but his words moved through her like Paul's music did, somehow both inside and outside her at once. David poured more wine and changed the subject, and then they were standing, stepping into the brightly lit living room. David pulled his series of black-and-white photos from his portfolio, and he and Howard launched into an intent discussion about the qualities of light.

Norah lingered. The photographs they were discussing were all of her: her hips, her skin, her hands, her hair. And yet she was excluded from the conversation: object, not subject. Now and then when she went into an office in Lexington, Norah would find a photo, anonymous yet eerily familiar too—some curve of her body or a place she had visited with David, stripped of its original meaning and transformed: an image of her own flesh that had become abstract, an idea. She had tried, by posing for David, to ease some of the distance that had grown between them. His fault, hers—it didn't really matter. But watching David now, absorbed in his explanation, she understood that he did not really see her and hadn't for years.

Anger rose up in a rush that left her trembling. She turned and walked from the room. Since the day with the wasps she had drunk very little, but now she went into the kitchen and poured herself a red plastic glass brimming with wine. All around her were dirty pots and congealing butter, the fiery red husks of lobsters like the shells of dead cicadas. Such a lot of work for such brief pleasure! Usually David did the dishes, but tonight Norah tied an apron around her waist and filled the sink and put the remaining oyster stew away in the refrigerator. In the living room the voices went on and on, rising and falling like the sea. What had she been thinking, putting on this dress, falling into Howard's voice? She was Norah Henry, the wife of David, the mother of Paul, a son nearly grown. There were strands of gray in her hair, which she did not believe anyone could see except herself, squinting in the harsh light of the bathroom. Still, it was true. Howard had come to discuss photography with David, and that was that.

She stepped outside, carrying the garbage to the dumpster. The sand was faintly cold against her bare feet, the air as warm as her own skin. Norah walked to the edge of the ocean and stood gazing at the vivid white sweep of stars. Behind her the screen door opened and swung shut. David and Howard came out, walking through the sand and darkness.

"Thanks for cleaning up," David said. He touched his hand briefly to her back and she tensed, making an effort not to move away. "Sorry not to help. I guess we got talking. Howard has some good ideas."

"Actually, I was mesmerized by your arms, " Howard noted, referring to the hundreds of shots David had taken. He picked up a piece of driftwood and flung it, hard. They heard it splash and the waves licking, pulling it out to sea.

Behind them the house was like a lantern, casting a bright circle, but the three of them stood in a darkness so complete that Norah could barely see David's face, or Howard's, or her own hands. Only shadowy shapes and disembodied voices in the night. The conversation meandered, circling back to technique and process. Norah thought she might scream. She put one bare foot behind the other, meaning to turn and leave, when suddenly a hand brushed her thigh. She paused, startled. Waiting. In a moment Howard's fingers ran lightly up the seam of her dress, and then his hand was slipping inside her pocket, a sudden secret warmth against her flesh.

Norah held her breath. David talked on about his pictures. She was still wearing the apron, and it was very dark. After a moment she made a slight turn, and Howard's hand flowered open against the thin cloth, the flatness of her stomach.

"Well, that's true," Howard said, his voice low and easy. "You'd sacrifice something in clarity if you were to use that filter. But the effect would certainly be worth it."

Norah let her breath out, slowly, slowly, wondering if Howard could feel the wild rapid pulsing of her blood. Warmth radiated from his fingers; she was filled with such yearning that she ached. The waves rose and eased away and rose again. Norah stood very still, listening to the rush of her own breath.

"Now, with the camera obscura you're one step closer to the process," Howard said. "It's really quite remarkable, the way it frames the world. I wish you'd come by and see it. Will you?" he asked.

"I'm taking Paul deep-sea fishing tomorrow," David said. "Maybe the next day."

"I think I'll go inside," Norah said faintly.

"Norah gets bored," David said.

"Who can blame her?" Howard said, and his hand pressed low on her belly, hard and swift, like the beat of a wing. Then he slid it from her pocket. "Come tomorrow morning if you want," he said. "I'm making some drawings with the camera obscura."

Norah nodded without speaking, imagining the single shaft of light piercing through darkness, casting marvelous images on the wall.

He left a few minutes later, disappearing almost at once into the darkness.

"I like that guy," David said later, when they were inside. The kitchen was immaculate now, all evidence of her dreamy afternoon hidden away.

Norah was standing at the window looking out at the dark beach, listening to the waves, both hands sunk deeply in the pockets of her dress.

"Yes," she agreed. "So do I."

. . .

The next morning, David and Paul rose before sunrise to drive up the coast and catch the fishing boat. Norah lay there in the dark while they got ready, the clean cotton sheet soft against her skin, listening to them bump around awkwardly in the living room, trying not to make any noise. Footsteps, then, and the roar of the car starting, then fading into silence, the sound of waves. She lay there, languid, as a line of light formed where sky and ocean met. Then she showered and got dressed and made herself a cup of coffee. She ate half a grapefruit, washed her dishes and put them neatly away, and walked out the door. She was wearing shorts and a turquoise blouse patterned with flamingos. Her white sneakers were tied together and swinging from her hand. She had washed her hair and the ocean wind was blowing it dry, tangling it around her face.

Howard's cottage, a mile down the beach, was nearly identical to her own. He was sitting on the porch, bent over a darkly finished wooden box. He was wearing white shorts and an orange plaid madras shirt, unbuttoned. His feet, like hers, were bare. He stood up as she drew near.

"Want some coffee?" he called. "I've been watching you walk down the beach."

"No, thanks," she said.

"You sure? It's Irish coffee. With a little jolt, if you know what I mean."

"Maybe in a minute." She climbed the steps and ran her hand over the polished mahogany box. "Is this the camera obscura?"

"It is," he said. "Come. Take a look."

She sat down on the chair, still warm from his flesh, and looked through the aperture. The world was there, the long stretch of beach and the cluster of rocks, and a sail moving slowly in the horizon. Wind lifted in the piney casuarina trees, everything tiny and rendered in such sharp detail, framed and contained, yet alive, not static. Norah looked up then, blinking, and found that the world had been transformed as well: the flowers, so sharply drawn against the sand, the chair with its bright stripes, and the couple walking at the edge of the water. Vivid, startling, so much more than she'd realized.

"Oh," she said, looking back into the box. "It's astonishing. The world is so precise, so rich. I can even see the wind moving in the trees."

Howard laughed. "It's wonderful, isn't it? I knew you'd like it."

She thought of Paul as an infant, his mouth rounded in a perfect O as he lay in his crib staring up at some ordinary amazement. She bent her head again to view the world contained, then looked up to see it transformed. Released from its surrounding frame of darkness, even the light was shimmering, alive. "It's so beautiful," she whispered. "I almost can't stand how beautiful it is."

"I know," Howard said. "Go. Be in it. Let me draw you."

She rose and walked out into the hot sand, the glare. She turned and stood before Howard, his head bent over the aperture, watching his hand move across the sketch pad. Her hair kindled—already the sun was a hot flat hand—and she remembered posing the day before, and the day before that. How many times had she stood just this way, the subject and an object too, posed to evoke or to preserve what really did not exist, her true thoughts locked away?

So she stood now, a woman reduced to a perfect miniature of herself, every fact of her cast by light onto a mirror. The ocean wind, warm and damp, moved in his hair, and Howard's hands, with their long fingers and trim nails, moved quickly as he sketched her, fixing her image on the page. She remembered the sand shifting beneath her hips as she posed for David's camera, and how they had talked about her later, David and Howard, not as a flesh-and-blood woman in the room but rather as an image, a form. Remembering this, her body seemed fragile suddenly, as if she were not the accomplished self-sufficient woman who'd taken a group to China and back but rather someone who might be swept away by the next gust of wind. Then she remembered Howard's hand, warming her pocket and her flesh. That hand, the one moving now, the one that drew her.

She reached down to her waist and caught the hem of her blouse. Slowly, but without hesitation, she pulled it over her head and let it fall on the sand. On the porch, Howard stopped drawing, though he did not lift his head. The small muscles in his arms and shoulders had ceased moving. Norah unzipped her shorts. They slid down over her hips and she stepped out of them. So far it was nothing unfamiliar, just the same swimsuit she had modeled in so many times before. But now she reached behind and unhooked the straps of the top. She pushed the bottoms over her hips and down her legs, kicking them away. She stood feeling the sun and wind move across her skin.

Howard slowly raised his head from the camera obscura and sat staring.

For an instant it had a nightmare quality, that sense of panic and shame when she realized, in the middle of a dream, shopping or walking in a crowded park, that she had forgotten to get dressed. She started to reach for her suit.

"No, don't," Howard whispered, and she paused, straightening. "You're so beautiful." He rose then, carefully, slowly, as if she were a bird he might startle into flight. But Norah stood very still, intently present in her body, feeling as if she were made out of sand, sand meeting fire and about to be transformed, smoothed, made glittering. Howard crossed the few feet of beach. It seemed to take him forever, his feet sinking into the warm sand. When he finally reached her he stopped, without touching her, and stared. The wind moved in her hair and he pushed a strand from her lip, tucking it, very gently, behind her ear.

"I could never capture this," he said, "what you are in this moment. I could never capture it."

Norah smiled and splayed her hand flat on his chest, feeling the thin madras cotton and the warm flesh, the layers of muscle, bone. The sternum, she remembered, from the days when she had studied bones in order to better understand David and his work. The manubrium and the gladiolus, shaped like a sword. The true ribs and the false, the lines of union.

He cupped his hands lightly around her face. She let her own hand fall. Together, without speaking, they walked to the little cottage. She left her clothes on the sand; she did not care about that either, that anyone might see them. The boards of the porch gave slightly beneath her feet. The cloth over the camera obscura was thrown back and she saw with satisfaction that Howard had sketched the beach and horizon, the scattered rocks and trees; all these were perfect reproductions. He had sketched her hair, a soft cloud, amorphous, but that was all. Where she had stood the page was blank. Her clothes had fallen like leaves, and he had looked up to see her standing there.

For once, it was she who had stopped time.

The room seemed dim after the light of the beach, and the world was framed in the window as it had been in the lens of the camera obscura, so bright and vivid that it brought tears to her eyes. She sat on the edge of the bed. *Lie down,* he said, pulling his shirt over his head. *I just want to look at you for a moment.* She did, and he stood over her, his eyes moving across her skin. *Stay with me,* he said, and he shocked her by kneeling and resting his head on her belly, his unshaven cheek bristling against the flatness of her stomach. She felt his weight with every breath she took, and his own breath traveled on her skin. She reached down, weaving her hands through his thinning hair, and pulled him up to kiss her.

Later, she would be astonished, not that she had done these things or any of those that followed, but that she had done them on Howard's bed beneath the open unscreened window, framed like an image in a camera. David was gone, far out at sea with Paul, fishing. Still, anyone might have walked by and seen them.

Yet she did not stop, then or later. He was with her like a fever, a compulsion, an open door into her own possibilities, into what she believed was freedom. Strangely, she found that her secret made the distance between herself and David seem more bearable too. She went back to Howard again and again, even after David remarked about how many walks she was taking, how far she went. Even when, lingering in bed while Howard fixed them both a drink, she fished his shorts off the floor and found a photo of his smiling wife and three small children, inside a letter that said *My mother is better, we all miss and love you and will see you next week.*

This happened in the afternoon, sunlight glittering on the

moving water, heat shimmering up from the sand. The ceiling fan clicked in the dim room and she held the photo, gazed outside into the landscape of the imagination, the brilliant light. In real life, this photo would have cut, swift and sure, but here she felt nothing. Norah slid the photo back and let his shorts slip back to the floor. Here, this did not matter. Only the dream mattered, and the fevered light. For the next ten days, she met him.

August 1977

I

D AVID RAN UP THE STAIRS AND STEPPED INTO THE QUIET
foyer of the school, pausing for a moment to get his breath
and his bearings. He was late for Paul's concert, very late. He'd
planned to leave the hospital early, but ambulances had pulled in
with an older couple as he was walking out the door: the husband
had fallen off a ladder and landed on his wife. His leg was broken,
and her arm; the leg needed a plate and pins. David called Norah,
hearing the barely contained anger in her voice, angry enough himself that he didn't care, was glad, even, to annoy her. She had married him knowing what his work was, after all. The silence had
pulsed between them for a long moment before he hung up.

The terrazzo floor had a faintly pinkish cast, and the lockers that
lined the walls of the hallway were dark blue. David stood listening, hearing only his own breathing for a moment, and then a burst
of applause drew him down the hall to the big double wooden
doors of the auditorium. He pulled one door open and stepped inside, letting his eyes adjust. The place was packed; a sea of darkened heads flowed downward to the brightly lit stage. He scanned
them, looking for Norah. A young woman handed him a program,
and as a boy in low-slung jeans walked out onto the stage and sat

down with his saxophone, she pointed to the fifth name down. David took a deep grateful breath and felt his tension ease. Paul was number seven; he had made it just in time.

The saxophonist began, playing with passion and intensity, hitting one screeching wrong note that sent chills down David's spine. He scanned the audience again and found Norah in the center near the front, with an empty seat beside her. So she had thought of him, at least, saving him this place. He hadn't been sure she would; he wasn't sure, anymore, of anything. Well, he was sure of his anger, and of the guilt that kept him silent about what he'd seen in Aruba; those things certainly stood between them. But he did not have the smallest glimpse into Norah's heart, her desires or motivations.

The sax player finished with a flourish and stood up to bow. During the applause, David made his way down the dimly lit aisle, climbing awkwardly past those already seated to take his place by Norah.

"David," she said, moving her coat. "So. You made it after all."

"It was emergency surgery, Norah," he said.

"Oh, I know, I'm used to it. It's only Paul who concerns me."

"Paul concerns me too," David said. "That's why I'm here."

"Yes. Indeed." Her voice was sharp and clipped. "So you are."

He could feel her anger, radiating in waves. Her short blond hair was perfectly styled, and she was all shades of cream and gold, wearing a natural silk suit she'd bought on her first trip to Singapore. As the business had grown, she'd traveled more and more, taking tour groups to places both mundane and exotic. David had gone with her a few times in the early days, when the trips were smaller and less ambitious: down to Mammoth Cave or on a boat ride on the Mississippi. Each time he'd marveled at Norah, at the person she'd become. The people on the tours came to her with their worries and concerns: the beef was undercooked, the cabin too small, the airconditioning on the fritz, the beds too hard. She listened to them thoughtfully and stayed calm through every crisis, nodding, touching a shoulder, reaching for the phone. She was beautiful still, though her beauty had an edge to it now. She was good at her work, and more than one blue-haired woman had taken him aside to make sure he knew how lucky he was.

He had to wonder what they would have thought, those women, if they'd been the ones to find her clothes discarded in a pile on the beach.

"You have no right to be angry with me, Norah," he whispered. She smelled very faintly of oranges, and her jaw was tense. Onstage, a young man in a blue suit sat down at the piano, flexing his fingers. After a moment he plunged in, the notes rippling. "No right at all," David said.

"I'm not angry. I'm just nervous about Paul. You're the one who's angry."

"No, it's you," he said. "You've been like this ever since Aruba."

"Look in the mirror," she whispered back. "You look like you swallowed one of those little lizards that used to hang on the ceiling."

A hand fell on his shoulder, then. He turned to see a heavy woman sitting next to her husband, a long chain of children extending out beside them.

"Excuse me," she said. "You're Paul Henry's father, aren't you? Well, that's my son Duke playing the piano, and if you don't mind, we'd really like to hear him."

David met Norah's eyes then, in a brief moment of connection; she was even more embarrassed than he was.

He settled back and listened. This young man, Duke, a friend of Paul's, played the piano with an intent self-consciousness, but he was very good, technically proficient and passionate too. David watched his hands move over the keys, wondering what Duke and Paul talked about when they rode their bikes through the quiet neighborhood streets. What did they dream, those boys? What did Paul tell his friends that he would never tell his father?

Norah's clothes, discarded in a bright pile against the white sand, the wind lifting the edge of her wildly colored blouse: that was one thing they would never discuss, though David suspected that Paul had seen them too. They'd risen very early that morning for their fishing trip and had driven up the coast in the predawn darkness, passing little villages along the way. They weren't talkers, either he or Paul, but there was always a sense of communion in the early hours, in the rituals of casting and reeling, and David looked forward to this chance to be with his son, growing so fast, such a mystery to him now. But the trip had been canceled; the motor on the boat had given out and the owner was waiting for new parts. Disappointed, they'd lingered for a while on the dock, drinking bottled orange soda and watching the sun rise over the glassy ocean. Then they drove back to the cottage.

The light was good that morning, and David, though disappointed, was also eager to get back to his camera. He'd had another idea, in the middle of the night, about his photos. Howard had pointed out a place where one more image would tie the whole series together. A nice guy, Howard, and perceptive. Their conversation had been on David's mind all night, generating a quiet excitement. He'd hardly slept, and now he wanted to get home and shoot another roll of Norah on the sand. But they found the cottage still and cool and empty, washed with light and with the sound of waves. Norah had left a bowl of oranges centered on the table. Her coffee cup was neatly washed and draining in the sink. *Norah?* he called, and then again, *Norah?* But she didn't answer. *I think I'll take a run,* Paul said, a shadow in the bright doorway, and David nodded. *Keep an eye out for your mother,* he said.

Alone in the cottage, David moved the bowl of oranges to the counter and spread his photos on the table. They fluttered in the breeze; he had to anchor them with shot glasses. Norah complained that he was becoming obsessed with photography—why else would he bring his portfolio on vacation?—and maybe that was true. But Norah was wrong about the rest. He didn't use the camera to escape the world. Sometimes, watching images emerge in the bath of developer, he glimpsed her arm, the curve of her hip, and was stilled by a deep sense of his love for her. He was still arranging and rearranging the photos when Paul returned, the door slamming hard behind him.

"That was fast," David said, looking up.

"Tired," Paul said. "I'm tired." He walked straight through the dining room and disappeared into his room.

"Paul?" David said. He went to the door and turned the handle. Locked.

"I'm just tired," Paul said. "Everything's fine."

David waited a few more minutes. Paul was so moody lately. Nothing David did seemed to be the right thing, and the worst were talks with Paul about his future. It could be so bright. Paul was gifted in music and sports, with every possibility open to him. David often thought that his own life—the difficult choices he had made—would be justified if Paul would only realize his potential, and he lived with the constant, nagging fear that he'd failed his son somehow; that Paul would throw his gifts away. He knocked again, lightly, but Paul didn't answer.

Finally, David sighed and went back into the kitchen. He admired the bowl of oranges on the counter, the curves of fruit and dark wood. Then, following an impulse he could not explain, he went outside and started walking down the beach. He'd gone at least a mile before he glimpsed the bright flutter of Norah's shirt from a distance. When he got closer, he realized that they were her clothes, left lying on the beach in front of what must be Howard's cottage. David stopped in the bright glare of the sun, puzzled. Had they gone for a swim, then? He scanned the water but didn't see them, and then he kept walking, until Norah's familiar laughter, low and musical, drifted out of the cottage windows and stopped him. He heard Howard's laugh too, an echo of Norah's. He knew then, and he was gripped by a pain as gritty and searing as the hot sand beneath his feet.

Howard, with his thinning hair and his sandals, standing in the living room the night before, giving cool advice about photography.

With Howard. How could she?

And yet, all the same, he had expected this moment for years.

The sand pressed up hotly against David's feet and the light glared. He was filled with the old, sure sense that the snowy night when he had handed their daughter to Caroline Gill would not pass without consequence. Life had gone on, it was full and rich; he was, in all visible ways, a success. And yet at odd moments—in the middle of surgery, driving into town, on the very edge of sleep—he'd start suddenly, stricken with guilt. He had given their daughter away. This secret stood in the middle of their family; it shaped their lives together. He knew it, he saw it, visible to him as a rock wall grown up between them. And he saw Norah and Paul reaching out and striking rock and not understanding what was happening, only that something stood between them that could not be seen or broken.

Duke Madison finished playing with a flourish, stood, and bowed. Norah, clapping hard, turned to the family sitting behind them.

"He was wonderful," she said. "Duke is so talented."

The stage was empty then, and the applause faded. One moment passed, and another. People began to murmur.

"Where is he?" David asked, glancing down at his program. "Where's Paul?"

"Don't worry, he's here," Norah said. To David's surprise, she took his hand. He felt it, cool in his own, and was washed with an inexplicable relief, believing, for a moment, that nothing had changed; that nothing stood between them after all. "He'll be out soon."

Even as she spoke there was a stirring, and then Paul was walking onto the stage. David took him in: tall and lanky, wearing a clean white shirt with the sleeves rolled up and flashing a wry, crooked smile at the audience. David felt briefly astonished. How had it come to be that Paul was nearly grown, standing up here before this darkened room full of people with such confidence and ease? It was nothing David himself would ever have dreamed of doing, and a wave of intense nervousness washed through him. What if Paul failed up there before all these people? He was aware of Norah's hand in his own as Paul leaned over the guitar, testing a few notes, and then began to play.

It was Segovia, the program noted: two short pieces, "Estudio" and "Estudio Sin Luz." The notes of these songs, delicate and precise, were intimately familiar. David had heard Paul play these pieces a hundred times, a thousand times, before. All during the vacation in Aruba this music had spilled out of his room, faster or slower, measures and bars repeated again and again. The patterns were as familiar to him now as Paul's long deft fingers, moving with such sureness over the strings, weaving music in the air. And yet David felt he was hearing it for the first time, and maybe he was seeing Paul for the first time also. Where was the toddler who had pulled off his shoes to taste them, the boy climbing trees and standing up on his bike with no hands? Somehow, that sweet daredevil boy had become this young man. David's heart filled, beating with such intensity that he wondered for a moment if he might be having a heart attack—he was young for that, only forty-six, but such a thing might happen.

Slowly, slowly, David let himself relax into this darkness, closing his eyes, letting the music, Paul's music, move through him in waves. Tears rose in his eyes, and his throat ached. He thought of his sister, standing on the porch and singing in her clear sweet voice; music was a silvery language it seemed she'd been born speaking, just as Paul had. A deep sense of loss rose up in him, so forceful, woven of so many memories: June's voice, and Paul slamming the door shut behind him, and Norah's clothes scattered on the beach. His newborn daughter, released into Caroline Gill's waiting hands.

Too much. Too much. David was on the verge of weeping. He opened his eyes and made himself go through the periodic table— *hydrogen, helium, lithium*—so the knot in his stomach would not twist into tears. It worked, as it always worked in the operating room, to focus his attention. He pushed it all back: June, the music, the powerful rushing love he felt for his son. Paul's fingers came to rest on the guitar. David pulled his hand from Norah's. Fiercely, he applauded.

"Are you all right?" she asked, glancing at him. "Are you okay, David?"

He nodded, still not quite trusting himself to speak.

"He's good," he said at last, barking the words out. "He's good."

"Yes." She nodded. "That's why he wants to go to Juilliard." She was still clapping, and when Paul looked in their direction she blew him a kiss. "Wouldn't that be wonderful, if it could happen? He has a few years left to practice still, and if he gives it everything he has—who knows?"

Paul bowed, left the stage with his guitar. The applause swelled high.

"Everything he has?" David repeated. "What if it doesn't work out?"

"What if it does?"

"I don't know," David said slowly. "I just think he's too young to shut doors."

"He's so talented, David. You heard him. What if this is a door opening?"

"But he's only thirteen."

"Yes, and he loves music. He says he's most alive when he's playing the guitar."

"But—it's such an unpredictable life. Can he make a living?"

Norah's face was very serious. She shook her head. "I don't know. But what's that old saying? *Do what you love, and the money will follow.* Don't shut the door on his dream."

"I won't," David said. "But I worry. I want him to be secure in life. And Juilliard is a long shot, no matter how good he is. I don't want Paul to get hurt."

Norah opened her mouth to speak, but the auditorium grew quiet as a young woman in a dark red dress came on with her violin, and they turned their attention to the stage.

David watched the young woman and all those who followed, but it was Paul's music that was with him still. When the performances were over, he and Norah made their way to the lobby, stopping to shake hands every few feet, hearing praise for their son. When they finally reached Paul, Norah pushed through the crowd and hugged him, and Paul, embarrassed, patted her on the back. David caught his eye and grinned, and Paul, to his surprise, grinned back. An ordinary moment: again David let himself believe that things would be all right. But seconds later Paul seemed to catch himself. He pulled away from Norah, stepping back.

"You were great," David said. He hugged Paul, noting the tension in his shoulders, the way he was holding himself: stiff, aloof. "You were fantastic, son."

"Thanks. I was kind of nervous."

"You didn't seem nervous."

"Not at all," Norah said. "You had wonderful stage presence."

Paul shook his hands at his sides, loosely, as if to release leftover energy.

"Mark Miller invited me to play with him at the arts festival. Isn't that the best?"

Mark Miller was David's guitar instructor, with a growing reputation. David felt another surge of pleasure.

"Yes, it is the best," Norah said, laughing. "That's absolutely the best, indeed."

She looked up and caught Paul's pained expression.

"What?" she asked. "What is it?"

Paul shifted, shoving his hands in his pockets, and glanced around the crowded lobby. "It's just—I don't know—you sound kind of ridiculous, Mom. I mean, you're not exactly a teenager, okay?"

Norah flushed. David watched her grow still with hurt, and his own heart ached. She didn't know the source of Paul's anger, or his own. She did not know that her discarded clothes fluttered in a wind that he himself had set in motion so many years ago.

"That's no way to talk to your mother," he said, taking on Paul's anger. "I want you to apologize right now."

Paul shrugged. "Right. Sure. Okay. Sorry."

"Like you mean it."

"David"—Norah's hand was on his arm now—"let's not make a federal case out of this. Please. Everyone is just a little excited, that's all. Let's go home and celebrate. I was thinking I'd invite some people over. Bree said she'd come, and the Marshalls—wasn't Lizzie good on the flute? And maybe Duke's parents. What do you think, Paul? I don't know them very well, but maybe they'd like to come over too?"

"No," Paul said. He was distant now, looking past Norah at the crowded foyer.

"Really? You don't want to invite Duke's family?"

"I don't want to invite anyone," Paul said. "I just want to go home."

For a moment they stood, an island of silence in the midst of the buzzing room.

"All right then," David said at last, "let's go home."

The house was dark when they got there, and Paul went straight upstairs. They heard his footsteps moving to the bathroom and back again; they heard his door shutting softly, the turn of the lock.

"I don't understand," Norah said. She had slipped off her shoes and she looked very small to him, very vulnerable, standing in her stocking feet in the middle of the kitchen. "He was so good onstage. He seemed so happy—and then what happened? I don't understand." She sighed. "Teenagers. I'd better go talk to him."

"No," he said. "Let me."

He climbed the stairs without turning on the light, and when he reached Paul's door he paused for a long moment in the darkness, remembering how his son's hands had moved with such delicate precision over the strings, filling the wide auditorium with music. He had done the wrong thing all those years ago; he had made a mistake when he handed his daughter to Caroline Gill. He'd made a choice, and so he stood here, on this night, in the darkness outside Paul's room. He knocked on the door, but Paul didn't answer. He knocked again, and when there was still no answer, David went to the bookcase and found the thin nail he kept there and slid it into the hole in the doorknob. There was a soft click, and when he turned the knob the door swung open. It did not surprise him to see that the room was empty. When he turned on the light, a breeze caught the pale white curtain and lifted it to the ceiling.

"He's gone," he told Norah. She was still in the kitchen, standing with her arms folded, waiting for the teakettle to boil.

"Gone?"

"Out the window. Down the tree, most likely."

She pressed her hands to her face.

"Any idea where he went?"

She shook her head. The kettle started to whistle and she didn't respond right away, and the thin persistent wailing filled the room.

"I don't know. With Duke, maybe."

David crossed the room and pulled the kettle from the burner.

"I'm sure he's okay," he said.

Norah nodded, then shook her head.

"No," she said. "That's the thing. I really don't think he is."

She picked up the phone. Duke's mother gave Norah the address of a post show party, and Norah reached for her keys.

"No," David said, "I'll go. I don't think he wants to talk to you right now."

"Or to you," she snapped.

But he saw her understand, even as she spoke. In that moment something was stripped away. It all stood between them then, her long hours away from their cottage, the lies and the excuses and the clothes on the beach. His lies too. She nodded once, slowly, and he was afraid of what she might say or do, of how the world might be forever changed. He wanted, more than anything, to fix this moment in place, to keep the world from moving forward.

"I blame myself," he said. "For everything."

He took the keys and went out into the soft spring night. The moon was full, the color of rich cream, so beautiful and round and low on the horizon. David kept glancing at it as he drove through the silent neighborhood, along streets solid and prosperous, the sort of place he'd never even imagined as a child. This is what he knew that Paul didn't: the world was precarious and sometimes cruel. He'd had to fight hard to achieve what Paul simply took for granted.

He saw Paul a block before the party, walking down the sidewalk with his hands shoved into his pockets, his shoulders hunched. There were cars parked all along the road, no place to pull over, so David slowed and tapped the horn. Paul looked up, and for a moment David was afraid he might run.

"Get in," David said. And Paul did.

David started driving. They didn't speak. The moon cast the world with a beautiful light, and David was aware of Paul sitting beside him, aware of his soft breathing and his hands lying still in his lap, aware that he was staring out the window at the silent lawns they passed.

"You were really good tonight. I was impressed."

"Thanks."

They drove two blocks in silence.

"So. Your mother says you want to go to Juilliard."

"Maybe."

"You're good," David said. "You're good at so much, Paul. You'll have a lot of choices in your life. A lot of directions you can go. You could be anything."

"I like music," Paul said. "It makes me feel alive. I guess I don't expect you to understand that."

"I understand it," David said. "But there's being alive, and there's making a living."

"Right. Exactly."

"You can talk like this because you've never wanted for a thing," David said. "That's a luxury you don't understand."

They were close to home now, but David turned in the opposite direction. He wanted to stay with Paul in the car, driving through the moonlit world where this conversation, however strained and awkward, was possible.

"You and Mom," Paul said, his words bursting out, as if he'd been holding them back a long time. "What's wrong with you, anyway? You live like you don't care about anything. You don't have any joy. You just get through the days, no matter what. You don't even give a damn about that Howard guy."

So he did know.

"I give a damn," David said. "But things are complicated, Paul. I'm not going to talk about this with you, now or ever. There's a lot you don't understand."

Paul didn't speak. David stopped at a traffic signal. There were no other cars around and they sat in silence, waiting for the light to change.

"Let's stay focused here," David said at last. "You don't need to worry about your mother and me. That's not your job. Your job is to find your way in the world. To use all your many gifts. And it can't all be for yourself. You have to give something back. That's why I do that clinic work."

"I love music," Paul said softly. "When I play, I feel like I'm doing that—giving something back."

"And you are. You are. But Paul, what if you have it in you to discover, say, another element in the universe? What if you could discover the cure for some rare and awful disease?"

"Your dreams," Paul said. "Yours, not mine."

David was silent, realizing that once, indeed, those had been exactly his dreams. He'd set out to fix the world, to change it and shape it, and instead he was driving in the flooding moonlight with his nearly grown son, and every aspect of his life seemed beyond his grasp.

"Yes," he said. "Those were my dreams."

"What if I could be the next Segovia?" Paul asked. "Think of it, Dad. What if I have it in me to do that, and I don't try?"

David didn't answer. He'd reached their street again, and this time he turned toward home. They pulled into the driveway, bouncing a little over the uneven edge where it met the street, and stopped in front of the detached garage. David turned off the car, and for a few seconds they sat in silence.

"It's not true that I don't care," David said. "Come on. I want to show you something."

He led Paul out into the moonlight and up the exterior stairs to the darkroom above the garage. Paul stood by the closed door, his arms folded, radiating impatience, while David set up the developing process, pouring out the chemicals and sliding the negative into the enlarger. Then he called Paul over.

"Look at this," he said. "What do you think it is?"

After a moment's hesitation, Paul crossed the room and looked. "A tree?" he said. "It looks like a silhouette of a tree."

"Good," David said. "Now look again. I took this during surgery, Paul. I stood up on the balcony of the operating theater with a telephoto lens. Can you see what else it is?"

"I don't know . . . is it a heart?"

"A heart, yes. Isn't that amazing? I'm doing a whole perception series, images of the body that look like something else. Sometimes I think the entire world is contained within each living person. That mystery, and the mystery of perception—I care about that. So I understand what you mean about music."

David sent concentrated light through the enlarger, then slid the paper into the developer. He was deeply aware of Paul standing next to him in the darkness and the silence.

"Photography is all about secrets," David said, after a few minutes, lifting the photo with a pair of tongs and slipping it into the fixer. "The secrets we all have and will never tell."

"That's not what music is like," Paul said, and David heard the rejection in his son's voice. He looked up, but it was impossible to read Paul's expression in the soft red light. "Music is like you touch the pulse of the world. Music is always happening, and sometimes you get to touch it for a while, and when you do you know that everything's connected to everything else."

Then he turned and walked out of the darkroom.

"Paul!" David called, but his son was already clattering angrily down the exterior steps. David went out to the window, watching him run through the moonlight and up the back stairs and disappear inside. Moments later a light went on in his room, and the precise notes of Segovia drifted clearly and delicately through the air.

David, running over their conversation in his mind, considered going after him. He'd wanted to connect with Paul, to have a moment when they understood each other, but his good intentions had spiraled into argument and distance. After a moment, he turned and went back to the darkroom. The soft red light was very soothing. He considered what he'd said to Paul—that the world was made of hidden things, of secrets; built of bones that never saw the light. It was true that he'd once sought unity, as if the underlying correspondences between tulips and lungs, veins and trees, flesh and earth, might reveal a pattern he could understand. But they had not. In a few minutes he would go inside and get a drink of water. He would walk upstairs and find Norah already asleep, and he would stand watching her—this mystery, a person he would never really know, curled around her secrets.

David went to the mini refrigerator where he kept his chemicals and film. The envelope was tucked far in the back, behind several bottles. It was full of twenty dollar bills, new and crisp and cold. He counted out ten, then twenty, and put the envelope away, behind the bottles. The bills sat neatly on the counter.

Usually he mailed the money, wrapped in a sheet of blank paper, but tonight, Paul's anger lingering in the room, his music floating on the air, David sat down and wrote a letter. He wrote swiftly, letting the words pour out, all his regrets about the past, all his hopes for Phoebe. Who was she, this child of his flesh, the girl he had given away? He had not expected that she would live this long, or that she would have the sort of life Caroline wrote him about. He thought of his son, sitting all alone on the stage, and of the loneliness Paul carried with him everywhere. Was it the same for Phoebe? What would it have meant to them to grow up together, like Norah and Bree, different in every way yet intimately connected too? What would it have meant to David if June had not died? *I would like very much to meet Phoebe,* he wrote. *I would like her to know her brother, and for him to know her.* Then he folded the letter around the money without rereading it, put it all in an envelope, and addressed it. Sealed it, stamped it. He would mail it tomorrow.

Moonlight poured in through the windows in the gallery space. Paul had stopped playing. David gazed at the moon, higher in the sky now, yet distinct and sharply rendered against the darkness. He'd made a choice, on the beach; he'd left Norah's clothes lying on the sand, her laughter spilling into the light. He'd gone back to the cottage and worked with the photos, and when she'd come in, an hour or so later, he hadn't said a thing about Howard. He'd kept this silence because his own secrets were darker, more hidden, and because he believed that his secrets had created hers.

Now he went back into the darkroom and searched through his most recent roll of film. He'd taken some candid photos during the dinner party: Norah, carrying a tray of glasses, Paul standing by the grill with his cup lifted, various shots of them all relaxing on the porch. It was the final image he wanted; once he found it, he cast it with light onto the paper. In the developing bath, he watched the image emerge slowly, grain by tiny grain, something appearing where nothing had been. This was always, for David, an experience of intense mystery. He watched as the image took shape, Norah and Howard on the porch, lifting their glasses of wine in a toast, laughing. A moment both innocent and charged; a moment when a choice was being made. David took the photograph from the developer, but he didn't slide it into the fixer. Instead, he went into the gallery room and stood in the moonlight with the wet photo in his hands, looking at his house, darkened now, Paul and Norah inside, dreaming their private dreams, moving in their own orbits, their lives constantly shaped by the gravity of the choice he'd made so many years ago.

In the darkroom again, he hung the photograph of that moment to dry. Unfinished, unfixed, the image wouldn't last. Over the next hours, light would work on the exposed paper. The picture of Norah laughing with Howard would slowly darken until—within a day or two—it would be completely black.

II

THEY WERE WALKING ON THE TRACKS, DUKE MADISON WITH his hands shoved in the pockets of the leather jacket he'd found at Goodwill, Paul kicking at stones that zinged against the rails. A train whistle sounded, distant. In silent accord, the two boys stepped to the edge of the tracks, their feet still on the westward rail, balancing. The train was coming for a long time, the rail beneath them vibrating, the engine a speck, growing steadily larger and darker, the driver blasting on the horn. Paul looked at Duke, whose eyes were alive with the risk and danger, and felt that rising excitement in his own flesh, too much to bear almost, with the train closer and closer and the wild horn sounding through all the neighborhood streets and far beyond. There was the light and the engineer visible in the high window and the horn again, warning. Closer, the wind off the engine flattening weeds, he waited, looking at Duke, who stood balanced on the rail beside him, the train rushing, almost on them, and still they waited and waited and Paul thought he might never jump. And then he did, he was in the weeds and the train was rushing a foot from his face. For an instant only the conductor's expression, pale shock, and then the train—darkness and flash, darkness and flash—as the cars passed, and then it passed into the distance, and even the wind was gone.

Duke, a foot away, sat with his face raised to the overcast sky.

"Damn," he said. "What a rush."

The two boys brushed themselves off and started walking toward Duke's place, a little shotgun house right by the tracks. Paul had been born over here, a few streets down, but even though his mother sometimes drove him over to see the little park with the gazebo and the house across from it where he'd first lived, she didn't like him coming over here or to Duke's. But what the hell, she was never around, and as long as his homework was done, which it was, and as long as he'd mowed the lawn and practiced the piano for an hour, which he had, he was free.

What she didn't see wouldn't hurt her. What she didn't know.

"He was royally pissed off," Duke said. "That train dude."

"Yeah," Paul said. "He sure as hell was."

He liked swearing, and the memory of the hot wind on his face, and the way it quelled, for the moment anyway, this quiet rage. He'd gone running on the beach that morning in Aruba with a carefree heart, pleased at how the wet sand at the water's edge gave just slightly beneath his feet, strengthening the muscles in his legs. Pleased, too, because the fishing trip with his father had fallen through. His father loved to fish, long hours sitting in silence in a boat or on a dock, casting and recasting and—every once in a while—the drama of a catch. Paul had loved it too, as a child, not the ritual of fishing as much as the chance to spend time with his father. But as he'd grown older, the fishing trips had come to seem more and more obligatory, like something his father planned because he couldn't think what else to do. Or because they might bond; Paul imagined him reading it in some manual for parents. He'd gotten the facts of life on one vacation, sitting trapped in the boat on a lake in Minnesota as his father, turning red beneath his sunburn, talked about the realities of reproduction. These days, Paul's future was his father's favorite topic, his ideas about as interesting to Paul as a glassy flat expanse of water.

So he'd been happy to run on the beach, he'd been relieved, and he'd thought nothing of the pile of clothes at first, discarded in front of one of the little cottages so widely spaced beneath the casuarina trees. He had run right past them, deep in a rhythmic stride, his muscles making a kind of music that sustained him all the way to the rocky point. Then he stopped, walked circles for a while, and started running back, more slowly. The clothes had shifted: the sleeve of the blouse was flapping in the ocean wind, and the flamingos, bright pink, danced against the dark turquoise background. He slowed. It could have been anybody's shirt. But his mother had one like it. They had laughed about it in the tourist shop in town; she had held it up, amused, and bought it as a joke.

So, okay, maybe there were a hundred, a thousand shirts like this around. Still, he leaned down and picked it up. His mother's bathing suit, nubby, the color of flesh and unmistakable, fell out of the sleeve. Paul stood still, unable to move, as if he'd been caught stealing, as if a camera had flashed and pinned him. He dropped the shirt, but he still couldn't move. Finally, he started walking, and then he was running back to their own cottage as if seeking sanctuary. He stood in the doorway, trying to pull himself together. His father had moved the bowl of oranges to the counter. He was arranging photos on the big wooden table. *What's wrong?* he asked, looking up, but Paul couldn't say. He went to his room and slammed the door and didn't look up, not even when his father came and knocked on the door.

His mother was back two hours later, humming, the flamingo shirt tucked neatly into her tan shorts. "I thought I'd take a swim before lunch," she said, as if everything might still be normal. "Want to come?" He shook his head and that was that, the secret, his secret, hers and now his, between them like a veil.

His father had secrets too, a life that happened at work or in the darkroom, and Paul had figured it was all normal, just the way families were, until he started hanging out with Duke, an awesome piano player he'd met in the band room one afternoon. The Madisons didn't have much money, and the trains were so close the house shook and the windows rattled in their frames every time they passed, and Duke's mom had never been on an airplane in her life. Paul knew he ought to feel sorry for her, his parents would; she had five kids and a husband who worked at the GE plant and wouldn't ever make much money. But Duke's dad liked to play ball with his boys, and he came home every night at six when the shift was over, and even though he didn't talk any more than Paul's own father did he was right there, and when he wasn't they always knew where to find him.

"So whaddaya want to do?" Duke asked him.

"Dunno," Paul said. "How about you?" The metal rails were still humming. Paul wondered where the train would finally stop. Wondered if anyone had seen him standing at the edge of the track, so close he could have reached out and touched a moving car, the wind slicing through his hair, stinging his eyes. And if they had seen him, what had they thought? Images moving past the train windows like a series of still photographs: one and another; a tree, yes; a rock, yes; a cloud, yes; and none the same. And then a boy, himself, with his head flung back, laughing. And then gone. A bush, electric lines, the flash of road.

"We could shoot some hoops."

"Nah."

They walked along the tracks. When they had crossed Rosemont Garden and were surrounded by tall grass, Duke stopped, fishing in the pockets of his leather jacket. His eyes were green, flecked with blue. Like the world, Paul thought. That's how Duke's eyes were. Like the view of the earth from the moon.

"Look here," he was saying. "I got this last week from my cousin Danny."

It was a small plastic bag full of dried green clippings.

"What is it," Paul asked, "a bunch of dead grass?" As he spoke he understood, and he flushed, embarrassed, at what a geeky dork he was.

Duke laughed, his voice loud in the silence, the rustle of weeds.

"That's right, man, *grass*. You ever get high?"

Paul shook his head, shocked despite himself.

"You don't get hooked, if that's what's scaring you. I've done it twice. It's totally amazing. I'm telling you."

The sky was still gray, and the wind was moving in the leaves, and far away another train whistle sounded.

"I'm not scared," Paul said.

"Sure. Nothing to be scared of," Duke said. "You wanna try it?"

"Sure." He looked around. "But not here."

Duke laughed. "Who do you think is going to catch us out here?"

"Listen," Paul said. They did, and then the train was visible, approaching from the opposite direction, a small dot growing ever larger, its whistle slicing the air. They got off the tracks and stood facing each other on either side of the metal rails.

"Let's go to my place," Paul shouted, as the train bore down. "No one's home." He imagined them smoking pot on his mother's new chintz sofa, and he laughed out loud. Then the train was rushing between them; there was the roar and silence, roar and silence, of the passing cars. He glimpsed Duke in flashes, like photographs hanging in his father's darkroom, all those moments from his father's life like glimpses from a train. Trapped and caught. Rush and silence. Like this.

So they walked back to Duke's house and got on their bicycles, crossing over Nicholasville Road and meandering through the neighborhoods to Paul's.

The house was locked, the key hidden under the loose flagstone by the rhododendron. Inside the air was warm, faintly stale. While Duke called home to say he'd be late, Paul opened a window, and the breeze lifted the curtains his mother had made. Before she'd started working, she'd redecorated the whole house every year. He remembered her bent over the sewing machine, swearing when the lining snagged and bunched. These curtains had a creamy background with country scenes in dark blue that matched the dark-striped wallpaper. Paul remembered sitting at the table staring at them, as if the figures might suddenly start to move, might step out of their houses and hang up their clothes and wave goodbye.

Duke hung up and looked around. Then he whistled. "Man," he said. "You're rich.' He sat at the dining room table and spread out a thin rectangular paper. Paul watched, fascinated, as Duke arranged a line of ragged weed, then rolled a thin white tube.

"Not in here," Paul said, uneasy at the last minute. They went outside and sat on the back steps, and the joint flared orange on the tip and moved back and forth between them. Paul felt nothing at first. It began to sprinkle, then stopped, and after a while—he wasn't sure how long—he realized that he had been staring at a drop of water on the pavement, watching it spread slowly and merge with another drop and then spill off the edge into the grass. Duke was laughing hard.

"Man, you should see yourself," he said. "Are you ever stoned!"

"Leave me alone, you asshole," Paul said, and then he started laughing too.

They went inside at some point, though not before the rain had started again, leaving them soaked and suddenly chilled. His mother had left a casserole on the stove but Paul ignored it. Instead, he opened a jar of pickles and another of peanut butter, and then Duke ordered a pizza and Paul got out his guitar and they went into the living room, where the piano was, to jam. Paul sat on the edge of the raised hearth and strummed a few chords, and then his fingers started moving in the familiar patterns of the Segovia pieces he'd played the night before: "Estudio" and "Estudio Sin Luz." The titles made him think of his father, tall and silent, bending over the enlarger in the darkroom. The songs felt like light and shadow, one set against the other, and now the notes had been woven into his own life, into the silence in the house and the vacation on the beach and the high-windowed classrooms of his school. Paul played, and he felt himself being lifted up, the waves riding in and he was on them, he was making the music and then he *was* the music and it was carrying him up and up, rising to a crest.

When he finished there was silence for a minute, before Duke said, *Damn, that was good!* He ran a scale on the piano and launched into his piece from the recital, Grieg's *March of the Trolls*, with its energy and dark joy. Duke played and then Paul did and they didn't hear the doorbell or the knocking; suddenly the pizza delivery boy was standing in the open door. It was dusk by then; a darkening wind surged into the house. They ripped open the boxes and ate furiously, quickly and without tasting, burning their tongues. Paul felt the food settling in him, holding him down like a stone. He looked up through the French doors to the bleak gray sky beyond, and then at Duke's face, so pale his zits stood out, his dark hair falling flatly over his forehead, a smear of red sauce on his lips.

"Damn," Paul said. He put his hands flat on the oak floor, glad to find it there and himself on it and the room around him totally intact.

"No joke," Duke agreed. "Some stuff. What time is it?"

Paul stood up and walked to the grandfather clock in the foyer. Minutes or hours earlier, they had stood here, convulsing with laughter as the seconds ticked off, a gaping stretch of time between each one. Now all Paul could think of was his father, who paused to set his watch by this clock every morning, looking up across the table full of photos, and he was filled with sadness. He looked back on the afternoon and saw it gone, condensed into a memory no larger than that drop of rain, and the sky already nearly dark.

The phone rang. Duke was still lying flat out on the living room rug, and it seemed like hours passed before Paul picked up the receiver. It was his mother.

"Sweetie," she said, over noise and silverware in the background. He pictured her in her suit, maybe the dark blue one, fingers running through her short hair, rings flashing. "I've got to take these clients out to dinner. It's the IBM account, it's important. Is your father home yet? Are you okay?"

"I did my homework," he said, studying the grandfather clock, so recently hilarious. "I practiced the piano. Dad's not home."

There was a pause. "He promised he'd be home," she said.

"I'm okay," he said, remembering last night, how he'd sat on the edge of the windowsill and thought about jumping, and then he was in the air, falling; he was landing with a soft thud on the ground, and no one heard. "I'm not going anywhere tonight," he said.

"I don't know, Paul. I'm worried about you."

So come home, he wanted to say, but in the background laughter rose and fell, breaking like a wave. "I'm okay," he said again.

"You're sure?"

"Sure."

"Well, I don't know." She sighed, covered the receiver, and spoke to someone else, then came back on the line. "Well, that's good about your homework, anyway. Look, Paul, I'll call your father, and no matter what, I'll be no later than another two hours myself. I promise. Is that okay? Are you sure you're okay? Because I'll drop everything if you need me."

"I'm okay," he said. "You don't need to call Dad."

Her tone, when she answered, was cool, clipped.

"He told me he'd be home," she said. "He promised me."

"These people," he asked, "from IBM. Do they like flamingos?"

There was a pause, the roar of laughter and clinking glasses.

"Paul," she said at last. "Are you all right?"

"I'm fine," he said. "It was just a joke. Never mind."

When she'd hung up, Paul stood alone for a moment, listening to the dial tone. The house rose around him, silent. It wasn't like the silence in the auditorium, expectant and charged, but rather an emptiness. He reached for his guitar, wondering about his sister. If she hadn't died, would she be like him? Would she like to run? Would she sing?

In the living room, Duke was still lying with an arm over his face. Paul picked up the empty pizza box and the thin sheets of waxy paper and carried them out to the garbage can. The air was cool, the world brand new. He was thirsty like a desert, like a ten-mile run, and he carried a half gallon of milk back with him to the living room, drinking straight from the jug and then passing it to Duke. He sat down and played again, more quietly. The guitar notes fell through the air, slowly, gracefully, like winged things.

"You got any more of that stuff?" he asked.

"Yeah. But this'll cost."

Paul nodded, kept on playing, while Duke got up and went to make a phone call.

He had drawn his sister once, when he was just a kid, maybe in kindergarten. His mother had told him all about her, so he'd drawn her into the picture he made called "My Family": his father, outlined in brown, his mother with dark yellow hair, and himself holding hands with a mirror figure. Drawn at school, tied up with a ribbon, he'd presented this gift to his parents over breakfast, and had felt some darkness open up inside him when he saw his father's face, emotions that, at five, Paul couldn't explain or describe but that he knew already had to do with sorrow. His mother, too, when she'd taken the picture from his father, was touched with sadness, but she slipped a mask over it, the same bright mask she wore with clients now. He remembered how her hand had lingered on his cheek. She still did that sometimes, looking at him hard as if he might disappear. *Oh, it's beautiful,* she'd said that day. *It's a beautiful picture, Paul.*

Later, when he was older, maybe nine or ten, she had taken him to the quiet cemetery in the country where his sister was buried. It was a cool spring day, and his mother had planted morning glory seeds along the cast-iron border. Paul stood, reading the name— PHOEBE GRACE HENRY—and his own birth date, feeling an uneasiness, a weight, he could not explain. *Why did she die?* he asked, when his mother finally joined him, slipping off her gardening gloves. *No one knows,* she said and then, seeing his expression, she put her arm around him. *It wasn't your fault,* she said fiercely. *It was nothing to do with you.*

But he hadn't really believed her, and he didn't now. If his father secluded himself in his darkroom every evening and his mother worked long past dinner most days and, on their vacations, shed her clothes and slipped into the cottages of strange men, whose fault could it be? Not his sister's, who had died at birth and left this silence. It all made a knot in his stomach, which started each morning the size of a penny and grew throughout the day and made him sick to his stomach. He was alive, after all. He was here. So surely it was his job to protect them.

Duke appeared in the doorway, and he stopped playing.

"He's coming over, Joe is," he said. "If you have the cash."

"Yeah," Paul said. "Follow me."

They went out the back door and down the wet concrete steps and up the side stairs to the big open room above the garage. This room had tall windows on every wall, and during the day it was filled with light from every direction. A darkroom, windowless, was inset like a closet just next to the entrance. A few years ago, once his photographs had started to get noticed, his father had built this. Now he spent most of his free time here, developing film, doing experiments with light. Almost no one else came up here—

his mother, never. Sometimes his father invited Paul, who looked forward to these days with a yearning that embarrassed him.

"Hey, these are cool," Duke said, walking around the exterior wall, studying the framed prints.

"We're not supposed to be inside," Paul said. "We can't hang out here."

"Hey, I've seen this one," Duke said, stopping before the photo of smoldering ruins of the ROTC building, dogwood petals pale against the charred walls. This was his father's breakthrough photograph. It had been picked up by the wire services and flashed across the country, years before. *It started everything,* his father was fond of saying. *It put me on the map.*

"Yeah," Paul said. "My father took that. Don't touch anything, okay?"

Duke laughed. "Be cool, man. Everything's cool."

Paul went into the darkroom, where the air was warmer and stiller. Prints were strung, drying. He opened the little refrigerator where his father kept the film and took a cool manila envelope from the back. Inside was another envelope, full of twenty-dollar bills. He slipped one out, then another, and put the rest of the money back.

He came here with his father, and other times, secretly, he came here by himself. That was how he'd found the money, one afternoon when he'd been playing the guitar up here, angry because his father had promised to teach him to use the enlarger and then canceled at the last minute. Angry and disappointed and finally hungry. He'd rummaged through the refrigerator and found this envelope with cool bills, new, inexplicable. He'd taken one twenty that first time, more later. His father never seemed to notice. So now and then he came up here and took more.

It made Paul uneasy, the money and his thefts and the not being caught. It was the same feeling he had when he stood here with his father in the dark, images taking shape before their eyes. There was not only one photo in a negative, his father said; there were multitudes. A moment was not a single moment at all, but rather an infinite number of different moments, depending on who was seeing things and how. Paul listened to his father talk, feeling a pit open up inside him. If all this was true, his father was someone he could never really know, which scared him. Still, he liked being there amid the soft light and the smell of chemicals. He liked the series of precise steps from beginning to end, the sheet of exposed paper sliding into the developing fluid and the images rising out of nowhere, the timer going off and then the paper slipping into the fixer. The images drying, fixed in place, glossy and mysterious.

He paused to study them. Strange swirling shapes, like petrified flowers. Coral, he realized, from the trip to Aruba, brain coral with its flesh receded, leaving only the intricate skeletal framework. The other photos were similar, porous openings blooming in white, like a landscape of complex craters transmitted from the moon. *Brain coral/bones,* said his father's notes, placed neatly on the table by the enlarger.

On that day in the cottage, in the instant before he felt Paul's presence and looked up, his father's expression had been utterly open, washed with emotions like rain—some old love and loss. Paul saw it and longed to say something, to do something, anything that would make the world right. At the same time, he wanted to break away, to forget all their problems, to be free. He glanced away, and when he looked back his father's expression was distant again, impassive. He might have been thinking of a technical problem with his film, or diseases of the bone, or lunch.

A moment might be a thousand different things.

"Hey," Duke said, pushing open the door. "You ever coming out, or what?"

Paul slipped the cool bills into his pocket and went back into the larger room. Two other boys had arrived, seniors, who hung out in the vacant lot across from the school during lunch, smoking. One of them had a six-pack and handed him a beer, and Paul almost said *Let's go downstairs, let's do this outside,* but it was raining harder now and the boys were older than he was and bigger too, so he just sat down and joined them. He gave Duke the money and then the lit ember moved around the circle. Paul became fascinated with Duke's fingertips, how delicately they held the joint, remembering how they flew over the keys with wild precision. His father was meticulous too. He mended people's bones, their bodies.

"You feeling it?" Duke asked after a while.

Paul heard him from a long way off, as if through water, past the distant whistle of a train. This time there was no wild laughter, no giddiness, only a deep interior well through which he was falling. The well inside became part of the darkness outside, and he couldn't see Duke, and he was scared.

"What's wrong with him?" someone asked and Duke said, *He's just getting paranoid, I guess,* and the words were so big, they filled the room up and pressed him against the wall.

Long rolls of laughter filled the room, and the faces of the others grew distorted with mirth. Paul couldn't laugh; he was frozen in place. His throat was dry and he felt his hands getting too large for his body, and he studied the door as if at any moment his father might burst through, his anger shattering over them like waves. Then the laughter was gone and the others were getting up. They were going through the drawers, looking for food, but they only found his father's careful files. *Don't* he tried to say as the oldest one, the one with a beard, started pulling files out and opening them up. *Don't:* it was a scream inside his head, yet nothing came out of his mouth. The others were standing up now too, taking out folder after folder, spreading the prints and the negatives, so carefully arranged, on the floor.

"Hey," Duke said, turning to show him a glossy 8 by 10. "This you, Paul?"

Paul sat very still, his arms folded around his knees, his breath a wild rush in his lungs. He didn't move, he couldn't. Duke let the photo slip to the floor and joined the others, who had gone a little wilder now, scattering photos and negatives all over the shiny painted floors.

He sat very, very still. For a long time he was too scared to move but then he had moved, he was inside the darkroom, hunched in a warm corner, against the filing cabinet his father kept locked, listening to what was going on outside: swirls of noise, laughter, and then a bottle crashing. Finally, it grew quieter. The door opened and Duke said, *Hey, man, you in here, you okay?* And when Paul didn't answer there was a hurried conversation outside and then they left, clattering down the stairs. Paul stood slowly and walked through the darkness, stepping into the gallery space filled with piles of ruined photos. He stood in the window, watching Duke coast silently down the driveway on his bike, his right leg swinging over the bar before he disappeared into the street.

Paul was so tired. Drained. He turned and surveyed the room: photos everywhere, lifting in the breeze from the window, the negatives strewn like streamers from the counters and the lights. A bottle had been broken. Green glass was scattered over the floor, and the counters were splashed with beer. There were words on the walls, crude drawings and graffiti. He leaned against the door, then slid down until he was sitting on the floor in the mess. He would have to stand up again soon, he would have to clean this up, sort the photographs, put them right.

He lifted his hand, looked at the photo beneath it, then picked it up. It was no place he knew: a ramshackle house fastened to the side of a hill. In front of it stood four people: a woman in a dress to her calves, wearing an apron, her hands clasped in front of her. Wind blew a stray strand of hair across her face. A man, gaunt, bent like a comma, stood next to her, holding a hat to his chest. The woman was turned slightly toward the man, and they both had suppressed smiles on their faces, as if one of them had just made a joke and in another instant they would burst out in laughter. The mother's hand rested on a girl's blond head, and between them was a boy, not far from his own age, staring seriously straight into the camera. The image looked strangely familiar. He closed his eyes, feeling drained from the pot, near tears with exhaustion.

. . .

He woke to dawn blazing in through the eastern windows and his father silhouetted, speaking from the center of the light.

"Paul," he said. "What the hell?"

Paul sat up, struggling to realize where he was and what had happened. Ruined photographs and film scattered the floor, covered with muddy footprints. Negatives unfurled like streamers. Broken glass littered the room and had left deep scratches in the floor. Fear rushed through Paul; he felt like throwing up. He shaded his eyes from the blinding morning light with his hand.

"Good God, Paul!" his father was saying. "What happened here?" He moved out of the light at last, he was bending down, squatting. He lifted the photo of the unknown family from the chaos on the floor and studied it for a moment. Then he sat back against the wall, the photo still in his hands, and surveyed the room.

"What happened here?" he asked again, more quietly.

"Some friends came over. I guess things got kind of out of control."

"I guess," his father said. He pressed one hand to his forehead. "Was Duke here?"

Paul hesitated, then nodded. He was fighting back tears, and every time he looked at the ruined papers something tightened like a fist in his chest.

"Did you do this, Paul?" his father asked, his voice oddly gentle.

Paul shook his head. "No. But I didn't stop them."

His father nodded.

"It will take weeks to clean it up," he said at last. "You'll do it. You'll help me reconstruct the files. It will be a lot of work. A lot of time. You'll have to give up rehearsals."

Paul nodded, but the tightness in his chest grew stronger and he couldn't hold it back. "You just want an excuse to make me stop playing."

"That's not true. Damn it, Paul, you know that's not true."

His father shook his head and Paul was afraid he was going to stand up and leave, but instead he looked down at the photo in his hand. It was black and white, with a scalloped white border around the family standing in front of the low small house.

"Do you know who this is?" he asked.

"No," Paul said, but even as he spoke he realized that he did. "Oh," he said, pointing to the boy on the steps. "Oh. That's you."

"Yes. I was your age. That's my father right behind me. And beside me is my sister. I had a sister, did you know that? Her name was June. She was good at music, like you. This is the last photo that was ever taken of us all. June had a heart condition, and she died the next fall. It just about killed my mother, losing her."

Paul was looking at the photo differently now. These people weren't strangers after all, but his own flesh and blood. Duke's grandmother lived in an upstairs room and made apple pies and watched soap operas every afternoon. Paul studied the woman in the picture with her barely suppressed laughter—this woman he had never known was his grandmother.

"Did she die?" he asked.

"My mother? Yes. Years later. Your grandfather too. They weren't very old, either of them. My parents had hard lives, Paul. They didn't have money. I don't mean that they weren't rich. I mean that sometimes they didn't know if we were going to have food to eat. It pained my father, who was a hard-working man. And it pained my mother, because they couldn't get much help for June. When I was about your age, I got a job so I could go to high school in town. And then June died, and I made a promise to myself. I was going to go out and fix the world." He shook his head. "Well, of course I didn't really do that. But here we are, Paul. We have plenty of everything. We never worry about having enough to eat. You'll go to any college you want. And all you can think to do is get drugged up with your friends and throw it all away."

The tightness in his stomach had moved to his throat, and Paul couldn't answer. The world was still too bright and not quite steady. He wanted to make the sadness in his father's voice go away, to erase the silence that filled up their house. More than anything, he longed for this moment—his father sitting next to him and telling him family stories—to never end. He was afraid he would say the wrong thing and ruin everything, like too much light flooding onto the paper ruined the picture. Once that happened you could never go back.

"I'm sorry," he said.

His father nodded, looking down. Briefly, lightly, his hand passed over Paul's hair.

"I know," he said.

"I'll clean it all up."

"Yes," he said. "I know."

"But I love music," Paul said, knowing this was the wrong thing, the pulse of sudden light that turned the paper black, yet unable to stop himself. "Playing is my life. I'll never give it up."

His father sat in silence for a moment, his head bent. Then he sighed and stood.

"Don't close any doors just now," he said. "That's all I'm asking."

Paul watched his father disappear into the darkroom. Then he got on his knees and began to pick up shards of broken glass. Distantly, trains rushed, and the sky beyond the windows opened up forever, clear and blue. Paul paused for a moment in the harsh morning light, listening to his father work inside the darkroom, imagining those same hands moving carefully inside a person's body, seeking to repair what had been broken.

September 1977

CAROLINE CAUGHT THE CORNER OF THE POLAROID BETWEEN her thumb and first finger as it slipped from the camera, the image already emerging. The table with its white cloth appeared to float on a sea of dark grass. Moonflowers, white and faintly luminous, climbed the hillside. Phoebe was a pale blur in her confirmation dress. Caroline waved the photo dry in the fragrant air. There was thunder far away, a late summer storm gathering; a rising breeze stirred the paper napkins.

"One more," she said.

"Oh, Mom," Phoebe protested, but she stood still.

The minute the camera clicked she was off, running across the lawn to where their neighbor Avery, age eight, was holding a tiny kitten with hair the same dark orange as her own. Phoebe, at thirteen, was short for her age, chubby, still impulsive and impassioned, slow to learn but moving from joy to pensiveness to sadness and back to joy with an astonishing speed. "I'm confirmed!" she shouted now, turning once on the lawn with her arms flung high in the air, causing the guests to glance her way, drinks in their hands, and smile. Skirt swirling, she ran to Sandra's son, Tim, now a

221

teenager too. She wrapped her arms around him, kissing him exuberantly on the cheek.

Then she caught herself and glanced back anxiously at Caroline. Hugging had been a problem earlier this year, at school. "I *like* you," Phoebe would announce, enveloping a smaller child; she didn't understand why not. Caroline had told her again and again, *Hugs are special. Hugs are for family;* slowly Phoebe had learned. Now, however, seeing Phoebe rein in her love, she wondered if she'd done the right thing.

"It's okay, honey," Caroline called. "It's okay to hug your friends at the party."

Phoebe relaxed. She and Tim went off to pet the kitten. Caroline looked at the Polaroid in her hand: the luminous garden and Phoebe's smile, a fleeting moment caught, already gone. There was more thunder in the distance, but the evening was still lovely, warm and beautiful with flowers. All across the lawn people moved, talking and laughing and filling their plastic cups. A cake, three tiers and frosted white, stood on the table, decorated with dark red roses from the garden. Three layers, for three celebrations: Phoebe's confirmation, her own wedding anniversary, and Doro's retirement, a bon voyage.

"It's *my* cake." Phoebe's voice floated over the rise and fall of conversations, the physics professors and neighbors and choir members and school friends, families from the Upside Down Society, all sorts of children, running. Caroline's new friends from the hospital, where she'd started working part-time once Phoebe was in school, were here too. She had brought all these people together; she had planned this beautiful party unfolding in the dusk like a flower. "It's my cake." Phoebe's voice came again, high and floating. "I'm confirmed."

Caroline sipped her wine, the air warm as breath on her skin. She didn't see Al arrive but he was suddenly there, sliding a hand around her waist and kissing her cheek, his presence, his scent, sweeping through her. Five years ago they had married at a garden party much like this one, strawberries floating in champagne and the air full of fireflies, the scent of roses. Five years, and the novelty had not worn off. Caroline's room on the third floor of Doro's house had become a place as mysterious and sensual as this garden. She loved waking to the warm, heavy length of Al sleeping beside her, his hand coming to rest, lightly, on the flat of her belly, the scent of him—fresh soap and Old Spice—slowly infusing the room, the sheets, the towels. He was there, so vividly present she felt him in every nerve. There, and then as quickly gone.

"Happy anniversary," he said now, pressing his hands lightly on her waist.

Caroline smiled, filled with pleasure. The evening had deepened and people were moving and laughing in the lingering warmth and fragrance, dew gathering on the darkening grass, the white froth of flowers everywhere. She took Al's hand, solid and sure, and almost laughed because he'd just arrived and didn't yet know the news. Doro was leaving on a year-long cruise around the world with her lover, a man named Trace. Al knew that already; plans had been evolving for months. But he didn't know that Doro, in what she called a joyful liberation from the past, had given Caroline the deed to this old house.

Doro was arriving even now, coming down the stairs from the alley in a silky dress. Trace was just behind her, carrying a bag of ice. He was a year younger than she, sixty-five, with short gray hair, a long narrow face, full lips. He was naturally pale, conscious of his weight, and fussy about his food, a lover of opera and sports cars. Trace had been an Olympic swimmer once, had almost won a bronze medal, and he thought nothing, still, of diving into the Monongahela and swimming to the opposite shore. One afternoon he'd risen out of the water and staggered up the riverbank, pale and dripping, into the middle of the annual picnic for the department of physics. That was the story of their meeting. Trace was kind and good to Doro, who clearly adored him, and if he seemed aloof to Caroline, a bit distant and reserved, it really wasn't any of her business.

A gust swept a pile of napkins off the table and Caroline stooped to catch them.

"You're bringing the wind," Al said, as Doro drew near.

"It's so exciting," she said, lifting her hands. She had come to resemble Leo more and more, her features sharper, her hair, short
now, pure white.

"Al's like those old mariners," Trace said, putting the ice on the
table. Caroline used a small stone to weigh down the napkins. "He's
attuned to atmospheric changes. Oh, Doro, stay just as you are," he
exclaimed. "God, but you're beautiful. Honestly. You look like a
goddess of the wind."

"If you're the wind goddess," Al said, catching the paper plates as
they lifted, "you'd better cool your jets so we can have this party."

"Isn't it glorious?" Doro asked. "It's such a beautiful party, a
wonderful farewell."

Phoebe ran up, holding the tiny kitten, a ball of pale orange, in
her arms. Caroline reached out and smoothed her hair, smiling.

"Can we keep him?" she asked.

"No," Caroline replied as she always did. "Aunt Doro's allergic."

"Mom," Phoebe complained, but she was distracted at once by
the wind, the beautiful table. She tugged on Doro's silky sleeve.
"Aunt Doro. It's my cake."

"Mine too," Doro said, putting one arm around Phoebe's shoulders. "I'm going on a trip, don't forget, so it's my cake too. And your
mother's and Al's because they've been married five years."

"I'm coming on the trip," Phoebe said.

"Oh, no, sweetie," Doro said. "Not this time. This is a grown-up
trip, honey. For me and Trace."

Phoebe's expression was touched with a disappointment as acute
as her earlier joy. Mercurial, quicksilver—whatever she felt in each
moment was the world.

"Hey, sweetie," Al said, squatting down. "What do you think?
You think that kitty cat might like some cream?"

She fought a smile and then gave in, nodding, distracted for the
moment from her loss.

"Great," Al said, taking her hand, winking at Caroline.

"Don't take that cat inside," Caroline warned.

She filled a tray with glasses and moved among her guests, still
marveling. She was Caroline Simpson, mother of Phoebe, wife of
Al, organizer of protests—a different person altogether from the

timid woman who had stood in a silent snow-swept office thirteen years ago with an infant in her arms. She turned to look at the house, the pale brick strangely vivid against the graying sky. *It's my house,* she thought, echoing Phoebe's earlier chant. She smiled at her next thought, strangely apropos: *I'm confirmed.*

Sandra was laughing with Doro by the honeysuckle bush, and Mrs. Soulard was walking up the alley with a vase full of lilies. Trace, wind pushing his gray hair into his face, cupped a match in his hand, trying to light the candles. The flames flickered, sputtered, but finally held, illuminating the white linen tablecloth, the small transparent votive cups, the vase of white flowers, the whipped-cream cake. Cars rushed past, muted by the laughing voices, the fluttering leaves. For a moment Caroline stood still, thinking of Al, his hands reaching for her in the darkness of the night to come. *This is happiness,* she told herself. *This is what happiness means.*

The party lasted until eleven. Doro and Trace lingered after the last guests had left, carrying trays of cups and leftover cake, vases of flowers, putting tables and chairs away in the garage. Phoebe was asleep by then; Al had carried her inside after she dissolved into tears, tired and overstimulated, overcome with Doro's leaving, weeping with great heaving sobs that left her breathless.

"Don't do anymore," Caroline said, stopping Doro at the top of the steps, brushing past the dense, supple leaves of the lilacs. She had planted this hedge three years ago, and now the bushes, just twigs for so long, had taken root and shot up. Next year, they would be heavy with flowers. "I'll clean up tomorrow, Doro. You have an early flight. You must be eager to be off."

"I am," Doro said, her voice so soft Caroline had to strain to hear her. She nodded to the house where Al and Trace were working in the bright kitchen, scraping plates. "But Caroline, it's so bittersweet. Earlier, I walked through all the rooms, one last time. I've spent my whole life here. It's strange to leave it. Yet, all the same, I'm excited to be going."

"You can always come back," Caroline said, fighting a sudden swell of emotion.

"I hope I won't want to," Doro said. "Not for more than a visit, anyway." She took Caroline's elbow. "Come on," she said. "Let's go sit on the porch."

They walked along the side of the house, under arching wisteria, and sat in the swing, a river of cars moving by on the parkway. The high leaves of the sycamores, big as plates, fluttered against the streetlights.

"You won't miss the traffic," Caroline said.

"No, that's true. It used to be so quiet. They used to close the whole street off in the winter. We rode our sleds straight down the middle of the road, right here."

Caroline pushed the swing, remembering that long-ago night when moonlight flooded the lawns and fell through the bathroom windows, Phoebe coughing in her arms and herons rising from the fields of Doro's childhood.

The screen door swung open and Trace stepped out.

"Well?" he asked. "Are you about ready, Doro?"

"Just about," she said.

"I'll go get the car, then, and bring it around front."

He went back inside. Caroline counted cars, up to twenty. A dozen years ago she had come to this door, Phoebe an infant in her arms. She had stood right here, waiting to see what would happen.

"What time is your flight?" she asked.

"Early. At eight. Oh, Caroline," Doro said, leaning back and stretching her arms wide. "After all these years, I feel so free. Who knows where I might fly?"

"I'll miss you," Caroline said. "Phoebe will too."

Doro nodded. "I know. But we'll see each other. I'll send postcards from everywhere."

Headlights poured down the hill, and then the rental car was slowing and Trace's long arm was lifting in a wave.

"It's the call of the road!" he shouted.

"Be well," Caroline said. She hugged Doro, feeling her soft cheek. "You saved my life all those years ago, you know."

"Honey, you saved mine too." Doro pulled away. Her dark eyes were wet. "It's your house now. Enjoy it."

And then Doro was down the steps, her white sweater catching in the wind. She was in the car and waving goodbye; she was gone.

Caroline watched the car merge onto the crosstown and disappear into the river of rushing lights. The storm was still circling in the hills, flashing the sky white, dull thunder echoing far away. Al came out with drinks, pushing the door open with his foot. They sat down in the swing.

"So," Al said. "Nice party."

"It was," Caroline said. "It was fun. I'm exhausted."

"Have enough energy to open this?" Al asked.

Caroline took the package and undid the clumsy wrapping. A wooden heart fell out, carved from cherry, smooth as a water-worn stone in her palm. She closed her hand around it, remembering the way the medallion had glinted in the cold light of Al's cab and how, months later, Phoebe's tiny hand had caught it.

"It's beautiful," she said, pressing the smooth heart against her cheek. "So warm. It fits right here exactly, in the palm of my hand."

"I carved it myself," Al said, pleasure in his voice. "Nights, on the road. Thought it might be kind of hokey, but this waitress I know in Cleveland said you'd like it. I hope you do."

"I do," Caroline said, linking her arm in his. "I got something for you too." She handed him a small cardboard box. "I didn't have time to wrap it."

He opened the box and took out a new brass key.

"What's this, the key to your heart?"

She laughed. "No. It's a key to this house."

"Why? Did you change the locks?"

"No." Caroline pushed at the swing. "Doro gave it to me, Al. Isn't that amazing? I have the deed inside. She said she wanted a completely fresh start."

One heartbeat. Two, three, and the creak of the swing, back and forth.

"That's pretty extreme," Al said. "What if she wants to come back?"

"I asked her that same thing. She said Leo had left a lot of money. Patents, savings, I don't know what-all. And Doro was thrifty her whole life, so she doesn't need the money. If they come back, she and Trace will get a condo or something."

"Generous," Al said.

"Yes."

Al was silent. Caroline listened to the porch swing creaking, the wind, the cars.

"We could sell it," he mused. "Take off ourselves. Go anywhere."

"It's not worth much," Caroline said slowly. The idea of selling this house had never crossed her mind. "Anyway, where would we go?"

"Oh, I don't know, Caroline. You know me. I've spent life wandering. I'm just speculating here. Taking in the news."

The comfort of the darkness, the steady swing, gave way to a deeper unease. Who was this man next to her, Caroline wondered, this man who arrived every weekend and slipped so familiarly into her bed, who tipped his head at a particular angle every morning to slap Old Spice on his neck and chin? What did she really know about his dreams, his secret heart? Next to nothing, it suddenly seemed, or he of hers.

"So you'd rather not have a house?" she pressed.

"It's not that. This was good of Doro."

"But it ties you down."

"I like coming home to you, Caroline. I like coming down that last stretch of highway and knowing you and Phoebe are here, in the kitchen cooking, or planting flowers, or whatever. But sure, it's appealing, what they're doing. Packing up. Taking off. Wandering the world. It would be nice, I think. That freedom."

"I don't have those urges anymore," Caroline said, looking out into the dark garden, the scattering of city lights and the dark red letters of the Foodland sign, mosaic pieces amid the dense summer foliage. "I'm happy right where I am. You'll get bored with me."

"Naw. That just makes us compatible, honey," Al said.

They sat in silence for a time, listening to the wind, the rush of cars.

"Phoebe doesn't like change," Caroline said. "She doesn't handle it well."

"Well, there's that too," Al said.

He waited a moment, and then he turned to her.

"You know, Caroline. Phoebe's starting to grow up. She's starting not to be a little girl anymore."

"She's barely thirteen," Caroline said, thinking of Phoebe with the kitten, how easily she slipped back into the carefree joys of childhood.

"That's right. She's thirteen, Caroline. She's—well, you know—starting to develop. I feel uncomfortable picking her up like I did tonight."

"So don't," Caroline said sharply, but she was remembering Phoebe in the pool earlier in the week, swimming away and then returning, grabbing hold of her underwater, the soft rising buds of her breasts pressed against her arm.

"You don't have to get mad, Caroline. It's just that we've never once talked about it, have we? What's going to become of her. What it'll be like for us when we retire, like Doro and Trace." He paused, and she had the sense that he was choosing his words carefully. "I'd like to think we might consider traveling. It makes me a little claustrophobic, that's all, to imagine staying in this house forever. And what about Phoebe? Will she live with us forever?"

"I don't know," Caroline said, weariness around her, dense as night. She had fought so many fights already to make a life for Phoebe in this indifferent world. For the time being she had all the problems solved, and for the last year or so she'd been able to relax. But where Phoebe would work and how she might live when she grew up—all this remained unknown. "Oh Al, I can't think about all this tonight. Please."

The porch swing glided back and forth.

"We'll need to think about it sometime."

"She's just a little girl. What are you suggesting?"

"Caroline. I'm not suggesting anything. You know I love Phoebe. But you or I, we could die tomorrow. We're not always going to be around to take care of her, that's all. And there may come a time when she doesn't want us to. I'm just asking if you've thought about this. What you're saving all that money for. I'm just raising the topic for discussion. I mean, think about it. Wouldn't it be nice if you could come on the road with me now and again? Just for a weekend?"

"Yes," she said softly. "That would be nice."

But she wasn't sure. Caroline tried to imagine Al's life, a different room every night, a different city, and the road unfurling in the same gray ribbon. His first thought had been a restless one: sell the house, hit the road, roam the world.

Al nodded, drained his glass, and started to stand up.

"Don't go just yet," she said, putting her hand lightly on his arm. "I have to talk to you about something."

"Sounds serious," he said, settling back into the swing. He gave a nervous laugh. "You're not leaving me, are you? Now that you've come into this inheritance and all?"

"Of course not; it's nothing like that." She sighed. "I got a letter this week," she said. "It was a strange letter, and I need to talk about it."

"A letter from who?"

"From Phoebe's father."

Al nodded and folded his arms, but he didn't speak. He knew about the letters, of course. They'd been arriving for years, bearing cash in varying amounts and a note with a single scrawled sentence. *Please let me know where you are living.* She had not done this, but in the early years she'd told David Henry everything else. Heartfelt confessional letters, as if he were a friend close to her heart, a confidant. As time passed she'd become more efficient, sending photos and a line or two, at best. Her life had become so full and rich and complicated; there was no way to get it all down on paper, so she had simply stopped trying. What a shock it had been, then, to find a fat letter from David Henry, three full pages, written in his tight script, a passionate letter that started with Paul, his talent and his dreams, his rage and his anger.

> *I know it was a mistake. What I did, handing you my daughter, I know it was a terrible thing, and I know I can't undo it. But I would like to meet her, Caroline, I would like to make amends, somehow. I'd like to know something more about Phoebe, and about your lives.*

She was unnerved by the images he'd given her—Paul, a teenager, playing the guitar and dreaming of Juilliard, Norah with her own business, and David, fixed in her mind all these years, as clearly as a photograph in a book, bent over this piece of paper, filled with regret and yearning. She'd slipped the letter into a drawer, as if that might contain it, but the words had hovered in her mind through every moment of this task-filled and emotional week.

"He wants to meet her," Caroline said, fingering the fringe of a shawl Doro had tossed over the arm of the swing. "To be a part of her life again somehow."

"Nice of him," Al said. "What a stand-up guy, after all this time."

Caroline nodded. "He *is* her father, though."

"Which makes me what, I wonder?"

"Please," Caroline said. "You're the father Phoebe knows and loves. But I didn't tell you everything, Al, about how I came to have Phoebe. And I think I'd better."

He took her hand in his.

"Caroline. I hung around in Lexington after you left. I talked to that neighbor of yours, and I heard lots of stories. Now, I didn't get much schooling, but I'm not a stupid man, and I know that Dr. David Henry lost a baby girl about the time you left town. What I'm saying is that whatever happened between the two of you doesn't matter. Not to me. Not to us. So I don't need the details."

She sat in silence, watching cars rush by on the highway.

"He didn't want her," she said. "He was going to put her in a home—an institution. He asked me to take her there, and I did. But I couldn't leave her. It was an awful place."

Al didn't speak for a while. "I've heard of things like that," he said at last. "I've heard those kinds of stories, on the road. You were brave, Caroline. You did the right thing. It's hard to think of Phoebe growing up in a place like that."

Caroline nodded, tears in her eyes. "I'm so sorry, Al. I should have told you years ago."

"Caroline," he said. "It's okay. It's water under the bridge."

"What do you think I should do?" she asked. "I mean, about this letter. Should I answer it? Let him meet her? I don't know, it's been tearing at me all week. What if he took her away?"

"I don't know what to tell you," he said, slowly. "It's not for me to decide."

She nodded. That was fair, the consequence of having kept this to herself.

"But I'll support you," Al added, pressing her hand. "Whatever you feel is best, I'll support you and Phoebe one hundred percent."

"Thank you. I was so worried."

"You worry too much about the wrong things, Caroline."

"It doesn't touch us, then?" she asked. "The fact that I didn't tell you this before—it doesn't touch you and me?"

"Not with a hundred-foot pole," he said.

"Okay, then."

"Okay." He stood up, stretching. "Long day. You coming up?"

"In a minute, yes."

The screen door squeaked open, fell shut. The wind moved through the place where he'd been sitting.

It began to rain, softly against the roof at first, and then a drumming. Caroline locked the house—her house, now. Upstairs, she paused to check on Phoebe. Her skin was warm and damp; she stirred and her mouth worked around unspoken words, and then she settled back into her dreams. *Sweet girl,* Caroline whispered, and covered her. She stood for a minute in the rain-echoing room, moved by Phoebe's smallness, by all the ways she would not be able to protect her daughter in the world. Then she went to her own room, slipping between the cool sheets next to Al. She remembered his hands on her skin, the press of his beard against her neck, and her own cries in the darkness. A good husband to her, a good father to Phoebe, a man who would get up on Monday morning and shower and dress and disappear in his truck for the week, trusting her to do whatever she felt was best about David Henry and his letter. Caroline lay for a long time, listening to the rain, her hand resting on his chest.

·   ·   ·

She woke at dawn, Al thundering down the stairs to take the rig in early for an oil change. Rain cascaded from the gutters and the downspouts, teemed in puddles, and poured downhill in a stream.

Caroline went downstairs and made coffee, so absorbed in her own thoughts, in the strangeness of the silent house, that she didn't hear Phoebe until she was standing in the doorway behind her.

"Rain," Phoebe said. Her bathrobe hung loosely around her. "Cats and dogs."

"Yes," Caroline said. They'd spent hours once, learning this idiom, working with a poster Caroline made of angry clouds, cats and dogs teeming from the sky. It was one of Phoebe's favorites. "More like giraffes and elephants today."

"Cows and pigs," Phoebe said. "Pigs and goats."

"Do you want some toast?"

"Want a cat," Phoebe said.

"What do you want?" Caroline asked. "Use your sentences."

"I want a cat, please," Phoebe said.

"We can't have a cat."

"Aunt Doro went away," Phoebe said. "I can have a cat."

Caroline's head ached. *What will become of her?*

"Look, Phoebe, here's your toast. We'll talk about the cat later, okay?"

"I want a cat," Phoebe insisted.

"Later."

"A cat," Phoebe said.

"Damn it." The palm of Caroline's hand came down flat on the counter, startling them both. "Don't talk to me anymore about a cat. Do you hear?"

"Sit on the porch," Phoebe said, sullen now. "Watch the rain."

"What do you want? Use your sentences."

"I want to sit on the porch and watch the rain."

"You'll get cold."

"I want—"

"Oh, fine," Caroline interrupted, waving one hand. "Fine. Go out, sit on the porch. Watch the rain. Whatever."

The door opened and swung shut. Caroline looked out to see Phoebe sitting on the porch swing with her umbrella open and her toast on her lap. She was angry with herself for losing her patience. It wasn't about Phoebe. It was just that Caroline didn't know how to answer David Henry, and she was afraid.

She collected the photo albums and the stray pictures she'd been meaning to sort, and sat on the sofa where she could keep an eye on Phoebe, masked by her umbrella, rocking in the porch swing. She spread the recent photos on the coffee table, then took out a piece of paper and wrote to David.

Phoebe was confirmed yesterday. She was so sweet in her white dress, eyelet fabric with pink ribbons. She sang a solo at the church. I'm sending a picture of the garden party we had later. It's hard to believe how big she's gotten, and I'm starting to feel worried about what the future holds. I suppose this was what was on your mind the night you handed her to me. I've fought so hard all these years and sometimes I'm terrified of what will happen next, and yet—

Here she paused, wondering at her impulse to reply. It wasn't for the money. Every cent of it went into the bank; over the years Caroline had saved nearly $15,000, all of it held in trust for Phoebe. Perhaps it was simply old habit, or to keep their connection alive. Perhaps Caroline had simply wanted him to understand what he was missing. *Here,* she wanted to say, grabbing David Henry by the collar, *here is your daughter: Phoebe, thirteen years old, a smile like the sun on her face.*

She put her pen down, thinking of Phoebe in her white dress, singing with the choir, holding the kitten. How could she tell him all this and then not honor his request to meet his daughter? Yet if he came here, after all these years—what would happen then? She didn't think she loved him anymore, but maybe she did. Maybe she was still angry with him, too, for the choices he'd made, for never really seeing who she was. It troubled her to discover this hardness in her own heart. What if he'd changed, after all? But what if he hadn't? He might hurt Phoebe as he'd once hurt her, without even knowing it had happened.

She pushed the letter aside. Instead, she paid some bills, then stepped outside to slip them in the mailbox. Phoebe was sitting on the front steps, holding her umbrella high against the rain. Caroline watched her for a minute before she let the door fall shut and went to the kitchen to get another cup of coffee. She stood for a long time at the back door, gazing out at the dripping leaves, the wet lawn, the little stream running down the sidewalk. A paper cup was lodged under a bush, a napkin turned to pulp by the garage. In a few hours Al would drive away again. She glimpsed it, for a moment, how that might feel like freedom.

The rain came harder suddenly, hitting the roof. Something opened up in her heart, some powerful instinct that made Caroline turn and walk into the living room. She knew before she stepped out on the porch that she'd find it empty, the plate set neatly on the concrete floor, the swing still.

Phoebe gone.

Gone where? Caroline went to the edge of the porch and searched up and down the street, through the teeming rain. A train sounded in the distance; the road to the left climbed the hill to the tracks. To the right, it ended in the freeway entrance ramp. *All right, think. Think! Where would she go?*

Down the street the Swan children were playing barefoot in the puddles. Caroline remembered Phoebe saying, earlier that morning, *I want a cat,* and Avery standing at the party with the furry bundle in her arms. Remembered Phoebe, fascinated by its smallness, its tiny sounds. And sure enough, when she asked the Swan children about Phoebe, they gestured across the road to the copse of trees. The kitten had run away. Phoebe and Avery had gone to rescue it.

At the first break in traffic, Caroline darted across the road. The earth was saturated, water pooling in her footprints. She pushed through the brushy copse and broke at last into the clearing. Avery was there, kneeling by the pipe that drained water from the hills into the concrete ditch. Phoebe's yellow umbrella was discarded, like a flag, beside her.

"Avery!" She squatted down beside the girl, touched her wet shoulder. "Where's Phoebe?"

"She went to get the cat," Avery said, pointing into the pipe. "It went in there."

Caroline swore softly and knelt in the edge of the pipe. Cold water rushed against her knees, her hands. *Phoebe!* she cried, and her voice echoed in the darkness. *It's Mom, honey, are you here?*

Silence. Caroline inched her way inside. The water was so cold. Already her hands were numb. *Phoebe!* she shouted, her voice swelling. *Phoebe!* She listened hard. A sound then, faint. Caroline crawled a few feet farther in, feeling her way through cold invisible rushing water. Then her hand brushed fabric, cold flesh, and Phoebe, trembling, was in her arms. Caroline held her close, remembering the night she'd carried Phoebe in the damp purple bathroom, urging her to breathe.

"We have to get out of here, honey. We have to get out."

But Phoebe wouldn't move.

"My cat," she said, her voice high, determined, and Caroline felt the squirming beneath Phoebe's shirt, heard the small mewing. "It's my cat."

"Forget the cat," Caroline shouted. She pulled Phoebe gently in the direction she had come. "Come on, Phoebe. Right now."

"My cat," Phoebe said.

"Okay," Caroline said, water rushing higher now, around her knees. "Okay, okay, it's your cat. Just go!"

Phoebe began to move, inching slowly toward the circle of light. Finally they emerged, cold water streaming around them in the concrete ditch. Phoebe was soaked, her hair plastered against her face, the kitten wet too. Through the trees Caroline glimpsed her house, solid and warm, like a raft in the dangerous world. She imagined Al, traveling some distant highway, and the familiar comfort of these rooms that were her own.

"It's all right." Caroline put her arm around Phoebe. The kitten twisted, thin claws scratching the backs of her hands. The rain fell, dripping off the dark, vivid leaves.

"There's the mailman," Phoebe said.

"Yes," Caroline said, watching him climb the porch and slide the bills she'd put out into his leather bag.

Her letter to David Henry sat unfinished on the table. She had stood at the back door watching the rain, thinking only of Phoebe's father, while Phoebe wandered into danger. It seemed like an omen suddenly, and she let herself turn the fear she'd felt at Phoebe's disappearance into anger. She wouldn't write to David again; he wanted too much from her, and he wanted it too late. The mailman walked back down the steps, his bright umbrella flashing.

"Yes, honey," she said, stroking the kitten's bony head. "Yes. There he is."

1982

April 1982

I

CAROLINE STOOD AT THE BUS STOP NEAR THE CORNER OF Forbes and Braddock, watching the kinetic energy of the children on the playground, their happy shouts lifting up over the steady roar of the traffic. Beyond them, on the baseball field, figures in blue and red from competing local taverns moved with silent grace against new grass. It was spring. Evening was gathering. In a few minutes the parents sitting on the benches or standing with their hands in their pockets would start calling the children to go home. The grown-ups' game would continue to the edge of darkness, and when it ended the players would slap each other on the back and depart too, settling in for drinks at the tavern, their laughter loud and happy. She and Al saw them there when they made it out for an evening. An early show at the Regent, then dinner and—if Al wasn't on call—a couple of beers.

Tonight he was gone, however, speeding far away through the gathering night, south from Cleveland to Toledo, then Columbus. Caroline had his routes hung on the refrigerator. Years ago, in those strange days after Doro left, Caroline had hired someone to watch Phoebe while she traveled with Al, hoping to bridge the distance between them. Hours slid away; she slept and woke and lost track

241

of time, the road spinning out beneath them forever, a dark ribbon bisected by the steady flashes of white, seductive and mesmerizing. Finally Al, bleary himself, would pull into a truck stop and take her to a restaurant that didn't differ appreciably from the one they had left behind in whatever city they'd stayed in the day before. Life on the road seemed like falling through strange holes in the universe, as if you might walk into a restroom in one city in America and then walk out the same door to find yourself somewhere else: the same strip malls and gas stations and fast-food places, the same hum of wheels against the road. Only the names were different, the light, the faces. She'd gone with Al twice, then never again.

The bus rounded the corner and roared to a stop. The doors folded open and Caroline climbed in and took a window seat, trees flashing as they roared over the bridge and the hollow below. Flying past the cemetery, lurching through Squirrel Hill, then lumbering on through the old neighborhoods to Oakland, where Caroline got off. She stood before the Carnegie Museum for a moment, collecting herself, looking up at the grand stone building with its cascading steps and ionic columns. A banner strung along the top of the portico fluttered in the wind: MIRROR IMAGES: PHOTOGRAPHS BY DAVID HENRY.

Tonight was the opening: he would be here to speak. Hands trembling, Caroline slid the newspaper clipping from her pocket. She had carried it for two weeks, her heart surging every time she touched it. A dozen times, perhaps more, she had changed her mind. What good could come of it?

And then, in the next breath, what harm?

If Al had been here, she would have stayed home. She would have let the opportunity slip away unremarked, glancing at the clock until the opening was over and David Henry had disappeared back into whatever life he now led.

But Al had called to say he'd be away tonight, and Mrs. O'Neill was home to keep an eye on Phoebe, and the bus had been on time.

Caroline's heart was roaring now. She stood still, taking deep breaths, while the world moved around her, the squeal of brakes and the scent of spent fuel, and the faint stirrings of the feathery new leaves of spring. Voices swelled as people drew near, then receded, scraps of conversation drifting like bits of paper borne on the wind. Streams of people, dressed in silk and heels and dark expensive suits, flowed up the museum's stone steps. The sky was a darkening indigo and the streetlights had come on; the air was full of the scent of lemon and mint from the festival at the Greek Orthodox Church one block down. Caroline closed her eyes, thinking of black olives, which she had never tasted until she reached this city. Thinking of the wild mosaic of Saturday morning market at the Strip, fresh bread and flowers and fruits and vegetables, a riot of food and color for blocks along the river, something she would never have seen except for David Henry and an unexpected snowstorm. She took one step and then another, merging with the crowd.

The museum had high white ceilings and oak floors, polished to a dark, gleaming gold. Caroline was given a program of thick creamy paper with David Henry's name across the top. A list of photos followed. "Dunes at Dusk," she read. "A Tree in the Heart." She walked into the gallery room and found his most famous photo, the undulating beach that was more than a beach, the curve of a woman's hip, then the smooth length of her leg, hidden among the dunes. The image trembled, on the edge of being something else, and then it suddenly *was* something else. Caroline had stared at it for a good fifteen minutes the first time she saw it, knowing that the swell of flesh belonged to Norah Henry, remembering the white hill of her belly rippling with contractions, the powerful force of her grip. For years she had consoled herself with her disdainful opinion of Norah Henry, a bit imperial, used to ease and order, a woman who might have left Phoebe in an institution. But this image exploded that idea. These photos showed a woman she had never known.

People milled in the room; the seats filled. Caroline sat down, watching everything intently. The lights dimmed once and went on again, and then suddenly there was applause and David Henry was walking in, tall and familiar, fleshier now, smiling at the audience. It shocked her to see that he was not a young man anymore. His hair was turning gray and there was a slight bend to his shoulders.

He walked to the podium and gazed out at the audience and Caroline caught her breath, sure he must have seen her, must have known her at once, as she knew him. He cleared his throat and made a joke about the weather. As the laughter spilled out around her and died down, as he looked at his notes and began to speak, Caroline understood that she was just another face in the crowd.

He spoke with melodious assurance, though Caroline paid almost no attention to what he was saying. Instead, she studied the familiar gestures of his hands, the new lines at the corners of his eyes. His hair was longer, thick and luxurious despite the gray, and he seemed satisfied, settled. She thought of that night, almost twenty years ago now, when he'd woken and lifted his head from the desk and caught her in the doorway, naked in her love for him, the two of them as vulnerable to each other in that moment as it was possible to be. She had recognized something then, something he kept hidden, some experience or expectation or dream too private to share. And it was true, she could see that still: David Henry had a secret life. Her mistake twenty years ago had been in believing that his secret had to do with any kind of love for her.

When his talk was over, the applause rose, strong, and then he was stepping from behind the podium, taking a long drink from his glass of water, answering questions. There were several—from a man with a notebook, a matron with gray hair, a young woman dressed in black with dark cascading hair who asked something rather angrily about form. Tension grew in Caroline's body and her heart pounded until she could barely breathe. The questions ended and the silence grew, and David Henry cleared his throat, a smile forming as he thanked the audience and turned away. Caroline felt herself rising then, almost beyond her own volition, her purse in front of her like a shield. She crossed the room and joined the little group collecting around him. He glanced at her and smiled politely, without recognition. She waited through more questions, growing somewhat calmer as the moments passed. The curator of the show hovered at the edge of the group, anxious for David to mingle, but when a break came in the questions, Caroline stepped forward and put her hand on David's arm.

"David," she said. "Don't you know me?"

He searched her face.

"Have I changed so much?" she whispered.

She saw him understand, then. His face altered, the shape of it even, as if gravity had suddenly gotten stronger. A flush crept up his neck and a muscle pulsed in his cheek. Caroline felt something strange happening with time, as if they were back in the clinic again all those years ago, the snow falling down outside. They stared at each other without speaking, as if the room and all the people in it had fallen utterly away.

"Caroline," he said at last, recovering. "Caroline Gill. An old friend," he added, speaking to the people still clustering around them. He reached up with one hand and adjusted his tie, and a smile broke across his face, though it did not touch his eyes. "Thank you," he said, nodding to the others. "Thank you all for coming. Now, if you'll excuse us."

And then they were crossing the room. David walked beside her, one hand lightly but firmly against her back, as if she might disappear unless he held her in place.

"Come in here," he said, stepping behind a display panel, where an unframed door was barely visible in the white wall. He guided her inside, swiftly, and shut the door behind them. It was a storage closet, small, one bare bulb raining light down on shelves full of paint and tools. They stood face-to-face, just inches apart. His scent filled the room, that sweetish cologne, and beneath it was a smell she remembered, something medicinal and tinged with adrenaline. The little room was hot, and she felt suddenly dizzy, silverfish flashing in her vision.

"Caroline," he said. "Good God, do you live here? In Pittsburgh? Why wouldn't you tell me where you were?"

"I wasn't hard to find. Other people found me," she said slowly, remembering Al walking up the alley, understanding for the first time the depth of his persistence. For if it was true that David Henry had not looked very hard, it was also true that she had wanted to be lost.

Outside the door there were footsteps, drawing near and then pausing. The rush and murmur of voices. She studied his face. All these years she'd thought about him every single day, and yet now she couldn't imagine what to say.

"Shouldn't you be out there?" she asked, glancing at the door.

"They'll wait."

They looked at each other then, not speaking. Caroline had held him in her mind all this time like a photograph, a hundred or a thousand photographs. In each of these David Henry was a young man full of a restless, determined energy. Now, staring at his dark eyes and fleshy cheeks, his hair so carefully styled, she realized that if she had passed him on the street she might not have known him, after all.

When he spoke again his tone had softened, though a muscle still worked in his face. "I went to your apartment, Caroline. That day, after the memorial service. I went there, but you were already gone. All this time——" he began, and then he fell silent.

There was a light tap on the door, a muffled questioning voice.

"Give me a minute," David called back.

"I was in love with you," Caroline said in a rush, astonished at her confession, for it was the first time she had ever voiced this, even to herself, though it was knowledge she had lived with for years. The admission made her feel light-headed, reckless, and she went on. "You know, I spent all sorts of time imagining a life with you. And it was in that moment by the church when I realized I hadn't crossed your mind at all, not really."

He'd bent his head as she spoke, and now he looked up.

"I knew," he said. "I knew you were in love with me. How could I have asked you to help me, otherwise? I'm sorry, Caroline. For years now, I have been—so sorry."

She nodded, tears in her eyes, that younger version of herself still alive, still standing by the edge of the memorial service, unacknowledged, invisible. It made her angry, even now, that he had not really seen her then. And that, not knowing her at all, he hadn't hesitated to ask her to take away his daughter.

"Are you happy?" he asked. "Have you been happy, Caroline? Has Phoebe?"

His question, and the gentleness in his voice, disarmed her. She thought of Phoebe, struggling to learn to shape letters, to tie her shoes. Phoebe, playing happily in the backyard while Caroline made phone call after phone call, fighting for her education. Phoebe, putting her soft arms around Caroline's neck for no reason at all and saying, *I love you, Mom*. She thought of Al, gone too much but walking through the door at the end of a long week, carrying flowers or a bag of fresh rolls or a small gift, something for her, always, and something for Phoebe. When she'd worked in David Henry's office she had been so young, so lonely and naïve, that she imagined herself as some sort of vessel to be filled up with love. But it wasn't like that. The love was within her all the time, and its only renewal came from giving it away.

"Do you really want to know?" she asked at last, looking him straight in the eye. "Because you never wrote back, David. Except for that one time, you never asked a single thing about our lives. Not for years."

As Caroline spoke, she realized that this was why she had come. Not out of love at all, or any allegiance to the past, or even out of guilt. She had come out of anger and a desire to set the record straight.

"For years you never wanted to know how I was. How Phoebe was. You just didn't give a damn, did you? And then that last letter, the one I never answered. All of a sudden, you wanted her back."

David gave a short, startled laugh. "Is that how you saw it? Is that why you stopped writing?"

"How else could I see it?"

He shook his head slowly. "Caroline, I asked you for your address. Again and again—every time I sent money. And in that final letter I simply asked you to invite me back into your life. What more could I do? Look, I know you don't realize this, but I kept every letter you ever sent. And when you stopped writing, I felt like you'd slammed a door in my face."

Caroline thought of her letters, all her heartfelt confessions flowing into ink on paper. She couldn't remember anymore what she'd written: details about Phoebe's life, her hopes and her dreams and her fears.

"Where are they?" she asked. "Where do you keep my letters?"

He looked surprised. "In my darkroom filing cabinet: bottom drawer. It's always locked. Why?"

"I didn't think you even read them," Caroline said. "I felt I was writing into a void. Maybe that's why I felt so free. Like I could say anything at all."

David rubbed his hand on his cheek, a gesture she remembered him using when he was tired or discouraged. "I read them. At first I had to force myself, to be honest. Later, I wanted to know what was happening, even though it was painful. You gave me little glimpses of Phoebe. Little scraps from the fabric of your lives. I looked forward to that."

She didn't answer, remembering the satisfaction she'd felt on that rainy day, when she'd sent Phoebe upstairs with her kitten, Rain, to change out of her wet clothes while she stood in the living room, tearing his letter in four pieces, then eight, then sixteen, and dropping it like confetti in the trash. Satisfaction, and a sense of pleasure at having the matter closed. She'd felt those things, oblivious— unconcerned, even—about what David had been feeling.

"I couldn't lose her," she said. "I was angry with you for a long, long time, but by then I was mostly afraid that if you met her you'd take her away. That's why I stopped writing."

"That was never my intention."

"You didn't intend any of this," Caroline answered. "But it happened anyway."

David Henry sighed, and she imagined him in her deserted apartment, walking from room to room and realizing she was gone for good. *Tell me your plans,* he'd said. *That's all I ask.*

"If I hadn't taken her," she added softly. "You might have chosen differently."

"I didn't stop you," he said, meeting her gaze again. His voice was rough. "I could have. You wore a red coat that day at the memorial service. I saw you and I watched you drive away."

Caroline felt suddenly depleted, almost faint. She did not know what she had hoped for from this night, but when she had imagined this conversation, she had not imagined this contention: his grief and anger, and her own.

"You saw me?" she said.

"I went straight to your apartment afterward. I expected you to be there."

Caroline closed her eyes. She had been driving toward the highway, then, on her way here, to this life. She'd probably missed David Henry's visit by minutes, an hour. How much had turned on that moment. How differently her life might have unfolded.

"You didn't answer me," David said, clearing his throat. " Have you been happy, Caroline? Has Phoebe? Is her health okay? Her heart?"

"Her heart's fine," Caroline said, thinking of the early years of constant worry over Phoebe's health—all the trips to the doctors and dentists and cardiologists and ear, nose, and throat specialists. But she had grown up; she was well; she shot baskets in the driveway and loved to dance. "The books I read when she was still small predicted she'd be dead by now, but she's fine. She was lucky, I guess; she never had a problem with her heart. She loves to sing. She has a cat named Rain. She's learning how to weave. That's where she is right now. At home. Weaving." Caroline shook her head. "She goes to school. Public school, with all the other kids. I had to fight like hell for them to take her. And now she's nearly grown I don't know what will happen. I have a good job. I work part-time in an internal medicine clinic at the hospital. My husband—he travels a lot. Phoebe goes to a group home each day. She has a lot of friends there. She's learning how to do office work. What else can I say? You missed a lot of heartache, sure. But David, you missed a lot of joy."

"I know that," he said. "Better than you think."

"And you?" she asked, struck again by how he'd aged, still trying to assimilate the fact of his presence, here with her, in this small room after all these years. "Have you been happy? Has Norah? And Paul?"

"I don't know," he said slowly. "As happy as anyone ever is, I suppose. Paul's so smart. He could do anything. What he wants is to go to Juilliard and play the guitar. I think he's making a mistake, but Norah doesn't agree. It's caused a lot of tension."

Caroline thought of Phoebe, how she loved to clean and organize, how she sang to herself while washing the dishes or mopping the floors, how she loved music with her whole heart and would never have a chance to play the guitar.

"And Norah?" she asked.

"She owns a travel agency," David said. "She's away a lot too. Like your husband."

"A travel agency?" Caroline repeated. "Norah?"

"I know. It surprised me too. But she's owned it for years now. She's very good at it."

The doorknob turned, and the door swung open a few inches. The curator of the show stuck his head inside, his blue eyes bright with curiosity and concern. He ran one hand through his dark hair nervously, as he spoke. "Dr. Henry?" he said. "You know, there are a lot of people out here. There's a kind of expectation that'll you'll—ah—mingle. Is everything all right?"

David looked at Caroline. He was hesitating, but he was impatient too, and Caroline knew that in an instant he would turn, adjust his tie, and walk away. Something that had endured for years was ending in this moment. *Don't,* she thought, but the curator cleared his throat and gave an uncomfortable laugh, and David said, "No problem. I'm coming. . . . You'll stay, won't you?" he said to Caroline, taking her elbow.

"I need to get home," she said. "Phoebe's waiting."

"Please." He paused outside the door. She met his eyes and saw the same sadness and compassion she remembered from so long ago, when they were both much younger. "There so much to say, and it's been so many years. Please say you'll wait? It shouldn't be long." She felt sick to her stomach, an uneasiness she couldn't place, but she nodded slightly, and David Henry smiled. "Good. We'll have dinner, all right? All this glad talk—I have to do it. But I was wrong, all those years ago. I want more than just the scraps."

His hand was on her arm and they were moving back into the crowd. Caroline couldn't seem to speak. People were waiting, glancing frankly in their direction, curious and whispering. She reached into her purse and handed David the envelope she'd prepared, with the latest photographs of Phoebe. David took it, met her eyes and nodded seriously, and then a slight woman in a black linen dress was taking him by the arm. It was the woman from the audience again, beautiful and faintly hostile, asking another question about form.

Caroline stood where she was for a few minutes, watching him gesture to a photo that resembled the dark branches of a tree, talking to the woman in the black dress. He had been handsome and he was still. Twice he glanced in Caroline's direction and then, seeing her, turned his attention fully to the moment. *Wait,* he'd said. *Please wait.* And he'd expected that she would. The sick feeling rose up in her stomach again. She didn't want to wait; that was it. She'd spent too much of her young life waiting—for recognition, for adventure, for love. It wasn't until she'd turned with Phoebe in her arms and left the home in Louisville, not until she packed up her things and moved away, that her life had really begun. Nothing good had ever come to her from waiting.

David was standing with his head bent, nodding, listening to the woman with dark hair, the envelope clasped in his hands, behind his back. As she watched, he reached up and put the envelope casually in his pocket, as if it contained something trivial and mildly unpleasant—a utility bill, a traffic ticket.

In moments she was outside, hurrying down the stone steps into the night.

It was spring, the air crisp and damp, and Caroline was too agitated to wait for the bus. Instead she walked quickly, block after block, oblivious to the traffic or the people passing or even the slight danger involved in being out by herself at this hour. Moments came back to her, in swirls and glimpses, strange disconnected details. There had been a patch of dark hair over his right ear, and his fingernails had been clipped down to the quick. Square-tipped fingers, she remembered those, but his voice had changed, become more gravelly. It was disconcerting: the images she'd kept in her mind all this time had altered the moment she had seen him.

And for herself? How had she seemed to him tonight? What had he seen, what had he ever seen, of Caroline Lorraine Gill? Of her secret heart? Nothing. Nothing at all. And she'd known that too, she'd known it for years, ever since the moment outside the church when the circle of his life had closed against her, when she had turned and left. In some deep place in her heart, Caroline had

kept alive the silly romantic notion that somehow David Henry
had once known her as no one else ever could. But it was not true.
He had never even glimpsed her.

She had walked five blocks. It had started to rain. Her face was
wet, her coat and shoes. The chill night seemed to have entered her,
seeped beneath her skin. She was near a corner when a 61B
squealed to a stop and she ran to catch it, brushing off her hair, sitting on the cracked plastic of the seat. Lights, neon, and the watery
red blur of headlights moved across the windows. The early spring
air was cool and damp on her face. The bus lumbered through the
streets, picking up speed as it reached the dark stretches of the park,
the long low hill.

She got off in the center of Regent Square. A roar, shouts,
swelled out of the tavern as she passed, and through the glass she
glimpsed the shadowy figures of the players she'd seen earlier,
glasses in their hands now and fists pumping in the air as they gathered around the television. Light from the jukebox cast stripes of
neon blue across the arm of the waitress as she turned from the table
nearest the window. Caroline paused, the wild adrenaline rush of
her meeting with David Henry suddenly gone, dissipating into the
spring night like mist. She felt her own isolation acutely, the figures
in the bar joined by a common purpose, the people moving around
her on the sidewalk drawn along the lines of their lives to places she
could not even imagine.

Tears rose in her eyes. The television screen flickered and another cheer swelled through the glass. Caroline moved off, jostling
a woman carrying a paper sack of groceries, stepping over a pile of
fast-food trash someone had left on the sidewalk. Down the hill and
then up the alley to her house, the city lights giving way to those so
well known and so familiar: the O'Neills, where a golden glow
spilled out over the dogwood tree; the Soulards, with their dark
stretch of garden, and finally the Margolis lawn, moonflowers
growing wild up the hillside in the summertime, beautiful and
chaotic. Houses in a row like so many steps down a hill and then, finally, her own.

She paused in the alley, looking at her tall, narrow house. She had closed the blinds, she was sure of it, but now they were open and she could see clearly through the dining room windows. The chandelier glowed over the table where Phoebe had spread out her yarns. She was bent over the loom, moving the shuttle back and forth, calmly, intently. Rain was curled on her lap, a fluffy orange ball. Caroline watched, worried at how vulnerable her daughter seemed, how exposed to the world that swirled so mysteriously in the darkness behind her. She frowned, trying to remember that moment—her hand turning the narrow plastic stick and the blinds falling closed. Then she glimpsed a movement deeper in the house, a shadow shifting beyond the French doors to the living room.

Caroline caught her breath, startled but not yet alarmed, and then the shadow took shape and she relaxed. This was no stranger but only Al, home early from his travels, puttering through the house. She was surprised and strangely gladdened; Al had been taking more jobs and was often gone two weeks at a time. But here he was; he had come home. He had opened the blinds, giving her this moment to savor, this glimpse of her life, contained within these brick walls, framed by the buffet she had refinished, the ficus tree she had not yet managed to kill off, the layers of glass and paint she'd washed so lovingly all these years. Phoebe glanced up from her work, staring unseeing out the window at the dark wet lawn, running her hand along the cat's soft back. Al walked through the room, holding a cup of coffee in one hand. He stood beside her and gestured to the rug she was weaving with his cup.

It was raining harder now, her hair was soaked, but Caroline didn't move. What had been an emptiness outside the tavern window, a bleak vacancy real enough and fearful, was banished by the sight of her family. Rain hit her cheeks and streaked down the windows, beaded on her good wool coat. She took off her gloves and fumbled in her purse for her keys, then realized that the door would be unlocked. In the darkness of the lawn, as the eternal cars swooshed past on the freeway, their headlights catching in the dense lilac bushes she'd planted as a screen so many years ago, Caroline stood still a moment longer. This was her life. Not the life she had once dreamed of, not a life her younger self would ever have imagined or desired, but the life she was living, with all its complexities. This was her life, built with care and attention, and it was good.

She shut her purse, then. She climbed the steps. She pushed the back door open and went home.

II

SHE WAS A PROFESSOR OF ART HISTORY AT CARNEGIE MELLON and she was asking him about form. *What is beauty?* she wanted to know, her hand on his arm, guiding him across the gleaming oak floors, between the white walls on which his photos hung. *Is beauty to be found in form? Is meaning?* She turned, and her hair swung back; she swept it behind her ear with one hand.

He stared down at her, at the white part in her hair, at her smooth pale face.

"Intersections," he said mildly, glancing back to where Caroline lingered by a photo of Norah on the beach, relieved to see her still there. With an effort, he turned back to the professor. "Convergence. That's what I'm after. I don't take a theoretical approach. I photograph what moves me."

"No one lives outside of theory!" she exclaimed. But she paused in her questions then, eyes narrowing, lightly biting the edge of her lip. He couldn't see her teeth but he imagined them, straight and white and even. The room swirled around him, voices rose and fell; in an instant of silence he became aware that his heart was pounding, that he still held the envelope Caroline had given him. He glanced across the room again—yes, good, she was still there—and tucked it carefully into his shirt pocket; his hands were trembling faintly.

Her name was Lee, the dark-haired woman was saying now. She was the visiting critic-in-residence. David nodded, only half listening. Did Caroline live in Pittsburgh, or had she seen the show advertised and come from somewhere else, from Morgantown or Columbus or Philadelphia? She had mailed letters to him from all these places, and then she had stepped forward out of this anonymous audience, looking so much the same yet older, tauter and tougher somehow, the softness of her youth long gone. *David, don't you know me?* And he had, even when he hadn't let that knowledge in.

He scanned the room for her again and did not see her, and the first threads of panic began, tiny, pervasive, like the filaments of mushrooms hidden in a log. She had come all this way; she had said she would stay; surely she would not leave. Someone passed with a tray of champagne glasses and he took one. The curator was there again, introducing him to the sponsors of the show. David pulled himself together enough to speak intelligently, but he was still thinking of Caroline, hoping to glimpse her at the edge of the room. He had walked away believing that she'd wait, but now, uneasily, he remembered that long-ago morning at the memorial service, Caroline standing on the fringes in her red coat. He remembered the coolness of the new spring air, and the sunny sky, and Paul kicking beneath the blankets in his carrier. He remembered that he'd let her walk away.

"Excuse me," he murmured, interrupting the speaker. He walked with purpose across the hardwood floors to the foyer of the main entrance, where he paused and turned back to survey the gallery room, searching the crowd. Surely, having found her after all this time, he couldn't possibly lose her again.

But she was gone. Beyond the windows, the lights of the city glittered seductively, scattered like sequins all over the undulating, dramatic hills. Somewhere, here or nearby, Caroline Gill washed dishes, swept the floor, paused to look out a darkened window. Loss and grief: they rushed up through him like a wave, so powerful that he leaned against the wall and bent his head, fighting a deep nausea. They were excessive, his emotions, disproportionate. He'd lived without seeing Caroline Gill for many years, after all. He took a deep breath, running through the periodic table in his mind—*silver cadmium indium tin*—but he could not seem to still himself.

David reached into his pocket and took out the envelope she'd given him; maybe she'd left an address or a phone number. Inside were two Polaroids, stiff, the color poor, muted and toned with gray. The first showed Caroline, smiling, her arm around the girl beside her, who wore a stiff blue dress, low-waisted, with a sash. They were outside, posed against the brick wall of a house, and the sun-washed air bleached the scene of color. The girl was sturdy; the dress fit her well but did not make her graceful. Her hair fell around her face in soft waves and she smiled a bright smile, her eyes nearly closed in her pleasure at the camera or whoever stood behind it. Her face was wide, gentle-seeming, and it might have been only the angle of the camera that made her eyes slant slightly upward. *Phoebe on her birthday,* Caroline had written on the back. *Sweet Sixteen.*

He slid the first photo behind the second, more recent one. Here was Phoebe again, playing basketball. She was poised to shoot, her heels lifting off the asphalt. Basketball, the sport Paul refused to play. David looked at the back and checked the envelope again, but there was no address. He drained his champagne and put his glass down on a marble-topped table. The gallery was still crowded, buzzing with conversation. David paused in the doorway and watched for a moment with curious detachment, as if this scene were something he'd stumbled on by accident, nothing to do with him. Then he turned away and stepped out into the soft, cool, rain-dampened air. He slipped Caroline's envelope with its photos in his breast pocket and, without knowing where he was going, he began to walk.

Oakland, his old college neighborhood, was changed and yet not changed. Forbes Field, where he had spent so many afternoons hunched high in the bleachers, soaking in the sun, cheering when bats cracked and the balls rose over the bright green fields, was gone. A new university building, square and blunt, rose into the air where the cheers of thousands had once roared. He paused, turning to the Cathedral of Learning, that slender gray monolith, a shadow against the night sky, to regain his bearings.

He walked on, down the dark city streets, past people emerging from restaurants and theaters. He did not really think about where he was going, though he knew. He saw he'd been caught, frozen for all these years in that moment when he handed Caroline his daughter. His life turned around that single action: a newborn child in his arms—and then he reached out to give her away. It was as if he'd taken pictures all these years since to try and give another moment similar substance, equal weight. He'd wanted to try and still the rushing world, the flow of events, but of course that had been impossible.

He kept walking, agitated, muttering to himself now and then. What had been held still in his heart all this time had been set in motion again by his meeting with Caroline. He thought of Norah, who had become a self-sufficient and powerful woman, who courted corporate accounts with glittery assurance and came in from dinners smelling of wine and rain, traces of laughter, triumph, and success still on her face. She'd had more than one affair over the years, he knew that, and her secrets, like his own, had grown up into a wall between them. Sometimes in the evening he glimpsed, for the briefest instant, the woman he had married: Norah, standing with Paul as an infant in her arms; Norah, her lips stained with berries, tying on an apron; Norah as a fledgling travel agent, staying up late to balance her accounts. But she had shed these selves like skins, and they lived together now like strangers in their vast house.

Paul suffered for it, he knew that. David had tried so hard to give him everything. He had tried to be a good father. They'd collected fossils together, organizing and labeling them and displaying them in the living room. He'd taken Paul fishing at every chance. But however hard he worked to make Paul's life smooth and easy, the fact remained that David had built that life on a lie. He had tried to protect his son from the things he himself had suffered as a child: poverty and worry and grief. Yet his very efforts had created losses David never anticipated. The lie had grown up between them like a rock, forcing them to grow oddly too, like trees twisting around a boulder.

The streets converged, coming together at odd angles, as the city narrowed to the point where the great rivers met, the Monongahela and the Allegheny, their confluence forming the Ohio, which traveled to Kentucky and beyond before it poured itself into the Mississippi and disappeared. He walked to the very tip of the point. As a young man, a student, David Henry had come here often, standing at the edge of land, watching the two rivers converge. Time and again he had stood here with his toes suspended above the dark skin of the river, wondering in a detached way how cold this black water might be, whether he would be strong enough to swim to shore if he fell in. Now, as then, the wind cut through the fabric of his suit, and he looked down, watching the river move between the tips of his shoes. He edged out an inch farther, changing the composition. A glimmer of regret flashed through his weariness: this would be a good photo, but he'd left his camera in the hotel safe.

Far below the water swirled, foamed white against the cement piling, surged away. The arch of his foot, that's where David felt the pressure of the concrete edge. If he fell or jumped and couldn't finally swim to safety, they would find these things: a watch with his father's name inscribed on the back, his wallet with $200 in cash, his driver's license, a pebble from the stream near his childhood home that he had carried with him for thirty years. And the photos, in the envelope tucked into the pocket above his heart.

His funeral would be crowded. The cortege would stretch for blocks.

But it would stop there, the news. Caroline might never know. Nor would word travel any farther, back to where he'd been born.

Even if it did, no one there would recognize his name.

The letter had been waiting for him, tucked behind the empty coffee can of the corner store, one day after school. No one said anything, but everyone watched him, knowing what it was; the University of Pittsburgh logo was clear. He'd carried the envelope upstairs and placed it on the table by his bed, too nervous to open it. He remembered the gray sky of that afternoon, flat and blank beyond the window, broken by the leafless branch of an elm.

For two hours he had not allowed himself to look. And then he did, and the news was good: he had been accepted with a full scholarship. He sat on the edge of the bed, too stunned, too wary of good news—as he would always be, all his life—to allow himself real joy. *It is my pleasure to inform you . . .*

But then he noticed the error, the dull truth rising up and fitting just where he'd expected it, in that hollow place just below his ribs: the name on the letter was not his. The address was right, and every other detail from his date of birth to his social security number—all these were correct. And his first two names, David for his father and Henry for his grandfather, those were fine as well, typed precisely by a secretary who had perhaps been interrupted by a phone call, by a visitor. Or maybe it was only the lovely spring air that made her look up from her work, dreaming herself into the evening, her fiancé there with flowers in his hands and her own heart trembling like a leaf. Then a door slammed. Footsteps sounded, her boss. She started, drew herself together and back into the present. Blinking, she hit the return carriage and went back to work.

David Henry she had typed already, correctly.

But his last name, McCallister, had been lost.

He had never told anyone. He had gone off to college and registered, and no one ever knew. It was, after all, his true name. Still, David Henry was a different person from David Henry McCallister, that much he knew, and it seemed clear it was as David Henry he was meant to go to college, a person with no history, unburdened by the past. A man with a chance to make himself anew.

And he had done just that. The name had allowed it; to some extent, the name had demanded it: strong and a bit patrician. There had been Patrick Henry, after all, a statesman and an orator. In the early days, during those conversations where he had felt himself to be at sea, surrounded by people wealthier and better connected than he would ever be, by people utterly at ease in the world he was so desperately trying to join, he would sometimes allude, though never directly, to a distant but important lineage, invoking false ancestors to stand behind him and lend support.

This was the gift he'd tried to give Paul: a place in the world that no one could question.

The water between his feet was brown, edged with a sickly white foam. The wind rose, and his skin became as porous as his suit. The wind was in his blood, and the swirling water flashed, drew closer, and then there was acid in his throat and he was on his hands and knees, the stones cold beneath his hands, vomiting into the wild gray river, heaving until nothing more could be expelled. He lay there for a long time, in the darkness. Finally, slowly, he stood, wiped the back of his hand against his mouth, and walked back into the city.

. . .

He sat in the Greyhound terminal all night, dozing and jerking awake, and in the morning he caught the first bus to his childhood home in West Virginia, traveling deep into the hills that surrounded him like an embrace. After seven hours, the bus stopped where it always had, on the corner of Main and Vine, and then roared away, leaving David Henry in front of the grocery store. The street was quiet, a newspaper plastered against a telephone pole and weeds growing up through cracks in the sidewalk. He'd worked in this store to earn his room and board above it, the smart kid come down from the hills to study, astonished by the sounds of bells and traffic, the housewives shopping, the schoolchildren clustering to buy sodas at the fountain, the men gathering in the evenings, spitting tobacco and playing cards and passing the time with stories. But that was gone now, all of it. Red and black graffiti covered the plywood-covered windows, bleeding into the grain, unreadable.

Thirst was a fire in David's throat. Across the street, two men, middle-aged, one bald, one with thin graying hair to his shoulders, sat playing checkers on the porch. They looked up, curious, suspicious, and for a moment David saw himself as they would, his pants stained and wrinkled, his shirt a day and night old, his tie gone, his hair flattened from his fitful sleep on the bus. He did not belong here, never had. In the narrow room above the store, books spread out on his bed, he'd been so homesick he couldn't concentrate, and yet when he went back to the mountains, his yearning did not diminish. In the small clapboard house of his parents, set firmly into the hill, the hours stretched and grew, measured out by the tamping of his father's pipe against the chair, his mother's sighs, the stirrings of his sister. There was the life below the creek and the life above it, and loneliness opening everywhere, a dark flower.

He nodded at the men, then turned and started walking, feeling their stares.

A light rain, delicate as mist, began to fall. He walked, though his legs ached. He thought of his bright office, a lifetime or a dream away. It was late afternoon. Norah would still be at work and Paul would be up in his room, pouring his loneliness and anger into music. They expected him home tonight, but he would not be there. He'd have to call, later, once he knew what he was doing. He could get on another bus and go back to them right now. He knew this, but it also seemed impossible for that life to exist in the same world as this one.

The sidewalk, uneven, was soon broken up by lawns on the edge of town, a stop-and-start pattern like some sort of Morse code, abandoned for intervals and then gone entirely. Shallow ditches ran along the edges of the narrow road; he remembered them full of daylilies, swelling orange masses like running flames. He slid his hands under his arms to warm them. It was a season earlier here. The lilacs of Pittsburgh and the warm rain were nowhere. Crusts of snow broke under his feet. He kicked the blackened edges into the ditches, where more snow lingered, broken through with weeds, debris.

He'd reached the local highway. Speeding cars forced him to the grassy shoulder, spraying him with a fine mist of slush. This had once been a quiet road, cars audible for miles before they came in sight, and usually it was a familiar face behind the windshield, the car slowing, stopping, and a door swinging open to let him in. He was known, his family was, and after the small talk—*How's your mama, your daddy; how's the garden doing this year?*—a silence would fall, in which the driver and the other passengers thought carefully about what might be said and what might not to this boy so smart he had a scholarship, to this boy with a sister too sick to go to school. There was in the mountains, and perhaps in the world at large, a theory of compensation that held that for everything given something else was immediately and visibly lost. *Well, you've got the smarts, even if your cousin did get the looks.* Compliments, seductive as flowers, thorny with their opposites: *Yes, you may be smart but you sure are ugly; You may look nice but you didn't get a brain.* Compensation; balance in the universe. David heard accusation in each remark about his studies—he'd taken too much, taken everything—and in the cars and trucks silence had swelled until it seemed impossible that a human voice could ever break it.

The road curved, then curved again: June's dancing road. The hillsides steepened and streams cascaded down and the houses grew steadily sparser, poorer. Mobile homes appeared, set into the hills like tarnished dime-store jewelry, turquoise and silver and yellow faded to the color of cream. Here was the sycamore, the heart-shaped rock, the curve where three white crosses, decorated with faded flowers and ribbons, had been pounded into the earth. He turned and went up the next stream, his stream. The path was overgrown; almost, but not quite, disappeared.

It took him nearly an hour to reach the old house, now weather-beaten a soft gray, the roof sagging at the center of the ridgepole and some of the shingles missing. David stopped, taken so powerfully into the past that he expected to see them again: his mother coming down the steps with a galvanized tin tub to collect water for the laundry, his sister sitting on the porch, and the sound of the ax striking logs from where his father chopped firewood, just out of sight. He had left for school and June had died, and his parents had stayed on here as long as they could, reluctant to leave the land. But they had not thrived, and then his father died, too young, and his mother finally went north, traveling to her sister and the promise of work in the auto factories. David had come home from Pittsburgh rarely and never again since his mother died. The place was as familiar as breath but as far from his life now as the moon.

The wind rose. He walked up the steps. The door hung crookedly on its hinges and would not close. The air inside was chilly, musty. It was a single room, the sleeping loft compromised now by the sagging ridgepole. The walls were water-stained; through chinks, he glimpsed pale sky. He'd helped his father put this roof on, sweat pouring down their faces and sap on their hands, their hammers rising into the sun, into the sharp fragrance of fresh-cut cedar.

As far as David knew, no one had been here for years. Yet a frying pan sat on the old stove, cold, the grease congealed but not, when he leaned to smell it, rancid. In the corner there was an old iron bed covered with a worn quilt like his grandmother and his mother had made. The cloth was cool, faintly damp, beneath his hand. There was no mattress, only a thick layering of blankets against boards set into the frame. The plank floor was swept clean, and there were three crocuses in a jar in the window.

Someone was living here. A breeze moved through the room, stirring the paper cutouts that hung everywhere—from the ceiling, from the windows, above the bed. David walked around, examining them with a growing sense of wonder. They were a little like the snowflakes he'd cut out in school, but infinitely more intricate and detailed, showing entire scenes to the last detail: the state fair, a tidy living room before a fire, a picnic with exploding fireworks. Delicate and precise, they gave the old house an air of rustling mystery. He touched the scalloped edge of a hay-wagon scene, the girls wearing lace-trimmed bonnets, the boys with their pants rolled to their knees. Ferris wheels, fluttering carousels, cars traveling down highways: these hung above the bed, moving lightly in the drafts, as fragile as wings.

Who had made these with such skill and patience? He thought of his own photographs: he tried so hard to catch each moment, pin it in place, make it last, but when the images emerged in the darkroom they were already altered. Hours, days had passed by then; he had become a slightly different person. Yet he had wanted so much to catch the fluttering veil, to capture the world even as it disappeared, once and again and then again.

He sat on the hard bed. His head still throbbed. He lay down and pulled the damp quilt around him. There was a soft gray light in all the windows. The bare table, and the stove: everything smelled faintly of mildew. The walls were covered with layers of newspaper that had begun to peel. His family had been so poor; everyone they knew had been poor. It wasn't a crime, but it might as well have been. That's why things got saved, old engines and tin cans and milk bottles scattered across the lawns and hills: a spell against need, a hedge against want. When David was small, a boy named Daniel Brinkerhoff had climbed into an old refrigerator and suffocated to death. David remembered the hushed voices, and then the body of a boy his own age lying in a cabin much like this one, with candles lit. The mother had wept, which had made no sense to him; he had been too young to understand grief, the magnitude of death. But he remembered what had been said, outside but within his mother's hearing, by the anguished father who had lost his son: *Why my child? He was whole, he was strong. Why not that sickly girl? If it had to be someone, why not her?*

He closed his eyes. It was so quiet. He thought of all the sounds that filled up his life in Lexington: footsteps and voices in the hallways and the phone ringing, shrill in his ear; his pager beeping through the sounds of the radio as he drove; and at home, always, Paul on the guitar and Norah with the phone cord wrapped around one wrist as she talked to clients; and in the middle of the night more calls, he was needed at the hospital, he must come. And, rising in the darkness, the cold, he went.

Not here. Here there was only the sound of the wind fluttering the old leaves and, distantly, the soft murmuring of water in the stream beneath the ice. A branch tapped on the exterior wall. Cold, he lifted himself up, rising on his heels and the upper part of his back so he could tug the quilt free and pull it more fully over him. The photos in his pocket poked his chest as he turned, pulling the quilt closer. Still, he shivered for a few minutes longer, from the cold and the residue of travel, and when he closed his eyes he thought of the two rivers meeting, converging, and the dark waters swirling. Not to fall but to jump: that was what had hung there in the balance.

He closed his eyes. Just for a few minutes, to rest. There was, beneath the mustiness and mildew, the scent of something sweet, sugary. His mother had bought sugar in town, and he could almost taste the birthday cake, yellow and dense, so rich and sweet it seemed to explode in his mouth. Neighbors from below, their voices carrying all the way up the hollow, the dresses of the women multicolored and joyous, brushing against the tall grass. The men in their dark trousers and their boots, the children scattering wildly, shouting, across the yard, and later they all gathered and made ice cream, packed in salty brine beneath the porch, freezing hard, until they lifted the icy metal lid and scooped the sweet cold cream high into their bowls.

Maybe that was after June was born, after her baptism maybe, that day with the ice cream. June was like other babies, her small hands waving in the air, brushing against his face when he leaned down to kiss her. In the heat of that summer day, ice cream cooling under the porch, they celebrated. Fall came, and winter, and June did not sit up and did not, and then it was her first birthday and she was too weak to walk far. Fall came again and a cousin visited with her son, almost the same age, her son not only walking but running through the rooms and starting to talk, and June was still sitting, watching the world so quietly. They knew, then, that something was wrong. He remembered his mother watching the little boy cousin, tears sliding silently down her face for a long time before she took a deep breath and turned back into the room and went on. This was the grief he had carried with him, heavy as a stone in his heart. This was the grief he had tried to spare Norah and Paul, only to create so many others.

"David," his mother had said that day, drying her eyes briskly, not wanting him to see her cry, "pick up those papers from the table and go outside for wood and water. Do it right now. Make yourself useful."

And he had. And they had all gone on, that day and every day. They had drawn into themselves, not even visiting people except for the rare christening or funeral, until the day Daniel Brinkerhoff had shut himself in the refrigerator. They came home from that wake in the dark, working their way up the streamside path by feel, by memory, June in his father's arms, and his mother had never left the mountain again, not until the day she moved to Detroit. . . .

• • •

"Don't suppose you're anyways useful," the voice was saying, and David, still half asleep, not sure if he was dreaming or hearing voices in the wind, shifted at the tugging at his wrists, at the muttering voice, and ran his dry tongue against the roof of his mouth. Their lives were hard, the days long and full of work, and there was no time and no patience for grief. You had to move on, that was all you could do, and since talking about her would not bring June back, they had never mentioned her again. David turned and his wrists hurt. Startled, he half woke, his eyes opening and drifting over the room.

She was standing at the stove, just a few feet away, olive fatigues tight around her slim hips, flaring fuller around her thighs. She wore a sweater the color of rust shot through with luminous strands of orange, and over this a man's green-and-black plaid flannel shirt. She had cut the fingertips from her gloves, and she moved around the stove with deft efficiency, poking at some eggs in the frying pan. It had grown dark outside—he had slept a long time—and candles were strewn around the room. Yellow light softened everything. The delicate paper scenes stirred softly.

Grease spattered and the girl's hand flew up. He lay still for several minutes, watching her, every detail vivid: the black stove handles his mother had scrubbed, and this girl's bitten nails, and the flicker of candles in the window. She reached to the shelf above the stove for salt and pepper, and he was struck by the way light traveled across her skin, her hair, as she moved in and out of shadow, by the fluid nature of everything she did.

He had left his camera in the hotel safe.

He tried to sit up then, but was stopped again by his wrists. Puzzled, he turned his head: a filmy red chiffon scarf tied him to one bedpost; the strings from a mop to the other. She noticed his movement and turned, tapping her palm lightly with a wooden spoon.

"My boyfriend's coming back any minute now," she announced.

David let his head fall back heavily on the pillow. She was slight, no older and perhaps even younger than Paul, out here in this abandoned house. *Shacking up,* he thought, wondering about the boyfriend, realizing for the first time that maybe he ought to be afraid.

"What's your name?" he asked.

"Rosemary," she said, and then looked worried. "You can believe that or not," she added.

"Rosemary," he said, thinking of the piney bush Norah had planted in a sunny spot, its wands of fragrant needles, "I wonder if you would be good enough to untie me."

"No." Her voice was swift and bright. "No way."

"I'm thirsty," he said.

She looked at him for a moment; her eyes were warm, sherry-tinted brown, wary. Then she went outside, releasing a wedge of cold air into the room, setting all the paper cuttings fluttering. She came back with a metal cup of water from the stream.

"Thanks," he said, "but I can't drink this lying down."

She attended to the stove for a minute, turning the sputtering eggs, then rummaged through a drawer, coming up with a plastic straw from some fast-food place, dirty at one end, which she thrust into the metal cup.

"I suppose you'll use it," she said, "if you're thirsty enough."

He turned his head and sipped, too thirsty to do more than note the taste of dust in the water. She slid the eggs onto a blue metal plate speckled with white and sat down at the wooden table. She ate quickly, pushing the eggs onto a plastic fork with the forefinger of her left hand, delicately, without thinking, as if he weren't in the room at all. In that moment he understood somehow that the boyfriend was fiction. She was living here alone.

He drank until the straw sputtered dry, water like a dirty river in his throat.

"My parents used to own this place," he said, when he finished. "In fact, I still do own it. I have the deed in a safe. Technically, you're trespassing."

She smiled at this and put her fork down carefully in the center of the plate. "You come here to claim it then? Technically?"

Her hair, her cheeks, caught the flickering light. She was so young, yet there was something fierce and strong about her too, something lonely but determined.

"No." He thought of his strange journey from an ordinary morning in Lexington—Paul taking forever in the bathroom and Norah frowning as she balanced the checkbook at the counter, coffee steaming—to the art show, and the river, and now here.

"Then why did you come?" she said, pushing the plate to the

middle of the table. Her hands were rough, her fingernails broken. He was surprised that they could have made the delicate, complex paper art that filled the room.

"My name is David Henry McCallister." His real name, so long unspoken.

"I don't know any McCallisters," she said. "But I'm not from around here."

"How old are you?" he asked. "Fifteen?"

"Sixteen," she corrected. And then, primly, "Sixteen or twenty or forty, take your pick."

"Sixteen," he repeated. "I have a son older than you. Paul."

A son, he thought, and a daughter.

"Is that so?" she said, indifferent.

She picked up the fork again, and he watched her eating the eggs, taking such delicate bites and chewing them carefully, and with a sudden powerful rush he was living another moment in this same house, watching his sister June eat eggs in this same way. It was the year she died, and it was hard for her to sit up at the table, but she did; she had dinner with them every night, lamplight in her blond hair and her hands moving slowly, with deliberate grace.

"Why don't you untie me," he suggested softly, his voice hoarse with emotion. "I'm a doctor. Harmless."

"Right." She stood and carried her blue metal plate to the sink.

She was pregnant, he realized with shock, catching her profile as she turned to take the soap from the shelf. Not very far along, just four or five months, he guessed.

"Look, I really am a doctor. There's a card in my wallet. Take a look."

She didn't answer, just washed her plate and fork and dried her hands carefully on a towel. David thought how strange it was that he should be here, lying once again in this place where he'd been conceived and born and mostly raised, how strange that his own family should have disappeared so completely and that this girl, so young and tough and so clearly lost, should have tied him to the bed.

She crossed the room and pulled his wallet from his pocket. One by one she placed his things on the table: cash, credit cards, the miscellaneous notes and bits of paper.

"This says photographer," she said, reading his card in the wavering light.

"That's right," he said. "I'm that, too. Keep going."

"Okay," she said a moment later, holding up his ID. "So you're a doctor. So what? What difference does that make?"

Her hair was pulled back in a ponytail and stray wisps fell around her face; she pushed them back over her ear.

"It means I'm not going to hurt you, Rosemary. *First, do no harm.*"

She gave him a quick, assessing glance. "You'd say that no matter what. Even if you meant me harm."

He studied her, the untidy hair, the clear dark eyes.

"There are some pictures," he said. "Somewhere here. . . ." He shifted and felt the sharp edge of the envelope through the cloth of his shirt pocket. "Please. Take a look. These are pictures of my daughter. She's just about your age."

When she slipped her hand into his pocket, he felt the heat of her again and smelled her scent, natural but clean. What was sugary? he wondered, remembering his dream and the tray of cream puffs that had passed by at the opening of his show.

"What's her name?" Rosemary asked, studying first one photo, then the other.

"Phoebe."

"Phoebe. That's pretty. She's pretty. Is she named for her mother?"

"No," David said, remembering the night of her birth, Norah telling him just before she went under the names she wanted for her child. Caroline, listening, had heard this and had honored it. "She was named for a great-aunt. On her mother's side. Someone I didn't know."

"I was named after both my grandmothers," Rosemary said softly. Her dark hair fell across her pale cheek again and she brushed it back, her gloved finger lingering near her ear, and David imagined her sitting with her family around another lamplit table. He wanted to put his arm around her, take her home, protect her. "Rose on my father's side, Mary on my mother's."

"Does your family know where you are?" he asked.

She shook her head. "I can't go back," she said, both anguish and anger woven in her voice. "I can't ever go back. I won't."

She looked so young, sitting at the table, her hands closed in loose fists and her expression dark, worried. "Why not?" he asked.

She shook her head and tapped the photo of Phoebe. "You say she's my age?"

"Close, I'm guessing. She was born March sixth, 1964."

"I was born in February, 1966." Her hands trembled a little as she put the photos down. "My mom was planning a party for me: sweet sixteen. She's into all the pink frilly stuff."

David watched her swallow, brush her hair behind her ear again, gaze out the dark window. He wanted to comfort her some-how, just as he had so often wanted to comfort others—June, his mother, Norah—but now, as then, he couldn't. Stillness and mo-tion: there was something here, something he needed to know, but his thoughts kept scattering. He felt caught, as fixed in time as any of his photographs, and the moment that held him was deep and painful. He had only wept once for June, standing with his mother on the hillside in the raw evening wind, holding the Bible in one hand as he recited the Lord's Prayer over the newly turned earth. He wept with his mother, who hated the wind from that day on, and then they hid their grief away and went on. That was the way of things, and they did not question it.

"Phoebe is my daughter," he said, astonished to hear himself speaking, yet compelled beyond reason to tell his story, this secret he'd kept for so many years. "But I haven't seen her since the day she was born." He hesitated, then forced himself to say it. "I gave her away. She has Down's syndrome, which means she's retarded. So I gave her away. I never told anyone."

Rosemary's glance was darting, shocked. "I see that as harm," she said.

"Yes," he said. "So do I."

They were silent for a long time. Everywhere David looked he was reminded of his family: the warmth of June's breath against his cheek, his mother singing as she folded laundry at the table, his fa-ther's stories echoing against these walls. Gone, all of them gone, and his daughter too. He struggled against grief from old habit, but tears slipped down his cheeks; he could not stop them. He wept for June, and he wept for the moment in the clinic when he handed Phoebe to Caroline Gill and watched her turn away. Rosemary sat at the table, grave and still. Once their eyes met and he held her gaze, a strangely intimate moment. He remembered Caroline watching him from the doorway as he slept, her face softened with love for him. He might have walked with her down the museum steps and back into her life, but he'd lost that moment too.

"I'm sorry," he said, trying to pull himself together. "I haven't been here for a long time."

She didn't answer and he wondered if he sounded crazy to her. He took a deep breath.

"When is your baby due?" he asked.

Her dark eyes widened in surprise. "Five months, I guess."

"You left him behind, didn't you?" David said softly. "Your boyfriend. Maybe he didn't want the baby."

She turned her head, but not before he saw her eyes fill.

"I'm sorry," he said at once. "I don't mean to pry."

She shook her head a little. "It's okay. No big deal."

"Where is he?" he asked, keeping his voice soft. "Where's home?"

"Pennsylvania," she said, after a long pause. She took a deep breath, and David understood that his story, his grief, had made it possible for her to reveal her own. "Near Harrisburg. I used to have an aunt here in town," she went on. "My mother's sister, Sue Wallis. She's dead now. But when I was a little girl we came here, to this place. We used to wander all over these hills. This house was always empty. We used to come here and play, when we were kids. Those were the best times. This was the best place I could think of."

He nodded, remembering the rustling silence of the woods. Sue Wallis. An image stirred, a woman walking up the hill, carrying a peach pie beneath a towel.

"Untie me," he said, softly still.

She laughed bitterly, wiping her eyes. "Why?" she asked. "Why would I do that, with us alone up here and no one around? I'm not a total idiot."

She rose and gathered her scissors and a small stack of paper from the shelf above the stove. Shards of white flew as she cut. The wind moved, and the candle flames flickered in the drafts. Her face was set, resolute, focused and determined like Paul when he played music, setting himself against David's world and seeking another place. Her scissors flashed and a muscle worked in her jaw. It had not occurred to him before that she might harm him.

"Those paper things you make," he said. "They're beautiful."

"My Grandma Rose taught me. It's called *scherenschnitte*. She grew up in Switzerland, where I guess they make these all the time."

"She must be worried about you."

"She's dead. She died last year." She paused, concentrating on her cutting. "I like making these. It helps me remember her."

David nodded. "Do you start with an idea?" he asked.

"It's in the paper," she said. "I don't invent them so much as find them."

"You find them. Yes." He nodded. "I understand that. When I take pictures, that's how it is. They're already there, and I just discover them."

"That's right," Rosemary said, turning the paper. "That's exactly right."

"What are you going to do with me?" he asked.

She didn't speak, kept cutting.

"I need to piss," he said.

He had hoped to shock her into speaking, but it was also painfully true. She studied him for a moment. Then she put her scissors down, her paper, and disappeared without comment. He heard her moving outside, in the darkness. She came back with an empty peanut butter jar.

"Look," he said. "Rosemary. Please. Untie me."

She put the jar down and picked up the scissors again.

"How could you give her away?" she asked.

Light flashed on the blades of her scissors. David remembered the glint of the scalpel as he made the episiotomy, how he'd floated out of himself to watch the scene from above, how the events of that night had set his life in motion, one thing leading to another, doors opening where none had been and others closing, until he reached this particular moment, with a stranger seeking the intricate design hidden in her paper and waiting for him to answer, and there was nothing he could do and nowhere he might go.

"Is that what worries you?" he asked. "That you'll give your baby away?"

"Never. I'll never do that," she said fiercely, her face set. So someone had done that to her, one way or another, and tossed her out like jetsam to sink or swim. To be sixteen and pregnant and alone, to sit at this table.

"I realized it was wrong," David said. "But by then it was too late."

"It's never too late."

"You're sixteen," he said. "Sometimes, trust me, it's too late."

Her expression tightened for an instant and she didn't answer, just kept cutting, and in the silence David started talking again, trying to explain at first about the snow and the shock and the scalpel flashing in the harsh light. How he had stood outside himself and watched himself moving in the world. How he had woken up every morning of his life for eighteen years thinking maybe today, maybe this was the day he would put things right. But Phoebe was gone and he couldn't find her, so how could he possibly tell Norah? The secret had worked its way through their marriage, an insidious vine, twisting; she drank too much and then she began to have affairs, that sleazy realtor at the beach and then others; he'd tried not to notice, to forgive her, for he knew that in some real sense the fault was his. Photo after photo, as if he could stop time or make an image powerful enough to obscure the moment when he turned and handed his daughter to Caroline Gill.

His voice, rising and falling. Once he began he couldn't stop, any more than he could stop rain, the stream running down the mountainside, or the fish, persistent and elusive as memory, flashing beneath the ice across the stream. *Bodies in motion,* he thought, that old scrap of high school physics. He had handed his daughter to Caroline Gill and that act had led him here, years later, to this girl in motion of her own, this girl who had decided *yes,* a brief moment of release in the back of a car or in the room of a silent house, this girl who had stood up later, adjusting her clothes, with no knowledge of how that moment was already shaping her life.

She cut and listened. Her silence made him free. He talked like a river, like a storm, words rushing through the old house with a force and life he could not stop. At some point he began to weep again, and he could not stop that either. Rosemary made no comment whatsoever. He talked until the words slowed, ebbed, finally ceased.

Silence welled.

She did not speak. The scissors glinted; the half-cut paper slid from the table to the floor as she stood. He closed his eyes, fear rising, because he had seen anger in her eyes, because everything that happened had been his fault.

Her footsteps and then the metal, cold and bright as ice, slid against his skin.

The tension in his wrists released. He opened his eyes to see her stepping back, her eyes, bright and wary, fixed on his, her scissors glinting.

"All right," she said. "You're free."

III

P AUL," SHE CALLED. HER HEELS WERE A SHARP STACCATO ON
the polished stairs and then she was standing in the doorway,
slender and stylish in a navy suit with a narrow skirt and thickly
padded shoulders. Through barely opened eyes, Paul saw what she
was seeing: clothes scattered on the floor, a cascade of albums and
sheet music, his old guitar propped in a corner. She shook her head
and sighed. "Get up, Paul," she said. "Do it now."

"Sick," he mumbled, pulling the covers over his head, making
his voice hoarse. Through the loose weave of the summer blanket he could still see her, hands on her hips. The early light caught
in her hair, frosted yesterday, glinting with red and gold. He'd
heard her on the phone with Bree, describing the little strands of
hair wrapped up in foil and baked.

She'd been sautéing ground beef as she talked, her voice calm,
her eyes red from crying, earlier. His father had disappeared, and
for three days no one knew if he was dead or alive. Then last night
his father had come home, walking through the door as if he'd
never been gone, and their tense voices had traveled up the stairs for
hours.

"Look," she said now, glancing at her watch. "I know you're not sick, anymore than I am. I'd like to sleep all day. God *knows* I'd like to. But I can't, and neither can you. So get yourself out of that bed and get dressed. I'll drop you at school."

"My throat's on fire," he insisted, making his voice as rough as possible.

She hesitated, closed her eyes, and sighed again, and he knew he'd won.

"If you stay home, you stay home," she warned. "There'll be no hanging out with that quartet of yours. And—listen to me—you have to clean up this pigsty. I'm serious, Paul. I have all I can deal with on my plate right now."

"Right," he croaked. "Yep. I will."

She stood a moment longer without speaking. "This is hard," she said at last. "It's hard for me too. I'd stay with you, Paul, but I promised to take Bree to the doctor."

He pushed up on his elbows then, alerted by her somber tone. "Is she okay?"

His mother nodded, but she was looking out the window and wouldn't meet his eyes. "I think so. But she's having some tests and she's a little worried. Which is natural. I promised her last week that I'd go. Before all this with your father."

"It's okay," Paul said, remembering to make his voice sound hoarse. "You should go with her. I'll be okay." He spoke with assurance, but part of him hoped she'd pay no attention, that she'd stay home instead.

"It shouldn't take long. I'll come straight back."

"Where's Dad?"

She shook her head. "I have no idea. Not here. But how unusual is that?"

Paul didn't answer, just lay back down and closed his eyes. *Not very,* he thought. *Not unusual at all.*

His mother put her hand on his cheek lightly, but he didn't move, and then she was gone, leaving a coolness on his face where her hand had rested. Downstairs, doors slammed; Bree's voice rose from the foyer. Over these last years they'd become very close, his mother and Bree, so close they'd even started to look alike, Bree with her hair streaked too, a briefcase swinging from her hand. She was still a very cool and together person, she was still the one who'd take a risk, the one who told him to follow his heart and apply to Juilliard like he wanted. Everyone liked Bree: her sense of adventure, her exuberance. She brought in a lot of business. She and his mother were complementary forces, he'd heard her say. And Paul saw that. Bree and his mother moved through their lives like point and counterpoint, one impossible without the other, one pulling always against the other. So, their voices, mingling, back and forth, and then his mother's unhappy laugh, the door slamming. He sat up, stretching. Free.

The house was quiet, the hot water heater ticking. Paul went downstairs and stood in the cool light of the refrigerator, eating macaroni and cheese from a Corningware dish with his fingers, studying the shelves. Not much. In the freezer he found six boxes of Girl Scout cookies, thin mints. He ate a handful, rinsing down the cool chocolate disks with milk drunk straight from the plastic jug. Another handful, then, the milk jug swinging from his hand, he walked back through the living room, where his father's blankets were piled neatly on the couch, to the den.

The girl was still there, sleeping. He slipped another cookie in his mouth, letting the mint and chocolate melt slowly, studying her. Last night the familiar angry voices of his parents had risen up to his room, and although they were arguing, the stone he had felt in his throat at the thought of his father lying dead somewhere, his father gone forever—immediately, that had dissolved. Paul got out of bed and started down the stairs, but on the landing he stopped, taking in the scene: his father in a white shirt that had gone unwashed for days, his dress pants stained everywhere with mud, limp and bedraggled, a full beard on his face and his hair barely combed; his mother in her peach satin robe and slippers, curved around her folded arms, her eyes narrowed, and this girl, this stranger, standing in the doorway in a black coat that was too big, clutching at the edges of the sleeves with her fingertips. His parents' voices mingling, rising. This girl had looked up, past the swirling anger. Her eyes had met his. He'd stared, taking her in: her paleness and her uncertain glance, her ears so delicately sculpted. Her eyes were such a clear brown, so tired. He had wanted to walk down the steps and cup her face in his hands.

"Three days," his mother was saying, "and then you come home like—my God, look at you, David—like *this* and with this girl. Pregnant, you say? And I'm supposed to take her in, no questions asked?"

The girl flinched then and looked away, and Paul's eyes had fallen to her stomach, flat enough beneath the coat, except that she had rested one hand there protectively and he saw the slight swell beneath her sweater. He stood very still. The argument went on; it seemed to last a long time. Finally, his mother, silent and tight-lipped, had pulled sheets, blankets, pillows from the linen closet and thrown them down the stairs at his father, who had taken the girl very formally by the elbow and led her to the den.

Now she slept on the fold-out couch, her head turned to the side, one hand resting near her face. He studied her, the way her eyelids moved, the slow rise and fall of her chest. She was lying on her back; her belly rose up like a low wave. Paul's own flesh quickened, and he was afraid. He'd had sex with Lauren Lobeglio six times since March. She had hung around during quartet rehearsals for weeks, watching him, not speaking: a pretty, wasted, eerie chick. One afternoon she had stayed after the rest of the band left, and it was just the two of them in the silence of the garage, light moving through the leaves outside and making patterns of flickering shadow on the concrete floor. She was strange but sexy, with her long thick hair, her black eyes. He had sat in the old lawn chair, adjusting the strings on his guitar and wondering if he should go over to where she was standing by the wall of tools and kiss her.

But it was Lauren who crossed the room. She stood in front of him for a heartbeat, then slid onto his lap, her skirt hiking up, revealing slender white legs. This was what people said: that Lauren Lobeglio would do it if she liked you. He'd never really thought it was true, but there he was, slipping his hands beneath her T-shirt, her skin so warm, her breasts so soft beneath his hands.

It wasn't right. He knew that, but it was like falling: once you started you couldn't stop until something stopped you. She hung around like before, except now the air was charged, and when they were alone he would cross the room and kiss her, sliding his hands up the smooth satin skin of her back.

The girl in the bed sighed, her lips working. *Jailbait,* his friends warned him about Lauren. Duke Madison especially, who had dropped out of school to marry his girlfriend the year before, who hardly played the piano anymore and had a haggard glancing-at-the-clock kind of look when he did. *Get her pregnant and you're more than screwed.*

Paul studied this girl, her paleness and long dark hair, her scattered freckles. Who was she? His father, methodical, predictable as a ticking clock, had simply disappeared. On the second day his mother called the police, who had remained noncommittal and jocular, until his father's briefcase was found in the cloakroom of the museum in Pittsburgh, his suitcase and camera in his hotel. Then they got serious. He'd been seen at the reception, arguing with a woman with dark hair. She turned out to be an art critic; her review of the show had been in the Pittsburgh papers, and it wasn't pretty.

Nothing personal, she had told the police.

Then last night a key had turned in the lock and his father had walked into the house with this pregnant girl he claimed to have just met, a girl whose presence he would not explain. She needs help, he said, tersely

There are plenty of ways to help, his mother had pointed out, talking about the girl as if she weren't standing in the foyer in her too-big coat. *You give money. You take her to a place for unmarried mothers. You don't disappear for days on end without a word and then show up with a pregnant stranger. My God, David, don't you have any idea? We called the police! We thought you were dead.*

Maybe I was, he said, the strangeness of his answer quelling his mother's protests, fixing Paul in his place on the stairs.

And now she slept, oblivious, and within her the baby grew in its dark sea. Paul reached out, touched her hair lightly, then let his hand fall. He had a sudden urge to get into the bed with her, to hold her. It wasn't like with Lauren somehow, it wasn't about sex; he just wanted to feel her near him, her skin and her warmth. He wanted to wake up next to her, to run his hand over the rising curve of her belly, to touch her face and hold her hand.

To find out what she knew about his father.

Her eyes blinked open, and for a moment she stared at him, unseeing. Then she sat up quickly, pushing her hands through her hair. She was wearing one of his old faded T-shirts, blue with the Kentucky Wildcats logo across the front, that he'd worn a couple of years ago while running track. Her arms were long and lean, and he caught a glimpse of her underarm, stubbled and tender, and of the smooth rising curve of her breast.

"What are you looking at?" She swung her feet to the floor.

He shook his head, unable to speak.

"You're Paul," she said. "Your father told me about you."

"He did?" he asked, hating the need in his voice. "What'd he say?"

She shrugged, pushing her hair behind her ears, and stood up. "Let's see. You're headstrong. You hate him. You're a genius on the guitar."

Paul felt the heat rising to his face. Usually, he thought his father didn't even see him, or saw only the ways he didn't measure up.

"I don't hate him," he said. "It's the other way around."

She leaned down to gather up the blankets, then sat with them in her arms, looking around.

"This is nice," she said. "Someday I'm going to have a place like this."

Paul gave a startled laugh. "You're pregnant," he said. It was his own fear in the room, the fear that rose up each time when, trembling, he crossed the garage to Lauren Lobeglia, drawn by the irresistible power of his desire.

"Right. So what? I'm pregnant. Not dead."

She spoke defiantly but she sounded scared, as scared as Paul sometimes felt himself, waking up in the middle of the night, dreaming of Lauren, all warmth and silk and her voice low in his ear, knowing he could never stop though they were heading for disaster.

"You might as well be," he said.

She looked up sharply, actual tears in her eyes, as if he'd slapped her.

"I'm sorry," he said. "I didn't mean anything."

She kept crying.

"What are you doing here anyway?" he demanded, angry at her tears, at her very presence. "I mean, who do you think you are to latch on to my father and show up here?"

"I don't think I'm anyone," she said, but his tone had startled her and she dried her tears, grew tougher and more distant. "And I didn't ask to come here. It was your father's idea."

"That doesn't make sense," Paul said. "Why would he do that?"

She shrugged. "How should I know? I was living in that old house where he grew up, and he said I couldn't stay there anymore. And it's his place, right? What could I say? In the morning we walked into town and he bought bus tickets and here we are. The bus was a drag. It took forever to make all the crazy connections."

She pulled her long hair back and yanked it into a ponytail, and Paul watched her, thinking how pretty her ears were, wondering if his father thought she was pretty too.

"What old house?" Paul asked, feeling something sharp and hot in his chest.

"Like I said. The one where he grew up. I was living there. I didn't have anywhere else to go," she added, glancing at the floor.

Paul felt something fill him then, some emotion he couldn't name. Envy, maybe, that this girl, this thin pale stranger with the beautiful ears, had been to a place that mattered to his father, a place he himself had never seen. *I'll take you there someday,* his father had promised, but years had passed and he had never mentioned it again. Yet Paul had never forgotten it, the way his father had sat down amid the wreckage of his darkroom, picking up the photos one by one, so carefully. *My mother, Paul, your grandmother. She had a hard life. I had a sister, did you know that? Her name was June. She was good at singing, at music, just like you.* He remembered to this day the way his father smelled that morning, clean, already dressed for the hospital, yet sitting on the floor of the darkroom, talking, like he had all the time in the world. Telling a story Paul had never heard.

"My father's a doctor," Paul said. "He just likes to help people."

She nodded and then looked at him straight on, her expression full of something—pity for him, that's what he read there, and the thin hot flare traveled to his fingertips.

"What?" he asked.

She shook her head. "Nothing. You're right. I needed help. That's all."

A strand of hair slipped from her ponytail and fell across her face, very dark with reddish highlights, and he remembered how soft it had been when he touched it as she slept, soft and warm, and he resisted an urge to reach over and brush it behind her ear.

"My father had a sister," Paul said, remembering the story and his father's soft steady voice, pushing to see if it was true, that she'd been there.

"I know. June. She's buried on a hillside above the house. We went there too."

The thin flare widened, making his breathing low and shallow. Why should it matter that she knew this? What difference did it make? And yet he could not stop imagining her there, walking up some hillside, following his father to this place he'd never seen.

"So what?" he said. "So what that you've been there, so what?"

She seemed about to speak for a moment, but then she turned and started walking across the room to the kitchen. Her dark hair, in a long rope, bounced against her back. Her shoulders were lean and delicate, and she walked slowly, with careful grace, like a dancer.

"Wait," Paul called after her, but when she paused he did not know what to say.

"I needed a place to stay," she said softly, looking back over her shoulder. "That's all there is to know about me, Paul."

He watched her go into the kitchen, heard the refrigerator door open and shut. Then he went upstairs and got the folder he'd hidden in his bottom drawer, full of the photos he'd saved from the night he'd talked with his father.

He took the pictures and his guitar and went out on the porch, shirtless, barefoot. He sat on the swing and played, keeping an eye on this girl as she moved through the rooms inside: the kitchen, the living room, the dining room. But she did very little, just ate some yogurt and then stood for a long time in front of his mother's bookshelves before she pulled down a novel and sat on the couch.

He kept on playing. It soothed him, the music, in a way that nothing else did. He entered some other plane where his hands seemed to move automatically. The next note was right there, and then the next and the next. He reached the end and stopped, eyes closed, letting the notes die away into the air.

Never again. Not this music, this moment, ever again.

"Wow." He opened his eyes and she was leaning against the doorjamb. She pushed open the screen door and came out onto the porch, carrying a glass of water, and sat down. "Wow, your father was right," she said. "That was amazing."

"Thanks," he said, ducking his head to hide his pleasure, hitting a chord. The music had released him; he was not so angry anymore. "What about you? You play?"

"No. I used to take piano lessons."

"We have a piano," he said, nodding at the door. "Go ahead."

She smiled, though her eyes were still serious. "That's okay. Thanks. I'm not in the mood. Besides, you're really, really good. Like a professional. I'd be embarrassed to pound out "Für Elise' or something."

He smiled too. " 'Für Elise.' I know that one. We could do a duet."

"A duet," she repeated, nodding, frowning a little. Then she looked up. "Are you an only child?" she asked.

He was startled. "Yes and no. I mean, I had a sister. A twin. She died."

Rosemary nodded. "Do you ever think about her?"

"Sure." He felt uncomfortable and looked away. "Not *about* her, exactly. I mean, I never knew her. But about what she might have been like."

He flushed then, shocked to have revealed so much to this girl, this stranger who'd disrupted all their lives, this girl he didn't even like.

"So okay," he said. "Now it's your turn. Tell me something personal. Tell me something my father doesn't know."

She gave him a searching look.

"I don't like bananas," she said at last, and he laughed, and then she did. "No, honestly, I don't. What else? When I was five, I fell off my bike and broke my arm."

"Me too," Paul said. "I broke my arm too, when I was six. I fell out of a tree." He remembered it then, the way his father had lifted him, the way the sky had flashed, full of sun and leaves, as he was carried to the car. He remembered his father's hands, so focused and so gentle as he set the bones, and coming home again, into the bright golden light of the afternoon.

"Hey," he said. "I want to show you something."

He laid the guitar flat on the swing and picked up the grainy black-and-white photos.

"Was it this place?" he asked, handing one to her. "Where you met my father?"

She took the photo and studied it, then nodded. "Yes. It looks different now. I can see from this picture—those sweet curtains in the windows and the flowers growing—that it was a nice house once. But no one lives there now. It's just empty. The wind comes through because the windows are broken. When I was a kid we used to play there. We used to run wild in those hills, and I used to play house with my cousins. They said it was haunted, but I always liked it. I don't know exactly why. It was like my secret place. Sometimes I just sat inside, dreaming about what I was going to be."

He nodded, taking the photo back and studying the figures as he had so many times before, as if they might answer all his questions about his father.

"You didn't dream this," he said at last, looking up.

"No," she said softly. "Never this."

Neither of them spoke for a few minutes. Sunlight slanted through the trees and cast shadows on the painted floor of the porch.

"Okay. It's your turn again," she said after a minute, turning back to him.

"My turn?"

"Tell me something your father doesn't know."

"I'm going to Juilliard," he said, the words coming in a rush, bright as music in the room. He'd told no one but his mother yet. "I was first on the wait list, and I got accepted last week. While he was gone."

"Wow." She smiled a little sadly. "I was thinking more in terms of your favorite vegetable," she said. "But that's great, Paul. I always thought college would be great."

"You were going to go," he said, realizing suddenly what she'd lost.

"I will go. I will definitely go."

"I'll probably have to pay my own way," Paul offered, recognizing her fierce determination, the way it covered fear. "My father's set on me having some kind of secure career plan. He hates the idea of music."

"You don't know that," she said, looking up sharply. "You don't really know the whole story about your father at all."

Paul did not know how to answer this, and they sat silently for several minutes. They were screened from the street by a trellis, clematis vines climbing all over it and the purple and white flowers blooming, so when two cars pulled into the driveway, one after the other, his mother and his father home so oddly in the middle of the day, Paul glimpsed them in flashes of color, bright chrome. He and Rosemary exchanged looks. The cars doors slammed shut, echoing against the neighboring house. Then there were footsteps, and the quiet, determined voices of his parents, back and forth, just beyond the edge of the porch. Rosemary opened her mouth, as if to call out, but Paul held up one hand and shook his head, and they sat together in silence, listening.

"This day," his mother said. "This week. If you only knew, David, how much pain you caused us."

"I'm sorry. You're right. I should have called. I meant to."

"That's supposed to be enough? Maybe *I'll* just go away," she said. "Just like that. Maybe I'll just take off and come back with a good-looking young man and no explanation. What would you think of that?"

There was a silence, and Paul remembered the discarded pile of bright clothes on the beach. He thought of the many evenings since when his mother had not made it home before midnight. Business, she always sighed, slipping off her shoes in the foyer, going straight to bed. He looked at Rosemary, who was studying her hands, and he held himself very still, watching her, listening, waiting to see what would happen next.

"She's just a child," his father said at last. "She's sixteen and pregnant, and she was living in an abandoned house, all alone. I couldn't leave her there."

His mother sighed. Paul imagined her running a hand through her hair.

"Is this a midlife crisis?" she asked quietly. "Is that what this is?"

"A midlife crisis?" His father's voice was even, thoughtful, as if he were considering the evidence carefully. "I suppose it might be. I know I hit some kind of wall, Norah. In Pittsburgh. I was so driven as a young man. I didn't have the luxury of being anything else. I went back to try and figure out some things. And there was Rosemary, in my old house. That doesn't feel like a coincidence. I don't know, I can't explain it without sounding kind of crazy. But please trust me. I'm not in love with her. It's not like that. It never will be."

Paul looked at Rosemary. Her head was bent so he couldn't see her expression, but her cheeks were flushed pink. She picked at a torn fingernail and wouldn't meet his eye.

"I don't know what to believe," his mother said slowly. "This week, David, of all weeks. Do you know where I was just now? I was with Bree, at the oncologist's. She had a biopsy done last week: her left breast. It's a very small lump, her prognosis is good, but it's malignant."

"I didn't know, Norah. I'm sorry."

"No, don't touch me, David."

"Who's her surgeon?"

"Ed Jones."

"Ed's good."

"He'd better be. David, your midlife crisis is the last thing I need."

Paul, listening, felt the world slow down a little bit. He thought of Bree, with her quick laugh, who would sit for an hour listening to him play, the music moving between them so they didn't need to speak. She'd close her eyes and stretch out in the swing, listening. He couldn't imagine the world without her.

"What do you want?" his father was asking. "What do you want from me, Norah? I'll stay, if you want, or I'll move out. But I can't turn Rosemary away. She has no place to go."

There was a silence and he waited, hardly daring to breathe, wanting to know what his mother would say, and wanting her never to answer.

"What about me?" he asked, startling himself. "What about what *I* want?"

"Paul?" His mother's voice.

"Right here," he said, picking up his guitar. "On the porch. Me and Rosemary."

"Oh, good grief," his father said. Seconds later, he came around to the steps. Since last night he'd showered and shaved and put on a clean suit. He was thin, and he looked tired. So did his mother, coming to stand beside him.

Paul stood and faced him. "I'm going to Juilliard, Dad. They called last week: I got in. And I'm going."

He waited, then, for his father to start in as usual: how a musical career wasn't reliable, not even a classical one. How Paul had so many options open to him; he could always play, and always take joy in playing, even if he made his living another way. He waited for his father to be firm and reasonable and resistant, so that Paul could give vent to his anger. He was tense, ready, but to his surprise his father only nodded.

"Good for you," his father said, and then his face softened for a moment with pleasure, the frown of worry easing from his forehead. When he spoke his voice was quiet and sure. "Paul, if it's what you want, then go. Go and work hard and be happy."

Paul stood uneasily on the porch. All these years, each time he and his father talked, he'd felt he was running into a wall. And now the wall was mysteriously gone but he was still running, giddy and uncertain, in open space.

"Paul?" his father said. "I'm proud of you, son."

Everyone was looking at him now, and he had tears in his eyes.

He didn't know what to say, so he started walking, at first just to get out of sight, so he wouldn't embarrass himself, and then he was truly running, the guitar still in his hand.

"Paul!" his mother called after him, and when he turned, running backward for a few steps, he saw how pale she was, her arms folded tensely across her chest, her newly streaked hair lifting in the breeze. He thought of Bree, what his mother had said, how much they'd come to be like each other, his mother and his aunt, and he was afraid. He remembered his father in the foyer, his clothes filthy, dark stubble taking the rough shape of a beard, his hair wild. And now, this morning, clean and calm, but still changed. His father—impeccable, precise, sure of everything—had turned into someone else. Behind, half screened by the clematis, Rosemary stood listening, her arms folded, her hair, set free, falling over her shoulders now, and he imagined her in that house set into the hill, talking with his father, riding the bus with him for so many long hours, somehow a part of this change in his father, and again he was afraid of what was happening to them all.

So he ran.

It was a sunny day, already warm. Mr. Ferry, Mrs. Pool, waved from their porches. Paul lifted the guitar in salute and kept running. He was three blocks away from home, five, ten. Across the street, in front of one low bungalow, an empty car stood running. The owner had forgotten something probably, had run inside to grab a briefcase or a jacket. Paul paused. It was a tan Gremlin, the ugliest car in the universe, edged with rust. He crossed the street, opened the driver's door, and slipped inside. No one shouted; no one came running from the house. He yanked the door shut and adjusted the seat, giving himself leg room. He put the guitar on the seat beside him. The car was an automatic, scattered with candy wrappers and empty cigarette packs. A total loser owned this car, he thought, one of those ladies who wore too much makeup and worked as a secretary somewhere dead and plastic spastic, like the dry cleaners, maybe, or the bank. He put the car in gear and backed up.

Still nothing: no shouts, no sirens. He geared into DRIVE and pulled away.

He hadn't driven much, but it seemed to be a lot like sex: if you pretended to know what was going on, then pretty soon you did know, and then it was all second nature. By the high school, Ned Stone and Randy Delaney were hanging out on the corner, tossing butts into the grass before they went inside, and he looked for Lauren Lobeglio, who sometimes stood there with them, whose breath was often dark and smoky when he kissed her.

The guitar slipped. He pulled over and strapped it in with a seat belt. A Gremlin, shit. Through town now, stopping carefully at every light, the day vibrant and blue. He thought of Rosemary's eyes, filling with tears. He hadn't meant to hurt her, but he had. And something had happened, something had changed. She was part of it and he was not, though his father's face had filled, for just an instant, with happiness at his news.

Paul drove. He did not want to be in that house for whatever happened next. He reached the interstate where the road split and went west, to Louisville. California glimmered in his mind: music there, and an endless beach. Lauren Lobeglio would latch herself onto someone new. She didn't love him and he didn't love her; she was like an addiction, and what they were doing had a darkness to it, a weight. California. Soon he'd be on the beach, playing in a band and living cheap and easy all summer long. In the fall, he'd find a way to get to Juilliard. Hitchhike across the country, maybe. He cranked his window all the way down, letting the spring air rush in. The Gremlin barely hit 55 even with his foot pressing the pedal to the floor. Still, it felt like he was flying.

He had come this way before, on orderly school trips to the Louisville Zoo and earlier, on those wild rides his mother had taken when he was small, when he lay in the backseat watching leaves and branches and phone lines flashing in the window. She had sung, loudly, with the radio, her voice lurching, promising him they'd stop for ice cream, for a treat, if he'd just be good, be quiet. All these years he had been good, but it hadn't made any difference. He'd discovered music and played his heart out into the silence of that house, into the hole his sister's death had made in their lives, and that hadn't mattered either. He had tried as hard as he could to make his parents look up from their lives and hear the beauty, the joy that he'd discovered. He'd played so much and he'd gotten so fine. And yet all this time they'd never looked up, not once, not until Rosemary had stepped through the door and altered everything. Or maybe she hadn't changed anything at all. Maybe it was just that her presence cast a new, revealing light on their lives, shifting the composition. After all, a picture could be a thousand different things.

He put his hand on the guitar, feeling the warm wood, comforted. He pressed the pedal to the floor, climbing between the limestone walls where the highway had been cut into the hill, and then he descended toward the curve of the Kentucky River, flying. The bridge sang under his tires. Paul drove and drove, trying to do anything but think.

IV

BEYOND NORAH'S GLASS-PANELED DOOR, THE OFFICE HUMMED. Neil Simms, the personnel manager from IBM, walked through the outer doors, a flash of dark suit, polished shoes. Bree, who had paused in the reception room to collect the faxes, turned to greet him. She was wearing a yellow linen suit and dark yellow shoes; a fine gold bracelet slipped down her wrist as she reached to shake his hand. She'd gotten thin and sharp-boned beneath her elegance. Still, her laugh was light, traveling through the glass to where Norah sat with the phone in one hand, the glossy folder she'd spent weeks preparing on her desk, IBM in bold black letters across the front.

"Look, Sam," Norah said. "I told you not to call me, and I meant it."

A cool deep current of silence welled up against her ear. She imagined Sam at home, working by the wall of windows overlooking the lake. He was an investment analyst, and Norah had met him in the parking garage six months ago, in the murky concrete light near the elevator. Her keys had slipped and he had caught them in midair, fast and fluid, his hands flashing like fish. *Yours?* he'd asked, with a quick, easy smile—a joke, since they were the only two around. Norah, filled with a familiar rush, a kind of dark delicious plummeting, had nodded. His fingers brushed her skin; the keys fell coldly against her palm.

That night he left a message on her machine. Norah's heart had quickened, stirred at his voice. Still, when the tape ended, she had forced herself to sit down and count up her affairs—short-lived and long, passionate and detached, bitter and amicable—over the years.

Four. She had written the number down, dark blunt streaks of graphite on the edge of the morning paper. Upstairs, water was dripping in the tub. Paul was in the family room, playing the same chord over and over again on his guitar. David was outside, working in his darkroom—so much space between them, always. Norah had walked into each of her affairs with a sense of hope and new beginnings, swept up in the rush of secret meetings, of novelty and surprise. After Howard, two more, transitory and sweet, followed by one other, longer. Each had begun at moments when she thought the roar of silence in her house would drive her mad, when the mysterious universe of another presence, any presence, had seemed to her like solace.

"Norah, please, just listen," Sam was saying now: a forceful man, something of a bully in negotiations, a person she didn't even particularly like. In the reception room, Bree turned to glance at her, inquiring, impatient. Yes, Norah gestured through the glass, she would hurry. They had courted this IBM account for almost a year; she would certainly hurry. "I just want to ask about Paul," Sam was insisting. "If you've heard anything. Because I'm here for you, okay? Do you hear what I'm saying, Norah? I'm totally, absolutely, here for you."

"I hear you," she said, angry with herself—she didn't want Sam talking about her son. Paul had been gone for twenty-four hours now; a car three blocks down was missing too. She'd watched him leave after that strained scene on the porch, trying to remember what she'd said, what he'd overheard, pained at the confusion on his face. David had done the right thing, giving Paul his blessing, but somehow that too, the very strangeness of it, had made the moment worse. She'd watched Paul run off, carrying his guitar, and she'd nearly gone after him. But her head ached, and she'd let herself think that maybe he needed some time to work this out on his own. Plus, surely, he wouldn't go far—where could he go, after all?

"Norah?" Sam said. "Norah, are you okay?"

She closed her eyes briefly. Ordinary sunlight warmed her face. Sam's bedroom windows were full of prisms, and on this brilliant morning light and color would be shifting, alive, on every surface. *It's like making love in a disco,* she'd told him once, half complaining, half enchanted, long shafts of color moving on his arms, her own pale skin. That day, as on every day since they'd met, Norah had intended to end things. Then Sam had traced the shaft of variegated light on her thigh with his finger, and slowly she'd felt her own sharp edges begin to soften, to blur, her emotions bleeding one into another in mysterious sequence, from darkest indigo to gold, reluctance transforming, mysteriously, to desire.

Still, the pleasure never lasted past the drive home.

"I'm focusing on Paul right now," she said, and then, sharply, she added, "Look, Sam, I've had it, actually. I was serious the other day. Don't call me again."

"You're upset."

"Yes. But I mean it. Don't call me. Never again."

She hung up. Her hand was trembling; she pressed it flat on her desk. She felt Paul's disappearance like a punishment: for David's long anger, for her own. The car he'd stolen had been found deserted on a side street in Louisville last night, but there had been no trace of Paul. And so she and David were waiting, moving helplessly through the silent layers of their house. The girl from West Virginia was still sleeping on the pull-out sofa in the den. David never touched her, hardly even spoke to her except to ask if she needed anything. And yet Norah sensed something between the two of them, an emotional connection, alive and positively charged, which pierced her as much, perhaps more, than any physical affair would have done.

Bree knocked on the glass, then opened the door a few inches.

"Everything okay? Because Neil's here, from IBM."

"I'm fine," Norah said. "How are you doing? Are you okay?"

"It's good for me to be here," Bree said brightly, firmly. "Especially with everything else that's going on."

Norah nodded. She had called Paul's friends, and David called the police. All night and into this morning she had paced the house in her bathrobe, drinking coffee and imagining every possible disaster. The chance to come to work, to put at least part of her mind on something else, had felt like sanctuary. "I'll be right there," she said.

The phone started ringing again as she stood, and Norah let a rush of weary anger push her through the door. She would not let Sam rattle her, she would not let him ruin this meeting, she would not. Her other affairs had ended differently, swiftly or slowly, amicably or not, but none with this element of uneasiness. *Never again,* she thought to herself. *Let this be finished, and never again.*

She hurried through the lobby, but Sally stopped her at the reception desk, holding out the phone. "You'd better take this, honey," she said. Norah knew at once; she took the receiver, trembling.

"They found him." David's voice was quiet. "The police just called. They found him in Louisville, shoplifting. Our son was caught stealing cheese."

"He's okay, then," she said, releasing a breath she hadn't realized she'd been holding all this time, blood rushing back into her fingertips. Oh! She'd been half dead and hadn't known it.

"Yes, he's fine. Hungry, apparently. I'm on my way to get him. Do you want to come?"

"Maybe I should go. I don't know, David. You might say the wrong thing." *You stay here with your girlfriend,* she almost added.

He sighed. "I wonder what would be the right thing to say, Norah? I'd really like to know. I'm proud of him, and I told him that. He ran away and stole a car. So what, I wonder, would be the right thing to say?"

Too little, too late, she wanted to say. *And what about your girlfriend?* But she said nothing.

"Norah, he's eighteen. He stole a car. He has to take responsibility."

"You're fifty-one," she snapped. "So do you."

There was a silence then; she imagined him standing in his office, so reassuring in his white coat, his hair alive with silver. No one seeing him would imagine the way he'd come back home:

unshaven, his clothes torn and filthy, a pregnant girl in a shabby black coat by his side.

"Look, just give me the address," she said. "I'll meet you there."

"He's at the police station, Norah. Central booking. Where do you think, the zoo? But sure, hang on. I'll give you the address."

As Norah was writing it down, she looked up to see Bree closing the front door behind Neil Simms.

"Paul's okay?" Bree asked.

Norah nodded, too moved, too relieved, to speak. Hearing his name had made the news real. Paul was safe, maybe in handcuffs but safe. Alive. The office staff, hovering in the reception room, began to clap, and Bree crossed the room to hug her. So thin, Norah thought, tears in her eyes; her sister's shoulder blades were delicate and sharp, like wings.

"I'll drive," Bree said, taking her arm. "Come on. Tell me as we go."

Norah let herself be led down the hall and into the elevator, to the car in the garage. Bree drove through the crowded downtown streets while Norah talked, relief rushing through her like a wind.

"I can't believe it," she said. "I was awake all night. I know Paul's an adult now. I know in a few months he'll be off to college, and I won't have a clue where he is at any given moment. But I couldn't stop worrying."

"He's still your baby."

"Always. It's hard, letting him go. Harder than I thought."

The were passing the low dull buildings of IBM, and Bree waved at them. "Hey, Neil," she said. "Be seeing you soon."

"All that work." Norah sighed.

"Oh, don't worry. We won't lose the account," Bree said. "I was very, very charming. And Neil's a family man. He's also, I suspect, the sort who likes a damsel in distress."

"You're setting back the cause," Norah retorted, remembering Bree in the filtered light of the dining room long ago, waving pamphlets on lactation.

Bree laughed. "Not at all. I've just learned to work with what I have. We'll get the account, don't worry."

Norah didn't reply. White fences flashed and blurred against the lush grass. Horses stood calmly in their fields; tobacco barns, weathered gray, were set against one hillside, then another. Early spring, Derby time soon, the redbuds bursting into bloom. They crossed the Kentucky River, muddy and glinting. In a field just beyond the bridge a single daffodil waved, a bright flash of beauty, gone. How many times had she traveled this road, the wind in her hair, the Ohio River luring her with its promise, its swift and undulating beauty? She had given up the gin, the windswept drives; she had bought this travel business and made it grow; she had changed her life. But a realization came to her now clearly, suddenly, like a harsh new light in the room: she had never stopped running. To San Juan and Bangkok, London and Alaska. Into the arms of Howard and the others, all the way to Sam and to this moment.

"I can't lose you, Bree." she said. "I don't know how you're being so calm about everything, because I feel like I've run into a wall." She remembered David saying the same thing yesterday, standing in the driveway, trying to explain why he'd brought young Rosemary home. What had happened to him in Pittsburgh, to leave him so changed?

"I'm calm," Bree said, "because you're not going to lose me."

"Good. I'm glad you're so sure. Because I couldn't stand it."

They drove in silence for a few miles.

"Do you remember that ratty old blue sofa I had?" Bree asked at last.

"Vaguely," Norah said, wiping her eyes. "What about it?"

A tobacco barn, another, and a long stretch of green.

"I always thought it was so beautiful, that sofa. Then one day—it was during a really bleak time in my life—the light was coming in the room differently, snow outside or something, and I realized that old sofa was utterly decrepit, only held together by dust. I knew I had to make some changes." She glanced across the car, smiling. "So I came to work for you."

"A bleak time?" Norah repeated. "I always imagined your life was so glamorous. Next to mine, anyway. I didn't know you went through a bleak time, Bree. What happened?"

"It doesn't matter. It's ancient history. But I was awake last night too. I have the same kind of feeling: something's changing. It's funny how things seem different, suddenly. This morning I found myself staring at the light coming in the kitchen window. It made a long rectangle on the floor, and the shadows of new leaves were moving in it, making all their patterns. Such a simple thing, but it was beautiful."

Norah studied Bree's profile, remembering her as she had been, carefree, bold, and assured in her boldness, standing on the steps of the administration building. Where had that young girl gone? How had she become this woman, so lean and determined, so forceful and so solitary?

"Oh, Bree," Norah managed, at last.

"It's not a death sentence, Norah." Bree was speaking crisply now, focused and determined, as if she were giving an overview of accounts receivable. "More like a wake-up call. I did some reading, and my chances really are very good. And I was thinking this morning that if there's not a support group for women like me, I'm going to start one."

Norah smiled. "That sounds just like you. That's the most reassuring thing you've said yet." They drove in silence for a few minutes longer, and then Norah added, "But you didn't tell me. All those years ago, when you were unhappy. You never told me."

"Right," Bree said. "I'm telling you now."

Norah put her hand on Bree's knee, feeling her sister's heat, her thinness.

"What can I do?"

"Just go on, day by day. I'm on the prayer list at church, and that helps."

Norah looked at her sister, her short stylish hair, her sharp profile, wondering how to respond. About a year ago Bree had started attending a small Episcopalian church near her home. Norah had gone with her once, but the service, with its complex rituals of kneeling and standing, prayer and silence, had made her feel inept, an outsider. She had sat stealing glances at the others in the pews, wondering what they were feeling, what had made them get out of bed and come here to church on this beautiful Sunday morning. It was hard to see any mystery, hard to see anything but the clear light and a group of tired, hopeful, dutiful people. She'd never gone back, but now she found herself suddenly, fiercely grateful for whatever solace her sister had gathered, for whatever she'd found in that quiet church that Norah hadn't seen.

The world flashed by: grass, trees, sky. Then, increasingly, buildings. They had entered Louisville now, and Bree was merging into the heavy traffic on I-71, into swift lanes full of rushing cars. The parking lot of the police station was nearly full, shimmering faintly in the noon sun. They got out of the car, their slammed doors echoing, and walked along a concrete sidewalk bordered by a series of small tired bushes, through the revolving doors, and into the dim underwater light inside.

Paul was on a bench on the far side of the room, hunched over, his elbows on his knees and his hands dangling loosely between them. Norah's heart caught. She walked past the desk and the officers, wading through that thick sea-green air to her son. It was hot in the room. A fan turned almost imperceptibly against the stained acoustic tiles on the ceiling. She sat down beside Paul on the bench. He hadn't bathed, his hair was thick and greasy, and beneath the stink of sweat and dirty clothes the odor of cigarettes clung to him. Acrid, sharp smells, the smells of a man. His fingers were calloused, tough from the guitar. He had his own life now, his secret life. It humbled her suddenly to find he was so much his own person. Of her, yes, always that, but no longer hers.

"I'm glad to see you," she said quietly. "I was worried, Paul. We all were."

He looked at her, his eyes darkly angry and suspicious, and turned away suddenly, blinking back tears.

"I stink," he said.

"Yeah," Norah agreed. "You really do."

He scanned the lobby, his gaze lingering on Bree, who stood at the desk, and then on the swirl and flash of the revolving doors.

"So. I guess I'm lucky he didn't bother to come."

David, he meant. Such pain in his voice. Such anger.

"He's coming," Norah said, keeping her voice even. "He'll be here any minute. Bree drove me over. Flew, really."

She had meant to make him smile, but he only nodded.

"Is she okay?"

"Yes," Norah said, thinking of their conversation in the car. "She's okay."

He nodded again. "Good. That's good. I'll bet Dad's pissed off."

"Count on it."

"Am I going to jail?" Paul's voice was very soft.

She took a breath. "I don't know. I hope not. But I don't know."

They sat in silence. Bree was talking to an officer, nodding, gesturing. Beyond, the revolving door turned and turned, flashing light and dark, spilling strangers inside or out, one by one, and then it was David striding across the terrazzo floor, his black shoes squeaking, his expression serious and impassive, impossible to read. Norah tensed and felt Paul tense beside her. To her astonishment, David walked straight to Paul and grabbed him in a powerful, wordless hug.

"You're safe," he said. "Thank God."

She drew a deep breath, grateful for this moment. An officer with a white crew cut and startling blue eyes crossed the room, a clipboard under one arm. He shook Norah's hand, David's. Then he turned to Paul.

"What I'd like to do is put you in the slammer," he said conversationally. "A smart-aleck boy like yourself. Don't know how many I've seen over the years, boys thinking they're so tough, boys who get let off again and again, until eventually they hit real trouble. Then they go to jail for a long time and find out that they're not tough at all. It's a shame. But it seems your neighbors think they're doing you a favor and won't press charges about the car. So since I can't lock you up, I'm releasing you in the custody of your parents."

Paul nodded. His hands were trembling; he shoved them in his pockets. They all watched as the officer tore a paper off his clipboard, handed it to David, and walked slowly back to the desk.

"I called the Bolands," David explained, folding the paperwork and tucking it into his breast pocket. "They were reasonable. This could have been much worse, Paul. But don't think you won't be paying back every red cent of what it will cost to get that car repaired. And don't think your life is going to be very happy for quite a while. No friends. No social life."

Paul nodded, swallowing.

"I have to rehearse," he said. "I can't just drop the quartet."

"No," David said. "What you can't do is steal a car from our neighbors and expect life to go on as usual."

Norah felt Paul, so tense beside her and so angry. *Leave it,* she found herself thinking, seeing the muscle move in David's jaw. *Leave it alone, both of you. That's enough.*

"Fine," Paul said. "Then I'm not coming home. I'd rather go to jail."

"Well, I can certainly arrange that," David answered, his tone dangerously cool.

"Go ahead," Paul said. "Arrange it. Because I'm a musician. And I'm good. And I'd rather sleep in the streets than give it up. Hell, I'd rather be dead."

There was a moment, a heartbeat. When David didn't respond, Paul's eyes narrowed.

"My sister doesn't know how good she's got it," he said.

Norah, who had been holding herself very still, felt the words like shards of ice, a harsh, bright, piercing grief. Before she knew what she'd done, she'd slapped Paul across the face. The stubble of his new beard was rough against her palm—he was a man, no longer a boy, and she'd hit him hard. He turned, shocked, a red mark already rising on his cheek.

"Paul," David said, "don't make things worse than they are. Don't say things you'll regret for the rest of your life."

Norah's hand was still stinging; her blood rushed. "We'll go home," she said. "We'll settle this at home."

"I don't know. A night in jail might do him good."

"I lost one child," she said, turning to him. "I will not lose another."

Now David looked stunned, as if she'd slapped him too. The ceiling fan clicked, and the revolving door spun with rhythmic *thunks.*

"All right," David said. "Maybe that's right. Maybe you're right to pay no attention to me. God knows I'm sorry for the things I've done to fail you both."

"David?" Norah said, as he turned away, but he didn't respond. She watched him walk across the room and enter the revolving door. Outside, he was visible for an instant, a middle-aged man in a dark jacket, part of the crowd, then gone. The ceiling fan clicked amid smells of sour flesh and French fries and cleaning fluid.

"I didn't mean—" Paul began.

Norah held up her hand. "Don't. Please. Don't say another word."

It was Bree, calm and efficient, who got them to the car. They opened the windows against Paul's stench, and Bree drove, her thin fingers steady on the wheel. Norah, brooding, paid little attention, and it was nearly half an hour before she realized that they were no longer on an interstate but were traveling more slowly, on smaller roads, through the vivid spring countryside. Fields, barely greening, flashed in the windows, and branches with their just-opening buds.

"Where are you going?" Norah asked.

"On a little adventure," Bree said. "You'll see."

Norah didn't want to look at Bree's hands, so bony, the blue veins visible. She glanced at Paul in the rearview mirror. He sat, pale and sullen, arms folded, slouching, clearly furious, clearly in pain. She had done the wrong thing back there, lashing out at David like that, slapping Paul; she had only made things worse. His angry eyes met hers in the mirror, and she remembered his soft plump infant hand pressed against her cheek, his laughter trilling through the rooms. Another boy altogether, that child. Where had he gone?

"What kind of adventure?" Paul asked.

"Well, actually I'm trying to find the Abbey of Gethsemani."

"What for?" Norah asked. "Is it nearby?"

Bree nodded. "It's supposed to be. I've always wanted to see it, and on the way here I realized how close we were. I thought, Why not? It's such a pretty day."

It was pretty, the sky a clear blue, pale at the horizon, the trees vivid and alive, fluttering in the breeze. They drove along the narrow roads for another ten minutes, and then Bree pulled over to the side of the road and started rummaging under the seat.

"I guess I didn't bring a map," she said, sitting up.

"You never bring a map," Norah replied, realizing in that moment that this had been true of Bree all her life. Yet it didn't seem to matter. She and David had started off with all sorts of maps, and look where they were now.

Bree had stopped near two farmhouses, modest and white, the doors shut tight and no one in sight, the tobacco barns, weathered silver, standing open on the far hills. It was planting season. Distantly, tractors crawled across the newly plowed fields, and people followed, reaching to set the bright green tobacco seedlings into the dark earth. Down the road, at the far end of the field, there was a small white church, shaded by old sycamores, bordered with a row of purple pansies. At the side of this church was a graveyard, the old stones tilting behind a wrought-iron fence. It was so like the place where her daughter was buried that Norah caught her breath, remembering that long-ago March day, damp grass beneath her feet, the low clouds pressing down, and David silent and distant beside her. *Ashes to ashes, dust to dust,* and the known world had shifted under their feet.

"Let's go to the church," she said. "Someone there might know."

They drove down the road, and she and Bree got out of the car by the church, feeling citified and out of place in their work clothes. The day was very still, almost hot, sunlight flickering through the leaves. The grass against Bree's yellow shoes was dark green and lush. Norah put her hand on Bree's thin arm, the yellow linen both soft and crisp.

"You're going to ruin those shoes," she said.

Bree looked down, nodded, and slipped them off. "I'll ask at the manse," she said. "The front door's open."

"Go on," Norah said. We'll wait here."

Bree stooped to pick up her shoes and then made her way through the rich green grass, something girlish and vulnerable about her pale legs, her stocking feet. Her yellow shoes were swinging from her hand. Norah remembered her, suddenly, running through a field behind their childhood home, laughter floating through the sunlit air. *Be well,* she thought, watching. *Oh, my sister, be well.*

"I'm going to take a walk," she told Paul, who was still slouching in the backseat. She left him there and followed the gravel path to the cemetery. The iron gate pushed open easily, and Norah wandered in among the stones, gray and worn. She had not been to the grave on Bentley's farm for years. She looked back at Paul. He was getting out of the car, stretching, his eyes masked by dark sunglasses.

The church door was red. It swung open silently when Norah touched it. The sanctuary was dim and cool, and the stained-glass windows were ablaze, jewel-like images of saints and biblical scenes, doves and fire. Norah thought of Sam's bedroom, the riot of colors there, and how tranquil this seemed in contrast, the colors stable, fixed, falling through the air. A guest book lay open, and she signed it in her fluid script, remembering the ex-nun who had taught her cursive writing. Norah lingered. Perhaps it was simply the silence that caused her to take a few steps down the empty center aisle: silence and this sense of peace and emptiness, the way the light fell through the stained-glass windows, the dusty air. Norah walked through this light: red, dark blue, gold.

The pews smelled of furniture polish. She slid into one. There were blue velvet kneelers, a little dusty. She thought of Bree's old sofa, and then she had a sudden memory of the women of her long-ago night circle, the women who had come to her house bearing gifts for Paul. She remembered helping them once to clean the church, how they'd polished the pews by sitting on rags and sliding across the long smooth planks on their bottoms. *More weight this way,* they'd joked, laughter filling the sanctuary. In her grief Norah had turned away from them and never gone back, but it occurred to her now that they had suffered too, had lost loved ones, experienced illnesses, failed themselves and others. Norah had not wanted to be one of them or to accept their comfort, and she had walked away. Remembering, her eyes filled with tears. Oh, this was silly, her loss had happened almost two decades ago. Surely this grief should not be welling up, fresh as water in a spring.

It was crazy. She was crying so hard. She'd run so fast, so far, to avoid this moment, and yet it was still happening: a stranger slept on the pull-out sofa, dreaming, a mysterious new life within her like a secret, and David shrugged and turned away. She would go home, she knew, to find him gone, a suitcase packed, perhaps, but nothing else taken. She wept for this knowledge and for Paul, the rage and lostness in his eyes. For her daughter, never known. For Bree's thin hands. For the multitude of ways in which their love had failed them all, and they, love. Grief, it seemed, was a physical place. Norah wept, unaware of anything except a kind of release she remembered from childhood; she sobbed until she was aching, breathless, spent.

There were birds, sparrows, nesting in the open rafters. As she came back to herself, Norah became aware, slowly, of their soft sounds, the flutter of wings. She was kneeling with her arms resting on the back of the pew in front of her. Light still fell through the windows in angled shafts, collecting in pools on the floor. Embarrassed, she sat up and wiped the tears from her face. A few gray feathers rested on the tile steps to the altar. Looking up, Norah caught sight of a sparrow winging lightly overhead, a shadow amid the greater shadows. Over the years so many others had sat here with their secrets and their dreams, dark and light. She wondered if their wild grief, like hers, had eased. It didn't make any sense to her, that this place should have brought her such peace, but it had.

When she stepped back outside, blinking, into the sunlight, Paul was sitting on a stone in front of the wrought-iron fence.

In the distance, Bree was walking through the grass, her shoes swinging.

He nodded at the scattered stones of the cemetery. "I'm sorry," he said, "for what I said. I didn't mean it. I was trying to make Dad angry, so I could be."

"Don't ever say it again," Norah told him. "That your life's not worth it. Don't ever, ever let me hear that again. Don't think it, either."

"I won't," he said. "I'm really sorry."

"I know you're angry," Norah said. "You have a right to whatever life you want to live. But your father's right too. There will be certain conditions. Break them, and you're on your own."

She said all this without looking at him, and when she turned she was shocked to see his face working, tears on his cheeks. Oh, the boy he'd been was not so far away, after all. She hugged him as well as she could. He was so tall; her head only reached his chest.

"Look, I love you," she said into his smelly shirt. "I'm so glad you're back. And you really, really stink," she added, laughing, and he laughed too.

She shaded her eyes, glancing across the field at Bree, closer now.

"It's not far," Bree called. "Just down the road a bit. She says we can't miss it."

They got back in the car and traveled once more along the narrow road, through the rolling hills. Within a few miles they began to glimpse white buildings through the cypress trees. Then suddenly the Abbey of Gethsemani stood revealed, magnificent and stark and simple against the rolling green landscape. Bree pulled into a parking lot beneath a row of rustling trees. As they got out of the car, bells began to ring, calling the monks to prayer. They stood listening, the clear sound fading into the clearer air, cows grazing in the near distance and clouds floating idly overhead.

"It's beautiful," Bree said. "Thomas Merton used to live here, did you know that? He went to Tibet to meet the Dalai Lama. I love imagining that moment. I love imagining all the monks inside, doing the same things day after day."

Paul had taken off his sunglasses. His dark eyes were clear. He reached into his pocket and spread some small stones on the hood of the car.

"Remember these?" he asked, as Norah picked one up, fingering the smooth white disk with a hole in the middle. "Crinoids. From sea lilies. Dad taught me about them, that day I broke my arm. I took a walk while you were in the church. They're all over the place out here."

"I'd forgotten," Norah said slowly, but then it came back in a rush: the necklace Paul had made, and how worried she'd been that he'd get caught in it and choke. The sound of bells faded in the clear air. The size of a shirt button, the fossil was light and warm in her hand. She remembered David lifting Paul and carrying him from the party, setting his broken arm. How hard David had worked to make things good for them all, to make things right, and yet somehow it had always been so difficult, for all of them, as if they were swimming the shallow sea that once had covered all this land.

1988

July 1988

I

DAVID HENRY SAT UPSTAIRS IN HIS HOME OFFICE. THROUGH the window, filmed with years of weather and faintly warped, the view of the street wavered, undulant and slightly distorted. He watched a squirrel retrieve a nut and run up the sycamore tree whose leaves pressed against the window. Rosemary was on her knees by the porch, her long hair swinging as she leaned to plant bulbs and annuals in the flower beds she had made. She had transformed the gardens, bringing daylilies from the gardens of friends, planting flax by the garage, where it bloomed, a profusion of pale blue, like mist. Jack sat near her, playing with a dump truck. He was a sturdy boy, five years old now, cheerful and good-natured, with dark brown eyes and traces of red in his blond hair. He had a stubborn streak. On the evenings when David watched him while Rosemary went to work, Jack insisted on doing everything by himself. *I'm a big boy,* he announced, several times a day, proud and important.

David let him take on what he wanted, within the limits of safety and reason. The truth was, he loved to watch the boy. He loved to read Jack stories, feeling his weight and warmth, his head falling against his shoulder as he drifted nearly into sleep. He loved to hold his small trusting hand when they walked down the sidewalk to the store. It pained David that his memories of Paul at this age were so sparse, so fleeting. He had been establishing his career then, of course, busy with his clinic—and his photography too—but really it was his guilt that had kept him distant. The patterns of his life were painfully clear now. He had handed their daughter to Caroline Gill and the secret had taken root; it had grown and blossomed in the center of his family. For years he'd come home to watch Norah, mixing drinks or tying on an apron, and he'd think how lovely she was and how he hardly knew her.

He had never been able to tell her the truth, knowing he would lose her entirely—and perhaps Paul too—if he did. So he had devoted himself to his work and, in those areas of his life he could control, had been very successful. But, sadly, from those years of Paul's childhood he remembered only a few moments in brief isolation, with the clarity of photos: Paul asleep on the sofa, one hand falling into the air, his dark hair tousled. Paul standing in the surf, shouting with fear and delight as the waves rushed around his knees. Paul sitting at the little table in the playroom, coloring seriously, so absorbed in his task that he did not notice David standing in the doorway, watching. Paul, casting a line out onto the quiet waters, holding still, hardly breathing, while they waited in the dusk for a bite.

Brief memories, almost unbearably beautiful. And then there were the years of adolescence, when Paul had traveled a distance greater even than Norah's, shaking the house with his music and his anger.

David tapped on the window and waved to Jack and Rosemary. He'd bought this house, a duplex, in such haste, looking at it only once and then going home to pack while Norah was at work. It was an old two-story house, split almost exactly in half, with thin partitions dividing what had been expansive rooms; even the stairway, once wide and elegant, had been cut in half. David had taken the larger apartment and given Rosemary the keys to the other; for the last six years they had lived side by side, separated by thin walls but seeing each other every day. Rosemary had tried to pay rent from time to time, but David had refused, telling her to go back to school and get a degree; she could pay him back later. He knew that his motives weren't entirely altruistic, yet he couldn't explain even to himself why she mattered so much to him. *I fill up that place left by the daughter you gave away,* she said once. He'd nodded, thinking it over, but that wasn't it either, not exactly. It was more, he suspected, that Rosemary knew his secret. He'd poured his story out to her in such a rush, the first and last time he had ever told it, and she had listened without judging him. There was freedom in that; David could be completely himself with Rosemary, who had listened to what he'd done without rejecting him and without telling anyone, either. Strangely, over the years Rosemary and Paul had established a friendship, grudging at first, then later a kind of earnest ongoing argument about issues that mattered to them both— politics and music and social justice—arguments that started over dinner during Paul's rare visits and lasted into the night.

Sometimes, David suspected that this was Paul's way of keeping a distance from him, a way of being in the house without having to talk about anything deeply personal. Now and then David made overtures, but Paul always chose that moment to leave, pushing back his chair and yawning, suddenly tired.

Now Rosemary looked up, brushing a wisp of hair from her cheek with her wrist, and waved back. David saved his files and walked down the narrow hallway. On the way he passed the door that opened into Jack's room. It was supposed to have been sealed when the house was converted to a duplex, but one evening David had, on an impulse, tried the handle and found that it was not. Now, quietly, he pushed the door open. Rosemary had painted the walls of Jack's room light blue, the bed and the dresser, found discarded on the curb, clean white. A whole series of *scherenschnitte,* intricate paper cuttings of mothers with children, of children playing beneath shady trees, delicate and full of motion, were mounted against midnight blue, framed and hung on the far wall. Rosemary had displayed these pieces in an art show a year ago, and to her surprise, orders had begun to come in, one after another. Nights, she often sat at her kitchen table, beneath a bright light, cutting one scene after another, each one different than any other. She couldn't promise people what she'd make; she refused to be tied down to any set of images. Because it was already there, she explained, hidden in the paper and the movements of her hands, and it could never be the same image twice.

David stood, listening to the sounds of the house: faint water dripping, and the hum of the old refrigerator. The smell of perfume and baby powder was strong; a slip was draped off the chair in the corner. He breathed in the scent of her, of Jack, and then he pulled the door firmly shut and carried on down the narrow hall. He'd never told Rosemary about the unsealed door, but he'd never walked through it either. It was a point of honor with him that, despite the scandal, he had never taken advantage of her, had never trespassed into her personal life.

Still, he liked knowing that the door was there.

There was more paperwork to do, but David went downstairs. His running shoes were on the back porch. He put them on, tying the laces tightly, and walked around to the front. Jack was standing by the trellis, pulling blossoms off the roses. David squatted down and pulled him close, feeling his soft weight, his steady breathing. Jack had been born in September, early in the evening, just as dusk began to settle. David had driven Rosemary to the hospital, and he sat with her during the first six hours of labor, playing chess and bringing her ice chips. Unlike Norah, Rosemary had no interest in a natural birth; as soon as she could, she had an epidural, and when the labor slowed, she had Pitocin to speed things along. David held her hand as the contractions grew strong, but when they took her to the delivery room he stayed behind. It was too private, not his place. Still, he'd been the first one after Rosemary to hold Jack, and he'd come to love the boy like his own.

"You smell funny," Jack said now, pushing at David's chest.

"It's my old stinky shirt," David said.

"Going running?" Rosemary asked. She sat back on her heels, brushing dirt from her hands. She was lean these days, almost bony, and he worried about the pace she kept, how hard she pushed herself at school and at her job. She wiped a fine sweat from her forehead with her wrist, leaving a streak of dirt.

"I am. I can't look at those insurance files another minute."

"I thought you hired someone."

"I did. She'll be good, I think, but she can't start until next week."

Rosemary nodded, pensive. Her pale eyelashes caught the light. She was young, just twenty-two, but she was tough and focused, carrying herself with the assurance of a woman years older.

"Class tonight?" he asked, and she nodded.

"My last one ever. July twelfth."

"That's right. I'd forgotten."

"You've been busy."

He nodded, feeling vaguely guilty, troubled by the date. July twelfth; it was hard to understand how time passed so quickly. Rosemary had gone back to school after Jack was born, the same dusky January in which he had left his former practice because a man who'd been his patient for twenty years had been turned away at the door for lack of health insurance. He'd started his own practice, and he took anyone who showed up, insurance or no. He wasn't in it for the money anymore. Paul was through college, and his own debts were long since paid off; he could do as he liked. These days, like old-time doctors, he was sometimes paid in produce, or yard work, or whatever anyone could offer. He imagined that he'd continue this way for another decade or so, seeing patients every day but gradually cutting back, until the parameter of his physical life was no larger than this house, this garden, the trips he would make to the grocer and the barber. Norah might still be winging around the globe like a dragonfly, but such a life was not for him. He was putting down roots; they were traveling deep.

"I have a chemistry final today," Rosemary said, pulling off her gloves, "and then, hooray, I'm done." Bees hummed in the honeysuckle. "There's something else I need to tell you," she said, tugging at her shorts and sitting next to him on the warm concrete steps.

"Sounds serious."

She nodded. "It is. I was offered a job yesterday. A good one."

"Here?"

She shook her head, smiling and waving to Jack as he tried to do a cartwheel and landed, sprawling, on the lawn. "That's the thing. It's in Harrisburg."

"Near your mother," he said, his heart sinking. He knew she'd been looking, and he'd been hoping she'd stay nearby. But moving had always been a very real possibility. Two years ago, after her father died quite suddenly, Rosemary had reconciled with her mother and her older sister, and they were anxious for her to come home and raise Jack nearby.

"That's right. It's the perfect job for me: four ten-hour days a week. They'll pay for me to go on to school too. I could work on getting my physical therapy degree. But mostly I'd have more time with Jack."

"And help," he said. "Your mother would help. And your sister."

"Yes. That would be really nice. And as much as I love Kentucky, it's never been home to me, not really."

He nodded, glad for her, not trusting himself to speak. He had sometimes imagined, theoretically, the possibility of having the house to himself: walls that might come down, space opening up, this duplex reverting in slow stages to the elegant single-family home it had once been. But all his conjectures had been about space and air, easily put aside for the pleasures of hearing her footsteps and soft movements next door, of waking in the night to Jack's distant cry.

There were tears in his eyes. He laughed.

"Well," he said, taking off his glasses, "I guess this was bound to happen. Congratulations, of course."

"We'll visit," she said. "You'll visit us."

"That's right," he said. "I'm sure we'll see a lot of each other."

"We will." She put her hand on his knee. "Look, I know we never talk about it. I don't even know how to bring it up, really. But what it meant to me—how you helped me—I'm so grateful. I will be forever."

"I've been accused of trying too hard to rescue people," he said.

She shook her head. "In many ways, you saved my life."

"Well. If that's true, I'm glad. God knows I've done enough damage elsewhere. I never could seem to do Norah much good."

There was a silence between them, the distant drone of a lawn mower.

"You ought to tell her," Rosemary said softly. "Paul too. You really must." Jack was squatting on the walkway now, making little piles of gravel, letting stones sift and cascade from his fingers. "It's not my place to say anything, I know that. But Norah ought to know about Phoebe. It isn't right, that she doesn't. It isn't right, what she's had to believe about us all this time, either."

"I told her the truth. That we're friends."

"Yes. And we are. But how could she believe it?"

David shrugged. "It's the truth."

"Not the whole truth. David, in some weird way we're connected, you and I, because of Phoebe. Because I know that secret. The thing is, I used to like that: feeling special because I knew something no one else did. It's a kind of power, isn't it, knowing a secret? But lately I don't like it so much, knowing this. It's not really mine to know, is it?"

"No." David picked up a lump of dirt and crumbled it between his fingers. He thought of Caroline's letters, which he'd carefully burned when he moved into this house. "I suppose it's not."

"So. You see? You will? Tell her, I mean."

"I don't know, Rosemary. I can't promise that."

They sat quietly in the sun for a few minutes, watching Jack try again to turn cartwheels on the grass. He was a towhead, agile, naturally athletic, a boy who liked to run and climb. David had come back from West Virginia set free from the grief and loss he'd locked away all those years. When June died he'd had no way to give voice to what had been lost, no real way to move on. It was unseemly, even, to speak of the dead in those days, so they had not. They had left all this grieving unfinished. Somehow, going back had allowed him to settle it. He had come home to Lexington drained, yes, but also calm and sure. After all these years, he'd finally had the strength to give Norah the freedom to remake her life.

. . .

When Jack was born, David set up an account for him in Rosemary's name, and one for Phoebe, in Caroline's name. It was easy enough; he'd always had Caroline's social security number, and he had her address too. It had taken a private investigator less than a week to find Caroline and Phoebe, living in Pittsburgh, in a tall narrow house near the freeway. David had driven there and parked on the street, meaning to go up the steps and knock on the door. What he wanted was to tell Norah what had happened, and he couldn't do that without telling her where Phoebe was. Norah would want to see their daughter, he was sure, so it wasn't only his own life he might change, or Norah's or Paul's. He had come here to tell Caroline what he was hoping to do.

Was it the right thing? He didn't know. He sat in the car. It was dusk, and headlights flashed off the sycamore leaves. Phoebe had grown up here, the street so familiar she took it for granted, this sidewalk pushed up by the roots of a tree, the caution sign quivering slightly in the wind, the rush of traffic—all of these would be, for his daughter, emblems of home. A couple pushing a baby in a stroller walked by, and then a light went on in the living room of Caroline's house. David got out of the car and stood at the bus stop, trying to look inconspicuous even as he gazed across the darkening lawn at the window. Inside, moving in the square of light, Caroline picked up the living room, gathering newspapers and folding up a blanket. She wore an apron. Her movements were deft and focused. She stood and stretched, looked over her shoulder, and spoke.

And then David saw her: Phoebe, his daughter. She was in the dining room, setting the table. She had Paul's dark hair and his profile, and for an instant, until she turned to reach for the saltshaker, David felt as if he must be watching his son. He took a step forward, and Phoebe walked out of his line of vision and then came back with three plates. She was short and stocky, and her hair was thin, held back with barrettes. She wore glasses. Even so, the resemblance was still visible to David: there was Paul's smile, his nose, Paul's expression of concentration on Phoebe's face when she put her hands on her hips and surveyed the table. Caroline came into the room and stood beside her, then put her arm around Phoebe in a quick affectionate hug, and they both laughed.

By then it was fully dark. David stood, transfixed, glad there was little foot traffic. Leaves skittered along the sidewalk in the wind, and he pulled his jacket closer. He remembered how he'd felt on the night of the birth, as if he were standing outside his own life and watching himself move through it. Now he understood that he was not in control of this situation, he was excluded from it as completely as if he didn't exist. Phoebe had been invisible to him all these years: an abstraction, not a girl. Yet here she was, putting water glasses on the table. She looked up, and a man with bristly dark hair came in and said something that made Phoebe smile. Then they sat down at the table, the three of them, and began to eat.

David went back to his car. He imagined Norah, standing next to him in the darkness, watching their daughter move through her life, unaware of them. He had caused Norah pain; his deception had made her suffer in ways he had never imagined or intended. But he could spare her this. He could drive away and leave the past undisturbed. And that was what he did, finally, traveling all night across the flat expanse of Ohio.

• • •

"I don't understand." Rosemary was looking at him. "Why can't you promise? It's the right thing to do."

"It would cause too much grief."

"You don't know what will happen until you do it."

"I can make a pretty good guess."

"But David—promise me you'll think about it?"

"I think about it every single day."

She shook her head, troubled, then smiled a small, sad smile. "All right, then. There's one more thing."

"Yes?"

"Stuart and I are getting married."

"You're far too young to get married," he said at once, and they both laughed.

"I'm as old as the hills," she said. "That's how I feel half the time."

"Well," he said. "Congratulations again. It's no surprise, but it's good news all the same." He thought of Stuart Wells, tall and athletic. *Strapping* was the word that came to mind. He was a respiratory therapist. He'd been in love with Rosemary for years now, but she'd made him wait until she finished school. "I'm glad for you, Rosemary. He's a good young man, Stuart. And he loves Jack. Does he have a job in Harrisburg?"

"Not yet. He's looking. His contract here finishes this month."

"How's the job market in Harrisburg?"

"So-so. But I'm not worried. Stuart's very good."

"I'm sure he must be."

"You're angry."

"No. No, not at all. But your news makes me feel sad. Sad and old."

She laughed. "Old as the hills?"

Now he laughed too. "Oh, much, much older."

They were silent for a moment. "It all just happened," Rosemary said. "Everything came together in this last week. I didn't want to mention anything about the job until I was sure. And then, once I got the job, Stuart and I decided to get married. I know it must seem sudden."

"I like Stuart," David said. "I'll look forward to congratulating him too."

She smiled. "Actually, I wondered if you'd give me away."

He looked at her then, her pale skin, the happiness she could no longer contain shining through her smile.

"I'd be honored," he said gravely.

"It's going to be here. Very small and simple and private. In two weeks."

"You're not wasting any time."

"I don't need to think about it," she said. "Everything feels completely right." She glanced at her watch and sighed. "I'd better get going." She stood up, brushing off her hands. "Come on, Jack."

"I'll keep an eye on him, if you want, while you get dressed."

"That would be a lifesaver. Thanks."

"Rosemary."

"Yes?"

"You'll send me photos now and then? Of Jack, as he grows up? Of you both, in your new place?"

"Sure. Of course." She folded her arms and kicked at the edge of the step.

"Thanks," he said simply, troubled again by the ways he had managed to miss his own life, absorbed as he'd been by his lenses and his grief. People imagined he had quit taking pictures because of the dark-haired woman in Pittsburgh and her unflattering review. He'd fallen out of favor, people speculated, he'd become discouraged. No one would believe he had simply ceased caring, but it was true. He hadn't picked up a camera since he went to stand by the confluence of those rivers. He had given it up, art and craft, the intricate and exhausting task of trying to transform the world into something else, to turn the body into the world and the world into the body. Sometimes he came across his photographs, in textbooks or hanging on the walls of private offices or homes, and he was startled by their cold beauty, their technical precision—sometimes, even, by the hungry searching that their emptiness implied.

"You can't stop time," he said now. "You can't capture light. You can only turn your face up and let it rain down. All the same, Rosemary, I'd like to have some pictures. Of you and of Jack. They would give me a glimpse, anyway. They would give me great pleasure."

"I'll send a lot," she promised, touching his shoulder. "I'll inundate you."

He sat on the steps while she dressed, lazy in the sun. Jack played with his truck. *You should tell her.* He shook his head. After he'd sat watching Caroline's house like a voyeur, he'd called a lawyer in Pittsburgh and set up those beneficiary accounts. When he died, they would skip probate. Jack and Phoebe would be taken care of, and Norah would never need to know.

Rosemary came back, smelling of Ivory soap, dressed in a skirt and flat shoes. She took Jack's hand and hefted a turquoise backpack on her shoulder. She looked so young, strong and slender, her hair damp, her face concentrated in a frown. She would drop Jack at the sitter's house on the way.

"Oh," she said, "with everything else, I almost forgot: Paul called."

David's heart quickened. "Did he?"

"Yes, this morning. It was the middle of the night for him; he'd just come from a concert. He was in Seville, he said. He's been there for three weeks, studying flamenco guitar with someone—I don't remember who, but he sounded famous."

"Was he having a good time?"

"Yes. It sounded like he was. He didn't leave a number. He said he'd call again."

David nodded, glad Paul was safe. Glad he'd called.

"Good luck on your exam," he said, standing.

"Thanks. As long as I pass, that's all that matters."

She smiled, then waved and walked with Jack down the narrow stone path to the sidewalk. David watched her go, trying to fix this moment—the vivid backpack, her hair swinging against her back, Jack's free hand reaching out to grab leaves and sticks—forever in his mind. It was futile, of course; he was forgetting things with every step she took. Sometimes his photographs amazed him, pictures he came across stored in old boxes or folders, moments he could not remember even when he saw them: himself laughing with people whose names he had forgotten, Paul wearing an expression David had never seen in life. And what would he have of this moment in another year, in five? The sun in Rosemary's hair, and the dirt beneath her fingernails, and the faint clean scent of soap.

And somehow, that would be enough.

He stood, stretched, and loped off to the park. About a mile into his run, he remembered the other thing that had been nagging him all morning, the importance of this day beyond Rosemary's test: July twelfth. Norah's birthday. She was forty-six.

Hard to believe. He ran, falling into an easy stride, remembering Norah on their wedding day. They had walked outside, into the raw late-winter sun, and stood on the sidewalk shaking hands with their guests. The wind caught at her veil, whipped it against his cheek, late snow on the dogwood tree raining down like a cloud of petals.

He ran, veering away from the park, heading instead for his old neighborhood. Rosemary was right. Norah should know. He would tell her today. He would go to their old house, where Norah still lived, and wait until she returned, and he would tell her, though he could not imagine how Norah would respond.

Of course you can't, Rosemary had said. *That's life, David. Would you have imagined yourself, years ago, living in this dumpy little duplex? Would you, in a million years, ever have imagined me?*

Well, she was right; the life he lived was not the one he had imagined for himself. He had come to this town as a stranger, but now the streets flashing by were so familiar; not a step or an image remained unconnected to a memory. He had seen these trees planted, watched them grow. He passed houses he knew, houses where he had been for dinner or for drinks, where he'd gone on emergency calls, standing late in the night in hallways or foyers, writing out prescriptions, calling an ambulance. Layer on layer of days and images, dense and complex and particular to him alone. Norah could walk here, or Paul, and see something quite different but just as real.

David turned down his old street. He had not been over here in months, and he was surprised to find the porch columns of his house torn down, the roof supported by pairs of two-by-fours. Rot in the porch floor, it looked like, but no workmen were in sight. The driveway was empty; Norah wasn't home. He paced across the lawn a few times to catch his breath, then walked to where the key was still hidden beneath a brick beside the rhododendron. He let himself inside and got a drink of water. The house smelled stale. He pushed open a window. Wind lifted the sheer white curtains. These were new, as was the tile floor and the refrigerator. He got another glass of water. Then he walked through the house, curious to see what else had changed. Small things, everywhere: a new mirror in the dining room, the living room furniture reupholstered and re-arranged.

Upstairs, the bedrooms were the same, Paul's room a shrine to adolescent angst, with posters of obscure quartets taped to the wall, ticket stubs pinned to the bulletin board, the walls painted a hideous dark blue, like a cave. He'd gone to Juilliard, and although David had given his blessing and paid half his bills, what Paul still remembered was the deeper past, when David didn't believe his talent would be enough to sustain him in the world. He was always sending program flyers and reviews, along with postcards from every city where he'd performed, as if to say *Here, look, I'm a success.* As if Paul himself could hardly believe it. Sometimes David traveled a hundred miles or more, to Cincinnati or Pittsburgh or Atlanta or Memphis, to slip into the back of a darkened auditorium and watch

Paul perform. His head bent over the guitar, his fingers deft, the music a language both mysterious and beautiful, would move David to tears. It was all he could do sometimes not to stride down the dark aisles and take Paul in his arms. But of course he never did; sometimes, he slipped away unseen.

The master bedroom was perfectly arranged, unused. Norah had moved to the smaller front bedroom; here the bedspread was wrinkled. David reached to straighten it, but pulled his hand back at the last minute, as if this would be too great an intrusion. Then he went back downstairs.

He didn't understand; it was late in the afternoon and Norah should be home. If she did not come soon, he would simply leave.

There was a yellow legal pad on the desk by the phone, full of cryptic notes: *Call Jan before 8:00 reschedule; Tim's not sure; the delivery, before 10:00. Don't forget——Dunfree and tickets.* He tore this page off carefully, neatly, arranging it in the center of the desk, then carried the pad back to the breakfast nook, sat down, and began to write.

Our little girl did not die. Caroline Gill took her and raised her in another city.

He crossed this out.

I gave away our daughter.

He sighed and put the pen down. He couldn't do this; he could hardly imagine anymore what his life would be without the weight of his hidden knowledge. He'd come to think of it as a kind penance. It was self-destructive, he could see that, but that was the way things were. People smoked, they jumped out of airplanes, they drank too much and got into their cars and drove without seat belts. For him, there was this secret. The new curtains stirred against his arm. Distantly, the tap in the downstairs bathroom dripped, something that had driven him crazy for years, something he had always meant to fix. He tore the page off the legal pad into small pieces and put them in his pocket to discard later. Then he went out into the garage and rummaged around in the tools he had left until he found a wrench and a spare set of washers. Probably he had bought them one Saturday for just this reason.

It took him more than an hour to fix the faucets in the bathroom.

He took them apart and washed sediment from the screens, replaced the washers, tightened the fixtures. The brass was tarnished. He polished it, using an old toothbrush he found stuck in a coffee can beneath the sink. It was six o'clock when he finished, early on a midsummer evening, sunlight still pouring through the windows but lower now, slanting on the floor. David stood in the bathroom for a moment, feeling deeply satisfied by the way the brass was shining, by the silence. The phone rang in the kitchen and an unfamiliar voice came on, speaking urgently about tickets for Montreal, interrupting itself to say, *Oh damn, that's right, I forgot you were off to Europe with Frederic.* And he remembered too—she'd told him, but he'd let it slip from his mind; no, he'd pushed it from his mind— that she had gone to Paris on a holiday. That she had met someone, a Canadian from Quebec, someone who worked out at the boxy buildings of IBM and spoke French. Her voice had changed when she spoke of him, somehow softened, a voice he'd never heard her use before. He imagined Norah, holding the phone with her shoulder while she typed information into the computer, looking up to realize that it was hours past dinner. Norah, striding through airport corridors, leading her groups to their buses, restaurants, hotels, adventures, all of which she had so confidently arranged.

Well, at least she would be happy about the faucets. And he was too—he'd done a careful, meticulous job. He stood in the kitchen, stretching his arms wide as he prepared to finish his run, and picked the yellow legal pad up again.

I fixed the bathroom sink, he wrote. *Happy Birthday.*

Then he left, locking the door behind him, and ran.

II

NORAH SAT ON A STONE BENCH IN THE GARDENS AT THE Louvre, a book open in her lap, watching the silvery poplar leaves flutter against the sky. Pigeons waddled in the grass near her feet, pecking, shuffling their iridescent wings.

"He's late," she said to Bree, who sat beside her, long legs crossed at the ankle, leafing through a magazine. Bree, now forty-four, was very beautiful, tall and willowy, turquoise earrings brushing against her olive skin, her hair a pure silvery white. During the radiation she'd cut it very short, saying she didn't intend to waste another instant of her life being fashionable. She was lucky and knew it; they'd caught the tumor early and she'd been cancer free now for five years. Yet the experience had left her changed, in ways both large and small. She laughed more and took more time off work. She'd started volunteering weekends on Habitat houses; while building a house in eastern Kentucky she had met a warm, ruddy, fun-loving man, a minister recently widowed. His name was Ben. They met again on a project in Florida, and once more in Mexico. On that last trip, quietly, they had gotten married.

"Paul will come," Bree said now, looking up. "It was his idea, after all."

"That's true," Norah said. "But he's in love. I just hope he remembers."

The air was hot and dry. Norah closed her eyes, thinking back to the late-April day when Paul had surprised her at the office, home for a few hours between one gig and another. Tall and still lanky, he sat on the edge of her desk, tossing her paperweight from one hand to the other as he described his plans for a summer tour of Europe, with a full six weeks in Spain to study with guitarists there. She and Frederic had scheduled a trip to France, and when Paul discovered that they'd be in Paris on the same day, he grabbed a pen from her desk and scrawled *LOUVRE* on the wall calendar in Norah's office: Five o'clock, July 21. *Meet me in the garden, and I'll take you out to dinner.*

He'd left for Europe a few weeks later, calling her now and then from rustic pensions or tiny hotels by the sea. He was in love with a flautist, the weather was great, the beer in Germany spectacular. Norah listened; she tried not to worry or ask too many questions. Paul was grown now, after all, six feet tall, with David's dark coloring. She imagined him walking barefoot on the beach, leaning to whisper something to his girlfriend, his breath like a touch on her ear.

She was so discreet she'd never even asked him for an itinerary, so when Bree called from the hospital in Lexington she had not known how to reach him with the shocking news: David, running in the arboretum, had been stricken with a massive heart attack and died.

She opened her eyes. The world was both vivid and hazy in the late-afternoon summer heat, leaves shimmering against the blue sky. She had flown home alone, waking on the plane from uneasy dreams of searching for Paul. Bree helped her through the funeral, and wouldn't let her return to Paris alone.

"Don't worry," Bree said. "He'll come."

"He missed the funeral," Norah said. "I'll always feel awful about that. They never really resolved things, David and Paul. I don't think Paul ever got over David's leaving."

"And you did?"

Norah looked at Bree, her short spiky hair and clear skin, her green eyes, calm and penetrating. She looked away.

"That sounds like something Ben would ask. I think maybe you've been spending too much time with ministers."

Bree laughed, but she didn't let it go. "Ben's not asking," she said. "I am."

"I don't know," Norah replied slowly, thinking of David the last time she'd seen him, sitting on the porch with a glass of iced tea after a run. They had been divorced for six years and married for eighteen before that: she had known him twenty-five years, a quarter of a century, more than half her lifetime. When Bree had called with news of his death, she simply could not believe it. Impossible to imagine the world without David. It was only later, after the funeral, that grief had caught up with her. "There are so many things I wish I'd said to him. But at least we did talk. Sometimes he just stopped by: to fix something, to say hello. He was lonely, I think."

"Did he know about Frederic?"

"No. I tried to tell him once, but he didn't seem to take it in."

"That sounds like David," Bree observed. "He and Frederic are so different."

"Yes. Yes, they are."

An image of Frederic in Lexington, standing outside in the shadowy dusk, tapping ash into the dirt around her rhododendrons, rushed through her. They had met just over a year ago on another drought-stricken day, in another park. The IBM account, landed with such effort, was still one of Norah's most lucrative ones, so she had gone to the annual picnic despite her headache and the distant growl of thunder. Frederic was sitting alone, looking vaguely dour and uncommunicative. Norah fixed herself a plate and sat next to him. If he didn't want to chat, that would suit her just fine. But he'd smiled and greeted her warmly, stirring from his thoughts, speaking English with a faint French accent; he was from Quebec. They talked for hours as the storm gathered, as the other picnickers packed their things and left. When the rain started, he'd asked her out to dinner.

"Where is Frederic anyway?" Bree asked. "Didn't you say he was coming?"

"He wanted to, but he got called to Orléans to work. He has

some family connection there from way back. Some distant second cousin who lives in a place called Châteauneuf. Wouldn't you like to live in a place named that?"

"They probably have traffic jams and bad hair days even there."

"I hope not. I hope they walk to market every morning and come home with fresh bread and pots full of flowers. Anyway, I told Frederic to go. He and Paul are great friends, but it's better that I give him this news alone."

"Yes. I'm planning to slip away too, once he comes."

"Thank you," Norah said, taking her hand. "Thank you for everything. For helping so much with the funeral. I couldn't have gotten through the last week without you."

"You owe me big-time," Bree said, smiling. Then she grew pensive. "I thought it was a beautiful funeral, if you can say such a thing. There were so many people. It surprised me to know how many lives David touched."

Norah nodded. She had been surprised too, Bree's little church filled up with people, so that by the time the service began they were standing three deep in the back. The preceding days had been a blur, Ben guiding her gently through choosing the music and the scriptures, the casket and the flowers, helping her write the obituary. Still, it had been a relief to have these concrete things to do, and Norah moved through the tasks in a protective cloud of numb efficiency—until the service began. People must have thought it odd, how deeply she'd wept then, the beautiful old words newly significant, but it was not only for David that she grieved. They had stood together at the memorial service for their daughter all those years ago, their loss even then growing between them.

"It was the clinic," Norah said. "The clinic he ran for all those years. Most of the people had been his patients."

"I know. It was amazing. People seemed to think he was a saint."

"They weren't married to him," Norah said.

Leaves fluttered against the hot blue sky. She scanned the park again, looking for Paul, but he was nowhere in sight.

"Oh," Norah said, "I can't believe David is really dead." Even now, days later, the words sent a little shock through her body. "I feel so old, somehow."

Bree took her hand, and they sat quietly for several minutes. Bree's palm was smooth and warm against her own, and Norah felt the moment extending, growing, as if it could contain the whole world. She remembered a similar feeling, all those long years ago when Paul was an infant and she sat in the soft dark nights, nursing him. Grown now, he stood in a train station or on the sidewalk beneath fluttering leaves or strode across a street. He paused in front of shop windows, or reached into his pocket for a ticket, or shaded his eyes against the sun. He'd grown from her body and now, astonishingly, he moved through the world without her. She thought of Frederic too, sitting in a meeting room, nodding as he scanned papers, placing his hands flat on the table as he prepared to speak. He had dark hair on his arms and long square fingernails. He shaved twice a day, and if he forgot, his new beard scraped against her neck when he pulled her close in the night, kissing her behind the ear to rouse her. He did not eat bread or sweet things; if the morning paper was late it made him exceptionally cross. All these small habits, alternately endearing and irritating, belonged to Frederic. Tonight she would meet him at their pension by the river. They would drink wine and she would wake in the night, moonlight flooding in, his steady breath soft in the room. He wanted to get married, and that was a decision too.

Norah's book slipped from her hand, and she leaned over to pick it up. Van Gogh's *Starry Night* wheeled across the brochure she'd been using as a bookmark. When she sat up again, Paul was crossing the park.

"Oh," she said, with the sudden rush of pleasure she always felt on seeing him: this person, her son, here in the world. She stood up. "There he is, Bree. Paul's here!"

"He's so handsome," Bree observed, standing up too. "He must get that from me."

"He must," Norah agreed. "Though where he gets the talent is anybody's guess, when neither one of us nor David could carry a tune in a bucket."

Paul's talent, yes. She watched him walk across the park. A mystery, that, and a gift.

Paul raised one hand to wave, grinning widely, and Norah started walking toward him, leaving her book on the bench. Her heart was beating with excitement and gladness, as well as grief and trepidation; she was trembling. How it changed the world, his being there! She reached Paul at last and hugged him hard. He wore a white shirt with the sleeves rolled up, khaki shorts. He smelled clean, as if he had just showered. She felt his muscles through the fabric, his strong bones, the very heat of him, and she understood, just for an instant, David's desire to fix the world in place. You couldn't blame him, no, you couldn't fault him for wanting to go deeper into every fleeting moment, to study its mystery, to shout against loss and change and motion.

"Hey, Mom," Paul said, pulling back to look at her. His teeth were white, straight, perfect; he'd grown a dark beard. "Fancy meeting you here," he said, laughing.

"Yes, fancy that."

Bree was beside her then. She stepped forward and hugged Paul too.

"I have to go," she said. "I was just hanging around to say hello. You're looking good, Paul. The wandering life agrees with you."

He smiled. "Can't you stay?"

Bree glanced at Norah. "No," she said. "But I'll see you soon, okay?"

"Okay," Paul said, leaning to kiss her on the cheek. "I guess."

Norah wiped the back of her wrist against her eye as Bree turned and walked away.

"What is it?" Paul asked; then, suddenly serious, "What's wrong?"

"Come and sit," she said, taking his arm.

Together, they crossed back to her bench, causing a cluster of pigeons, their feathers iridescent, to burst into flight. She picked up her book, fingering her bookmark.

"Paul, I have bad news. Your father died nine days ago. A heart attack."

His eyes widened in shock and grief and he looked away, staring without speaking at the path he'd walked to reach her, to reach this moment.

"When was the funeral?" he asked at last.

"Last week. I'm so sorry, Paul. There was no time to find you. I thought about contacting the embassy to help me track you down, but I didn't know where to start. So I came here today, hoping you'd show up."

"I almost missed the train," he said, pensive. "I almost didn't make it."

"But you did," she said. "Here you are."

He nodded and leaned forward with his elbows on his knees, his hands clasped between them. She remembered him sitting just this way as a child, struggling to hide his sadness. He clenched his fists, then released them. She took her son's hand in hers. His fingertips were calloused from years of playing. They sat for a long while, listening to the wind rustling through the leaves.

"It's okay to be upset," she said at last. "He was your father."

Paul nodded, but his face was still closed like a fist. When he finally spoke, his voice was on the edge of breaking.

"I never thought he'd die. I never thought I'd care. It's not like we ever really talked."

"I know." And she did. After the call from Bree, Norah had walked down the leaf-canopied street, weeping freely, angry with David for leaving before she'd had a chance to settle things with him, once and for all. "But before, at least talking was always an option."

"Yes. I kept waiting for him to make the first move."

"I think he was waiting for the same thing."

"He was my father," Paul said. "He was supposed to know what to do."

"He loved you," she said. "Don't ever think he didn't."

Paul gave a short, bitter laugh. "No. That sounds pretty, but it's just not true. I'd go over to his house and I'd try; I'd hang out and talk with Dad about this and that, but we never went any further. I could never get anything right for him. He'd have been happier with another son altogether." His voice was still calm, but tears had gathered in the corners of his eyes and were slipping down his cheeks.

"Honey," she said. "He loved you. He did. He thought you were the most amazing son."

Paul pushed the tears roughly off his cheeks. Norah felt her own grief and sadness gather in her throat, and it was a moment before she could speak.

"Your father," she said at last, "had a very hard time revealing himself to anyone. I don't know why. He grew up poor, and he was always ashamed of that. I wish he could have seen how many people came to the funeral, Paul. Hundreds. It was all the clinic work he did. I have the guest book; you can see for yourself. A lot of people loved him."

"Did Rosemary come?" he asked, turning to face her.

"Rosemary? Yes." Norah paused, letting the warm breeze move lightly over her face. She'd glimpsed Rosemary when the service ended, sitting in the last pew in a simple gray dress. Her hair was still long but she looked older, more settled. David had always insisted there had never been anything between them; in her heart, Norah knew this was true. "They weren't in love," Norah said. "Your father and Rosemary. It wasn't what you think."

"I know." He sat up straighter. "I know. Rosemary told me. I believed her."

"She did? When?"

"When Dad brought her home. That first day." He looked uncomfortable, but he went on. "I'd see her at his place sometimes. When I stopped in to visit Dad. Sometimes we'd all have dinner together. Sometimes Dad wasn't home, so I'd hang out for a while with Rosemary and Jack. I could tell there wasn't anything between them. Sometimes she'd have a boyfriend there. I don't know. It was a little weird, I guess. But I got used to it. She was okay, Rosemary. She wasn't the reason I couldn't ever really talk to him."

Norah nodded. "But Paul, you mattered to him. Look, I know what you're saying, because I felt it too. That distance. That reserve. That sense of a wall too high to get over. After a while I gave up trying, and after a longer while I gave up waiting for a door to appear in it. But behind that wall, he loved us both. I don't know how I know that, but I do."

Paul didn't speak. Every now and then he brushed tears from his eyes.

The air was cooler, and people had begun to stroll through the gardens, lovers holding hands, couples with children, solitary walkers. An elderly couple approached. She was tall, with a flash of white hair, and he walked slowly, stooping slightly, with a cane. She had her hand tucked around his elbow and was leaning down to speak to him, and he was nodding, pensive, frowning, looking across the gardens, beyond the gates, at whatever she wanted him to note. Norah felt a pang to see this intimacy. Once she had imagined herself and David moving into such an old age, their histories woven together like vines, tendril around shoot, leaves meshed. Oh, she'd been so old-fashioned; even her regret was old-fashioned. She had imagined that, married, she would be some sort of lovely bud, wrapped in the tougher, resilient calyx of the flower. Wrapped and protected, the layers of her own life contained within another's.

But instead she had found her own way, building a business, raising Paul, traveling the world. She was petal, calyx, stem, and leaf; she was the long white root running deep into the earth. And she was glad.

As they passed, the couple spoke in English, arguing about where to have dinner. Their accents were from the south—from Texas, Norah guessed—and the man wanted to find a place with steak, with food that was familiar.

"I'm so tired of Americans," Paul said, once they were out of earshot. "Always so glad to find another American. You'd think there weren't two hundred and fifty million of us. You'd think they'd want to be seeking out some French people, since they're in France."

"You've been talking to Frederic."

"Sure. Why not? Frederic is right on the mark when it comes to American arrogance. Where is he, anyway?"

"Away on business. He'll come tonight."

It rushed through her again, the image of Frederic walking

through the door of the hotel room, dropping his keys on the dresser and patting his pockets to make sure he had his wallet. He wore bright white shirts that caught the last light, with crisp button-down collars, and each evening he came in and tossed his tie over a chair, his low voice shaping her name. Perhaps it was his voice she had loved first. They had so much in common—grown children, divorces, demanding jobs—but because Frederic's life had happened in another country, half in another language, it felt exotic to Norah, familiar and unknown at once. An old country and a new.

"Has your visit been good?" Paul asked. "Do you like France?"

"I've been happy here," Norah said, and it was true. Frederic felt congestion had ruined Paris, but for Norah the charm was infinite, the boulangeries and the patisseries, the crêpes sold from street stands, the spires of ancient buildings, the bells. The sounds, too, of the language flowing like a stream, a word here and there emerging like a pebble. "How about you? How's the tour? Are you still in love?"

"Oh, yes," he said, his face easing a little. He looked straight at her. "Are you going to marry Frederic?"

She ran her finger around the sharp corner of the brochure. This was the question, of course, woven through all her moments: Should she change her life? She loved Frederic, she had never been happier, though she could see through that happiness to a time when his endearing habits might get on her nerves, and hers on his. He liked things just so; he was meticulous about everything from mitered corners to tax forms. In that way, though in no others, he reminded her of David. She was old enough now, experienced enough, to know that nothing was perfect. Nothing stayed the same, herself included. But it was also true that when Frederic walked into a room the air seemed to shift, grow charged, to pulse straight through her. She wanted to see what might happen next.

"I don't know," she said slowly. "Bree's willing to buy the business. Frederic has two more years on his contract, so we don't have to make any decisions for a while. But I can imagine myself in a life with him. I suppose that's the first step."

Paul nodded. "Is that how it was last time? You know, with Dad?"

Norah looked at him, wondering how to answer this.

"Yes and no," she said at last. "I'm much more pragmatic now. Then, I just wanted to be taken care of. I didn't know myself very well."

"Dad liked to take care of things."

"Yes. Yes, he did."

Paul gave a short, sharp laugh. "I can't believe he's dead."

"I know," Norah said. "Neither can I."

They sat for a time in silence, air moving lightly around them. Norah turned her brochure, remembering the coolness in the museum, the echo of footsteps. She'd stood for nearly an hour before this painting, studying the swirls of color, the sure and vivid brush-strokes. What was it Van Gogh had touched? Something that shimmered, something elusive. David had moved through the world, focusing his camera on its smallest details, obsessed with light and shadow, trying to fix things in place. Now he was gone and the way he'd seen the world was gone as well.

Paul was standing up, waving across the park, the sadness on his face giving way to a joyous smile, intense, clearly focused, and exclusive. Norah followed his gaze across the dry grass to a young woman with a long delicate face and skin the color of ripe acorns, her dark hair in dreadlocks to her waist. She was slender, wearing a soft print dress; she carried herself with a dancer's grace and reserve.

"It's Michelle," Paul said, already standing. "I'll be right back. It's Michelle."

Norah watched him move toward her as if pulled by gravity, Michelle's face lifting at the sight of him. He cupped her face lightly in his hands as they kissed, and then she raised her hand and their palms touched briefly, lightly, a gesture so intimate that Norah looked away. They crossed the park then, heads bent, talking. At one point they paused, and Michelle rested her hand on Paul's arm, and Norah knew he had told her.

"Mrs. Henry," she said, shaking hands when they reached the bench. Her fingers were long and cool. "I am so sorry about Paul's father."

Her accent, too, was faintly exotic: she had spent many years in

London. For a few minutes they all stood in the garden, talking. Paul suggested that they go for dinner, and Norah was tempted to say yes. She wanted to sit with Paul and talk long into the night, but she hesitated, aware that between Paul and Michelle there was a warmth, a radiance, a restlessness to be alone. She thought of Frederic again, perhaps already back in their pension, his tie falling across the back of a chair.

"How about tomorrow?" she said. "What if we meet for breakfast? I want to hear all about your trip. I want to know all about the flamenco guitarists in Seville."

On the street, walking to the metro, Michelle took Norah's arm. Paul walked just ahead of them, broad-shouldered, lanky.

"You raised a wonderful son," she said. "I'm so sorry I won't get to know his father."

"That would have been hard in any case—to get to know him. But yes, I'm sorry too." They walked a few steps. "Have you enjoyed your tour?"

"Oh, it's a wonderful freedom, traveling," Michelle observed.

It was a soft evening, the bright lights of the metro station a shock as they descended. A train clattered in the distance, echoed through the tunnel. There were mingled scents: perfume and, underneath, the sharper tang of metal, oil.

"Come by around nine tomorrow," Norah told Paul, raising her voice over the noise. And then, as the train came nearer, she leaned forward, close to his ear, shouting.

"He loved you! He was your father, and he loved you!"

Paul's face opened for an instant: grief and loss. He nodded. There was no time for more. The train was rushing now, rushing toward them all, and in its sudden wind she felt her heart fill up. Her son, here in the world. And David, mysteriously, gone. The train stopped, squealing, and the hydraulic doors burst open with a sigh. Norah got on and sat by the window, watching a flash, a final glimpse of Paul, walking, his hands in his pockets, his head down. There, then gone.

By the time she reached her stop, the air had filled up with the grainy light of dusk. She walked across cobblestones to the pension, painted pale yellow and faintly luminous, its window boxes spilling flowers. The room was quiet, her own strewn things undisturbed; Frederic had not arrived. Norah went to the window overlooking the river and stood there for a moment, thinking of David carrying Paul on his shoulders through their first house, thinking of the day he had proposed, shouting at her over the rush of water, the cool ring slipping down her finger. Thinking of Paul's hand and Michelle's, palm to palm.

She went to the little desk and wrote a note: *Frederic, I am in the courtyard.*

The courtyard, lined with potted palms, overlooked the Seine. Tiny lights were woven into the trees, the iron railings. Norah sat where she could see the river and ordered a glass of wine. She'd left her book somewhere—probably in the garden at the Louvre. Its loss filled her with a vague regret. It was not the sort of book one bought twice, just something light, something to pass the time. Something about two sisters. Now she would never know how the story ended.

Two sisters. Maybe someday she and Bree would write a book. The thought made Norah smile, and the man who was sitting at an adjacent table, dressed in a white suit, a tiny aperitif glass by his hand, smiled back. So these things began: there was a time when she would have crossed her legs or pushed back her hair, small gestures of invitation, until he rose and left his table and came to ask if he might join her. She had loved the power of this dance and the sense of discovery. But tonight she looked away. The man lit a cigarette, and when it was finished he paid his bill and left.

Norah sat watching the flow of people against the dark shimmer of the river. She did not see Frederic arrive. But then his hand was on her shoulder, she was turning, and he was kissing her, one cheek, and then the other, and then his lips on hers.

"Hello," he said, and sat down across the table. He was not a tall man, but he was very fit, with strong shoulders from years of swimming. He was a systems analyst, and Norah liked his sureness, his ability to grasp and discuss the larger whole and not get bogged down in the minutiae of the moment. Yet it was the very thing that sometimes irritated her too—his sense of the world as a steady and predictable place.

"Have you waited long?" he asked. "Have you eaten?"

"No." She nodded at her wineglass, nearly full. "Not long at all. And I'm famished."

He nodded. "Good. Sorry to be late. The train was delayed."

"It's all right. How was your day in Orléans?"

"Humdrum. But I had a nice lunch with my cousin." He began to talk and Norah sat back, letting the words wash over her. Frederic's hands were strong and deft. She remembered a day when he'd built her a set of bookshelves, working in the garage all weekend, curls of fresh wood falling off his planer. He was not afraid to work or to stop her in the kitchen while she cooked, sliding his hands around her waist and kissing her neck until she turned and kissed him back. He smoked a pipe, which she did not like, and worked too hard, and drove too fast on the highway.

"You told Paul?" Frederic asked. "Is he all right?"

"I don't know. I hope so. He's meeting us for breakfast. He wants to complain to you about arrogant Americans."

Frederic laughed. "Good," he said. "I like your son."

"He's in love. And she's quite lovely, this young woman he adores: Michelle. She'll come tomorrow too."

"Good," Frederic said again, weaving his fingers through her own. "It's good to be in love."

They ordered dinner, brochettes of beef on rice pilaf, more wine. The river moved below, darkly, silently, and as they talked Norah thought how lovely it was to sit quietly anchored in one place. To sit drinking wine in Paris, watching the birds burst into flight from the silhouetted trees, the river moving calmly below. She remembered her wild drives to the Ohio as a young woman, the strangely iridescent skin of the water, the sheerness of the limestone banks, the wind lifting her hair.

But now she sat still, and the birds flew up darkly against the indigo sky. She smelled water, and exhaust, and meat roasting, and the dank mud of the river. Frederic relit his pipe and poured more wine and people strolled by on the sidewalk, moving through this evening that was giving way to night, the nearby buildings fading slowly into the darkening air. One by one lights came on in windows. Norah folded her napkin and stood up. The world wheeled away; she was dizzy from the wine, the height, the scent of food after this long day of grief and joy.

"Are you all right?" Frederic asked, from far away.

Norah touched the table with one hand, caught her breath. She nodded, unable to speak above the sound of the river, the smell of its dark banks, the stars roaring everywhere, swirling, alive.

November 1988

H IS NAME WAS ROBERT AND HE WAS HANDSOME, WITH A shock of dark hair that fell across his forehead. He went up and down the aisle of the bus, introducing himself to everyone and commenting on the route, the driver, the day. He reached the end of the row, turned around, and went through the whole thing again. "I'm having a great time here," he announced, shaking Caroline's hand on his way. She smiled, patient; his grip was firm and confident. Other people would not meet his eye. They studied their books, their newspapers, the scenes slipping by outside the window. Yet Robert went on, undaunted, as if the people on the bus were as much to be remarked upon, and no more expected to respond, than trees, rocks, or clouds. Within his persistence, Caroline thought, watching from the last seat, deciding again every second not to intervene, was some deep desire to find a person who would really see him.

That person, it appeared, was Phoebe, who seemed to brighten, awash in some internal light, when Robert was around, who watched him move up and down the aisle as if he were some marvelous new creature, a peacock perhaps, beautiful and showy and proud. When he finally settled down in the seat next to her, still talking, Phoebe simply smiled up at him. It was a radiant smile; she held nothing back. No reserve, no caution, no waiting to make sure he felt the same surging love. Caroline closed her eyes at her daughter's naked expression of emotion—the wild innocence, the risk! But when she opened them again Robert was smiling back, as pleased by Phoebe, as wonderstruck, as if a tree had cried out his name.

Well, yes, Caroline thought, and why not? Wasn't such love rare enough in the world? She glanced at Al, who sat next to her, nodding off, his graying hair lifting as the bus traveled over bumps, around curves. He'd come in late last night and would leave again tomorrow morning, earning overtime to pay for the new roof and gutters. These last months, their days together had been mostly consumed with business. Sometimes a memory of their early marriage—his lips on hers, the touch of his hand on her waist— swept through Caroline, a bittersweet nostalgia. How had they become so busy and careworn, the two of them? How had so many days slipped away, one after another, to bring them to this moment?

The bus sped across the ravine, up the incline to Squirrel Hill. Headlights were already on in the early winter dusk. Phoebe and Robert sat quietly, facing the aisle, dressed for the Upside Down Society's annual dance. Robert's shoes were polished to a high shine; he wore his best suit. Beneath her winter coat, Phoebe wore a flowery white and red dress, a delicate white cross from her confirmation on a slender chain around her neck. Her hair had darkened and grown thinner and was cut in a short flyaway cap around her skull, clipped here and there with red barrettes. She was pale, with light freckles on her arms and face. She stared out the window, smiling faintly, lost in her thoughts. Robert studied the billboards above Caroline's head, ads for clinics and dentists, maps of the route. He was a good man, prepared in every moment to be delighted by the world, though he forgot conversations almost as soon as they were finished and asked Caroline for her phone number every time they met.

Still, he always remembered Phoebe. He always remembered love.

"We're almost there," Phoebe said, tugging on Robert's arm as they neared the top of the hill. The day facility was half a block away, its lights spilling softly across the brown grass, the crusts of snow. "I counted seven stops."

"Al," Caroline said, shaking his shoulder. "Al, honey, it's our stop."

They stepped off the bus into the damp chill of the November evening and walked in pairs through the dusky light. Caroline slid her hand around Al's arm.

"You're tired," she said, seeking to break the silence that, more and more, had come to be their habit. "You've had a long couple of weeks."

"I'm okay," he said.

"I wish you didn't have to be away so much." She regretted her words the moment she said them. The argument was old by now, a tender knot in the flesh of their marriage, and even to her own ears her voice sounded strident, shrill, as if she were deliberately picking a fight.

Snow crunched under their shoes. Al sighed heavily, his breath a faint cloud in the cold.

"Look, I'm doing the best I can, Caroline. The money's good just now and I have some seniority built up. I'm pushing sixty. I have to milk it while I can."

Caroline nodded. His arm beneath her hand was firm and steady. She was so glad to have him here, so tired of the strange rhythms of their lives that kept him away for days at a time. What she wanted, more than anything, was to have breakfast with him every morning and dinner every night; to wake with him in bed beside her, not in some anonymous hotel room a hundred or five hundred miles away.

"It's just that I miss you," Caroline said softly. "That's all I meant. That's all I'm saying." Phoebe and Robert walked ahead of them, holding hands. Caroline watched her daughter, wearing dark gloves, a scarf Robert had given her wrapped loosely around her neck. Phoebe wanted to marry Robert, to have a life with him; lately this was all she talked about. Linda, the day facility director, had warned, *Phoebe's in love. She's twenty-four, a bit of a late bloomer, and she's starting to discover her own sexuality, We need to discuss this, Caroline.* But Caroline, unwilling to admit that anything had changed, had put the discussion off.

Phoebe walked with her head slightly bent, intent on listening; now and then her sudden laughter floated back through the dusk. Caroline inhaled the sharp cold air, feeling a surge of pleasure at her daughter's happiness, taken back, in the same moment, to the clinic waiting room with its drooping ferns and rattling door, Norah Henry standing by the counter, pulling off her gloves to show the receptionist her wedding ring, laughing in this same way.

A lifetime ago, that was. Caroline had put those days from her mind almost completely. Then last week, while Al was still away, a letter had arrived from a law firm downtown. Caroline, puzzled, had ripped it open and read it on the porch, in the chill November air.

Please contact this office regarding an account in your name.

She called at once and stood at the window, watching the river of traffic, as the lawyer gave her the news: David Henry was dead. He'd been dead, in fact, for three months. They were contacting her to tell her about a bank account he'd left in her name. Caroline had pressed the phone to her ear, something sinking deeply and darkly through her at this news, studying the sparse remaining leaves of the sycamore trees as they fluttered in the cold morning light. The lawyer, miles away, went on talking. It was a beneficiary account: David had established it jointly in both their names, and therefore it stood outside the will and probate. They wouldn't tell her how much was in the account, not over the phone. Caroline would have to come in to the office.

After she hung up she went back out onto the porch, where she sat for a long time in the swing, trying to take in the news. It shocked her that David had remembered her this way. It shocked her more that he'd actually died. What had she imagined? That she and David would both somehow go on forever, living their separate lives yet still connected to that moment in his office when he stood up and put Phoebe in her arms? That somehow, someday, whenever it suited her, she would seek him out and let him meet his daugh-

ter? Cars rushed down the hill in a steady stream. She couldn't figure out what to do, and in the end she'd simply gone back inside
and gotten ready for work, sliding the letter into the top desk
drawer with the detritus of rubber bands and paper clips, waiting
for Al to get home and help her gain perspective. She hadn't mentioned it yet—he'd been so tired—but the news, unspoken, still
hung in the air between them, along with Linda's concern about
Phoebe.

Light spilled from the center onto the sidewalk, the brown stems
of grass. They pushed through the double glass doors into the hallway. A dance floor had been set up at the end of the hall and a disco
ball turned, scattering bright shards of light over the ceiling and the
walls and upturned faces. The music played , but no one was dancing. Phoebe and Robert stood on the edge of the crowd, watching
the light shifting on the empty floor.

Al hung up their coats and then, to Caroline's surprise, he took
her hand. "You remember that day in the garden, the day we decided to get hitched? Let's teach them how to rock and roll, what do
you say?"

Caroline felt quick tears, thinking of the leaves fluttering like
coins on that long-ago day, the brightness of the sun and the humming of distant bees. They had danced across the grass, and she had
taken Al's hand in the hospital, hours later, and said, *Yes, I will
marry you, yes.*

Al slid his hand around her waist and they stepped onto the floor.
Caroline had forgotten—it had been a long time—how easily and
fluidly their bodies moved together, how free it made her feel to
dance. She let her head rest against his shoulder, inhaling his spicy
aftershave, the clean scent of machine oil lingering beneath. Al's
hand was pressed firmly against her back, his cheek to hers. They
turned, and slowly other people drifted onto the dance floor, smiling in their direction. Caroline knew almost everyone in the room,
the staff of the day center, the other parents from Upside Down, the
residents from the facility next door. Phoebe was on a waiting list
for a room there, a place where she could live with several other
adults and a house parent. It seemed ideal in some ways—more independence and autonomy for Phoebe, at least a partial answer to

her future—but the truth was that Caroline could not imagine Phoebe living apart from her. The waiting list for the residence had seemed very long when they applied, but in the last year Phoebe's name had moved up steadily. Soon Caroline would have to make a decision. She glimpsed Phoebe now, smiling such a happy smile, her thin hair held back by the bright red barrettes, stepping shyly onto the dance floor with Robert.

She danced with Al for three more numbers, eyes closed, letting herself drift, following his steps. He was a good dancer, smooth and sure, and the music seemed to run straight through her. Phoebe's voice could do this to her too, the pure tones of her singing drifting through the rooms, making Caroline pause in whatever she was doing and stand still, the world pouring through her like light. *Nice,* Al murmured, pulling her closer, pressing his cheek to hers. When the music shifted to a fast rock number, he kept his arm around her as they left the floor.

Caroline, a little giddy, scanned the room for Phoebe by long habit, and felt the first filaments of worry when she didn't see her.

"I sent her down for more punch," Linda called from behind the table. She gestured to the dwindling refreshments on the table. "Can you believe this turnout, Caroline? We're running out of cookies too."

"I'll get some," Caroline offered, glad for an excuse to go after Phoebe.

"She'll be okay," Al said, catching her hand and gesturing to the chair beside him.

"I'll just check," Caroline said. "I won't be a minute."

She walked through the empty halls, so bright and quiet, Al's touch still present on her skin. She went down the stairs and into the kitchen, pushing open the swinging metal doors with one hand and reaching for the light switch with the other. The sudden fluorescence caught them like a photograph: Phoebe, in her flowered dress, her back against the counter, Robert standing close, his arms around her, one hand sliding up her leg. In the instant before they turned, Caroline saw that he was going to kiss her and Phoebe wanted to be kissed and was ready to kiss him back: this Robert, her first true love. Her eyes were closed, her face awash with pleasure.

"Phoebe," Caroline said, sharply. "Phoebe and Robert, that's enough."

They pulled away from each other, startled but not contrite.

"It's okay," Robert said. "Phoebe is my girlfriend."

"We're getting married," Phoebe added.

Caroline, trembling, tried to stay calm. Phoebe was, after all, a grown woman. "Robert," she said, "I need to talk to Phoebe for a minute. Alone, please."

Robert hesitated, then walked past Caroline, all his gregarious enthusiasm evaporated. "It's not bad," he said, pausing at the door. "Me and Phoebe—we love each other."

"I know," Caroline said, as the doors swung shut behind him.

Phoebe stood beneath the harsh lights, twisting her necklace. "You can kiss someone you love, Mom. You kiss Al."

Caroline nodded, remembering Al's hand on her waist. "That's right. But, honey, that looked like more than kissing."

"Mom!" Phoebe was exasperated. "Robert and me are getting *married*."

Caroline replied without thinking. "You can't get married, sweetie."

Phoebe looked up, her face set in a stubborn expression Caroline knew well. Fluorescent light fell through a colander and made a pattern on her cheeks.

"Why not?"

"Sweetheart, marriage . . ." Caroline paused, thinking of Al, his recent weariness, the distance he put between them every time he traveled. "Look, it's complicated, honey. You can love Robert without getting married."

"No. Me and Robert, we're getting married."

Caroline sighed. "All right. Say you do. Where are you going to live?"

"We'll buy a house," Phoebe said, her expression intent now, earnest. "We'll live there, Mom. We'll have some babies."

"Babies are an awful lot of work," Caroline said. "I wonder if you and Robert know how much work babies are? And they're expensive. How are you going to pay for this house? For food?"

"Robert has a job. So do I. We have a *lot* of money."

"But you won't be able to work if you're watching the babies."

Phoebe considered this, frowning, and Caroline's heart filled. Such profound and simple dreams, and they couldn't come true, and where was the fairness in that?

"I love Robert," Phoebe insisted. "Robert loves me. Plus, Avery had a baby."

"Oh, honey," Caroline said. She remembered Avery Swan pushing a carriage down the sidewalk, pausing so Phoebe could lean over and touch the new baby gently on the cheek. "Oh, sweetheart." She crossed the space between them and put her hands on Phoebe's shoulders. "Remember when you and Avery rescued Rain? And we love Rain, but he's a lot of work. You have to empty the litter box and comb his hair, you have to clean up the mess he makes and let him in and out, and you worry about him a lot when he doesn't come home. Having a baby is even more, Phoebe. Having a baby is like having twenty Rains."

Phoebe's face was falling, tears were slipping down her cheeks.

"It's not fair," she whispered.

"It's not fair," Caroline agreed.

The stood for a moment, quiet in the bright harsh lights.

"Look, Phoebe, can you help me?" she asked finally. "Linda needs some cookies, too."

Phoebe nodded, wiping her eyes. They walked back up the stairs and through the hallway, carrying boxes and bottles, not speaking.

Later that night, Caroline told Al what had happened. He was sitting beside her on the couch, arms folded, already half asleep. His neck was still tender, reddened from shaving earlier, and dark circles shadowed his eyes. In the morning he would rise at dawn and drive away.

"She wants so much to have her own life, Al. And it should be so simple."

"Mmm," he said, rousing. "Well, maybe it *is* simple, Caroline. Other people live in the facility and they seem to manage okay. We'd be right here."

Caroline shook her head. "I just can't imagine her out in the world. And she certainly can't get married, Al. What if she did get pregnant? I'm not ready to raise another child, and that's what it would mean."

"I don't want to raise another baby either," Al said.

"Maybe we should keep her from seeing Robert for a while."

Al turned to look at her, surprised. "You think that would be a good thing?"

"I don't know." Caroline sighed. "I just don't know."

"Look here," Al said gently. "From the minute I met you, Caroline, you've been demanding that the world not slam any doors on Phoebe. *Do not underestimate her*—How many times have I heard you say that? So why won't you let her move out? Why not let her try? She might like the place. You might like the freedom."

She stared at the crown molding, thinking it needed painting, while a difficult truth struggled to the surface.

"I can't imagine my life without her," she said softly.

"No one's asking you to do that. But she's grown up, Caroline. That's the thing. Why have you worked all your life, if not for some kind of independent life for Phoebe?"

"I suppose you'd like to be free," Caroline said. "You'd like to take off. To travel."

"And you wouldn't?"

"Of course I would," she cried, surprised at the intensity of her response. "But Al, even if Phoebe moves out, she'll never be completely independent. And I'm afraid you're unhappy because of it. I'm afraid you're going to leave us. Honey, you've been more and more distant these past years."

Al didn't speak for a long time. "Why are you so mad?" he asked at last. "What have I ever done to make you feel like I'm going to leave?"

"I'm not mad," she said quickly, because she heard in his voice that she'd hurt him. "Al, wait here a second." She walked across the room and took the letter from the drawer. "This is why I'm upset. I don't know what to do."

He took the letter and studied it for a long time, turning it over once as if its mystery might be answered by something written on the back, then reading it once more.

"How much is in this account?" he asked, looking up.

She shook her head. "I don't know yet. I have to go in person to find out."

Al nodded, studying the letter again. "It's strange, the way he did this: a secret account."

"I know. Maybe he was afraid I'd tell Norah. Maybe he wanted to make sure she had time to get used to his death. That's all I can imagine." She thought of Norah, moving through the world, never suspecting that her daughter was still alive. And Paul—what had become of him? Hard to imagine who he might be now, that dark-haired infant she'd seen only once.

"What do you think we should do?" she asked.

"Well, find out the details, first. We'll go down to see this lawyer fellow together when I get back. I can take off a day or two. After that, I don't know, Caroline. We sleep on it, I guess. We don't have to do anything right away."

"All right," she said, all her consternation of the last week falling away. Al made it sound so easy. "I'm so glad you're here," she said.

"Honestly, Caroline." He took her hand in his. "I'm not going anywhere. Except to Toledo, at six o'clock tomorrow morning. So I think I'll go up and hit the sack."

He kissed her then, full on the lips, and pulled her close. Caroline pressed her cheek against his, taking in his scent and warmth, thinking of meeting him that day in the parking lot outside of Louisville, the day that defined her life.

Al got up, his hand still in hers. "Come upstairs?" he invited.

She nodded and stood, her hand in his.

. . .

In the morning she rose early and made breakfast, decorating the plates of eggs, bacon, and hash browns with sprigs of parsley.

"That sure smells good," Al said, as he came in, kissing her cheek and tossing the paper on the table, along with yesterday's mail. The letters were cool, faintly damp, in her hands. There were two bills, plus a bright postcard of the Aegean Sea with a note from Doro on the back.

Caroline ran her fingers over the picture and read the brief message. "Trace sprained his ankle in Paris."

"That's too bad." Al snapped open the paper and shook his head at the election news.

"Hey, Caroline," he said after a moment, putting the paper down. "I was thinking last night. Why don't you come with me? Linda would take Phoebe for the weekend, I bet. We could get away, you and me. You'd get a chance to see how Phoebe might do with some time on her own. What do you say?"

"Right now? Just leave, you mean?"

"Yeah. Seize the day. Why not?"

"Oh," she said, flustered, pleased, though she didn't like the long hours on the road. "I don't know. There's so much to do this week. Maybe next time," she added quickly, not wanting to turn him away.

"We could take some side trips, this time," he coaxed. "Make it more interesting for you."

"It's a really good idea," she said, thinking with surprise that it was.

He smiled, disappointed, and leaned to kiss her, his lips brief and cool on hers.

After Al drove off, Caroline hung Doro's postcard on the refrigerator. It was a bleak November, the weather damp and gray and edging to snow, and she liked looking at that bright, alluring sea, the edge of warm sand. All that week, helping patients or making dinner or folding laundry, Caroline remembered Al's invitation. She thought about the passionate kiss she'd interrupted between Robert and her daughter, and about the residence where Phoebe wanted to live. Al was right. Someday the two of them would no longer be here, and Phoebe had a right to a life of her own.

Yet the world was no less cruel than ever. On Tuesday, while they were in the dining room eating meat loaf and mashed potatoes and green beans, Phoebe reached into her pocket and took out a little plastic puzzle, the kind with numbers printed on movable squares. The trick was to put the numbers in order, and she pushed at them in between bites.

"That's nice," Caroline said idly, drinking her milk. "Where did you get that, honey?"

"From Mike."

"Does he work with you?" Caroline asked. "Is he new?"

"No," Phoebe said. "I met him on the bus."

"On the bus?"

"Uh-huh. Yesterday. He was nice."

"I see." Caroline felt time slowing down a bit, all her senses growing more alert. She had to force herself to speak calmly, naturally. "Mike gave you the puzzle?"

"Uh-huh. He was nice. And he has a new bird. He wants to show me."

"Does he?" Caroline said, a cool wind rushing through her. "Phoebe, honey, you can't even think about going off with strangers. We talked about that."

"I know. I told him," Phoebe said. She pushed the puzzle away and squirted more ketchup on her meat loaf. "He said, Come home with me, Phoebe. And I said, Okay, but I have to tell my mom first."

"What a good idea," Caroline managed to say.

"So can I? Can I go to Mike's house tomorrow?"

"Where does Mike live?"

Phoebe shrugged. "I don't know. I see him on the bus."

"Every day?"

"Uh-huh. Can I go? I want to see his bird."

"Well, what if I come too?" Caroline said carefully. "What if we take the bus together tomorrow? That way I can meet Mike, and I'll come with you to see the bird. How's that?"

"That's good," Phoebe said, pleased, and finished her milk.

For the next two days, Caroline took the bus with Phoebe to and from her job, but Mike never showed up.

"Honey, I'm afraid he was lying," she told Phoebe on Thursday night as they washed the dishes. Phoebe was wearing a yellow sweater, and her hands sported a dozen little paper cuts from work. Caroline watched her pick up each plate and dry it carefully, grateful that Phoebe was safe, terrified that some day she would not be. Who was this stranger, this Mike, and what might he have done to

Phoebe if she had gone with him? Caroline filed a report with the police, but she had little hope that they'd find him. Nothing had actually happened, after all, and Phoebe couldn't describe the man, except to say that he'd worn a gold ring and blue sneakers.

"Mike is nice," Phoebe insisted. "He wouldn't lie."

"Sweetheart, not everyone is good or wants what's best for you. He didn't come back to the bus, like he promised. He was trying to trick you, Phoebe. You have to be careful."

"You always say that," Phoebe responded, throwing the dish towel on the counter. "You say that about Robert."

"That's different. Robert isn't trying to hurt you."

"I love Robert."

"I know." Caroline closed her eyes and took a deep breath. "Look, Phoebe, I love you. I don't want you to get hurt. Sometimes the world is dangerous. I think this man is dangerous."

"But I didn't go with him," Phoebe said, picking up on the sternness and fear in Caroline's voice. She put the last plate on the counter, suddenly near tears. "I didn't go."

"You were smart," Caroline said. "You did the right thing. Never go with anyone."

"Unless they know the word."

"Right. And the word is a secret, you don't tell anyone."

"Starfire!" Phoebe whispered loudly, beaming. "It's a secret."

"Yes." Caroline sighed. "Yes, it's a secret."

. . .

On Friday morning, Caroline drove Phoebe to work. That evening, she sat in her car, waiting, watching Phoebe through the window as she moved behind the counter, binding documents or joking with Max, her co-worker, a young woman with her hair pulled back in a ponytail who went out to lunch with Phoebe every Friday, and who was not afraid to take her to task if she messed up an order. Phoebe had worked here for three years now. She loved her job and she was good at it. Caroline, watching her daughter move behind the pane of glass, thought back to the long hours of organizing, all the presentations and the fights and paperwork it had taken to make this moment possible for Phoebe. Yet so much remained. The incident on the bus was just one concern. Phoebe didn't earn enough to live on, and she simply could not stay by herself, not even for a weekend. If a fire broke out or the electricity failed, she would be frightened and would not know what to do.

And then there was Robert. On the drive home, Phoebe chatted about work, about Max, and about Robert, Robert, Robert. He was coming over the next day to make a pie with Phoebe. Caroline listened, glad it was almost Saturday and Al would be back. One good thing about the stranger on the bus: he had given her an excuse to take Phoebe back and forth, thus limiting the time she spent with Robert.

When they walked in the door, the phone was ringing. Caroline sighed. It would be a salesman, or a neighbor collecting for the heart fund, or a wrong number. Rain mewed in welcome, weaving around her ankles. "Scat," she said, and picked up the phone.

It was the police, the officer on the other end clearing his throat, asking for her. Caroline was surprised, then pleased. Perhaps they had found the man on the bus, after all.

"Yes," she said, watching Phoebe pick up Rain and hug him. "This is Caroline Simpson."

He cleared his throat again and began.

Later, Caroline would remember this moment as being very large, time expanding until it filled the whole room and pressed her down into a chair, though the news was simple enough and could not have taken very long to say. Al's truck had left the road on a curve, breaking through a guardrail and flying into a low hill. He was in the hospital with a broken leg; the same trauma center where, so many years ago, Caroline had agreed to marry him.

Phoebe was humming to Rain, but she seemed to sense that something was wrong and looked up, questioning, the minute Caroline hung up the phone. Caroline explained what had happened as she drove. In the tiled hospital corridors, she found herself swimming in memories of that earlier day: Phoebe's lips swelling, her breathing labored, Al stepping in when she was so angry with that nurse. Now Phoebe was a grown woman, walking beside her in her work vest; she and Al had been married for eighteen years.

Eighteen years.

He was awake, his dark and silver hair standing out against the whiteness of the pillow. He tried to sit up when they came in but then grimaced in pain and lay back down slowly.

"Oh, Al." She crossed the room and took his hand.

"I'm okay," he said, and he closed his eyes for a moment and took a deep breath. She felt herself going very still inside, for she had never seen Al like this, so shaken he was trembling slightly, a muscle twitching in his jaw up near his ear.

"Hey, you're starting to scare me," she said, trying to keep her tone light.

He opened his eyes then, and for an instant they were looking straight at each other, everything between them falling away. He reached up and touched one large hand lightly against her cheek. She pressed it with her own hand, felt tears in her eyes.

"What happened?" she whispered.

He sighed. "I don't know. It was such a sunny afternoon. Bright, clear. I was moving right along, singing with the radio. Thinking about how great it would be if you were there, like we talked about. The next thing I knew, the truck was sailing through the guardrails. And after that I don't remember. Not until I woke up in here. I totaled the truck. The cops said another dozen yards either way down the road, and I'd have been history."

Caroline leaned forward and put her arms around him, smelling his familiar smells. His heart beat steadily in his chest. Just days ago, they had moved together on the dance floor, worried about the roof, the gutters. She fingered his hair, grown too long at the base of his neck.

"Oh, Al."

"I know," he said. "I know, Caroline."

Beside them, wide-eyed, Phoebe started to cry, pressing the sobs back into her mouth with her hand. Caroline sat up and put an arm around her. She stroked Phoebe's hair, felt the sturdy warmth of her body.

"Phoebe," Al said. "Look at you here, just getting off work. Did you have a good day, honey? I didn't get to Cleveland, so I didn't get those rolls you like so much, sorry to say. Next time, okay?"

Phoebe nodded, wiping her hands across her cheeks. "Where's

your truck?" she asked, and Caroline remembered the times Al had taken them both for a ride, Phoebe sitting high up in the cab and pulling her fist down when they passed other trucks to make them blow their horns.

"Honey, it's broken," Al said. "I'm sorry, but it's really smashed up."

Al was in the hospital for two days, and then he came home. Caroline's time passed in a blur of getting Phoebe to work and going to work herself, tending to Al, making meals, trying to make a dent in the laundry. She fell into bed exhausted each night, woke in the morning, and started all over again. It didn't help that Al was an awful patient, ornery at being so confined, short-tempered and demanding. She was reminded, unhappily, of those early days with Leo in this same house, as if time were not traveling in a straight line but circling around instead.

A week passed. On Saturday, Caroline, exhausted, put a load in the washer and went into the kitchen to get something made for dinner. She pulled a pound of carrots out of the refrigerator for a salad and rummaged in the freezer, hoping for inspiration. Nothing. Well, Al wouldn't like it, but maybe she'd order a pizza. It was five o'clock already, and in a few minutes she would have to leave to pick Phoebe up from work. She paused in the peeling, looking past her own faint reflection in the window to the Foodland sign flashing red through the bare branches of the trees, thinking of David Henry. She thought of Norah too, so objectified in his photographs, her flesh rising like hills and her hair filling the frame with unexpected light. The letter from the lawyer was still in the desk drawer. She'd kept the appointment she'd made before Al's accident, visiting the substantial oak-paneled office and learning the details of David Henry's bequest. The conversation had been in her mind all week, though she'd had no time to think about it or talk with Al.

There was a noise outside. Caroline turned, startled. Through the window in the back door she glimpsed Phoebe outside, on the porch. She'd gotten home on her own, somehow; she wasn't wearing her coat. Caroline dropped the peeler and went to the door, drying her hands on her apron. There she saw what had been hidden from inside: Robert, standing next to Phoebe, his arm around her shoulders.

"What are you doing here?" she asked sharply, stepping outside.

"I took the day off," Phoebe said.

"You did? What about your job?"

"Max is there. I'll work her hours on Monday."

Caroline nodded slowly. "But how did you get home? I was about to come and get you."

"We took the bus," Robert said.

"Yes." Caroline laughed, but when she spoke her voice was sharp with worry. "Right. Of course. You took the bus. Oh, Phoebe, I told you not to do that. It's not safe."

"Me and Robert are safe," Phoebe said, her lower lip protruding slightly, as it did when she got angry. "Me and Robert are getting married."

"Oh, for heaven's sake," Caroline said, pushed to the limit of her patience. "How can you get married? You don't know the first thing about marriage, either one of you."

"We know," Robert said. "We know about marriage."

Caroline sighed. "Look, Robert, you have to go home," she said. "You took the bus here, so you can take the bus home. I don't have time to drive you anywhere. It's too much. You have to go home."

To her surprise, Robert smiled. He looked at Phoebe, and then he walked into the shadowy part of the back porch and leaned under the swing. He came back carrying a sheaf of red and white roses, which seemed to glow slightly in the gathering dusk. He handed these to Caroline, the soft petals brushing her skin.

"Robert?" she said, taken aback, a faint perfume infusing the cold air. "What's this?"

"I got them at the grocery store," he said. "On sale."

Caroline shook her head. "I don't understand."

"It's Saturday," Phoebe reminded her.

Saturday—the day Al came home from his trips, always with a present for Phoebe and a bunch of flowers for his wife. Caroline imagined the two of them, Robert and Phoebe, taking the bus to the grocery store where Robert worked as a stocker, studying the prices of the flowers, counting out the exact change. There was a part of her that still wanted to scream, to put Robert back on the bus and out of their lives, a part of her that wanted to say, *It's too much for me. I don't care.*

Inside, the little bell she'd left with Al rang insistently. Caroline sighed and took a step back, gesturing to the kitchen, the light and warmth.

"All right," she said. "Come inside, the two of you. Come in before you freeze."

She hurried up the stairs, trying to pull herself together. How much was one woman supposed to do? "You're supposed to be patient," she said, walking into their room, where Al was sitting with his leg propped on an ottoman, a book in his lap. "*Patient.* Where do you think the word comes from, Al? I know it's exasperating, but healing takes time, for heaven's sake."

"You're the one who wanted me home more," Al retorted. "Be careful what you wish for."

Caroline shook her head and sat down on the edge of the bed. "I didn't wish for this."

He looked out the window for a few seconds. "You're right," he said at last. "I'm sorry."

"Are you okay?" she asked. "How's the pain?"

"Not so bad."

Beyond the glass, wind stirred the last leaves of the sycamore against the violet sky. Bags of tulip bulbs were under the tree, waiting to be planted. Last month she and Phoebe had put in chrysanthemums, bright bursts of orange and cream and dark purple. She had sat back on her heels to admire them, brushing dirt off her hands, remembering times when she had gardened like this with her mother, connected by their tasks though not by words. They had rarely talked about anything personal. There was so much, now, that Caroline wished she had said.

"I'm not going to do it anymore," he said, blurting the words out without looking at her "Drive a truck, I mean."

"All right," she said, trying to imagine what this might mean for their lives. She was glad—something in her had just shut down every time she imagined him driving away again—but she was suddenly a little apprehensive too. Not once since they were married had they spent more than a week together.

"I'll be getting in your hair all the time," Al said, as if reading her mind.

"Will you?" She looked at him intently, taking in his pallor, his serious eyes. "Are you planning to retire completely, then?"

He shook his head, still studying his hands. "Too young for that. I was thinking I could do something else. Transfer into the office, maybe; I know the system inside out. Drive a city bus. I don't know—anything, really. But I can't go out on the road again."

Caroline nodded. She'd driven out to the accident sight, seen the hole torn in the guardrail, the scarred piece of earth where the truck had fallen.

"I always had a feeling," Al said, glancing at his hands. He was letting his beard grow in; it stubbled his face. "Like this was bound to happen, one day or another. And now it has."

"I didn't know that," Caroline said. "You never said you were scared."

"Not scared," Al said. "I just had a feeling. It's different."

"Still. You never said anything."

He shrugged. "Wouldn't have made any difference. It was just a feeling, Caroline."

She nodded. Another few yards and Al would have died, the officers had said more than once. All week she'd kept herself from imagining what hadn't happened. But the truth was, she could be a widow, facing the rest of her life alone.

"Maybe you should retire," she said slowly. "I went down to the lawyer, Al. I'd already made the appointment, and I kept it. It's a lot of money that David Henry left for Phoebe."

"Well, it's not mine," Al said. "Even if it's a million dollars, it's not mine."

She remembered, then, how he'd responded when Doro had given them the house: this same reluctance to accept anything he hadn't earned with his own hands.

"That's true," she said. "The money is for Phoebe. But you and I, we raised her. If she's taken care of financially, we can worry less.

We can have more freedom. Al, we've worked hard. Maybe it's time for us to retire."

"What do you mean?" he asked. "You want Phoebe to move?"

"No. I don't want that at all. But Phoebe wants it. She and Robert are downstairs now." Caroline smiled a little, remembering the sheaf of roses she'd left lying on the counter by the pile of half-peeled carrots. "They went to the grocery store together. On the bus. They bought me flowers because it's Saturday. So, I don't know, Al. Who am I to say? Maybe they *will* be okay, more or less, together."

He nodded, thinking, and she was struck by how tired he looked, how fragile all their lives were, in the end. All these years she had tried to imagine every possibility, to keep everyone safe, and yet here was Al, grown a little older, with a broken leg—an outcome that had never crossed her mind.

"I'll make a pot roast tomorrow," she said, naming his favorite meal. "Will pizza be okay tonight?"

"Pizza's fine," Al said. "Get it from that place on Braddock, though."

She touched his shoulder and started down the stairs to make the call. On the landing she paused, listening to Robert and Phoebe in the kitchen, their low voices punctuated by a burst of laughter. The world was a vast and unpredictable and sometimes frightening place. But right now her daughter was in the kitchen, laughing with her boyfriend, and her husband dozed with a book in his lap, and she didn't have to cook dinner. She took a deep breath. The air held the distant scent of roses—a clean scent, fresh as snow.

1989

July 1, 1989

THE STUDIO OVER THE GARAGE, WITH ITS HIDDEN DARK-room, had not been opened since David moved out seven years ago, but now that the house was going up for sale Norah had no choice but to face it. David's work was in favor again, worth quite a lot of money; curators were coming tomorrow to view the collection. So Norah had been sitting on the painted floor since early morning, slicing through boxes with an X-Acto knife, lifting out folders full of photographs and negatives and notes, determined to remained detached, to be ruthless, in this process of selection. It should not have taken long; David had been so meticulous, and everything was neatly labeled. A single day, she'd thought, no more.

She hadn't counted on memory, the slow lure of the past. It was early afternoon already, growing hot, and she had only made it through one box. A fan whirred in the window and a fine sweat gathered on her skin; the glossy photos stuck to her fingertips. They seemed at once so near and so impossible, those years of her youth. There she was with a scarf tied gaily in her carefully styled hair, Bree beside her in sweeping earrings, a flowing patchwork skirt. And here was a rare photo of David, so serious, with a crew cut, Paul just an infant in his arms. Memories rushed up, too, filling the room, holding Norah in place: the scents of lilacs and ozone and Paul's infant skin; David's touch, the clearing of his throat; the sunlight of a lost afternoon moving in patterns on the wooden floors. What had it meant, Norah asked herself, that they had lived these moments in this particular way? What did it mean that the photos did not fit at all with the woman she remembered being? If she looked closely she could see it, the distance and longing in her gaze, the way she always seemed to be looking just beyond the photo's edge. But a stranger wouldn't notice, Paul wouldn't; from these images alone no one could suspect the intricate mysteries of her heart.

A wasp roamed and floated near the ceiling. Each year they returned and built a nest somewhere in the eaves. Now that Paul was grown, Norah had given up worrying about them. She stood and stretched and got a Coke from the refrigerator where David had once stored chemicals and slender packages of film. She drank it, gazing out the window at the wild irises and honeysuckle in the backyard. Norah had always meant to make something of it, do more than hang bird feeders from the honeysuckle branches, but in all these years she hadn't, and now she never would. In two months she would marry Frederic and leave this place forever.

He had been transferred to France. Twice the transfer had fallen through, and they had talked of moving in together in Lexington, selling both their places and starting fresh: something brand new, a place where no one else had ever lived. Their talk was idle, languorous, conversations that bloomed over their dinners together or while they lay together in the dusk, glasses of wine on the bedside tables, the moon a pale disk in the window above the trees. Lexington, France, Taiwan—it didn't matter to Norah, who felt she had already discovered another country with Frederic. Sometimes, at night, she closed her eyes and lay awake, listening to his steady breathing, filled with a deep sense of contentment. It pained her to realize how far she and David had drifted away from love. His fault, certainly, but hers too. She had held herself so close and tight, she had been so afraid of everything after Phoebe died. But those years were gone now; they had flowed away, leaving nothing but memory behind.

So France was fine. When the news came that the posting was just outside of Paris, she was glad. They had already rented a little cottage at the edge of the river in Châteauneuf. Frederic was there at this very moment, putting in a greenhouse for his orchids. Even now it filled Norah's imagination: the smooth red tiles of the patio, the slight river breeze in the birch tree by the door, and the way the sunlight fell on Frederic's shoulders, his arms, as he worked to frame the walls of glass. She could walk to the train station and be in Paris in two hours, or she could walk to the village and buy fresh cheese and bread, and dark gleaming bottles of wine, her cloth tote bags growing heavier with each stop. She could sauté onions, pausing to look up at the river moving slowly beyond the fence. On the patio in the evenings she'd spent there, the moonflowers had opened with their lemony fragrance and she and Frederic sat drinking wine and talking. Such simple things, really. Such happiness. Norah glanced at the boxes of photographs, wanting to take that young woman she had been by the arm and shake her gently. *Keep going,* she wanted to tell her. *Don't give up. Your life will be fine in the end.*

She drained her Coke and went back to work, bypassing the box in which she'd gotten so mired and opening another. Inside this one there were file folders neatly arranged, organized by year. The first held shots of anonymous infants, sleeping in their carriages, sitting on lawns or porches, held in the warm arms of their mothers. The photos were all 8-by-10s, glossy black-and-whites; even Norah could tell that they were David's early experiments in light. The curators would be pleased. Some were so dark the figures were barely visible; others were washed nearly white. David must have been testing the range of his camera, keeping the subject the same and varying the focus, the aperture, the available light.

The second folder was very similar, and the third and the fourth. Photos of girls, not infants anymore but two and three and four years old. Girls in their Easter dresses at church, girls running in the park, girls eating ice cream or clustered outside the school at recess. Girls dancing, throwing balls, laughing, crying. Norah frowned, flipping more quickly through the images. There wasn't one child she recognized. The photos were arranged carefully by age. When she skipped to the end, she found not girls but young women, walking, shopping, talking to each other. The last was a young woman in the library, her chin resting in her hand as she gazed out the window, a distant expression, familiar to Norah, in her eyes.

Norah let the folder fall into her lap, spilling photos. What was this? All these girls, young women: it could have been a sexual fixation, yet Norah knew instinctively that it was not. What the photos shared in common was not a darkness but an innocence. Children playing in the park across the street, wind lifting their hair and clothes. Even the older ones, the grown women, had this quality; they turned a distracted gaze on the world, wide-eyed, somehow, and questioning. Loss lingered in the play of lights and shadows; these were photos full of yearning. Of longing, yes, not lust.

She flipped back the box lid to read the label. SURVEY was all it said.

Quickly, careless of the disorder she was creating, Norah went through all the other boxes, pulling one off another. In the middle of the room she found another with that bold black word SURVEY. She opened it and pulled the folders out.

Not girls this time, not strangers, but Paul. Folder after folder of Paul in all his ages, his transformations and his growth, his turning-away rage. His intentness and his stunning gift of music, fingers flying over his guitar.

For a long time Norah sat very still, agitated, on the edge of knowing. And then suddenly the knowledge was hers, irrevocable, searing: all those years of silence, when he would not speak of their lost daughter, David had been keeping this record of her absence. Paul, and a thousand other girls, all growing.

Paul, but not Phoebe.

Norah might have wept. She longed suddenly to talk with David. All these years, he'd missed her too. All these photographs, all this silent, secret longing. She went through the images once more, studying Paul as a boy: catching a baseball, playing the piano, striking a goofy pose under the tree in the backyard. All these memories he'd collected, moments Norah had never seen. She studied them again and then again, trying to imagine herself in the world David had experienced, into his mind's eye.

Two hours passed. She was aware of being hungry, but she couldn't bring herself to leave or even to rise from her place on the floor. So many photos, all these pictures of Paul, all these anonymous girls and women, mirroring his age. Always, all these years, she had felt her daughter's presence, a shadow, standing just beyond every photo that was taken. Phoebe, lost at birth, lingered just out of sight, as if she had risen moments earlier and left the room, as if her scent, the brush of air from her passing, still moved in the spaces she'd left. Norah had kept this feeling to herself, fearing that anyone who heard her would think her sentimental, even crazy. It astonished her now, it brought tears to her eyes, to realize how deeply David, too, had felt their daughter's absence. He had looked for her everywhere, it seemed—in every girl, in each young woman—and had never found her.

Finally, into the expanding rings of silence in which she sat, gravel popped faintly: a car in the driveway. Someone was arriving. Distantly she heard a slammed door, footsteps, the doorbell ringing in the house. She shook her head and swallowed, but she did not get up. Whoever it was would go away and come back later, or not. She was wiping tears from her eyes; whoever wanted her could wait. But no. The furniture appraiser had promised to stop by this afternoon. So Norah pressed her hands across her cheeks and entered the house from the back, pausing to splash water, on her face and run a comb through her hair. "I'm coming," she called over the rush of water when the doorbell rang again. She walked through the rooms, the furniture all clustered into the center and covered with tarps: the painters were coming tomorrow. She calculated the days left, wondering if she could possibly get everything done. Remembering, for an instant, those evenings in Châteauneuf, where it seemed possible her life would always be serene, expanding into calm like a flower budding into air.

She opened the door, still drying off her hands.

The woman on the porch was vaguely familiar. She was dressed practically, in crisp dark-blue pants. She wore a white cotton sweater with short sleeves, and her thick hair was gray and cut very short. Even at first glance she gave the impression of being organized, efficient, the sort of person who wouldn't stand for any sort of nonsense, the sort of person who took charge of the world and got things done. She didn't speak, however. She seemed startled to see Norah, taking her in so intently that Norah folded her arms defensively, aware suddenly of her dust-streaked shorts, her sweat-damp T-shirt. She glanced across the street, then looked back at the woman on her porch. She caught the woman's gaze and focused on her wide-set eyes, so blue, and then she knew.

Her breath snagged. "Caroline? Caroline Gill?"

The woman nodded, her blue eyes falling shut for a moment as if something had been settled between them. But Norah did not know what. The presence of this woman from the long-lost past had set up a fluttering deep in her heart, taking her back to that dreamlike night when she and David had ridden to the clinic through the silent snow-filled streets, when Caroline Gill had administered gas and held her hand during the contractions, saying *Look at me, look at me now, Mrs. Henry, I'm right here with you and you're doing just fine.* Those blue eyes, the steady grip of her hand, as deeply woven into the fabric of those moments as her memory of David's methodical driving or Paul's first fluted cry.

"What are you doing here?" Norah asked. "David died a year ago."

"I know," Caroline said, nodding. "I know, I'm so sorry. Look, Norah—Mrs. Henry—I have something I need to talk with you about, something rather difficult. I wonder if you could spare me a few minutes. When it's convenient. I can come back if this isn't a good time."

There was both an urgency and a firmness in her voice, and against her better judgment Norah found herself stepping back and letting Caroline Gill step into the foyer. Boxes, neatly filled and taped, were stacked against the walls. "You'll have to excuse the house," she said. She gestured to the living room, the furniture all pushed to the center of the room. "I have painters coming in to give some bids. And a furniture appraiser. I'm getting married again," she added. "I'm moving."

"I'm glad I caught you then," Caroline said. "I'm glad I didn't wait."

Caught me *why?* Norah wondered, but from force of habit she invited Caroline into the kitchen, the only place they could comfortably sit. As they walked through the dining room, not speaking, Norah remembered the abruptness of Caroline's disappearance, the scandal. She glanced back twice, unable to shake the strange sensations Caroline's presence had stirred. Sunglasses hung from a chain around Caroline's neck. Her features had grown stronger over the years, her nose and chin more pronounced. She'd be formidable, Norah decided, in a business situation. Not a person to be taken lightly. Still, Norah realized, her uneasiness came from another source. Caroline had known her as a different person—a woman young and unsure, embedded in a life and a past she was not particularly proud to remember.

Caroline took a seat in the breakfast nook while Norah filled two glasses with ice and water. David's final note—*I fixed the bathroom sink. Happy Birthday*—was tacked onto the bulletin board just behind Caroline's shoulder. Norah thought impatiently of the photos waiting in the garage, of all she had to do that couldn't wait.

"You've got bluebirds," Caroline observed, nodding at the wild, chaotic garden.

"Yes. It took years to attract them. I hope the next people will feed them."

"It must be strange to be moving."

"It's time," Norah said, getting out two coasters and putting the glasses on the table. She sat down. "But you didn't come to ask about that."

"No."

Caroline took a drink, then placed her hands flat on the table as if, Norah sensed, to steady them. But when she spoke she seemed calm, resolved.

"Norah—may I call you Norah? That's how I've thought of you, all these years."

Norah nodded, still perplexed, increasingly unnerved. When was the last time Caroline Gill had crossed her mind? Not in ages, and never except as part of the fabric of the night when Paul was born.

"Norah," Caroline said, as if reading her mind, "what do you re-member about the night your son was born?"

"Why do you ask?" Norah's voice was firm, but she was already leaning back, pulling away from the intensity in Caroline's eyes, from some swirling undercurrent, from her own fear of what might be coming. "Why are you here, and why are you asking me that?"

Caroline Gill didn't answer right away. The lilting voices of the bluebirds flashed through the room like motes of light.

"Look, I'm sorry," Caroline said. "I don't know how to say this. There isn't an easy way, I suppose, so I'll just come out with it. Norah, that night when your twins were born, Phoebe and Paul, there was a problem."

"Yes," Norah said sharply, thinking of the bleakness she had felt after the birth, joy and bleakness woven together, and the long hard path she had taken to reach this moment of steady calm. "My daughter died," she said. "That was the problem."

"Phoebe did not die," Caroline said evenly, looking straight at her, and Norah felt caught in the moment as she had been all those years ago, holding on to that gaze as the known world shifted around her. "Phoebe was born with Down's syndrome. David believed the prognosis was not good. He asked me to take her to a place in Louisville where such children were routinely sent. It wasn't uncommon, in 1964, to do that. Most doctors would have advised the same. But I couldn't leave her there. I took her and moved to Pittsburgh. I've raised her all these years. Norah," she added gently, "Phoebe is alive. She's very well."

Norah sat very still. The birds in the garden were fluttering, call-ing. She was remembering, for some reason, the time she had fallen through an unmarked grate in Spain. She had been walking on a sunny street, carefree. Then a rush, and she was up to her waist in a ditch with a sprained ankle and long bloody scrapes on her calves. *I'm okay, I'm okay,* she had kept telling the people who helped her out, who took her to the doctor. Brightly, unconcerned, blood seep-ing from her cuts: *I'm okay.* It was only later, alone and safe in her room, when she closed her eyes and felt that rush again, that loss of control, and wept. She felt this way now. Shaking, she held onto the edge of the table.

"What?" she said. "What did you say?"

Caroline said it again: Phoebe, not dead but taken away. All these years. Phoebe, growing up in another city. Safe, Caroline kept saying. Safe, well cared for, loved. Phoebe, her daughter, Paul's twin. Born with Down's syndrome, sent away.

David had sent her away.

"You must be crazy," Norah said, though even as she spoke so many jagged pieces of her life were falling into place that she knew what Caroline was saying must be true.

Caroline reached into her purse and slid two Polaroids across the polished maple. Norah couldn't pick them up, she was trembling too hard, but she leaned close to take them in: a little girl in a white dress, chubby, with a smile that lit her face, her almond-shaped eyes closed in pleasure. And then another, this same girl years later, about to shoot a basketball, caught in the instant before she jumped. She looked a little like Paul in one, a little like Norah in the other, but mostly she was just herself: Phoebe. Not any of the images so neatly filed away in David's folders but simply herself. Alive, and somewhere in the world.

"But why?" The anguish in her voice was audible. "Why would he do this? Why would you?"

Caroline shook her head and looked out into the garden again.

"For years I believed in my own innocence," she said. "I believed I'd done the right thing. The institution was a terrible place. David hadn't seen it; he didn't know how bad it was. So I took Phoebe, and I raised her, and I fought many, many fights to get her an education and access to medical care. To make sure she would have a good life. It was easy to see myself as the hero. But I think I always knew, underneath, that my motives weren't entirely pure. I wanted a child and I didn't have one. I was in love with David too, or thought I was. From afar, I mean," she added quickly. "It was all in my own head. David never even noticed me. But when I saw the funeral announcement, I knew I had to take her. That I'd have to leave anyway, and I couldn't leave her behind."

Norah, caught in a wild turmoil, went back to those blurry days of grief and joy, Paul in her arms and Bree handing her the phone, saying, *You have to put this to rest.* She had planned the whole memorial service without telling David, each arrangement helping her return to the world, and when David had come home that night she'd fought his resistance.

What must it have been like for him, that night, that service?

And yet he had let it all happen.

"But why didn't he tell me?" she asked, her voice a whisper. "All these years, and he never told me."

Caroline shook her head. "I can't speak for David," she said. "He was always a mystery to me. I know he loved you, and I believe that as monstrous as this all seems, his initial intentions were good ones. He told me once about his sister. She had a heart defect and died young, and his mother never got over her grief. For what it's worth, I think he was trying to protect you."

"She is my child." Norah said, the words torn out of some deep place in her body, some old long-buried hurt. "She was born of my flesh. Protect me? By telling me she'd died?"

Caroline didn't answer, and they sat for a long time, the silence gathering between them. Norah thought of David in all those photos, and in all the moments of their lives together, carrying this secret with him. She hadn't known, she hadn't guessed. But now that she'd been told, it made a terrible kind of sense.

At last Caroline opened her purse and took out a piece of paper with her address and telephone number on it. "This is where we live," she said. "My husband, Al, and I, and Phoebe. This is where Phoebe grew up. She has had a happy life, Norah. I know that's not much to give you, but it's true. She's a lovely young woman. Next month, she's going to move into a group home. It's what she wants. She has a good job in a photocopy shop. She loves it there, and they love her."

"A photocopy shop?"

"Yes. She's done very well, Norah."

"Does she know?" Norah asked. "Does she know about me? About Paul?"

Caroline glanced down at the table, fingering the edge of the photo. "No. I didn't want to tell her until I'd talked to you. I didn't know what you'd want to do, if you'd want to meet her. I hope you will. But of course I won't blame you if you don't. All these years— oh, I'm so sorry. But if you want to come, we're there. Just call. Next week or next year."

"I don't know," Norah said slowly. "I think I'm in shock."

"Of course you are." Caroline stood up.

"May I keep the photos?" Norah asked.

"They're yours. They've always been yours."

On the porch, Caroline paused and looked at her, hard.

"He loved you very much," she said. "David always loved you, Norah."

Norah nodded, remembering that she'd said the same thing to Paul in Paris. She watched from the porch as Caroline walked to the car, wondering about the life Caroline was driving back to, what complexities and mysteries it held.

Norah stood on the porch for a long time. Phoebe was alive, in the world. That knowledge was a pit opening, endless, in her heart. Loved, Caroline had said. Well cared for. But not by Norah, who had worked so hard to let her go. The dreams she'd had, all that searching through the brittle frozen grass, came back to her, pierced her.

She went back in the house, crying now, walking past the shrouded furniture. The appraiser would come. Paul was coming too, today or tomorrow; he'd promised to call first but sometimes he just showed up. She washed the water glasses and dried them, then stood in the silent kitchen, thinking of David, all those nights in all those years when he rose in the dark and went to the hospital to mend someone who was broken. A good person, David. He ran a clinic, he tended those in need.

And he had sent their daughter away and told her she was dead.

Norah slammed her fist on the counter, making the glasses jump. She made herself a gin and tonic and wandered upstairs. She lay down, got up, called Frederic, and hung up when the machine answered. After a time she went back out to David's studio. Everything was the same, the air so warm, so still, the photographs and boxes scattered all over the floor, just as she'd left them. At least fifty thousand dollars, the curators had estimated. More if there were notes in David's hand about his process.

Everything was the same, yet not the same at all.

Norah picked up the first box and lugged it across the room. She heaved it up to the counter, then balanced it on the windowsill overlooking the backyard. She paused to catch her breath before she opened the screen and pushed the box firmly out, using both hands, hearing it land with a satisfying *thunk* on the ground below. She went back for the next one, and the next. She was everything she had wanted to be earlier: determined, brisk—yes, ruthless. In less than an hour, the studio was cleared. She walked back into the house, passing the broken boxes in the driveway, photographs spilling out and scuttling across the lawn in the late afternoon light.

Inside, she took a shower, standing beneath the rushing water until it ran cold. She put on a loose dress and made another drink and sat on the sofa. The muscles in her arms hurt from heaving the boxes. She got another drink and came back. When it got dark, hours later, she was still there. The phone rang, and she heard herself, recorded, and then Frederic, calling from France. His voice was so smooth and even, like a distant shore. She yearned to be there, to be in that place where her life had made sense, but she didn't pick up the phone or call him back. A train sounded, far away. She pulled the afghan up and slid into the darkness of that night.

She dozed, off and on, but didn't sleep. Now and then she got up to make another drink, walking through the empty rooms, shadowy with moonlight, filling her glass by touch. Not bothering, after a time, with tonic or lime or ice. Once she dreamed that Phoebe was in the room, emerging somehow from the wall where she had been all these years, Norah walking past day after day without seeing her. She woke then, weeping. She poured the rest of the gin down the sink and drank a glass of water.

She finally fell asleep at dawn. At noon, when she woke, the front door was standing wide open and in the backyard there were pictures everywhere: caught in the rhododendrons, plastered up against the foundation, stuck in Paul's old rusting swing set. Flashes of arms and eyes, of skin that resembled beaches, a glimpse of hair, blood cells scattered like oil across the water. Glimpses of their lives as David had seen them, as David had tried to shape them. Negatives, dark celluloid, scattered on the grass. Norah imagined the shocked and outraged voices of the curators, friends, of her son, even of a part of herself, imagined them crying out, *But you're destroying history!*

No, she answered, *I'm claiming it.*

She drank two more glasses of water and took some aspirin, then started hauling boxes to the far side of the overgrown yard. One box, the one full of images of Paul throughout his life, she pushed into the garage again to save. It was hot and her head ached; sparks of dizziness whirled before her eyes when she stood up too suddenly. She remembered that long-ago day on the beach, the glinting water and the silverfish of vertigo and Howard walking into her line of vision.

There were stones, piled behind the garage. She dragged these out, one by one, and arranged them in a wide circle. She dumped the first box, the glossy black and white images startling in the sunlight, all the unfamiliar faces of young women gazing up at her from the grass. Squatting in the harsh noon sun, she held a lighter to the edge of a glossy 8-by-10. When a flame licked and rose, she slid the burning photo into the shallow pile inside the ring of stones. At first the flame seemed not to catch. But soon a wavering heat rose up, a curl of smoke.

Norah went inside for another glass of water. She sat on the back step sipping, watching the flames. A recent city ordinance prohibited any sort of burning, and she worried that the neighbors might call the police. But the air remained quiet; even the flames were silent, reaching into the hot air, sending up a thin smoke the bluish color of mist. Wisps of blackened paper floated across the backyard, wafted on the shimmering waves of heat, like butterflies. As the fire in the circle of stones took hold and began to roar, Norah fed it more photos. She burned light, she burned shadow, she burned these memories of David's, so carefully captured and preserved.

You bastard, she whispered, watching the photographs flame high before they blackened and curled and disappeared.

Light to light, she thought, moving back from the heat, the roar, the powdery residue swirling in the air.

Ashes to ashes.

Dust, at last, to dust.

July 2–4, 1989

L OOK, IT'S FINE FOR YOU TO SAY THAT NOW, PAUL." MICHELLE was standing by the window with her arms folded, and when she turned her eyes were dark with emotion, veiled, too, by her anger. "You can say anything you want in the abstract, but the fact is, a baby would change everything—and mostly for me."

Paul sat on the dark-red sofa, warm and uncomfortable on this summer morning. He and Michelle had found it on the street when they first started living together here in Cincinnati, in those giddy days when it meant nothing to haul it up three flights of stairs. Or it meant exhaustion and wine and laughter and slow lovemaking later on its rough velvet surface. Now she turned away to look out the window, her dark hair swinging. An airy emptiness, a rushing, filled his heart. Lately, the world felt fragile, like a blown egg, as if it might shatter beneath a careless touch. Their conversation had begun amicably enough, a simple discussion of who would take care of the cat while they were both out of town: she in Indianapolis for a concert, he in Lexington to help his mother. And now, suddenly, they were here in this bleak territory of the heart, the place to which, lately, they both seemed constantly drawn.

Paul knew he should change the subject.

"Getting married doesn't translate directly into babies," he said instead, stubborn.

"Oh, Paul. Be honest. Having a child is your heart's desire. It's not me you want, even. It's this mythical baby."

"Our mythical baby," he said. "Someday, Michelle. Not right away. Look, I just wanted to raise the subject of getting married. It's not a big deal."

She gave a sound of exasperation. The loft had a pine floor and white walls and splashes of primary colors in the bottles, the pillows, the cushions. Michelle was wearing white too, her skin and hair as warm as the floors. Paul ached, looking at her, knowing she had, in some important sense, already made up her mind. She would leave him very soon, taking her wild beauty and her music with her.

"It's interesting," she said. "I find it very interesting, anyway. That all this is coming up just as my career is about to take off. Not before, but now. In a weird way, I think you're trying to break us up."

"That's ridiculous. Timing has nothing to do with it."

"No?"

"No!"

They didn't speak for several minutes and the silence grew in the white room, filled the space and pressed against the walls. Paul was afraid to speak and more afraid not to, but at last he could not hold back any longer.

"We've been together for two years. Either things grow and change or they die. I want us to keep growing."

Michelle sighed. "Everything changes anyway, with or without a piece of paper. That's what you're not factoring in. And no matter what you say, it *is* a big deal. No matter what you say, marriage changes everything, and it's *always* women who make the sacrifices, no matter what anyone says."

"That's theory. That's not real life."

"Oh! You're infuriating, Paul—so damned sure of everything."

The sun was up, touching the river and filling the room with a silvery light, casting wavering patterns on the ceiling. Michelle went into the bathroom and shut the door. A rummaging in drawers, the running of water. Paul crossed the room to where she had stood, taking in the view as if this might help him understand her. Then, quietly, he tapped on the door.

"I'm leaving," he said.

A silence. Then she called back. "You'll be back tomorrow night?"

"Your concert's at six, right?"

"Right." She opened the bathroom door and stood, wrapped in a plush white towel, rubbing lotion into her face.

"Okay, then," he said, and kissed her, taking in her scent, the smoothness of her skin. "I love you," he said, as he stepped back.

She looked at him for a moment. "I know," she said. "I'll see you tomorrow."

I know. He brooded on her words all the way to Lexington. The drive took two hours: across the Ohio River, through the dense traffic near the airport, and finally into the beautiful rolling hills. Then he was traveling through the quiet downtown streets, past empty buildings, remembering how it had been when Main Street still was the center of life, the place where people went to shop and eat and mingle. He remembered going into the drugstore, sitting at the ice cream fountain in the back. Scoops of chocolate in a metal cup frosted with ice, the whir of the blender; mingled scents of grilled meat and antiseptic. His parents had met downtown. His mother had ridden on an escalator and risen above the crowd like the sun, and his father had followed her.

He drove past the new bank building and the old courthouse, the empty place where the theater once stood. A thin woman was walking down the sidewalk, her head bent, her arms folded, her dark hair moving in the wind. For the first time in years Paul thought of Lauren Lobeglio, the silent determined way she had walked across the empty garage to him week after week. He had reached for her, again and then again; he had woken in the middle of so many dark nights, fearing with Lauren all he now so desired with Michelle: marriage, children, an interweaving of lives.

He drove, humming his newest song to himself. "A Tree in the Heart" it was called—maybe he would play this one tonight, at Lynagh's pub. Michelle would be shocked by that, but Paul didn't care. Lately, since his father died, he had been playing more at informal venues as well as concert halls: he'd pick up a guitar and play in bars or restaurants, classical pieces but also more popular works that he had always, in the past, disdained. He couldn't explain his change of heart, but it had something to do with the intimacy in those places, the connection he felt to the audience, close enough to reach out and touch. Michelle didn't approve; she believed it was a consequence of grief, and she wanted him to get over it. But Paul couldn't give it up. All the years of his adolescence, he had played out of anger and longing for connection, as if through music he could bring some order, some invisible beauty, into his family. Now his father was gone, and there was no one to play against. So he had this new freedom.

He drove to the old neighborhood, past the stately houses and deep front yards, the sidewalks and eternal quiet. The front door of his mother's house was closed. He turned off the engine and sat for a moment, listening to the birds and the distant sound of lawn mowers.

A tree in the heart. His father had been dead for a year and his mother was marrying Frederic and moving to France for a while, and he was here not as a child or as a visitor but as caretaker of the past. His to choose, what to keep and what to discard. He'd tried to talk with Michelle about this, his deep sense of responsibility, how what he kept from this house of his childhood would become, in turn, what he passed down to his own children someday—all they would ever know, in a tangible way, of what had shaped him. He'd been thinking of his father, whose past was still a mystery, but Michelle misunderstood; she stiffened at this casual mention of children. *That's not what I meant,* he protested, angry, and she was angry too. *Whether or not you knew it, that's what you meant.*

He leaned back, searching in his pocket for the house key. Once his mother understood that his father's work was valuable, she'd started keeping the doors locked, though the boxes sat unopened in the studio.

Well, he didn't want to look at that stuff either.

When Paul finally got out of the car he stood for a moment on the curb, looking around the neighborhood. It was hot; a high faint breeze moved through the tops of the trees. Pin oak leaves dug into the light, creating a play of shadows on the ground. Strangely, too, the air seemed to be full of snow, a feathery gray-white substance drifting down through the blue sky. Paul reached out into the hot, humid air, feeling as if he were standing in one of his father's photographs, where trees bloomed up in the pulse of a heart, where the world was suddenly not what it seemed. He caught a flake in one palm; when he closed his hand into a fist and opened it again, his flesh was smeared with black. Ashes were drifting down like snow in the dense July heat.

He left footprints on the sidewalk as he walked up the steps. The front door was unlocked, but the house was empty. *Hello?* Paul called, walking through the rooms, the furniture pushed into the middle of the floor and covered with tarps, the walls bare, ready for painting. He hadn't lived here for years but he found himself pausing in the living room, stripped of everything that had made it meaningful. How many times had his mother decorated this room? And yet it was just a room, finally. *Mom?* he called, but got no answer. Upstairs, he stood in the doorway of his own room. Boxes were piled here too, full of old things he had to sort. She hadn't thrown anything away; even his posters were rolled neatly and secured with rubber bands. There were faint rectangles on the walls where they'd once hung.

"Mom?" he called again. He went downstairs and onto the back porch.

She was there, sitting on the steps, wearing old blue shorts and a limp white T-shirt. He stopped, wordless, taking in the strange scene. A fire still smoldered in a circle of stones, and the ashes and wisps of burned paper that had fallen around him in the front yard were here too, caught in the bushes and in his mother's hair. Papers were scattered all over the lawn, pressed against the bases of trees, against the rusting metal legs of the ancient swing set. Paul realized with shock that his mother had been burning his father's photographs. She looked up, her face streaked with ashes and with tears.

"It's all right," she said, in an even voice. "I've stopped burning them. I was so angry with your father, Paul, but then it struck me: This is your inheritance too. I only burned one box. It was the box with all the girls, so I don't imagine it was very valuable."

"What are you talking about?" he asked, sitting down beside her.

She handed him a photo of himself, one he'd never seen. He was about fourteen, sitting in the porch swing, bent over his guitar, playing intently, oblivious to everything around him, caught up in the music. It startled him that his father had captured this moment—a private moment, completely unself-conscious, one of the moments of his life when Paul felt most alive.

"Okay. But I don't understand. Why are you so mad?"

His mother pressed her hands to her face, briefly, and sighed. "Do you remember the story of the night you were born, Paul? The blizzard, how we barely got to the clinic in time?"

"Sure." He waited for her to go on, not knowing what to say, yet understanding at some instinctive level that this had to do with his twin sister, who had died.

"Do you remember the nurse, Caroline Gill? Did we tell you about her?"

"Yes. Not her name. You said she had blue eyes."

"She does. Very blue. She came here yesterday, Paul. Caroline Gill. I haven't seen her since that night. She brought news, shocking news. I'm just going to tell you, since I don't know what else to do."

She took his hand. He didn't pull away. His sister, she told him calmly, had not died at birth after all. She'd been born with Down's syndrome, and his father had asked Caroline Gill to take her to a home in Louisville.

"To spare us," his mother said, and her voice caught. "That's what she said. But she couldn't go through with it, Caroline Gill. She took your sister, Paul. She took Phoebe. All these years your twin has been alive and well, growing up in Pittsburgh."

"My sister?" Paul said. "In Pittsburgh? I was just in Pittsburgh last week." It was not an appropriate response, but he did not know what else to say; he was filled with a strange emptiness, a kind of stunned detachment. He had a sister: that was news enough. She was retarded, not perfect, so his father had sent her away. It wasn't anger, strangely, but fear that rose up next, some old apprehension born of the pressure his father had focused on him as the only child. Born, too, of Paul's need to make his own way, even if his father might disapprove enough to leave. A fear Paul had transformed all these years, like a gifted alchemist, into anger and rebellion.

"Caroline went to Pittsburgh and started a new life," his mother said. "She raised your sister. I guess it was a struggle; it would have been, especially in those days. I keep trying to be thankful that she was good to Phoebe, but there's a part of me that's just raging."

Paul closed his eyes for a moment, trying to hold all these ideas together. The world felt flat, strange, and unfamiliar. All these years he'd tried to imagine his sister, what she would be like, but now he couldn't bring a single idea of her to mind.

"How could he?" he asked finally. "How could he keep this a secret?"

"I don't know," his mother said. "I've been asking myself the same thing for hours. How could he? And how dare he die and leave us to discover this alone?"

They sat there silently. Paul remembered an afternoon of developing photos with his father on the day after he'd trashed the darkroom, when he was full of guilt and his father was too, when the very air was charged with what they said and what they left unspoken. Camera, his father told him, came from the French *chambre,* room. To be *in camera* was to operate in secret. This was what his father had believed: that each person was an isolated universe. Dark trees in the heart, a fistful of bones: that was his father's world, and it had never made him more bitter than at this moment.

"I'm surprised he didn't give *me* away," he said, thinking of how hard he'd always fought against his father's vision of the world. He had gone out and played his guitar, music rising straight up through him and entering the world, and people turned, put down their drinks, and listened, and a room full of strangers was connected, each to each. "I'm sure he wanted to."

"Paul!" His mother frowned. "No. If anything, he wanted even more for you because of all this. Expected even more. Demanded perfection of himself. That's one of the things that's become clear to me. That's the terrible part, actually. Now that I know about Phoebe, so many mysteries about your father make sense. That wall I always felt—it was real."

She got up, went inside, and came back with two Polaroids. "Here she is," she said. "This is your sister: Phoebe."

Paul took them and stared from one to the other: a posed picture of a girl, smiling, and then a candid shot of her shooting a basket. He was still trying to take in what his mother had told him: that this stranger with the almond eyes and sturdy legs was his twin.

"You have the same hair," Norah said softly, sitting down next to him again. "She likes to sing, Paul. Isn't that something?" She laughed. "And guess what—she's a basketball fan."

Paul's laugh was sharp and full of pain.

"Well," he said, "I guess Dad chose the wrong kid."

His mother took the photos in her ash-stained hands.

"Don't be bitter, Paul. Phoebe has Down's syndrome. I don't know much about it, but Caroline Gill had a lot to say. So much I could hardly take it all in, really."

Paul had been running his thumb along the concrete edge of the step and now he stopped, watching blood seep up where he'd scraped it raw.

"Don't be bitter? We visited her grave," he said, remembering his mother walking through the cast-iron gate with her arms full of flowers, telling him to wait in the car. Remembering her kneeling the dirt, planting morning glory seeds. "What about that?"

"I don't know. It was Dr. Bentley's land, so he must have known too. Your father never wanted to take me there. I had to fight so hard. At the time I thought he was afraid I'd have a nervous break-down. Oh, it made me so mad—the way he always knew best."

Paul started at the vehemence in her voice, remembering his conversation that morning with Michelle. He pressed the edge of his thumb to his lips and sucked away the little beads of blood, glad for the sharp copper taste. They sat in silence for a time, looking at the backyard with its wisps of ash, its scattered photos and damp boxes.

"What does it mean," he asked at last, "that she's retarded? I mean, day-to-day."

His mother looked at the photographs again. "I don't know. Caroline said she's quite high-functioning, whatever that means. She has a job. A boyfriend. She went to school. But apparently she can't really live on her own."

"This nurse—Caroline Gill—why did she come here now, after all these years? What did she want?"

"She just wanted to tell me," his mother said softly. "That's all. She didn't ask for anything. She was opening a door, Paul. I really do believe that. It was an invitation. But whatever happens next is up to us."

"And what is that?" he asked. "What happens now?"

"I'll go to Pittsburgh. I know I have to see her. But after that, I don't know anything. Should I bring her back here? We'll be strangers to her. And I have to talk with Frederic; he has to know." She put her face in her hands for a moment. "Oh, Paul—how can I go to France for two years and leave her behind? I don't know what to do. It's too much for me, all at once."

A breeze fluttered the photographs scattered across the lawn. Paul sat quietly, struggling with many confused emotions: anger at his father, and surprise, and sadness for what he'd lost. Worry, too; it was terrible to be concerned about this, but what if he had to take care of this sister who couldn't live on her own? How could he possibly do that? He'd never even met a retarded person, and he found that the images he had were all negative. None of them fit with the sweetly smiling girl in the photograph, and that was disconcerting too.

"I don't know either," Paul said. "Maybe the first thing is to clean this mess up."

"Your inheritance," his mother said.

"Not just mine," he said thoughtfully, testing the words. "It's my sister's too."

They worked through that day and the next, sorting the photos and repacking the boxes, dragging them into the cool depths of the garage. While his mother met with the curators, Paul called Michelle to explain what had happened and to tell her he would not be at her concert after all. He expected her to be angry, but she listened without comment and hung up. When he tried to call back, the machine picked up; that happened all day long. More than once he considered getting in his car and driving like wild home to Cincinnati, but he knew it would do no good. Knew, too, that he didn't really want to go on this way, always loving Michelle more than she could love him back. So he forced himself to stay. He turned to the physical work of packing up the house, and in the evening he walked downtown to the library to check out books on Down's syndrome.

On Tuesday morning, quiet and distracted and full of apprehension, he and his mother got into her car and drove over the river and through the lush late-summer green of Ohio. It was very hot, the leaves of the corn shimmering against the expansive blue sky. They arrived in Pittsburgh amid returning Fourth of July traffic, traveling through the tunnel that opened onto the bridge in a breathtaking view of the two rivers merging. They crawled through downtown traffic and followed the Monongahela, traveling through another long tunnel. At last they pulled up at Caroline Gill's brick house on a busy tree-lined street.

She had told them to park in the alley and they did, getting out of the car and stretching. Beyond a strip of grass, steps led down into a narrow lot and the high brick house where his sister had grown up. Paul took the house in, so much like Cincinnati, so different from his own quiet childhood, its suburban ease and comfort. Traffic rushed by on the street, past the little postage-stamp yards, into the city sprawling all around them, hot and dense.

The gardens all along the alley were thick with flowers, hollyhocks and irises in every color, their white and purple tongues vivid against the grass. In this garden a woman was working, tending a row of lush tomato plants. A hedge of lilac bushes grew up behind her, the leaves flashing their pale green undersides in a breeze that pushed the hot air without cooling it. The woman, wearing dark blue shorts and a white T-shirt and bright flowered cotton gloves, sat up from where she was kneeling and ran the back of her hand across her forehead. The traffic rushed; she hadn't heard them coming. She broke a leaf off a tomato plant and pressed it to her nose.

"Is that her?" Paul asked. "Is that the nurse?"

His mother nodded. She had folded her arms tightly, protectively, across her chest. Her sunglasses masked her eyes, but even so he could see how nervous she was, how pale and tense.

"Yes. That's Caroline Gill. Paul, now that it's come to it, I'm not sure I can do this. Maybe we should just go home."

"We've driven all this way. And they're expecting us."

She smiled a small tired smile. She'd hardly slept in days; even her lips were pale.

"They can't possibly be expecting us," she said. "Not really."

Paul nodded. The back door swung open, but the figure on the porch was hidden in the shadows. Caroline stood, brushing her hands on her shorts.

"Phoebe," she called. "There you are."

Paul felt his mother grow tense beside him, but he didn't look at her. He looked instead at the porch. The moment stretched out, extended, and the sun pressed down against them. At last the figure emerged, carrying two glasses of water.

He stared hard. She was short, much shorter than he was, and her hair was darker, thinner and more flyaway, cut in a simple bowl shape around her face. She was pale, like his mother, and from this distance her features seemed delicate in a broad face, a face that seemed somewhat flattened, as if it had been pressed too long against a wall. Her eyes were slightly upslanted, her limbs short. She was not a girl anymore, as in the photographs, but grown, his own age, with gray in her hair. A few gray hairs flashed his beard too, when he let it grow. She wore flowered shorts and she was stocky, a little plump, her knees brushing together when she walked.

Oh, his mother said. She had placed one hand on her heart. Her eyes were hidden by the sunglasses, and he was glad; this moment was too private.

"It's okay," he said. "Let's just stand here for a while."

The sun was so hot, and the traffic rushed. Caroline and Phoebe sat side by side on the porch steps, drinking their water.

"I'm ready," his mother said at last, and they went down the steps to the narrow patch of lawn between the vegetables and flowers. Caroline Gill saw them first; she shaded her eyes, squinting against the sun, and stood up. Phoebe stood up too, and for a few seconds they looked at one another across the lawn. Then Caroline took Phoebe's hand in hers. They met by the tomato plants, the heavy fruit already starting to ripen, filling the air with a clean, acrid scent. No one spoke. Phoebe was gazing at Paul, and after a long moment she reached across the space between them and touched his cheek, lightly, gently, as if to see if he was real. Paul nodded without speaking, looking at her gravely; her gesture seemed right to him, somehow. Phoebe wanted to know him, that was all. He wanted to know her too, but he had no idea what to say to her this sudden sister, so intimately connected to him yet such a stranger. He was also terribly self-conscious, afraid of doing the wrong thing. How did you talk to a retarded person? The books he had read over the weekend, all those clinical accounts—none of this had prepared him for the real human being whose hand brushed so lightly against his face.

It was Phoebe who recovered first.

"Hello," she said, extending her hand to him formally. Paul took her hand, feeling how small her fingers were, still unable to say a single word. "I'm Phoebe. Pleased to meet you." Her speech was thick, hard to understand. Then she turned to his mother and did this again.

"Hello," his mother said, taking her hand, then clasping it between her own. Her voice was charged with emotion. "Hello, Phoebe. I'm very glad to meet you too."

"It's so hot," Caroline said. "Why don't we go inside? I have the fans on. And Phoebe made iced tea this morning. She's been excited about your visit, haven't you, honey?"

Phoebe smiled and nodded, suddenly shy. They followed her into the coolness of the house. The rooms were small but immaculate, with beautiful woodwork and French doors opening between the living room and dining room. The living room was full of sunlight and shabby, wine-colored furniture. A massive loom sat in the far corner.

"I'm making a scarf," Phoebe said.

"It's beautiful," his mother said, crossing the room to finger the yarns, dark pink and cream and yellow and pale green. She'd taken off her sunglasses and she looked up, her eyes watery, her voice still charged with emotion. "Did you choose these colors yourself, Phoebe?"

"My favorite colors," Phoebe said.

"Mine too," his mother said. "When I was your age, those were my favorite colors too. My bridesmaids wore dark pink and cream, and they carried yellow roses."

Paul was startled to know this; all the photos he had seen were black-and-white.

"You can have this scarf," Phoebe said, sitting down at the loom. "I'll make it for you."

"Oh," his mother said, and closed her eyes briefly. "Phoebe, that's lovely."

Caroline brought iced tea, and the four of them sat uneasily in the living room, talking awkwardly about the weather, about Pittsburgh's budding renaissance in the wake of the steel industry collapse. Phoebe sat quietly at the loom, moving the shuttle back and forth, looking up now and then when her name was mentioned. Paul kept casting sidelong glances at her. Phoebe's hands were small and plump. She concentrated on the shuttle, biting at her lower lip. At last his mother drained her tea and spoke.

"Well," she said. "Here we are. And I don't know what happens now."

"Phoebe," Caroline said. "Why don't you join us?" Quietly, Phoebe came over and sat next to Caroline on the couch.

His mother began, speaking too quickly, clasping her hands together, nervous. "I don't know what's best. There are no maps for this place we're in, are there? But I want to offer my home to Phoebe. She can come and live with us, if she wants to do that. I've thought about it so much, these last days. It would take a whole lifetime to catch up." Here she paused to take a breath, and then she turned to Phoebe, who was looking at her with wide, wary eyes. "You're my daughter, Phoebe, do you understand that? This is Paul, your brother."

Phoebe took hold of Caroline's hand. "This is my mother," she said.

"Yes." Norah glanced at Caroline and tried again. "That's your mother," she said. "But I'm your mother too. You grew in my body,

Phoebe." She patted her stomach. "You grew right here. But then you were born, and your mother Caroline raised you."

"I'm going to marry Robert," Phoebe said. "I don't want to live with you."

Paul, who had watched his mother struggle all weekend, felt Phoebe's words physically, as if she'd kicked him. He saw his mother feel them too.

"It's okay, Phoebe," Caroline said. "No one's going to make you go away."

"I didn't mean—I only wanted to offer—" His mother stopped and took another deep breath. Her eyes were deep green, troubled. She tried again. "Phoebe, Paul and I, we'd like to get to know you. That's all. Please don't be scared of us, okay? What I want to say— what I mean—is that my house is open to you. Always. Wherever I go in the world, you can come there too. And I hope you will. I hope you'll come and visit me someday, that's all. Would that be okay with you?"

"Maybe," Phoebe conceded.

"Phoebe," Caroline said, "Why don't you show Paul around for a while? Give Mrs. Henry and me a chance to talk a little bit. And don't worry, sweetheart," she added, resting her hand lightly on Phoebe's arm. "No one's going anywhere. Everything's okay."

Phoebe nodded and stood up.

"Want to see my room?" she asked Paul. "I got a new record player."

Paul glanced at his mother and she nodded, watching the two of them as they crossed the room together. Paul followed Phoebe up the stairs.

"Who's Robert?" he asked.

"He's my boyfriend. We're getting married. Are you married?"

Paul, pierced with a memory of Michelle, shook his head. "No."

"You have a girlfriend?"

"No. I used to have a girlfriend, but she went away."

Phoebe stopped on the top step and turned. They were eye to eye, so close that Paul felt uncomfortable, his personal space invaded. He glanced away and then looked back, and she was still looking straight at him.

"It's not polite to stare at people," he said.

"Well, you look sad."

"I am sad," he said. "Actually, I'm very, very sad."

She nodded, and for a moment she seemed to have joined him in his sadness, her expression clouding up and then, an instant later, clearing.

"Come on," she said, leading him down the hall. "I got some new records, too."

They sat on the floor of her room. The walls were pink, with pink and white checked curtains at the windows. It was a little girl's room, filled with stuffed animals, bright pictures on the walls. Paul thought of Robert and wondered if it was true that Phoebe would get married. Then he felt bad for wondering this; why shouldn't she get married, or do something else? He thought of the extra bedroom in his parents' house, where his grandmother stayed occasionally when he was a boy. That would have been Phoebe's room; she would have filled it with her music and her things. Phoebe put the album on and turned the volume up loud on her little record player, blasting "Love, Love Me Do," singing along to the music with her eyes half shut. She had a nice voice, Paul realized, turning the volume down a bit, flipping through her other albums. She had a lot of popular music but she had symphonies, too.

"I like trombones," she said, pretending to pull a long slide, and when Paul laughed, she laughed too. "I really love trombones." She sighed.

"I play the guitar," he said. "Did you know that?"

She nodded. "My mom said. Like John Lennon."

He smiled. "A little," he said, surprised to find himself in the middle of a conversation. He'd gotten used to her speech, and the more he talked to Phoebe, the more she was simply herself, impossible to label. "You ever hear of Andrés Segovia?"

"Uh-uh."

"He's really good. He's my favorite. Someday I'll play his music for you, okay?"

"I like you, Paul. You're nice."

He found himself smiling, charmed and flattered. "Thanks," he said. "I like you too."

"But I don't want to live with you."

"That's okay. I don't live with my mother either," he said. "I live in Cincinnati."

Phoebe's face brightened. "All by yourself?"

"Yes," he said, knowing he would go back to find Michelle gone. "All by myself."

"Lucky."

"I suppose," he said gravely, knowing suddenly that he was. The things he took for granted in life were the stuff of Phoebe's dreams. "I'm lucky, yes. It's true."

"I'm lucky too," she said, surprising him. "Robert has a good job, and so do I."

"What's your job?" Paul asked.

"I make copies." She said this with quiet pride. "Lots and lots of copies."

"And you like it?"

She smiled. "Max works there. She's my friend. We have twenty-three different colors of paper."

She hummed a little, content, as she put the first record carefully away and chose another. Her gestures were not fast, but they were efficient and focused. Paul could imagine her at the copy shop, doing her work, joking with her friend, pausing now and then to take pleasure in the rainbow of paper or a finished job. Downstairs he heard the murmur of voices as his mother and Caroline Gill worked out what to do. He realized, with a deep sense of shame, that his pity for Phoebe, like his mother's assumption of her dependence, had been foolish and unnecessary. Phoebe liked herself and she liked her life; she was happy. All the striving he had done, all the competitions and awards, the long and futile struggle to both please himself and impress his father—placed next to Phoebe's life, all this seemed a little foolish too.

"Where's your father?" he asked.

"At work. He drives a bus. Do you like *Yellow Submarine*?"

"Yes. Yes, I do."

Phoebe smiled a wide smile and put the album on.

September 1, 1989

NOTES SPILLED FROM THE CHURCH, INTO THE SUNLIT AIR. To Paul, standing just outside the bright red doors, the music seemed almost visible, moving among the poplar leaves, scattering on the lawn like motes of light. The organist was a friend of his, a woman from Peru named Alejandra, who wore her burgundy hair pulled back tightly in a long ponytail and who, in the bleak days after Michelle left, had appeared at his apartment with soup, iced tea, and admonishments. *Get up,* she told him briskly, flinging open curtains and windows, sweeping dirty dishes into the sink. *Get up, There's no use mooning around, especially not over a flautist. They're always flighty, didn't you know that? I'm surprised she lit down here as long as she did. Two years. Honestly, it must be a record.*

Now Alejandra's notes cascaded like silver water, followed by a bright crescendo, climbing, hanging suspended for an instant in the sunlight. His mother appeared in the doorway, laughing, one hand resting lightly on Frederic's arm. They stepped together into the sunlight, into a bright rain of bird seed and petals.

"Pretty," Phoebe observed, beside him.

She was wearing a dress of silvery green, holding the daffodils she'd carried in the wedding loosely in her right hand. She was

smiling, her eyes narrowed with pleasure, deep dimples in both
plump cheeks. The petals and the seeds arched against the bright
sky; Phoebe laughed, delighted, as they fell. Paul looked at her
hard: this stranger, his twin. They had walked together down the
aisle of this tiny church to where their mother waited with Frederic
by the altar. He'd walked slowly, Phoebe attentive and serious beside him, determined to do everything right, her hand cupped
around his elbow. There were swallows winging in the rafters during the exchange of vows, but his mother had been sure of this
church right from the beginning, just as she'd insisted, during all
the strange and unexpected and tearful discussions of Phoebe and
her future, that both of her children would stand with her at her
wedding.

Another burst, confetti this time, and a wave of laughter, rippling. His mother and Frederic bent their heads, and Bree brushed
bright specks of paper from their shoulders, their hair. Bright confetti scattered everywhere, making the lawn look like terrazzo.

"You're right," he said to Phoebe. "It's pretty."

She nodded, thoughtful now, and smoothed her skirt with both
hands.

"Your mother is going to France."

"Yes," Paul said, though he tensed at her choice of words: *your
mother.* A phrase you'd use for strangers, and of course they all
were. This, finally, was what had pained his mother most, the lost
years standing between them, their words so tentative and formal
where ease and love should have been. "You and me too, in a couple
of months," he said, reminding Phoebe of the plans they'd finally
agreed on. "We'll go to France and see them."

An expression of worry, fleeting as a cloud, crossed Phoebe's face.

"We'll come back," he added gently, remembering how scared
she'd been by his mother's suggestion that she move with her to
France.

She nodded, but she still looked worried.

"What is it," he asked. "What's wrong?"

"Eating snails."

Paul looked at her, surprised. He'd been joking with his mother
and Bree in the vestibule before the wedding, kidding about the

feast they'd have in Châteauneuf. Phoebe stood quietly at the edge of the conversation; he hadn't thought she was listening. This was a mystery too, Phoebe's presence in the world, what she saw and felt and understood. All he really knew of her he could put on an index card: she loved cats, weaving, listening to the radio, and singing in church. She smiled a lot, was prone to hugs, and was, like him, allergic to beestings.

"Snails aren't so bad," he said. "They're chewy. Kind of like garlic gum."

Phoebe made a face and then she laughed. "Gross," she said. "That's gross, Paul." The breeze moved lightly in her hair, and her gaze was still fixed on the scene before them: the moving guests, the sunlight, the leaves, all woven through with music. Her cheeks were scattered with freckles, just like his own. Far across the lawn, his mother and Frederic lifted a silver cake knife.

"Me and Robert," Phoebe said, "we're getting married too."

Paul smiled. He'd met Robert on that first trip to Pittsburgh; they'd gone to the grocery store to see him, tall and attentive, dressed in a brown uniform, wearing a name tag. When Phoebe introduced them, shyly, Robert had immediately taken Paul's hand and clapped him on the shoulder, as if they were seeing each other after a long absence. *Good to see you, Paul. Phoebe and me, we're getting married, so pretty soon you and me will be brothers; how about that?* And then, pleased, not waiting for a response, confident that the world was a good place and that Paul shared his pleasure, he'd turned to Phoebe and put his arm around her, and the two of them had stood there, smiling.

"It's too bad Robert couldn't come."

Phoebe nodded. "Robert likes parties," she said.

"That doesn't surprise me," Paul said.

Paul watched his mother slip a bite of cake into Frederic's mouth, touching the corner of his lip with her thumb. She was wearing a dress the color of cream and her hair was short, blond turning silver, making her green eyes look larger. He thought of his father, wondering what their wedding had been like. He'd seen the photos, of course, but that was just the surface. He wanted to know what the light had been like, how the laughter had sounded; he wanted to know if his father had leaned down, like Frederic was now doing, to kiss his mother after she'd licked a bit of frosting from her lips.

"I like pink flowers," Phoebe said. "I want lots and lots of pink flowers at my wedding." She grew serious then, frowned and shrugged, the green dress slipping a little against her collarbone. She shook her head. "But me and Robert, we have to save the money first."

The breeze lifted and Paul thought of Caroline Gill, tall and fierce, standing in the hotel lobby in downtown Lexington with her husband, Al, and Phoebe. They'd all met there yesterday, on neutral ground. His mother's house was empty, a FOR SALE sign in the yard. Tonight, she and Frederic would leave for France. Caroline and Al had driven in from Pittsburgh, and after a polite if somewhat uneasy brunch together they had left Phoebe here for the wedding while they went on a holiday to Nashville. Their first vacation alone, they'd said, and they seemed happy about it. Still, Caroline had hugged Phoebe twice, then paused on the sidewalk to look back through the window and wave.

"Do you like Pittsburgh?" Paul asked. He'd been offered a job there, a good job with an orchestra; he had an offer from an orchestra in Santa Fe, as well.

"I like Pittsburgh," Phoebe said. "My mother says it has a lot of stairs, but I like it."

"I might move there," Paul said. "What do you think?"

"That would be nice," Phoebe said. "You could come to my wedding." Then she sighed. "A wedding costs a lot of money. It's not fair."

Paul nodded. It wasn't fair, no. None of it was fair. Not the challenges Phoebe faced in a world that didn't welcome her, not the relative ease of his own life, not what their father had done—none of it. He suddenly, urgently, wanted to give Phoebe any wedding she wanted. Or at least a cake. It would be such small gesture against everything else.

"You could elope," he suggested.

Phoebe considered this, turning a green plastic bracelet on her wrist. "No," she said. "We wouldn't have a cake."

"Oh, I don't know. Couldn't you? I mean, why not?"

Phoebe, frowning hard, glancing at him to see if he was making fun of her. "No," she said firmly. "That's not how you have a wedding, Paul."

He smiled, touched by her sureness of how the world worked.

"You know what, Phoebe? You're right."

Laughter and applause drifted across the sunny lawn as Frederic and his mother finished with the cake. Bree, smiling, raised her camera to take a final picture. Paul nodded to the table where the small plates were being filled, passing from hand to hand. "The wedding cake has six layers. Raspberries and whipped cream in the middle. How about it, Phoebe? You want some?"

Phoebe smiled more deeply and nodded in reply.

"My cake is going to have *eight* layers," she said, as they walked across the lawn through the voices and the laughter and the music.

Paul laughed. "Only eight? Why not ten?"

"Silly. You're a silly guy, Paul," Phoebe said.

They reached the table. Bright confetti was scattered on his mother's shoulders. She was smiling, gentle in her motions, and she touched Phoebe's hair, smoothed it back, as if she were still a little girl. Phoebe pulled away, and Paul's heart caught; for this story, there were no simple endings. There would be transatlantic visits and phone calls, but never the ordinary ease of daily life.

"You did a good job," his mother said. "I'm so glad you were in the wedding, Phoebe, you and Paul. It meant a lot to me. I can't tell you."

"I like weddings," Phoebe said, reaching for a plate of cake.

His mother smiled a little sadly. Paul watched Phoebe, wondering how she understood what was happening. She seemed not to worry very much about things, but rather to accept the world as a fascinating and unusual place where anything might happen. Where one day, a mother and brother you never knew you had might appear at your door and invite you to be in a wedding.

"I'm glad you're coming to visit us in France, Phoebe," his mother went on. "Frederic and I, we're both so glad."

Phoebe looked up, uneasy again.

"It's the snails," Paul explained. "She doesn't like snails."

His mother laughed. "Don't worry. I don't like them either."

"And I'm coming back home," Phoebe added.

"That's right," his mother said gently. "Yes. That's what we agreed."

Paul watched, feeling helpless against the pain that had settled in his body like a stone. In the sharp light he was struck by his mother's age, a certain thinness to her skin, her blond hair giving way to silver. By her beauty too. She seemed lovely and vulnerable, and he wondered, as he had wondered so often in these past weeks, how his father could have betrayed her, betrayed them all.

"How?" he asked softly. "How could he never tell us?"

She turned to him, serious. "I don't know. I'll never understand it. But think how his life must have been, Paul. Carrying this secret with him all those years."

He looked across the table. Phoebe was standing next to a poplar tree whose leaves were just beginning to turn, scraping whipped cream off her cake with her fork.

"Our lives could have been so much different."

"Yes. That's true. But they weren't different, Paul. They happened just like this."

"You're defending him," he said slowly.

"No. I'm forgiving him. I'm trying to, anyway. There's a difference."

"He doesn't deserve forgiveness," Paul said, surprised at his bitterness, still.

"Maybe not," his mother said. "But you and I and Phoebe, we have a choice. To be bitter and angry, or to try and move on. It's the hardest thing for me, letting go of all that righteous anger. I'm still struggling. But that's what I want to do."

He considered this. "I was offered a job in Pittsburgh," he said.

"Really?" His mother's eyes were intent now, such a dark green in this light. "Are you going to take it?"

"I think so," he said, realizing he'd made up his mind. "It's a very good offer."

"You can't fix it," she said softly. "You can't fix the past, Paul."

"I know." And he did. He'd gone to Pittsburgh that first time believing that help was his to offer, or not. He'd been worried about the responsibility he'd have to undertake, how his life would change with the burden of a retarded sister, and he'd been surprised—astonished, really—to find this same sister saying *no, I like my life the way it is, no thank you.*

"Your life is your life," she went on, more urgently now. "You're not responsible for what happened. Phoebe's okay, financially."

Paul nodded. "I know. I don't feel responsible for her. I truly don't. It's just—I thought I'd like to get to know her. Day by day. I mean, she is my sister. It's a good job, and I *really* need a change. Pittsburgh's a beautiful city. So, I guess—why not?"

"Oh, Paul." His mother sighed, running her hand through her short hair. "Is it really a good job?"

"Yes. Yes it is."

She nodded. "It would be nice," she admitted slowly, "to have the two of you in the same place. But you have to think of the whole picture. You're so young, and you're just beginning to find your way. Know it's okay for you to do that."

Before he could answer, Frederic was there, tapping on his watch, saying they had to leave soon to catch their flight. After a moment's conversation Frederic went to get the car and his mother turned back to Paul, put one hand on his arm, and kissed his cheek.

"We're just about to go, I think. You'll be taking Phoebe home?"

"Yes. Caroline and Al said I could stay at their place."

She nodded. "Thank you," she said softly, "for being here. It can't have been easy for you, for all sorts of reasons. But it has meant so much to me."

"I like Frederic," he said. "I hope you'll be happy."

She smiled and touched his arm. "I'm so proud of you, Paul. Do you have any idea how proud I am of you? How much I love you?" She turned to gaze across the table at Phoebe; she had tucked the cluster of daffodils beneath her arm and the breeze moved her shiny skirt. "I'm proud of both of you."

"Frederic is waving," Paul said, speaking quickly to cover his emotion. "I think it's time. I think he's ready. Go and be happy, Mom."

She looked at him hard and long again, tears in her eyes, then kissed him on the check.

Frederic crossed the lawn and shook Paul's hand. Paul watched his mother embrace his sister and give Phoebe her bouquet; he watched Phoebe's tentative hug in return. Their mother and Frederic climbed into the car, smiling and waving, amid another shower of confetti. The car disappeared around the curve, and Paul made his way back to the table, pausing to say hello, to one guest after another, keeping Phoebe's figure in sight. When he drew near he heard her talking happily to another guest about Robert and her own wedding. Her voice was loud, her speech a little thick and awkward, her excitement uncontained. He saw the guest's reaction—a strained, uncertain, patient smile—and winced. Because Phoebe just wanted to talk. Because he himself had reacted to such conversations in the very same way, just a few weeks earlier.

"How about it, Phoebe," he said, walking over and interrupting. "You want to go?"

"Okay," she said, and put her plate down.

They drove through the lush countryside. It was a warm day. Paul turned off the air-conditioner and rolled down the windows, remembering the way his mother had driven so wildly through these same landscapes to escape her loneliness and grief, the wind whipping through her hair. He must have traveled thousands of miles with her, back and forth across the state, lying on his back, trying to guess where they were by the glimpses of leaves, telephone wires, sky. He remembered watching a steamship move through the muddy waters of the Mississippi, its bright wheels flashing light and water. He had never understood her sadness, though he had carried it with him later, wherever he went.

Now it was all gone, that sadness: that life was finished, gone, as well.

He drove fast, edges of autumn everywhere. The dogwoods were already turning, clouds of brilliant red against the hills. Pollen tickled Paul's eyes and he sneezed several times, but he still kept the windows open. His mother would have had the air-conditioning on, the car as chilly as a florist's case. His father would have opened his bag and found the antihistamine. Phoebe, sitting straight in the seat beside him, her skin so white, almost translucent, took a Kleenex from a small pack in her large black plastic purse and offered it to him. Veins, pale blue, traced just below the surface of her skin. He could see her pulse moving in her neck, calmly, steadily.

His sister. His twin. What if she'd been born without Down's? Or what if she'd been born as she was, simply herself, and their father had not raised his eyes to Caroline Gill, snow falling in the world outside and his colleague in a ditch? He imagined his parents, so young and so happy, bundling the two of them into the car, driving slowly through the watery streets of Lexington in the March thaw that followed their birth. The sunny playroom adjoining his would have belonged to Phoebe. She'd have chased him down the stairs, through the kitchen and into the wild garden, her face always with him, his laughter an echo of her own. Who would he have been, then?

But his mother was right; he could never know what might have happened. All he had were the facts. His father had delivered his own twins in the middle of an unexpected storm, following the steps he knew by heart, keeping his focus on the pulse and heart rate of the woman on the table, the taut skin, the crowning head. Breathing, skin tone, fingers and toes. A boy. On the surface, perfect, and a small singing started, deep in his father's brain. A moment later, the second baby. And then his father's singing stopped for good.

They were close to town now. Paul waited for a break in traffic, then turned into the Lexington cemetery, past the gatehouse made of stone. He parked beneath an elm tree that had survived a hundred years of drought and disease and got out of the car. He walked around to Phoebe's door and opened it, offering his hand. She looked at it, surprised, then up at him. Then she pushed herself out of the seat on her own, still holding the daffodils, their stems crushed and pulpy now. They followed the path for a while, past the monuments and the pond with the ducks, until he guided her across the grass to the stone that marked their father's grave.

Phoebe traced her fingers over the names and dates engraved in the dark granite. He wondered again what she was thinking. Al Simpson was the man she called her father. He did puzzles with her in the evenings, and brought her favorite albums home from his trips; he used to carry her on his shoulders so that she could touch the high leaves of the sycamores. It couldn't mean anything to her, this slab of granite, this name.

David Henry McCallister. Phoebe read the words out loud, slowly. They filled her mouth and fell heavily into the world.

"Our father," he said.

"Our father," she said, "who art in heaven hallowed be thy name."

"No," he said, surprised. "*Our* father. My father. Yours."

"Our father," she repeated, and he felt a surge of frustration, for her words were agreeable, mechanical, of no significance in her life.

"You're sad," she observed, then. "If my father died, I'd be sad too."

Paul was startled. Yes, that was it—he was sad. His anger had cleared, and suddenly he could see his father differently. His very presence must have must have reminded his father in every glance, with every breath, of the choice he'd made and could not undo. Those Polaroids of Phoebe that Caroline had sent over the years, found hidden in the back of a darkroom drawer after the curators had gone; the single photograph of his father's family too, the one Paul still had, standing on the porch of their lost home. And the thousands of others, one after another, his father layering image on image, trying to obscure the moment he could never change, and yet the past rising up anyway, as persistent as memory, as powerful as dreams.

Phoebe, his sister, a secret kept for a quarter of a century.

Paul walked a few feet back to the gravel path. He paused, his hands in his pockets, leaves swirling up in the eddies of wind, a scrap of newspaper floating over the rows of white stones. Clouds moved against the sun, making patterns on the land, and sunlight flashed on the headstones, the grass and trees. Leaves tapped lightly in the breeze, and the long grass rustled.

At first the notes were thin, almost an undercurrent to the breeze, so subtle that he had to strain to hear them. He turned. Phoebe, still standing by the headstone, her hand resting on its dark granite edge, had begun to sing. The grass over the graves was moving and the leaves were stirring. It was a hymn, vaguely famil- iar. Her words were indistinct, but her voice was pure and sweet, and other visitors to the cemetery were glancing in her direction, at Phoebe with her graying hair and bridesmaid's dress, her awkward stance, her unclear words, her carefree, fluted voice. Paul swallowed, stared at his shoes. For the rest of his life, he realized, he would be torn like this, aware of Phoebe's awkwardness, the difficulties she encountered simply by being different in the world, and yet propelled beyond all this by her direct and guileless love.

By her love, yes. And, he realized, awash in the notes, by his own new and strangely uncomplicated love for her.

Her voice, high and clear, moved through the leaves, through the sunlight. It splashed onto the gravel, the grass. He imagined the notes falling into the air like stones into water, rippling the invisible surface of the world. Waves of sound, waves of light: his father had tried to pin everything down, but the world was fluid and could not be contained.

Leaves lifted; sunlight swam. The words of this old hymn came back to him, and Paul picked up the harmony. Phoebe did not seem to notice. She sang on, accepting his voice as she might the wind. Their singing merged, and the music was inside him, a humming in his flesh, and it was outside, too, her voice a twin to his own. When the song ended, they stayed as they were in the clear pale light of the afternoon. The wind shifted, pressing Phoebe's hair against her neck, scattering old leaves along the base of the worn stone fence.

Everything slowed, until the whole world was caught in this single hovering moment. Paul stood very still, waiting to see what would happen next.

For a few seconds, nothing at all.

Then Phoebe turned, slowly, and smoothed her wrinkled skirt.

A simple gesture, yet it set the world back in motion.

Paul noted how short and clipped her fingernails were, how delicate her wrist looked against the granite headstone. His sister's hands were small, just like their mother's. He walked across the grass and touched her shoulder, to take her home.

A PENGUIN READERS GUIDE TO

THE MEMORY
KEEPER'S
DAUGHTER

Kim Edwards

An Introduction to
The Memory Keeper's Daughter

It is 1964 in Lexington, Kentucky, and a rare and sudden winter storm has blanketed the area with snow. The roads are dangerous, yet Dr. David Henry is determined to get his wife Norah to the hospital in time to deliver their first child. But despite David's methodical and careful driving, it soon becomes clear that the roads are too treacherous, and he decides to stop at his medical clinic instead. There, with the help of his nurse Caroline, he is able safely to deliver their son, Paul. But unexpectedly, Norah delivers a second child, a girl, Phoebe, in whom David immediately recognizes the signs of Down's Syndrome.

David is a decent but secretive man—he has shared his difficult past with no one, not even his wife. It is a past that includes growing up in a poor, uneducated family and the death of a beloved sister whose heart defect claimed her at the age of twelve. The painful memories of the past and the difficult circumstances of the present intersect to create a crisis, one in which his overriding concern is to spare his beloved Norah what he sees as a life of grief. He hands the baby girl over to Caroline, along with the address of a home to which he wants her taken, not imagining beyond the moment, or anticipating how his actions will serve to destroy the very things he wishes to protect. Then he turns to Norah, telling her, "our little daughter died as she was born."

From that moment forward, two families begin their new, and separate, lives. Caroline takes Phoebe to the institution but cannot bear to leave her there. Thirty-one, unmarried, and secretly in love with David, Caroline has been always been a dreamer, waiting for her real life to begin. Now when she makes her own split-second decision to keep and raise Phoebe as her own, she feels as if it finally has.

As Paul grows to adulthood, Norah and David grow more and more distant from each other. Norah, always haunted by the daughter she lost, takes a job that becomes an all-consuming career, and seeks the intimacy that eludes her with her own husband through a series of affairs. Feeling as if he's a disappointment to his father, Paul is angry and finds his only release through music. David, tormented by his secret, looks for solace through the lens of his camera, the "Memory Keeper," trying to make sense of his life through the images he captures.

But as *The Memory Keeper's Daughter* so eloquently shows, life is a moving image, unfolding and changing beyond our control. Despite our desire to freeze a moment or to go back into the past and alter events, time presses us forward. With her heart-wrenching yet ultimately hopeful novel, Kim Edwards explores the elusive mysteries of grief and love, and the power of the truth both to shatter and to heal.

A Conversation with Kim Edwards

1. The Memory Keeper's Daughter *is a powerful combination of a tragic and poignant family story as well as riveting page-turner, due primarily to the fact that it centers on such a shocking act by one individual that affects everyone he cares about. How did the idea for this novel come to you?*

A few months after my story collection, *The Secrets of a Fire King* was published, one of the pastors of the Presbyterian church I'd recently joined said she had a story to give me. I was pleased that she'd thought of me, if a bit surprised—I was back in church after a twenty-some year absence, and still quite skeptical of it all. Yet even to my critical eye it was clear that good things were happening: the congregation was vibrant and progressive and engaged; the co-pastors, a married couple who had both once been university professors, gave sermons that were beautifully crafted and thought-provoking, both intellectual and heartfelt. I'd already come to admire them very much. Still, it happens fairly often that people want to give me stories, and invariably those stories are not mine to tell. So I thanked my pastor, but didn't think much more about her offer.

The next week she stopped me again. *I really have to tell you this story*, she said, and she did. It was just a few sentences, about a man who'd discovered, late in life, that his brother had been born with Down's Syndrome, placed in an institution at birth, and kept a secret from his family, even from his own mother, all his life. He'd died in that institution, unknown. I remember being struck by the story even as she told it, and thinking right away that it really would make a good novel. It was the secret at the center of the family that intrigued me. Still, in the very next heartbeat, I thought: *of course, I'll never write that book*.

And I didn't, not for years. The idea stayed with me, however, as the necessary stories do. Eventually, in an unrelated moment, I was invited to do a writing workshop for adults with mental challenges through a Lexington group called Minds Wide Open. I was nervous about doing this, I have to confess. I didn't have much experience with people who have mental challenges, and I didn't have any idea of what to expect. As it turned out, we had a wonderful morning, full of expression and surprises and some very fine poetry. At the end of the class, several of the participants hugged me as they left.

This encounter made a deep impression on me, and I found myself thinking of this novel idea again, with a greater sense of urgency and interest. Still, it was another year before I started to write it. Then the first chapter came swiftly, almost fully formed, that initial seed having grown tall while I wasn't really paying attention. In her *Paris Review* interview, Katherine Anne Porter talks about the event of a story being like a stone thrown in water—she says it's not the event itself that's interesting, but rather the ripples the event creates in the lives of characters. I found this to be true. Once I'd written the first chapter, I wanted to find out more about who these people were and what happened to them as a consequence of David's decision; I couldn't stop until I knew.

2. Human motivation, the simple question of why we do what we do, is often very complex, as it is here with David and his fateful decision. As his creator, were you able to sympathize in any way with his motives?

Oh, yes, certainly. Even thought none of us may never experience a moment this dramatic, nonetheless we all have similar experiences, times when we react powerfully to an event in ways we may not completely understand until much later, if at all.

I knew from the beginning that David wasn't an evil person. He makes absolutely the wrong decision in that first chapter, but even so he acts out of what he believes are good intentions—the desire to protect Norah from grief, and even the desire to do what the medical community in that time and place had deemed best for a child with Down's Syndrome.

There's much more to this, of course. David's own grief at the loss of his sister is something he's never confronted, never resolved. I don't think this was unusual in that era. Grief counselors, after all, are relatively new. I remember stories, growing up, of adults in my town who had suffered terrible losses. There was a kind of silence around such people. Everyone knew their history, and the imprint of the loss was visible in the unfolding of their lives, but no one ever mentioned the person who had died.

So it was with David. His way of coping with the loss of his sister, and with the greater loss of his family that resulted, was to try to move on; to take control of his life and to push forward; to become a success in the eyes of the world. Yet even so, his grief was never far below the surface, and when Phoebe was born with Down's Syndrome, an event he could not anticipate or control, his old grief welled up. David's response in that moment is as much to the past as to the present, but it takes him decades, and a trip back to the place where he grew up, to understand this.

3. The novel begins in 1964. Do you think our attitudes toward people with disabilities have changed since then? Are we more enlightened or accepting now?

Yes, things have changed for the better over the past decades, but I'd say also that it's an ongoing process, with much more progress yet to be made.

Certainly, writing this novel was a process of enlightenment for me. When I began this book, I didn't know how to imagine Phoebe. I was compelled by the secret and its impact on the family, but I wasn't very knowledgeable about Down's Syndrome. To create a convincing character, one who was herself and not a stereotype, without being either sentimental or patronizing, seemed a daunting task.

I started reading and researching. Also, tentatively, I started having conversations. The first couple I spoke with has a daughter whom they'd raised during the time period of this book. They were a terrific help, candid and straightforward and wise. When I showed them the opening chapter, their immediate response was that I'd gotten the doctor exactly right: the attitudes David has about Down's Syndrome may seem outrageous to us now, but there was a time, not all that long ago, when these ideas were widely held.

The reason attitudes have changed, quite simply, is because the parents of children with Down's Syndrome refused, as Caroline does in this novel, to accept imposed limitations for their children. The fight that Caroline fights during this book is emblematic of struggles that took place all over the country during this era to change prevailing attitudes and to open doors that had been slammed shut.

The changes did not and do not happen easily, or without personal costs for those who struggled—and struggle still—to make their children visible to the world. Time and again as I researched this book I heard stories of both heartbreak and great courage. Time and again, also, I was impressed with the expansive generosity of people with Down's Syndrome and their families, who met with me, shared their life journeys and perceptions, their joys and struggles, and were eager to help me learn. Many of them have read the book and loved it, which for me is a profound measure of its success.

4. Your use of photography as a metaphor throughout the book is artfully done. Do you have a personal interest in photography, or did you educate yourself about it as part of the writing process?

I'm not a photographer, but for several years in college I was very good friends with people who were, some of whom, in fact, had darkrooms set up in their houses. Photography was woven into many of our conversations, and I sometimes went with my friends when they were seeking particular shots. I wasn't at all interested in the mechanics—apertures and f-stops left me cold— but I was always fascinated by the photographs appearing in the developer, what was invisible coaxed into image by the chemical bath. It's a slow emergence, a kind of birth, really; a moment of mystery. I was intrigued by the use of light, as well, the way too much light will erase an image on both film and paper.

I also remember being annoyed, more than once, when my friends' need to get a photo right interfered with the moment the photo was meant to capture: at a family reunion, for instance, or a birthday party. How did the presence of the photographer change the nature of the moment? What was gained and what was lost by having the eye of the camera present?

During the very early stages of writing this novel, I read a *New Yorker* essay about the photographer Walker Evans that discussed many of these questions quite eloquently, reminding me of my photographer friends. Norah gave David a camera, and from there I started doing quite a lot of research. Amid many other explorations, I spent time at Eastman Kodak Museum in Rochester and read Susan Sontag's fascinating and inspiring *On Photography*.

5. The city of Pittsburgh figures quite prominently in the story and is described in very affectionate terms. ("The city of Pittsburgh gleaming suddenly before her . . . so startling in its vastness and its beauty that she had gasped and slowed, afraid of losing control of the car" p. 91.) This is not a city that usually captures the imagination nor has it been a common setting for novels. Would you talk a bit about why you chose Pittsburgh and your personal connection, if any, to it?

I moved to Pittsburgh sight unseen—my husband and I were teaching in Cambodia when he was accepted into a Ph.D. program at the University of Pittsburgh. This was before e-mail; there were no telephones in Phnom Penh, and even electricity was often sporadic. With no clear image of Pittsburgh, we agreed to move there, visions of steel smoke and gritty industrialism hanging like a shadow when he sent in his acceptance.

Caroline's experience crossing the Fort Pitt bridge is my own. It's a spectacular moment: one emerges from the endless Fort Pitt tunnel onto a bridge spanning the Monogahela River, just before it merges with the Allegheny River and forms the Ohio River. Water gleams everywhere, and the buildings of the city narrow to the point between the rivers, and in the middle distance the greening hills rise up, studded with houses. The director of the MFA program at the University of Pittsburgh once confided to me how much he liked to drive visitors in from the airport, because they were invariably astonished by this view.

I spent four years in Pittsburgh and would have happily stayed there had circumstances allowed. It's a fascinating city, rich with history and parks. It's wonderful city for walking, too, with beautiful old neighborhoods and places where you find yourself suddenly standing on a bluff again, gazing out over the ever-changing rivers.

6. The Memory Keeper's Daughter, while ultimately redemptive and hopeful, reveals much of the dark side of the human experience. Actors often talk about how working on a very painful role can affect their psyche; others speak of being able simply to let it go and not have the work affect their daily lives. As a writer, how does working on such a heart-wrenching story affect your own state of mind? When you stop writing, are you able to let it go?

Well, they all struggle, don't they? They walk through a lot darkness. Yet I never found writing this book painful. In part, I think, I identified with all the characters in this book: the one who keeps a secret and the one from whom secrets have been kept; the parent who longs for a child and the child who longs for harmony and wholeness; the wanderer and the one who stays in place. I recognized their journeys of self-discovery, in any case. I was interested in them, and I wanted to know what happened to them, and who they were. The only way to discover all that was to write the book. Also, because the novel is told through four different points of view, moving from one character's mind to another, I was able step back from one point of view and work on another whenever I was stuck. This was very liberating, and allowed me to attain a certain level of detachment from one character while working on another.

7. As an award-winning short story writer, you are best known for your critically acclaimed collection The Secrets of a Fire King. *Would you talk a bit about how you came to write a novel, and the difference between working on a novel and a short story?*

When my story collection was published, several reviewers remarked that each one contained the scope of a novel. That interested me, because the stories always felt like stories; I couldn't imagine them being a word longer then they were. Likewise, *The Memory Keeper's Daughter* was a novel from the moment I started writing. Yet despite the difference in complexity and length, writing a novel was very much like writing stories. There's a bigger canvas in a novel, and thus more room to explore, but it's still a process of discovery, a leap into the unknown, and an intuitive seeking of the next moment, and the next. For me, writing is never linear, though I do believe quite ardently in revision. I think of revision as a kind of archeology, a deep exploration of the text to discover what's still hidden and bring it to the surface.

8. Who are some of your favorite authors, and what are you currently reading?

I read a great deal. Alice Munro and William Trevor are authors whose work I return to again and again. I have just finished Marilynne Robinson's *Gilead* and I will read it again soon simply to savor the beauty of the language. New books by both Ursula Hegi and Sue Monk Kidd are on my desk, along with the poems of Pablo Neruda. During the writing of *The Memory Keeper's Daughter* I returned to classic novels with secrets at their center, especially Dostoevsky's extraordinary *Crime and Punishment* and Hawthorne's *The Scarlet Letter*. I'm also midway through Thomas Mann's quartet of novels based on the story of Joseph and his brothers; these archetypal stories are informing the next novel I plan to write, as well.

9. What are you working on now?

I have begun a new novel, called *The Dream Master*. It's set in the Finger Lakes area of upstate New York where I grew up, which is stunningly beautiful, and which remains in some real sense the landscape of my imagination. Like *The Memory Keeper's Daughter*, this new novel turns on the idea of a secret—that seems to be my preoccupation as a writer—though in this case the event occurred in the past and is a secret from the reader as well as from the characters, so structurally, and in its thematic concerns, the next book is an entirely new discovery.

QUESTIONS FOR DISCUSSION

1. When David hands his baby girl over to Caroline and tells Norah that she has died, what was your immediate emotional reaction? At this early point, did you understand David's motivations? Did your understanding grow as the novel progressed?

2. David describes feeling like "an aberration" within his own family (p. 7) and describes himself as feeling like "an imposter" in his professional life as a doctor (p. 8). Discuss David's psyche, his history, and what led him to make that fateful decision on the night of his children's birth.

3. When David instructs Caroline to take Phoebe to the institution, Caroline could have flatly refused or she could have gone to the authorities. Why doesn't she? Was she right to do what she did and raise Phoebe as her own? Was Caroline morally obligated to tell Norah the truth right from the beginning? Or was her moral obligation simply to take care of Phoebe at whatever cost? Why does she come to Norah after David's death?

4. Though David wanted no part of her, Phoebe goes on to lead a full life, bringing much joy to Caroline and Al. Her story calls into question how we determine what kind of life is worth living. How would you define such a life? In contrast to Phoebe's, how would you describe the quality of Paul's life as he grew up?

5. Throughout the novel, the characters often describe themselves as feeling as if they are watching their own lives from the outside. For instance, David describes the moment when his wife is going into labor and says "he felt strangely as if he himself were suspended in the room . . . watching them both from above" (p. 10). What do you think Edwards is trying to convey here? Have you ever experienced similar feelings in your own life?

6. There is an obvious connection between David and Caroline, most aptly captured by a particular moment described through David's point of view: "Their eyes met, and it seemed to the doctor that he knew her—that they knew each other—in some profound and certain way" (p. 12). What is the significance of this moment for each of them? How would you describe the connection between them? Why do you think David married Norah and not Caroline?

7. After Norah has successfully destroyed the wasps' nest, Edwards writes that there was something happening in Norah's life, "an explosion, some way in which life could never be the same" (p. 139). What does she mean, and what is the significance of Norah's "fight" with these wasps?

8. When David meets Rosemary (p. 267) it turns out to be a cathartic experience for him. What is it about her that enables David to finally speak the truth? Why does he feel compelled to take care of her?

9. The secret that David keeps is enormous and ultimately terribly destructive to himself and his family. Can you imagine a circumstance when it might be the right choice to shield those closest to you from the truth?

10. What do you think Norah's reaction would have been if David had been honest with her from the beginning? How might Norah have responded to the news that she had a daughter with Down's Syndrome? How might each of their lives have been different if David had not handed Phoebe to Caroline that fateful day?

For more information about or to order other Penguin Readers Guides, please e-mail the Penguin Marketing Department at reading@us.penguingroup.com or write to us at:

> Penguin Books Marketing Dept.
> Readers Guides
> 375 Hudson Street
> New York, NY 10014-3657

Please allow 4–6 weeks for delivery.
To access Penguin Readers Guides online, visit the Penguin Group (USA) Web site at www.penguin.com.

FOR THE BEST IN PAPERBACKS, LOOK FOR THE

In every corner of the world, on every subject under the sun, Penguin represents quality and variety—the very best in publishing today.

For complete information about books available from Penguin—including Penguin Classics, Penguin Compass, and Puffins—and how to order them, write to us at the appropriate address below. Please note that for copyright reasons the selection of books varies from country to country.

In the United States: Please write to *Penguin Group (USA), P.O. Box 12289 Dept. B, Newark, New Jersey 07101-5289* or call 1-800-788-6262.

In the United Kingdom: Please write to *Dept. EP, Penguin Books Ltd, Bath Road, Harmondsworth, West Drayton, Middlesex UB7 0DA.*

In Canada: Please write to *Penguin Books Canada Ltd, 90 Eglinton Avenue East, Suite 700, Toronto, Ontario M4P 2Y3.*

In Australia: Please write to *Penguin Books Australia Ltd, P.O. Box 257, Ringwood, Victoria 3134.*

In New Zealand: Please write to *Penguin Books (NZ) Ltd, Private Bag 102902, North Shore Mail Centre, Auckland 10.*

In India: Please write to *Penguin Books India Pvt Ltd, 11 Panchsheel Shopping Centre, Panchsheel Park, New Delhi 110 017.*

In the Netherlands: Please write to *Penguin Books Netherlands bv, Postbus 3507, NL-1001 AH Amsterdam.*

In Germany: Please write to *Penguin Books Deutschland GmbH, Metzlerstrasse 26, 60594 Frankfurt am Main.*

In Spain: Please write to *Penguin Books S. A., Bravo Murillo 19, 1° B, 28015 Madrid.*

In Italy: Please write to *Penguin Italia s.r.l., Via Benedetto Croce 2, 20094 Corsico, Milano.*

In France: Please write to *Penguin France, Le Carré Wilson, 62 rue Benjamin Baillaud, 31500 Toulouse.*

In Japan: Please write to *Penguin Books Japan Ltd, Kaneko Building, 2-3-25 Koraku, Bunkyo-Ku, Tokyo 112.*

In South Africa: Please write to *Penguin Books South Africa (Pty) Ltd, Private Bag X14, Parkview, 2122 Johannesburg.*